Meet Me in Scotland

A Kilts and Quilts Novel

Patience Griffin

A SIGNET ECLIPSE BOOK

SIGNET ECLIPSE
Published by the Penguin Group
Penguin Group (USA) LLC, 375 Hudson Street,
New York, New York 10014

USA I Canada I UK I Ireland I Australia I New Zealand I India I South Africa I China
penguin.com
A Penguin Random House Company

First published by Signet Eclipse, an imprint of New American Library,
a division of Penguin Group (USA) LLC

First Printing, January 2015

Copyright © Patience Jackson, 2015
Penguin supports copyright. Copyright fuels creativity, encourages diverse voices, pro-
motes free speech, and creates a vibrant culture. Thank you for buying an authorized
edition of this book and for complying with copyright laws by not reproducing, scanning, or distributing any part of it in any form without permission. You are supporting
writers and allowing Penguin to continue to publish books for every reader.

SIGNET ECLIPSE and logo are trademarks of Penguin Group (USA) LLC.

ISBN 978-0-451-46830-7

Printed in the United States of America
10 9 8 7 6 5 4 3 2

PUBLISHER'S NOTE
This is a work of fiction. Names, characters, places, and incidents either are the product
of the author's imagination or are used fictitiously, and any resemblance to actual per-
sons, living or dead, business establishments, events, or locales is entirely coincidental.

If you purchased this book without a cover you should be aware that this book is stolen
property. It was reported as "unsold and destroyed" to the publisher and neither the
author nor the publisher has received any payment for this "stripped book."

PRAISE FOR
THE KILTS AND QUILTS NOVEL

Meet Me in Scotland

"A captivating story of four friends, two madcap romances, an idyllic Scottish town, and its endearingly stubborn but loyal inhabitants. Add scones, quilts, and kilts? Griffin sews this one up. Witty, warmhearted, and totally charming!"

—Shelley Noble, *New York Times* bestselling author of *Breakwater Bay*

To Scotland with Love

"A magnificent triple-hankie debut written straight from the heart, by turns tender, funny, heart-wrenching, and wise. Prepare to smile through your tears at this deft, brave, and deeply gratifying love story."

—Grace Burrowes, *New York Times* bestselling author of the Lonely Lords and the Windham series

"Griffin has quilted together a wonderful, heartwarming story that will convince you of the power of love."

—Janet Chapman, *New York Times* bestselling author of *The Highlander Next Door*

"Griffin's style is as warm and comfortable as a cherished heirloom quilt."

—Lori Wilde, *New York Times* bestselling author of the Cupid, Texas, Novels

"A life-affirming story of love, loss, and redemption. Patience Griffin seamlessly pieces compelling characters, a spectacular setting, and a poignant romance into a story as warm and beautiful as an heirloom quilt. Both heartrending and heartwarming, *To Scotland with Love* is a must-read romance and so much more. The story will touch your soul with its depth, engage you with its cast of endearing characters, and delight you with touches of humor."

—Diane Kelly, author of the Tara Holloway series

Also by Patience Griffin

To Scotland with Love

To the sisters of my heart . . .
you know who you are.

Acknowledgments

It is a truth universally acknowledged that a writer in possession of a manuscript is in want of a great editor. How lucky am I to have Tracy Bernstein on my side! Thank you, Tracy, for asking my stories all the right questions.

I'm grateful to Cynthia Stary Drajna of Iowa Star Quilts for designing the quilts for the Kilts and Quilts series, and to Marilyn Kidd of BeyondQuilting.com for quilting the quilts for the books. You, ladies, are incredible artists!

I wish to thank the indispensable Jacksons for standing by me—especially Elton, Kate, Matt, and Lori for their kind words when they were needed most. Also, a big thank-you goes to my brother, Phillip F. Jackson, MD, for being on call for writing help when it comes to all things medical.

Finally, there are those whom I can't do without on a day-to-day basis:

James, for being the Patron of the Arts.

Jamie, for talking writing twenty-four/seven.

And Kathleen Baldwin, for her friendship, phone calls, and plotting over pasta and salad.

PRONUNCIATION GUIDE

Aileen (AY-leen)
Ailsa (AIL-sa)
Bethia (BEA-thee-a)
Buchanan (byoo-KAN-uhn)
Cait (KATE)
Caitriona (kah-TREE-na)
Deydie (DI-dee)
Lochie (LAW-kee)
Macleod (muh-KLOUD)
Moira (MOY-ra)

DEFINITIONS

ceilidh (KAY-lee) — a party/dance
fash — trouble
Gandiegow — squall
Hogmanay — the Scottish celebration of the New Year
ken — understanding
kirk — church
lorry — truck
postie — postman
Sassenach (Sass-un-nak) — an English person

The Quilters of Gandiegow

Lesson #1
Quilting is the best kind of therapy.

Chapter One

Just as Emma Castle's plane landed in Scotland, she pulled out her phone and viewed the incriminating evidence once again. *Bollocks*. The damned video had gone viral. Exactly as her boss back in Los Angeles—now her ex-boss—had feared. She still couldn't believe it. *Fired*. Egghead Emma had been fired.

The video wasn't a sex tape, which her parents certainly would've preferred over the reality of what was hitting the Internet. She watched the forty-eight-second clip for a third time. How superior her British accent sounded, how smug she looked, like she had all the answers. Those forty-eight seconds had irrevocably changed her future. *Thirty years old and already a washout*. Oh, bloody hell, what would she do now?

Well, that's why she was here sitting on the tarmac—hoping to figure things out with her best friend, Claire.

As the other passengers pulled down their bags and left the plane, she stared out the window to what looked like midnight in the dead of winter. It was early evening, but a huge blizzard was brewing. An accurate metaphor for her life. She slid her phone back into her pocket.

Certainly I'm not the only marriage therapist in the world who doesn't believe in happily-ever-afters.

But she *was* the only one to get caught on hidden camera telling a couple how it really was. As a Brit working in America, she'd learned a thing or two about this time of year. At the clinic, they'd called them the Thanksgiving crowd. A week before the turkey and the dressing, marriages were either exploding or imploding because of the approaching holidays. Emma had apparently cracked up right along with them, telling one of her couples how it all was going to play out. Unfortunately, she'd been caught on tape. *Don't waste your money. Marriage therapy serves one purpose and one purpose only: getting you through the inevitable divorce.* In her defense, she'd only been telling her clients the truth. It was what she'd seen day in and day out.

She closed her eyes and laid her head back on the rest, trying to put the video out of her mind and trying not to imagine what her parents would say when they found out. Mum, the World's Leading Sex Therapist, and Dad, Hollywood's Marriage Counselor, would insist on having her professionally evaluated when the news reached them. But maybe then they would finally accept the truth. Emma wasn't cut out to be a couples counselor, and her controlling parents couldn't guilt her into doing it any longer. They'd have to find someone else to collaborate on their books and TV promotions. At times like these, Emma wished she had a sibling. Someone else to fulfill her parents' expectations. But having a sibling would require her parents to at least be in the same country at the same time, not to mention the same bed.

When the aisle cleared, she hurried off the plane and searched the waiting crowd. God, she'd missed her best friend. She'd hesitated only a moment when Claire had invited her to come to Gandiegow. Running away couldn't fix the predicament she'd gotten herself into, but it would give her a respite, and oh, how she needed a best friend booster shot to help make things better. Then she could head to London to face Mum. Hopefully, by then, she'd have a few things worked out, maybe even a plan for what to do next.

Emma's mobile rang; it was Claire.

"Where are you?" Emma scanned the faces around her. "Are you waiting at baggage reclaim?"

"Nay." Claire paused. "I sent Gabriel to pick you up."

"No," Emma cried. The people around her turned and stared. At the same time, her mother's voice rang in her ear: *Losing one's temper is not in a proper Englishwoman's repertoire.*

Hissing wasn't, either, but Emma did it anyway into the phone. "For your sake, Claire, I hope you're speaking of Gabriel the archangel and not the other one."

Claire gave her attitude right back. "Don't grumble at me. It's not my fault your flight was delayed. You know how early I have to get up."

"Why couldn't your husband take the morning shift for you?"

Claire tsked. "The scones are *my* specialty. The restaurant depends upon them."

Emma sighed heavily. "Yes, I know. But still."

"Gabriel was a saint to offer," Claire defended.

Yeah, right, Emma thought.

Her friend went on. "Is he there yet?"

"I don't know." Gabriel would be the perfect end to her perfectly horrible day.

"Buck up, Emma. You're a grown woman. You can handle a few hours with him." With that Claire said goodbye and hung up.

Emma's temples began to throb. Claire was testing her patience as only Claire could do. Gabriel MacGregor was incorrigible, plain and simple. Claire *knew* she couldn't stand being around him.

When Claire and Dominic had first coupled up, Emma had spent a fair amount of time in Gabriel's presence. Dominic and Gabriel were inseparable, closer than most brothers she knew. Not biological brothers, but Gabriel's father had taken Dominic in when he was orphaned.

Emma had visited Claire often back then and had been thrust into Gabriel's path over and over. He'd made a lasting impression, but not in a good way. He had a way of flustering her that was very uncomfortable. For years now she'd successfully avoided him, making sure she had plenty of excuses at the ready if Gabriel was to be present. The last time she'd actually seen him was at Claire and Dominic's wedding, ten years ago. He'd shown up late, roaring in on his motorcycle, wearing a leather jacket, leather pants, and an earring. Undignified and unrefined, especially for the occasion. Even worse, he had stirred something deep inside her she couldn't name. Ten minutes later, decked out in a tux, he'd smiled at her, tucked her arm into his, and walked her down the aisle, best man to her maid of honor. He'd behaved appropriately during the ceremony, but then at the reception he'd flirted with all the bridesmaids and had taken most of them back to his room for a pajama party. Emma sniffed. *Certainly no pajamas had been involved.* And Egghead Emma hadn't been invited, either. Gabriel MacGregor with his deep Scottish burr was a scoundrel—a rake.

She sighed heavily. There would be no helping it. She'd be forced to spend the next several hours with him in the car, but thankfully, it would only be that. Surely his visit to Gandiegow would be over soon and she wouldn't have to endure his presence in the small Scottish town for too long.

Emma stowed her phone and realized she was being stared at by an extraordinarily handsome man. Tall, dark, and devilish. A rake through and through. As a trained psychologist, she recognized within herself all the telltale signs of instant attraction. Her pulse raced, she involuntarily licked her lips, and she brushed her hair off her shoulders.

Then recognition hit. *Dr. Gabriel MacGregor.*
Bugger me.

At twenty he'd been handsome and she'd thought him a man. But now she saw she was wrong. Dead wrong. He made the twenty-year-old Gabriel look young and wiry and inconsequential. This man had muscles filling out his long-sleeved polo, the breadth of an American football player, and the stance of a Scottish warrior. She did it again. Licked her lips. *I'm in deep trouble.*

He made his way through the crowd to her, not smiling, not happy to see her, either. In truth, she couldn't blame him. She had been a pill at Claire's wedding, but she had wanted everything to run smoothly for her friend's big day. Emma might've crossed the line by scolding Gabriel at his tardiness. And she'd definitely given him plenty of attitude during the reception about his *tart-iness.* All those women, indeed. What could one man do with so many at once? From the novels she'd read—for pure research, mind you—she knew. Sex and lots of it.

"Do you have more luggage?" he said in his firm baritone burr.

It ran over her like warm syrup. *No, butter. No . . .* She fanned herself. She was incensed at her own visceral reaction. *And he hasn't given me a proper greeting.* At least she could be civilized.

"Hello, Gabriel." She felt her nose lift higher in the air. It might be misconstrued as snooty, but seriously, the man was six-three if he was an inch. She cranked her head back to inspect his face.

He gave her a one-sided frown and seemed to be inspecting her, too. But not her face.

"You filled out," he said.

Instinctively, she put an arm over her breasts. Her cheeks burned. She started to give him a piece of her mind, but then she got angry with herself for letting him provoke her.

Defiantly, she put her arm down and stuck out her chest. "Look all you want. They expanded all on their own. Without surgical intervention." Although her mother at one time had offered to pay for C cups if her nearly flat chest remained . . . *flat*.

Emma definitely wouldn't lower herself and explain to Gabriel—a doctor who should know these things— that Egghead Emma had been a late bloomer. In almost every area, except intelligence.

"No reason to get your panties in a twist. I only meant it as a compliment." He continued to feast his eyes on her.

She put her hands on her hips and glared back. "Are you done yet?"

"For now." He gave her an unrepentant grin. *Still the rogue.*

"Yes, I have more luggage," she said, answering his earlier question.

"Fine." Without permission, he reached for her carry-on.

She grabbed his arm, stopping him. In the process, her fingers landed on an anvil-hard biceps. She yanked her hand away and snipped at him, "I have it. Thank you." She tugged back her bag. "Your hands are filthy."

As he glanced down at the grease under his fingernails, she took the opportunity to head off to the baggage reclaim, all the while giving herself a stern lecture. Getting grease off her Louis Vuitton luggage wasn't the issue. He was a dog, and not the harmless type, either.

I can't be attracted to Gabriel MacGregor. Not again. I just can't. He was way out of her league. Besides, what self-respecting woman would want to get involved with a cad like him?

And those hands. His hands didn't look like doctors' hands—soft and delicate. He had the hands of an oil-rig mechanic.

She also noticed he didn't wear a wedding band.

Of course, Claire would've told her if Gabriel had married, wouldn't she? She'd told Emma when he'd suddenly gone off to medical school. Emma hadn't believed it at the time, assuring herself that a do-nothing like him would certainly work in a grimy garage for the rest of his life.

Oh, dear. Her thoughts did sound priggish, didn't they? But Gabriel seemed to bring out the worst in her. She'd treated him abominably back then, and she felt herself heading down the same path now. She would never be as serene and proper as her mother would like—all that etiquette training down the drain. Over the years, Emma had tried to be the person her mother wanted her to be, but she'd fallen short. She'd also fallen short of the person she wanted to be. But blast it, she was still trying to figure out who that person was.

With his long legs, Gabriel caught up to her. She automatically glanced over. He was all hard lines and pheromones.

"Why are you frowning?" he asked.

"I'm having a difficult time seeing you as a physician." She probably should keep her sentiments to herself, but they'd always spoken their minds to each other, the truth flowing easily between them. *Each of them giving the other more candor than Mum's society friends would ap-*

prove of. "Unless, of course, you use your title primarily as a way to pick up women."

He frowned at her. "Princess, are we going to get off on the wrong foot again?"

"That depends on you," she spouted. She did her best to sound assertive and unruffled, even though she felt unraveled and unsure. Seeing him didn't help. And the past thirty-six hours had her more than a little battered and bruised. She'd been fired and displaced. If he could see inside her—see the real Emma Castle—he'd know she wasn't such a snob. She didn't have all the answers. In fact, he'd see how she was questioning every aspect of her life and every choice she'd ever made.

She put the focus back on him to take the focus off herself. It helped her feel less uncomfortable. She raked her eyes over him unabashedly. Doctors were supposed to be old and nerdy. Doctors were supposed to instill a sense of calm and trust. Doctors were not supposed to conjure up all sorts of vivid images of a steamy nature. Yes, she could definitely imagine Dr. Gabriel MacGregor in his lab coat, *playing doctor*. Just the thought sent a warm nervous tingle zipping through her veins, throwing her limbic system into a tizzy. *Gads.*

It rankled that he, a former grease monkey, had made something of himself. Her only claim to fame was that she'd succeeded in becoming a huge failure. But she couldn't let him see how vulnerable she felt. No doubt he'd take advantage of it. She had to admit that he had every right to fling back one of her past sermons into her face. *It's time to become an actual adult and contribute something to society.* The amount of bull she'd dished out regularly to him in their younger days was embarrassing. Especially since, by anyone's standards, she was the screwup now. What had she ever done for society? Help people end their relationships?

At the baggage carousel, she intended to corral her own luggage, but she'd packed too heavily. In the end, Gabriel stepped in and hoisted her bag off, acting as if it was nothing more than cotton balls in his surgery. "Saint Gabriel," she muttered under her breath.

He raised a superior eyebrow at her. "*Thank you* is the *proper* response. Has Ms. Manners forgotten how to comport herself?"

Him and his bloody burr.

And accuracy.

Yes, she should've taken the high road and been grateful. But he made her forget she was supposed to be a lady.

With a huff, she pulled up the handle on her bag.

"What's in there, by the way?" He pointed to her rolling suitcase. "It weighs at least ten stone."

"Books." She would make no apologies. She'd packed as many books as clothes, planning to use reading as her escape from her disastrous life.

"Psychology books?" He frowned at her. "Certainly not your parents' books." His frown deepened.

"If you must know, they're novels." Books with happy endings. True, she didn't believe in happy endings, but she needed a dose of unreality right now. She'd had enough of the real world—its misfortune and misery.

"Well, we'd better get a move on. There's a winter storm blowing outside," he offered. "I was afraid you might be diverted to London. But you made it just in time." He looked up at the board as the announcement came over the loudspeaker: All flights were canceled.

As they hurried through the terminal, she couldn't stop peering over at him. He was so damned good-looking. A proper English deb did not swear, not even in her own thoughts, but once again Gabriel had her behaving quite horrendously.

"Emma," he said impatiently, "why are you staring?"

"I . . . uhhh." She sounded like an imbecile. Had his hair always looked this enticing? Enough so that she wanted to run her hands through it? She wondered if Gabriel was in a relationship.

"Well?" he said impatiently.

"Well, what?" She felt stupid for zoning out.

He frowned at her as if disappointed she couldn't keep up.

"Listen," she countered back, "I've been traveling for the past twenty-four hours. Cut me some slack." She'd been in America far too long, adopting some of their terrible language habits.

"Fine. *Slack cut*," he said.

She knew a few things about Gabriel. She'd met his father, the Reverend Casper MacGregor, at Dominic and Claire's wedding. He had officiated and they'd had a lovely chat afterward. Gabriel was raised in the Church of Scotland—Presbyterians. Which didn't exactly mesh with what she thought of him. Emma had been raised pragmatically—Mum insisted that religion was for those who needed it. Her parents had no need. They had money, fame, and high-profile careers.

Emma felt like they'd been trekking for miles through the terminal. Maybe she'd been rash by not allowing Gabriel to help. Her arms felt like deadweight, tired from maneuvering both her carry-on and the checked bag behind her.

Before they stepped outside, Emma stopped to button her suit jacket. But when she left the terminal, she found her effort was in vain. It was bloody miserable—cold as freezer frost. Wind blew up her long pencil skirt and froze both her legs and her nether regions. Her lined suit jacket couldn't keep out the cold, either, as the snow whirled all around them. "This is quite an adjustment," she hollered above the wind.

"Which? The cold weather or the darkness?"

"Both," she answered.

"The Highlands are extreme, Princess. If you think the short days are something, wait until the endless summer nights."

"I don't plan to be here that long." She pulled her scarf more tightly around her neck, clung to her cases, and hurried along.

He led her to his ancient Land Rover.

"The same auto you had ten years ago?" She wondered if he still had his motorcycle, too.

"Aye. I recently restored the interior." He unlocked her side of the car. "Get in."

Even though she was cold, she waited at the back with her bags.

He opened her door. "I said, get in. It's freezing."

"Just open the back." She was stubborn. She intended to prove to Gabriel she wasn't the pampered princess he thought she was.

He came around to the back and unlocked it. She started to lift her bag.

"Here, I've got it." He reached for her luggage, as well.

A small tug-of-war ensued. Determined to win the battle, she yanked as hard as she could, but the handle broke, sending her backward into the snow. If she'd thought it was cold before, she was mistaken. Instantly, she became crushed ice cold from head to toe.

He offered her his hand to help her up, but she swatted him away.

"I've got it." She stood and shook the snow out of her hair. When she bent over to get her carry-on, Gabriel started brushing snow off her bottom.

"What are you doing?" She leapt away from him. "Stop!"

"I'm just trying to help." He gave her a grin and one more brush.

"Just get the car going," she yelled.

"You get in first."

"Fine." As she huffed to the passenger's side, Gabriel threw her bags in, none too gently. When he slid into his seat, he had an nasty old blanket in his arms and moved to wrap it around her.

"Don't," she cried, scooting away from him. "What is that smell? Dog?"

"I don't know. Someone must've left it in the back when they borrowed the Land Rover." He tried again to wrap her in it, this time grazing her shoulder.

"Stop, Gabriel." She pushed it away.

"Listen, Your Majesty, if you don't raise your body temperature, you'll be in a heap of trouble. You've heard of hypothermia, haven't you?"

"I'd rather freeze to death than be asphyxiated by that smell."

"Suit yourself." He started the car and cranked up the heat. He glanced over at her. "You should probably take off your gloves and blow on your hands."

"Great medical advice," she said.

"Hey, I'm here to help."

She covered her nose. "Then put that blanket away. Better yet, throw it in the garbage. I can't handle the smell all the way to Gandiegow."

"Sure, Princess." He hopped out, taking the nasty blanket with him.

She wanted to tell him she wasn't a princess; she was a debutante. Big difference. A princess was a princess. A deb had to be introduced into society, which, in Emma's case, had been a lot of work.

She looked out the window, wondering what took so long. Gabriel was sweeping the snow from the windshield, rear window, and mirrors, but it seemed to be gathering quicker than he could remove it.

When he got back in, he rubbed his hands together. *"Brrr."*

Emma's teeth chattered a little, but she needed reassurances. "Are you sure we're going to make it to Gandiegow?"

"Aye. We'll do fine." He patted the steering wheel. "Her engine is newly rebuilt and she's purring like a kitten."

"So, the car's female?" She expected him to make a lewd comment, something about *all sweet rides are.* Or maybe she'd been too programmed by her mother; naughty talk was a huge part of Mum's Take Back Your Orgasm program. Emma glanced over at Gabriel. With all that masculinity oozing off him, his specialty was clear—*Meow.*

He gazed through the windshield up at the sky, which was white with blizzardlike snow. "It's damnable out there. How's your body temperature?"

"I'm fine." But sitting next to him made her nervous. "How long will it take to get to Claire?"

"In this weather? I don't know. We'll have to take it slow. Just sit back and relax."

Not even possible.

"Don't worry, Emma," Gabriel said, misreading her uneasiness and shocking her by using her name. "I promise to get you to Gandiegow safely."

Then he did the weirdest thing; he reached out and dusted the last of the snow from her shoulder.

She sat there, stunned. He looked a little embarrassed himself. He jerked his head forward and put the car in gear. Without a word, they made their way out of the airport. The streets beyond were relatively empty and even the highway had little traffic.

After a time, she felt safe to secretly peek over at him. Mr. Perfect handled the auto with ease, his large hands resting on the steering wheel, his uneasiness of a while ago gone. Maybe she'd imagined it. When they slid a bit on the curvy roads, he stayed calm, even then exuding confidence. His medium-length coffee dark hair was perfectly styled to fit his perfect head. When he was younger, his hair had been long and wild and out of control. He'd tamed it and it seemed to suit him now. The only part that spoke of rebellion was the beard stubble. But it wasn't a full rebellion, like he hadn't shaved in days. No, he must have trimmed it carefully this morning. Emma ached to run her hand over it to see if it felt prickly or soft or maybe a little of both. She turned away and shifted uncomfortably in her seat.

"Are you all right?" Concern pinched his eyebrows together.

"Sure. Why wouldn't I be?" The look he gave her made her feel vulnerable. "Did they teach that compassionate look in medical school?"

The doctor shot her a scowl.

Much better. That she could deal with. They drove on for several more miles, but she couldn't help sneaking another peek at him.

He sighed heavily. "Emma, ye're staring again."

She turned back to her window but saw only darkness. "It's just that," she said quietly, "you've filled out, too."

Did Gabe just hear Emma Castle turn his own words back on him? Shocking. So Miss Priss did have a little spunk. From his dealings with her before, he figured she was crammed full, from top to bottom, with her mama and papa's brand of snobbery. He'd seen Emma on the television recently, standing like a statue beside her famous parents while they'd peddled their books. *Books I wasted time reading. Books that were pure rubbish.* Relationships were more than manipulations, power struggles, and Kama Sutra sex.

Ah, hell, he shouldn't judge. It had taken him years to figure out that he wanted more than a nice ass in tight jeans. But now that he had, he was ready to settle down and find himself a warmhearted Scottish lass.

Gabe shifted uncomfortably in the driver's seat and turned on the radio. Usually, he was as easygoing as the next guy. But something about Emma Castle knocked him sideways. She was the one woman in the world who could make him feel off his game. It wasn't her beauty; he was bored with attractive women. Hell, back in the day, he'd cornered the market on gorgeous birds—blondes, brunettes, and redheads. He was looking for something more.

Out of nowhere, he found himself speculating . . . *What color is Emma's hair?* He glanced over. *Cinnamon?*

He swerved and muttered under his breath. What was wrong with him? *Cinnamon!* For Pete's sake, he wasn't a romantic. Sure, he could play the role to get a woman back to his flat—which he'd done many times—but still. *Cinnamon!* He almost reached down to make sure his balls were still intact.

But he had turned over a new leaf. No longer the hound dog of his youth, playing fast with the girls, or the rogue of his twenties. Now that he was thirty-one, he was ready for a real relationship. Not marriage per se, but something with more commitment than the string of one-nighters or two-nighters he'd enjoyed since his school days.

He glanced at Emma again on her side of the Land Rover. At Dom and Claire's wedding Emma had been much too uptight to have any fun. He'd tried to get her to loosen up, but to no avail. The more she'd given him her look of disapproval with those big evergreen eyes of hers, the harder he'd tried. In the end, he'd given up and overcompensated by taking a handful of women back to his room. He didn't stay, but returned downstairs to drink alone at the bar.

"Is the heat set all right for you?" he asked.

"Fine," she clucked at him with her full, enticing lips.

The conversation died once again. He wondered how long she planned to stay in Gandiegow. Hopefully, it wouldn't be too long.

Headlights appeared in front of them through the snow-induced whiteout. Gabe pumped the brakes to keep from hitting the car, but in vain. His Land Rover kept sliding toward them. He turned the wheel to avoid the crash, but his maneuver had them skidding into a ditch. Instinctively, he extended his arm to hold Emma in place. It registered that he pressed against her incredible breasts, but only for a moment, before they hit the far side of the embankment. *Bam.*

"Holy shit." He turned toward her. "Are you okay?"

The dash lights put off enough glow to illuminate her wide eyes staring at him.

"What is bloody wrong with you?" She glared down at his hand, still pressing up against her breasts.

He jerked his hand away. "Are you hurt?"

She peered down at her chest as if he'd left his imprint.

He flipped on the overhead light, not giving a rat's ass if she was angry with him or not. He had to know if she was okay. "Can you turn your head? Let me take a look in your eyes." He'd made damned sure her head hadn't hit the windshield. As evidence, his hand still tingled where he'd held her. But he wasn't entirely sure she hadn't impacted her side of the auto. "Humor me. I'm a doctor."

She rolled her eyes and shifted toward him. "Fine."

He looked in her eyes and her pupils looked good. He prided himself on his gentle touch and took extra care as he turned her chin. This little fender bender scared the shit of him. "If anything happened to you, Claire would kill me."

"Oh, so you're just worried about Claire taking the meat cleaver to you."

"Stop taking everything I say the wrong way." He scanned her body clinically from top to bottom. Or at least he tried to be clinical about it. "Anything else? Any other injuries?"

She rubbed her shoulder. "I hit my door a little."

"Hell." He leaned over her and pushed back her long hair to get better access. "Can you move it?"

She wiggled it around. "It's fine."

He gently ran his fingers over her shoulder, checking for a slight dislocation. Unfortunately, he got a whiff of her shampoo—apples? And of her—pure Emma. *Too damned intoxicating.* He tried to ignore it, but his pecker liked it. A lot.

"Ouch," she said.

"Sorry. I'm trying to be careful. I don't think anything's broken or dislocated. But you're probably going to have a bruise. We should get some ice on that." He opened his door and shoveled some snow into his hand, squeezing it into a brick. He pulled out a clean handkerchief, wrapped the ice pack in it, and leaned over her, holding it on her shoulder.

Her cheeks got red. "I can do it myself." When she took it from him, he noticed her hand trembled.

"Ah, Emma, we're going to be okay."

"I'm fine," she demanded.

"You're shaken up. It's a normal reaction to a car accident. Even minor ones. The adrenaline floods the body and overloads the nervous system."

"How come you're not shaking?"

He shrugged. Then rubbed his arm.

"Are you all right?" she asked.

"Aye." But his arm smarted where he'd braced it against the steering wheel so he didn't hit the windshield.

"What are we going to do now?" she asked.

He looked out the window and searched for the slow car that had caused the accident. It was gone. "We're going to get out of here. The Land Rover's a tank." When he put the vehicle in reverse, the wheels spun, but the tank didn't budge.

"And now?" she asked.

"We're going to call for a tow."

They both reached for their mobiles. Seconds later, they found out that neither one had a signal.

"Plan B," he said, pointing to the top of the hill. "See those lights?"

She looked, then turned back to him. "Yes?"

"We're going to wait there until the Land Rover is pulled out of this mess. What do you say, Ms. Castle? Are you up for a little snow trekking?"

She bent over and frowned at her red heels. "I guess I have to be."

"Wait here." He jumped out, tramped to the back, and retrieved her bag. The snow was really blowing now and the temperature had dropped here in the countryside. He knew they'd better hurry up to those lights before they both slipped into hypothermia.

He climbed into the backseat, as the bag and he wouldn't both fit in the front together.

She cranked her head around. "What are you doing with my suitcase?"

"You're damp from tumbling in the snow at the airport, right? And I have nothing good to say about your skirt in this weather. To traipse up that hill, you're going to have to be dressed warmer." He unzipped her bag and a pair of blue silk panties fell into his lap.

"Gabriel, stop," she said, panicked. She bent over the seat and reached for her bag. Then her eyes fell on her panties and she snatched them off his crotch, her cheeks turning bright pink.

But not before her fingertips accidentally brushed his cock. *Oh, God.*

"I'll get my clothes myself." She faced forward, reaching for the door handle.

He latched onto her good shoulder and anchored her to the seat. "What do you think you're doing? You're not going out there, not without being properly dressed. I'll turn your bag around so you can pull out what you need from where you are."

"Fine." She got on her knees and leaned over the seat.

Before he shifted the bag, he reached for a dry pair of her socks to stick in his pocket, but his thumb got hooked on a black bra.

Mortification once again swallowed her pretty face. She yanked her bra off his thumb. "You must stop handling my things."

She was so embarrassed. And so bloody cute about it. He'd never seen this side of her before. She'd always been so exact, restrained. And critical of him.

It was bad form to enjoy himself at her expense. But to see her so out of her element . . .

Not the in-control Emma now.

He peeked over the top of her luggage. "Any sweat-pants in there? You'll need them."

"Of course not. Do I look like an aerobics instructor?" She rummaged some more. "But I do have jeans." She yanked black jeans and a blue sweater from her luggage.

"What about sensible shoes? Like heavy boots or at least wellies?" He saw other underthings—items he'd like to get a closer look at—but she pulled the lid away, blocking his prying eyes.

"No boots. I've been living in southern California, remember? Just heels, flip-flops, and tennis shoes." She pulled out her sneakers and sat back down, speaking over her shoulder. "Close your eyes while I change. And don't peek."

He shrugged. "You don't have anything I haven't seen before."

"Please, Gabriel."

He closed his eyes but wasn't making any promises. His imagination went into overdrive.

Isn't that the way of things? As soon as a man decides he wants to live a more principled life, temptation is dropped into his lap. Literally. Her silk lace panties, lying there as they had, lit up his brain and other regions like high-wattage bulbs.

Sure, he was trying to change his past ways, but he wasn't *neutered*.

He heard her shuffling in the front seat and grunting.

"Need help with the zipper on that skirt?" He shouldn't have offered, but tomorrow he'd go back to working on being a gentleman.

"I've got it," she said in a strained voice.

He grinned at the images popping into his head. He did keep his eyes closed, though. For now.

He finally heard the zipper go down on her skirt.

Heard the sweater go over her head.

God, this is torture.

Heard her wriggle into her jeans.

He opened his eyes and found her big green eyes staring back from the visor mirror. He'd never seen eyes like hers.

"I knew it," she said, her glare turning dark again. "I knew you would break your promise."

"Sweetheart, I never promised you a damned thing."

She huffed while pulling up the zipper on her jeans.

He grinned at her reflection. "Hurry up and get your shoes on. Our objective is the top of that hill." He held up her extra socks. "You'll put these on when we get there." He shoved them in his pocket. He wished like hell he had a sled so he could drag her up the hill.

She gazed back at him. "What about you? Will you be warm enough? Your head is naked."

"I'm a Scot. This is only a wee chill to me." He gave her a confident smile, trying to assure her all would be well.

"What about the '*brrrr*' back at the airport?" She'd imitated his voice. "Not so Scottish then, huh?"

He ignored her and pulled another jacket from her bag, holding up the flimsy material. "Seriously, Emma, what were you thinking when you packed? This isn't heavy enough to handle a Highland summer breeze, let alone the winter."

"I left in a hurry."

He tossed the jacket upfront. "Put it on," he said gruffly. They wrapped their scarves around their necks and headed out into the bitter weather.

He'd only taken two steps when Emma tugged on his arm.

"Did you lock the car?" she asked.

"There's no need." He patted his pocket. "Besides, the keys are tucked away and I'm not pulling off my gloves to retrieve them."

"My belongings are in there," she complained.

"For heaven's sake." He spun her around, pointing her in the direction of the lights. "March, Your Highness. I promise if the Abominable Snowman ransacks your baggage before we get back, I'll be your personal mechanic for life. I mean it. Anytime, anywhere. I'm your guy. All right?"

"I don't own an auto," she grumbled, pulling away from him and huffing up the hill.

He trudged after her, muttering loud enough for her to hear, "The Sassenach would rather freeze to death than to be reasonable."

As they got closer, Gabe realized the cottage was not the beginning of civilization as he'd hoped. The lean-to of a cabin sat all alone with only a copse of trees to keep it company. "Let's see if anyone is home. There should be, with the lights on." He took Emma's elbow and helped her the last little bit, even though he knew she'd lecture him about it later.

Emma stopped, looking worried. "Do you think it's safe?"

"Aye. Ye're with me. I promise to take care of you."

She rolled her eyes. He knocked on the door and waited.

An old man with a gray beard and the girth of a two-ton lorry answered. With a jolly laugh, he greeted them as if they were expected. "Come in, come in."

Emma stepped closer to Gabe. He started to wrap his arm around her, but remembered himself. Surprisingly, she reached out and clung to his arm instead as they stepped into the small one-room cabin. There were a sink, a tiny stove, one rocking chair, a bed, and one pillow.

Gabe stepped forward and Emma dropped his arm. "We're sorry to bother you, sir, but we've had a bit of a run-in with the ditch down the way." He pulled off his gloves and stuck out a hand. "I'm Gabriel MacGregor."

The old guy took it, belly-laughing some more. "And this is your missus." He said it as if it were the truth and not a question.

Emma stepped up. "Heavens, no. We barely know each other."

The old man cocked an eyebrow and tilted his head as if to let her know what he thought of the fib.

Gabe frowned at her as well. "Nay, we're not married. May we stay by your fire while we wait for a tow?"

The old man chuckled again. "You think you'll get a tow truck out here at this hour? In this weather?"

"But my friend is expecting me." Emma pulled her cell from her pocket.

"I just finished making coffee and some oatcakes." The man slipped his coat on. "Help yourself."

"That would be grand." Gabe got his cell out, too. "Do you have a signal, Emma?"

"No. You?"

"Nay," he said, frowning.

"No worries. Use mine." The old guy pointed to an old-fashioned black rotary phone hanging on the wall. "It works, but I'm certain you'll be stuck here for the night." He grabbed his gloves. "Sorry I have to leave you, but I'm going out to sleep with Miz Flanders."

Gabe and Emma shared a glance. Was this guy a wee daft?

The big man laughed again. "Oh, you two, she's my prize sheep. She's feeling a mite under the weather. Gotta give her her medicine every hour, the veterinarian says." He picked up a vial from the table along with his mug of coffee. "There's only the one bed and one quilt. But I'm sure you'll manage." He winked at Gabe.

As the man opened the door, snow flew in; then he was gone. When the door shut, the two of them were left inside, alone.

Chapter Two

For a long moment, they both stared at the closed door. Then Gabe turned to the wall phone. "While I make that call, you"—he pointed to Emma—"get those shoes and socks off now." He tossed her the dry ones. "Put those on and get warm by the fire."

"You are the bossiest man I've ever met."

"Thank you."

She put her hands on her hips like she wanted to argue, but he assumed her cold feet convinced her otherwise. She slipped into the rocker by the fire and began untying her snow-covered laces.

He retrieved his auto card from his wallet and glanced at Emma as she slipped off the first shoe. When he picked up the receiver, he was relieved that there was a dial tone. As he placed the call, he turned back to her as the second shoe fell to the floor. "If you don't hurry and get those dry socks on, I'll come over and do it for you."

She glared at him, but the person on the other end picked up and he turned away. Gabe explained the situation to the auto club, but it didn't do any good. The earliest the tow company could get there would be in the morning. Basically, they insinuated he was crazy for suggesting otherwise.

He hung up. "*Great.*"

"What's the matter?" Emma leaned over and pulled on the second dry sock.

"We're not getting towed out."

"What?"

"The crews are stuck themselves. As soon as they can, they'll come to us."

"When is that?"

"Not tonight. Tonight you're stuck with me."

"*Marvelous.*" The frown she gave him said she'd rather take her chances with the old guy and Miz Flanders. She stood. "I'd better break it to Claire."

He put his hand up. "You stay by the fire. I'll call Dom's cell phone. I don't want to wake Claire. She has to get up early, remember?"

"Yes." Emma plopped down in the chair. "The blooming scones."

Gabe tsked at her, turned away, and smiled. He made the phone call and told Dom what was up.

When Gabe hung up, he saw Emma rocking in the chair with her hands in front of the hearth. With the fire as her backdrop, her cinnamon hair glowed.

He stopped breathing. The walls inched closer together. Suddenly the cottage felt too small and too cozy.

One bed.

One pillow.

One quilt.

Two adversaries.

He cleared his throat. But his voice still came out husky. "You take the bed. I'll sleep in the rocking chair." The rocker wasn't a high-back and would be uncomfortable as hell, but that's what he got for offering to help out Claire and Dom. He gazed down at the stone floor, looking for a soft spot to lie on, but it would be too cold.

"I can't let you do that," Emma argued. "I'll sleep in the chair."

"No, I insist." Given his past, he wouldn't dare offer for them to share the bed. She'd consider it an assault on her sensibilities.

She didn't understand, though, that she wasn't his type—too high maintenance. Even if Emma Castle was *naked and willing*, she wouldn't be able to coax him into doing more than sleeping. He was looking for a Scottish country lass, not a city woman. A girl who understood hard work and sharing the load. Not one with a maid who bustled around so she didn't have to lift a finger.

No, Emma Castle was too much trouble, by far.

He stared at the uncomfortable rocking chair. Another sleepless night wouldn't kill him. Last night, he'd delivered Amy and Coll's first baby. A boy, seven pounds, one ounce. "I'll take the chair and watch the fire." He hadn't seen any dry logs outside and there were only two left by the hearth. They were definitely going to get cold tonight.

Emma rose from the rocker and went to the small twin bed, which had been pushed into the corner. She stood over it, staring down, frowning. "Umm, I know this is going to make me sound awful, but you have to take the bed. I won't be able to lie down on this."

He walked over to inspect the bed, too. The quilt folded at the bottom of the mattress was pristine white with a few Red Cardinal blocks scattered about, perfectly clean. But the gray sheets pulled over the mattress looked like they'd never seen the inside of a washer. "I see what you mean. Not very sanitary."

"Maybe we should go back to the car?"

"Too cold. We'll have to stay here." He looked over at

the two logs. It wasn't much, but it was better than the prospect of carbon monoxide poisoning. "I have an idea."

He grabbed the quilt and spread it over the bed. "Here. Lie on this and I'll tuck it around you."

She looked pensively at the rocking chair and then back to him. "If you promise not to paw me, I have a better solution."

"Okay."

"We can both use the bed like a divan. If we sit and lean our heads against the wall, we could get some rest. There should be enough quilt to at least wrap around our legs to keep us warm."

Well . . . Gabe might have to adjust his perception of Emma Castle. She wasn't just an upper-crust beauty; she had brains, too. Usually he admired a good brain, but for some reason he wasn't happy that Emma might be more than what she appeared. "Then you won't mind me sitting next to you?"

She gazed at the expanse of him like he would cop a feel if given half the chance. "I'll suffer through."

"That's the spirit," he said.

"As long as you keep your hands to yourself."

"I assure you, that's the last thing on my mind."

She harrumphed, muttered something about an egghead, which made no sense, and busied herself adjusting the blanket.

"I didn't mean that the way it came out," he tried. She wouldn't believe him that he was a changed man. She ignored him, the damage already done.

Then she produced an extra-long yawn, her eyes watering.

"How many hours have you been up?"

"Don't worry yourself over it," she said, suppressing another yawn.

"Pick your spot." He went back to the hearth. "I'll put another log on the fire."

She put herself at the foot of the bed. He figured so she could make a fast getaway if necessary.

He glanced at his watch. "Who knows? Maybe we'll get lucky. The tow company could surprise us and get here sooner than expected."

"I do hope so." She wrapped the quilt over her legs. "Gabriel?"

"Hmm?"

"Good manners dictate that I thank you."

"For what?"

"For forcing me to change into warmer clothes."

"Don't mention it." He stoked up the fire. "I should apologize for causing you to fall in the snow at the airport. Sorry," he offered back.

"Oh yes, there is that." She looked like she might take back her thanks of a moment ago.

He lingered in front of the hearth. Not for warmth but for working on pinning his newfound principles in place. But old habits die hard. He was alone with a beautiful woman, and he was going to share a bed with her. Granted, it was more like sharing a sofa, since they would be sitting up with their backs against the wall. But still. In the past, he wouldn't have given a second thought to taking advantage of their cozy situation. He might've even gone as far as to believe it was a sign—that he was supposed to put the moves on her. But he was a changed man now. And, well, *Emma was Emma*. Not for him, that was for sure. He needed to stop visualizing her naked and tamp down the hard-on that threatened. She was not a potential mate—no matter how attractive she might be. Since they had to, the two of them would huddle together on the bed for warmth and nothing else.

He finished and wandered over to the bed. "Can I join you?" He kept telling himself to treat her like a sister. The only problem was, he'd never had one.

She scooted away from him, giving him plenty of room. He sat down and made sure he didn't touch one cell on her body. He wouldn't pull the cover over his legs just yet, either. She was already so skittish.

She leaned her head back and closed her eyes, and he thought she might be going to sleep. He relaxed against the wall, too, deciding that being holed up here with Emma Castle wasn't so bad. It gave him a respite from Gandiegow and his worries back there. It wasn't easy fitting in to a small town. Emma shocked him out of his thoughts by speaking.

"I still can't figure it out," she said with her eyes shut. "How in the world did you, of all people, come to be a doctor?"

He shook his head. "Aye, me of all people. Go to sleep, Princess."

Within minutes, her breathing turned even. According to her, she'd had a rough twenty-four hours. Emma seemed to think everything would be okay once she saw Claire. But the truth was, Claire had her own problems, and maybe Gabe should've warned Emma. Told her she should've thought twice and gone somewhere else, somewhere out of the line of fire. Anywhere but Scotland.

Emma woke slowly, feeling rested and contented. Things were a little hazy. Where was she? Whose body did she cling to? Why did she take such comfort in the arms around her? Slowly she became aware of the location of her hand and what lay underneath. *An erection.*

She rocketed to her feet, fully awake, appalled at what she'd been doing. Had she been rubbing him? Certainly not, but her hand had been on his . . . on his . . . *ohmigod,* his crotch. She wiped at a bit of drool from her face and saw in horror that she'd left some spittle on his jacket, where she'd been cuddled up to him. "Bloody hell," she muttered.

Gabriel came awake, looking dazed, too. "What's the matter? Is the tow here?"

"No. Just a bad dream." It was the truth. She couldn't admit to snuggling with him. Although she suspected he knew, because he eyed her closely. She glanced at his crotch. *Oh, why did I do that?* Even more dismaying, his hard-on didn't look diminished in the least. In fact it looked . . . bigger.

Her mother's teachings about men in the morning were very clear. *An erection in the morning is normal and should be expected. It doesn't mean that he's necessarily been stimulated by thoughts of you. But it also doesn't mean that you can't take advantage of his morning erection to get an orgasm.* Emma had been fourteen and appalled by her mother's info dump.

But Emma wasn't fourteen anymore. If she had to admit the truth, she was a little curious about what he looked like. How he felt. And gratified she'd played some part in causing such a response in him, no matter what facts her mother had spouted. And she was . . .

She licked her lips. *Turned on. Oh, God.*

Emma peeked at Gabriel's face and saw that the sadistic womanizer was blushing. *Blushing.* Cheeks red, sheepish look on his face. Why was Gabriel, the rogue, blushing?

"Emma, ye're staring again." He pulled the quilt over his manhood.

It was best to change the subject. She plastered on her politest smile. "What time is it? It's still dark out."

"It's well past seven," he said, apparently playing along with Let's Pretend This Never Happened.

"How about some tea?" she said.

He nodded. "Tea sounds fantastic. I wonder if the old guy has some."

"Great. Why don't you check and get it started?" She heard him mutter *Princess* under his breath as she flounced off to the bathroom. Hopefully, *her drool* on his jacket would dry before she came back.

She dawdled for quite a while in the restroom but finally had to emerge. "Is the tea ready?"

"Nay, just coffee. I hope you like yours black. I couldn't find cream or sugar."

"Savages," she muttered. That's what the Scots were. No tea. No cream. No sugar. "No, thank you."

"Just as well," he said. "There is only one mug, anyway." He took a sip of his coffee and went back to the rocker with a pad of paper.

"What are you doing?"

"Writing the old guy a note, in case he doesn't get back before we leave."

"What for?"

"Thanking him for the use of his cabin."

She felt stupid. Plus, she hadn't anticipated that Gabriel knew anything about polite manners.

Just as he took another sip from his mug, there was a knock at the door. He went to answer it.

A young man with bright red cheeks and red hair stood there. "Dr. MacGregor?"

"Aye."

"I got you pulled out of the ditch." Red handed him a clipboard. "Sign here, please. You'd better hurry and get down there. Your auto is blocking the roadway."

Emma rushed to pull on her shoes, anxious to see Claire. And to get away from Gabriel. Even though they had a drive ahead of them.

Gabriel held her coat open for her. *Another surprise.*

He could be a gentleman, too? Instead of stepping into it, she snatched it away from him. Not to be rude, but so she didn't have to be beholden to him. After she slid into it, she headed for the door. Out of the corner of her eye, she got another little shock: Gabriel had folded the Cardinal quilt and righted the bed. *More civilized than the man I remember.*

He followed behind her but stopped when he got outside the door and looked around.

"What's wrong?" she said.

"I don't see an outbuilding."

"So?"

"Then where did the old guy get off to?"

"I don't know. Maybe the outbuilding is on the other side of the hill." She turned back, and Red was halfway back to his lorry. She followed after him.

"I guess." Gabriel caught up to her. "When we get to the Land Rover, make sure you switch into dry socks again."

"Will you ever stop telling me what to do?"

"Doctor. Remember?"

"Bossy," she said.

"Princess," he shot back.

At the vehicle, Gabriel stuffed some bills into Red's hand. The kid tried to refuse them, but Gabriel insisted. She got in and traded out her socks, shoving her soaked sneakers under the vent.

When Gabriel started the Land Rover, she turned on the radio and chose a nice station with a soothing piano. He sighed loudly.

"What?" she said. "Need some head-banging music to get you going?"

"I don't mind a little classical music . . . if I'm going off to sleep. I'd like to stay awake and keep my wits about me. I expect we'll have an icy ride. Can't be too safe."

Considering the auto had just been pulled out of the ditch, she couldn't argue. She pointed to the radio. "By all means."

He scanned the channels until he found a nineties pop station.

She stared out the window, certain the sun would come up soon. In the meantime, she worked at putting Gabriel MacGregor out of her mind. Being near him had stressed her sensibilities. The next person she planned to speak to was Claire Douglas Russo. And no one else.

Finally, the sun made a brief appearance before slipping behind the clouds. At least Emma could get a better lay of the land now. It was vast, desolate, and beautiful. Snow either covered or dusted everything, and she wondered what it might look like in the bloom of summer. Her ramblings helped her to further ignore Gabriel while he hummed and sang along. She couldn't help but notice that he had a nice voice, though.

Sometime later, when they came over a hill, Gabriel slowed the Land Rover and pointed. "Down there. Gandiegow." His voice was laced with a harshness it hadn't had earlier.

The small village lay below, tucked into the curve of the sea under the rocky bluff. From this angle she could see the rooftops, most of them bright red with some gray ones scattered in between. Claire had told her there were only sixty-three houses in Gandiegow. Small by any standard.

"What a charming place," she said.

Gabriel turned off the radio. "Aye, charming." His sarcastic tone belied his true sentiment. One glance at him and she knew he'd put his armor on as if going into battle.

But she couldn't let herself care. They were here at last. Gabriel eased the auto down the hill and pulled the car into a parking lot on the far side of the town, where eight other vehicles sat.

"Why are we parking here?"

"It's a closed community. No roads in the town, no vehicles past this point. We walk from here."

Her arms stilled ached from yesterday after dragging her heavy luggage.

"Don't worry. I'll get your bags." It sounded more like, *I'll do this one last thing. Then I'll be done with ye.*

She shook her head. Since when did she hear deep Scottish accents in her brain?

"I'll take no argument from you today." He stepped out and slammed his door.

"What's wrong with you?" she asked, getting out, as well. A gannet flew above them and cackled. The waves crashed against the seawall. And she waited. "What happened to Mr. Good-Humored?"

He unlocked the back and frowned at her. His lips parted, and for a second he looked like he might tell her. But then he glanced away. "Nothing's the matter."

She chalked it up to him being tired. Maybe he hadn't slept well with her clinging to him like cellophane throughout the night.

"It's this way." He pulled her suitcases out. "The restaurant." He took off down the path.

The sidewalk had been shoveled and salted. The path forked and they headed toward the coastline with a long dock off to the east. She stared down the boardwalk at the buildings and cottages, which looked at if they were only inches from the sea. The first building they passed had a large sign that read THE FISHERMAN.

"What's that?" she asked.

"The pub." Gabriel gestured down the boardwalk. "The General Store is that way. In case you need to buy some boots." He shot her a pointed look. "And ye do."

He stopped in front of a three-and-a-half-story white building with a sharp slanted roof with plenty of windows. "There's no sign yet, but they're going to call it Dominic and Claire's Pastas & Pastries."

"Well, isn't this quaint?" Emma said.

"Not quite the savages you thought we were?" He raised his eyebrows at her.

"I get cranky when I can't have my morning tea."

"Of course you do. You Brits are such an emotional lot."

As he held the door open, Emma stepped inside, trying to think up a scathing comeback. And she almost missed it . . .

A pot rocketed across the room, banging against the wall just inches from Gabriel's head. "What the hell?"

Chapter Three

Emma stepped to the side as several people ran for the door, pushing past her to get outside. She saw Dominic glance to where the pot hit, but he didn't acknowledge either her or Gabriel. Instead he turned back to his wife, who'd lobbed it in the first place. "Claire, you've got to stop this."

Wild-eyed, Claire threw a plate at him this time. It shattered against the wall. "You're the backside of an Italian mule." She picked up a Goliath-sized metal spoon and slung it at Dominic's groin. "You always have to have your way."

The spoon didn't meet its mark, but it did hit Dominic's crotch-protecting hand. "Dammit, Claire. That hurt." He rubbed his knuckles.

She picked up a butcher knife and waved it. "Be grateful 'twasn't yere balls."

Emma stepped forward, afraid Dominic might indeed be parted from his testicles. "Put the knife down, Claire."

Recognition skidded across Claire's face. She withered, all the fire going out of her, as if someone had turned off the burner. The knife slipped from her hand, falling to the counter. "Emma," she breathed, and ran to her.

As they embraced, Emma glanced over at Dominic.

"Crazy Scots," Dominic muttered. "Always full of passion, but the wrong kind."

Claire's head shot up. "Keep yere opinions to yereself, Dominic Russo. Just so we're clear, from this moment on, ye've been cut off. Ye'll not be enjoying my *scones* anytime soon." She'd slung it across the room at him, too, saying it as if it was the most sexual thing in the world. She took Emma's arm and strutted for the stairs, that girl making sure her tail end stayed in Dominic's line of sight.

Emma saw the moment when *Oh, shit, what have I done?* crossed Dominic's face. He took in his wife's curvaceous body and his shoulders sank like a hungry man's with the proverbial feast being cleared away. Poor chap.

Emma followed Claire up the narrow steps. They didn't stop on the next floor at the grand dining room, but continued on up the next flight.

"What is going on with you two?" Emma demanded.

"Let's get you settled," Claire said as she tromped up each stair.

"What about my bags?" Emma said.

Claire pulled out her phone. "Gabriel, bring up Emma's things." She hung up without so much as a *please* or a *thank you.*

Claire went on. "Later, I'll show you around town."

Emma grabbed her arm. "No. We're going to talk. You're going to tell me why you were launching the kitchenwares at your husband's head."

"Dominic is a stubborn jackass." Claire opened the door to a flat. They walked into a warm parlor, decorated a little shabbily in blue chintz, but it felt homey. Claire burst into tears.

Emma closed the door and hugged her friend fiercely.

"Oh, sweeting," Emma said. "We'll work it out. We always do."

"But you came here so we can fix *you*. Not my jerk of a husband," Claire wailed.

"We'll just have to multitask," Emma declared.

That won her a little smile, but it didn't last. The gravity of the scene from downstairs returned quickly, sobering both of them.

There was a knock at the door. Gabriel stuck his head inside. "Is it safe to come in?" He stared directly at Emma.

She stared right back, hoping he could read her mind. "Yes, come." She wondered how much Gabriel, the rascal, had known beforehand about the Russos' problems.

Gabriel pushed the door all the way open and wheeled her bags into the parlor. He put his hands into his pockets, looking uncomfortable.

Despite Gabriel not warning her, Emma kind of felt bad for him in that moment. "Thank you for hauling my luggage up to the third floor. I don't think I could've managed it on my own."

"No problem."

She wondered if she should offer him something. A drink? A tip? Breakfast? *A right good kiss?*

"I'm off." Gabriel nodded his head to both of them and left.

Emma sat on the worn blue sofa and patted the spot next to her for Claire. "Come and tell me what's going on. You know I'll do anything to help." But then she amended her offer. "Except give you marriage advice. I'm the last person in the world to counsel you about your relationship with Dominic."

Claire pushed back her red hair. "There's nothing wrong with us that a good skillet to his head won't fix."

"What do you want that he won't give you?" Emma asked.

"A baby." Claire burst into tears, again. "We've been married ten years, Emms. Don't you think it's time? Every day, my ovaries shrivel a little bit more." Claire put her hand on her abdomen. "Nothing more than dried-up raisins by now."

"Claire." Emma grabbed her hand and pulled her closer. "What can I do?"

Claire broke into a sad smile. "Hold Dominic down while I ravish him?"

Emma hugged her. "You've got plenty of time. You're only thirty. Lots of women have babies well into their forties."

"But I'm tired of waiting. I want a bairn now."

Everyone knew about Claire, how she'd been baby crazy her whole life. Cooking and baking—that was her job. The only thing she'd ever really wanted was to be a mama. When Claire and Dominic had married, Emma had assumed Claire would start popping out moppets nine months later. No one had thought they'd still be childless at this point. Emma had assumed something was medically wrong.

"Are you two capable? I mean, have you been checked?"

"Right as rain," Claire said. "Dominic is as randy as ever. He has condoms stockpiled in every room of the flat."

Emma's cheeks flared and she turned away. She couldn't let Claire see. She'd lied to Claire forever about her own sex life and now wasn't the time to come clean. It was one thing to make up a bunch of sex stories about herself, but it was a completely different matter to glimpse inside someone's real sex life. Something that had happened way too often to Emma as a marriage therapist.

"Dominic says we can't afford to have a babe right now," Claire continued. "I think he's being ridiculous. Poor people have children all the time. Why should we be any different?"

Emma knew better than to offer money. Claire and Dominic had a stubborn streak that ran a kilometer wide when it came to what they considered charity.

"Well, sweeting," Emma said, "I'm with you. I will be your *yes-friend* until the end of time. If you want to have a baby, I think Dominic should go along with it."

Claire jumped up and paced the room. "That gorgeous, pigheaded Italian." With each step, she got more wound up. "I'm finally back in my hometown. I'm ready, willing, and able." She gestured wildly to the room. "Gandiegow is the perfect place to start a family. It's time. Right?"

Emma nodded in agreement.

"So what if the restaurant books say we don't have two shillings to rub together," Claire added. "Love is all that counts."

At that moment, Dominic dropped a platter or something; it could be heard all the way upstairs. Along with a litany of swear words, which reverberated through the ductwork. Claire slumped onto the blue couch, too. "What happens when love isn't enough?"

Seeing Claire crushed broke Emma's heart. She hadn't planned on hiding out long in Scotland, but she would have to stay for as long as Claire needed her. *Clearing the air with Mum and Dad will have to wait.*

Emma put her arm around her friend and Claire laid her head on her shoulder. *Just like we're eleven again.*

As girls, they'd bonded over being outsiders. Claire, the young Scottish lass from a small town, thrown into the hustle and bustle of London. Emma, left alone and adrift in her own famous family, to be raised by nannies who revolved in and out of her life. That is, until Claire's mom, Nessa, had come to be their housekeeper and brought Claire, and a sense of family, with her.

Emma, though, had something to say to her best friend. "We need to have a serious talk about your temper, Claire. You know how it gets you into trouble."

"I can't help myself," Claire said.

Emma patted her arm. "You're going to have to try. You mustn't go waving knives around." Not that throwing pots was much better. "Dominic could've gotten hurt."

"I know. But he's just such a . . . such a *man*."

"I know," Emma said. "One more thing. I hate to point out the obvious, but how do you expect to get pregnant if you just cut Dominic off?"

"Oh, shite," Claire sobbed. "I'm so tired. I wasn't thinking."

"I know. Come. You need to have a lie-down." Emma guided Claire down the hall. "I'll get you a cool washcloth for your forehead and you'll get some rest."

The master bedroom had nothing but a full-sized bed and a dresser in it. Emma pulled back the covers and tucked Claire in. She found the loo, prepared a washcloth, and took it back to her.

"I'm glad ye're here with me," Claire said.

Emma brushed back the hair on her friend's face. "Me, too. You rest. I'll go downstairs and see what I can do to get the kitchen cleaned up for later."

"Thank you," Claire said. "I don't want to see Dominic right now."

"I know." Emma left the bedroom but didn't immediately go back downstairs to the restaurant. She grabbed a quick shower to clean up from her long travels and to wash any residual dog-blanket smell off her, too. Afterward, she stared out the window into the cloudy sky, combing her hair and wondering what she'd gotten herself into. She wasn't a marriage counselor anymore. How exactly was she going to keep some distance and still be there for Claire?

Emma did a double take. In the center of town was a ship's mast. *A ship's mast?* She gave it a closer look. No, it was the white steeple of the church, jutting above the other roofs. It hadn't caught her eye before, but it did now. It stuck out.

With Emma's faux pas all over the Internet, her family would be even more in the limelight—and not in the fashion to which they were accustomed. Emma gazed upon the white steeple in the center of Gandiegow again and cringed. She was just like the steeple; she stuck out, too.

Gabe stood behind the restaurant's counter and poured himself a cup of coffee. "Well, that killed the lunch crowd."

Dom made a noncommittal grunt as he finished picking up the last dirty dish.

Gabe wiped off the counter. "I don't want to sound like a hen, but do you want to talk about it?"

"Hell, no." Dom shrugged his massive shoulders into his coat and snatched up the list. "I might as well get to Inverness and pick up the supplies now. Put a sign on the door when you leave. I should be back by three or four."

"Aren't you going to tell Claire that you're going?

Dom glared at him from the doorway. "Stay out of it, Gabe." He slammed the door behind him.

"If only I could." Gabe wrote up a ticket, put money in the register, and grabbed two of Claire's scones. When he turned around, Emma was standing there with her hands on her hips. Her hair looked perfect—down, damp, and wavy—and she was wearing a white blouse and blue jeans. Tight blue jeans. This woman was a combination of uptight professional and hot lay.

"How long has this been going on?" she demanded.

He glanced down at his plate. "I assume you're *not* talking about my scone habit."

"Did you know about their problems before you came here on holiday?"

He grabbed another plate, put one of his scones on it and laid it on the counter beside his. "Sit. I'll get water on for your tea."

"So, you knew and didn't warn me that Claire and Dominic were warring?" She glared at him. "Aren't you going to answer my questions?"

He grabbed a bag and put the scones in it. "Even better. Let's go where we can discuss this in private." He glanced up to gesture toward the flat on the third floor, like Claire might hear.

"Fine. I'll go grab my coat."

While she went back upstairs, he washed up the plates, put his coffee in a to-go cup, and put a sign on the door that the restaurant wouldn't open again until dinner.

When Emma came back down, she had a frown on her face. "I hadn't given it any thought before, but where are you staying? Is there a hotel or something in town?"

"Nay. I'm at the doctor's quarters."

"Hmm. That was nice of the doctor to share his place with you."

"Aye." He'd tell her, but not this minute. "Come."

They took the path behind the restaurant and walked away from the sea, toward the bluff. Between the red postbox and a small cottage with a blue door sat a two-story cottage known as the doctor's quarters. The downstairs was dedicated to caring for patients, and the upstairs was the doctor's flat. Gabe opened the front door and pointed for Emma to take the steps.

She looked toward the surgery. "Is the doctor not seeing patients today?"

"He was away overnight."

She looked around the entryway. "This is cozy."

"Aye." The walls were dark wood paneling, the floors dark wood, too. The cottage was more than a hundred years old and suited Gabe.

She pointed to the adjacent wall. "What a beautiful quilt."

"Yes." The quilt depicted trees and cottages in varying green and brown prints. The women's guild from his father's church had made it for him when he'd finished medical school.

"The handwoven rug?" she prodded, pointing to the earth-tone rug that had been here when he moved in.

"Not now," he said. *What am I? A blasted interior decorator?* He pointed up the stairs. "The kitchen is that way."

She glanced around once more. "I love this place. It feels like a home."

He shook his head. "And you've only seen the entryway."

"I don't believe in vibes, but if I did, I think the doctor's house has good ones." She spun around and sauntered up the stairs.

"At the top, to the right." He followed behind, doing his best to concentrate on the steps instead of her gluteus maximus.

"When does the doctor get back?" she asked.

"He's back," Gabe said. "Emma, I'm the—"

A man burst through the front door. "Doc, are you in?"

"What is it, Ramsay?" Gabe said.

Emma's mouth fell open. For a moment he enjoyed her shock. He hadn't *planned* to deceive her, but it sure entertained the hell out of him to pull the Scottish wool over her eyes. Especially after she'd made him feel so uncomfortable a few minutes ago.

Gabe headed back downstairs, with Emma following.

Ramsay held his arm up with a fishhook sticking out. "You said to come to you if we got injured instead of taking care of it ourselves." He frowned. "Well, here I am."

"Good." This was progress as far as Gabe was concerned. The townsfolk had pretty much shunned him so far. All because he wasn't their bloody precious Doc Fleming. They blamed Gabe for Doc Fleming's decision to retire to the south of France with his sister and her family. So to have one of the fishermen come here to the surgery, yes, it was progress.

"Go through," he said to Ramsay. "Emma, I won't be long."

She nodded but shot him a look that said he was in for a helluva lecture when he got upstairs.

Gabe took care of Ramsay. It was an easy fix. He clipped the end off the hook and pulled it through. Ramsay didn't need stitches, but a thorough cleaning, a bandage, and a tetanus shot were necessary. "It was right of you to come, Ramsay. You don't want to end up with lockjaw."

"Can I get back to the boat now?"

"Aye, but keep that wound dry. I don't want you to get an infection." Gabe sent him on his way and went back to Emma upstairs. He found her in the parlor, inspecting his pictures.

He pointed to one of them. "That's Dominic and me when we were ten. We were a couple of hellions. My father gave up on us at some point and concentrated on his parishioners instead of trying to wrangle us."

She set the picture back down and lit into him. "So, the doctor let you stay here, huh?"

"Sorry about that."

"How long have you been Gandiegow's doctor, anyway?"

"Three months." It had been the longest three months of his life. He'd never imagined the Highlanders would treat him like an outlander. He was a Scot from Edinburgh, dammit. How ridiculous could they be?

"So, you came before Claire and Dominic? You're the reason they moved all the way up here?"

"Nay. They were set to come, and then this position opened up. Dom talked me into it." The two of them were closer than brothers, always living near enough to see each other several times a week. When Dom and Claire took work in Glasgow, Gabe had found a position in one of the suburbs. "Doc Fleming, the old physician, insisted I come sooner rather than later."

"I see."

He wondered that Claire hadn't told her about him coming here—it was a hit to his ego that she hadn't. He assumed he had been discussed often, but apparently not as much as he liked to think.

"Let's go sit in the kitchen and have our breakfast. Well, lunch now." He pointed the way and followed her. She sat at the small dining table while he put on a kettle for her tea.

"When was the last time you saw Claire?" he asked.

"I came to Glasgow last summer for her birthday. I stayed a few days with her, saw Mum for a day in London, then flew back to LA. But we talk all the time."

"But since they moved here six weeks ago?"

Her frown deepened. "No, we haven't spoken. Work hasn't been going well for me."

"It's good ye're here now, is all I have to say."

"How bad is it?" she asked in her clipped British accent. "When did it all start?"

"Not long after they arrived," confessed Gabe. "It was like Claire being back in Gandiegow made her, I don't know, made her baby crazy. Like it had to happen now—or else."

"She's always been baby crazy," Emma said. "That's nothing new. But she does seem frantic. Which *is* new."

Gabe gazed at her in earnest. "Now that you're here, you can help them. You're the expert."

Emma thrust out her hands. "No. No, I can't."

"You're a marriage therapist and Claire's best friend." Emma flinched as if burned. "But—"

He sat across from her and reached for her hand to prove how important this was, but at the last second, he pulled back. "If you hadn't come now, you can be sure that I would've been calling you soon to come fix them."

The kettle whistled and Gabe rose to finish her tea. He looked over and saw Emma chewing her lip.

"Emma," Gabe encouraged, "it has to be you. I had some psychiatric training in my medical rotation, but that's it. You, though, you've been doing it full-time now for how many years?"

"Three." She sighed heavily, like it'd been a hundred.

"Well, then, it's settled. You'll take care of them and that will be that." He set a teacup in front of her.

"You have no idea why I've come to this remote part of Scotland, do you?" Her voice had an edge to it like she was teetering pretty damn close to hysteria.

"To see Claire?" he answered cautiously.

"To hide out." She hung her head for a moment, then looked back up at him. "I'm the laughingstock of marriage counselors everywhere. Or their greatest shame, would be more like it. I guess you didn't see my debut on YouTube. I'm a washout. Unless, of course, Claire and Dominic are planning a divorce. *Then I'm their girl*."

"What are you talking about?"

She told him about the video and how she'd come here to regroup. Finally, she finished with the bad news. "I mean, what I'm trying to say is, I can't help. I've given up the profession." She looked down at her feet and mumbled, "I just haven't told my parents yet."

Gabe poured the tea for her and pushed the sugar bowl closer. He'd seen Eleanor Hamilton, Emma's mother, on television more than once. He was no prude, but Eleanor's blunt talk about sexual positions, styles, tools, and toys was enough to put him off sex. And he liked sex a lot. Emma's father, Dean Castle, had accolades from countless movie stars. But Gabe had read his books and thought his techniques for saving relationships came down to a lot of manipulation and mind games. He wondered what Emma must have suffered through as a child with such infamous parents.

Gabe caught hold of Emma's arm and forced himself to ignore her soft skin. *I have to make her understand.* "Dominic and Claire *can't* get a divorce." He was surprised how forceful his voice sounded. He hated to admit even to himself how much he relied on Dom and Claire's marriage working. He wanted Dom to be happy; his foster brother had had such a hard time of it. *And Claire makes Dom happy, dammit.* Gabe had never met two people more in love, more in sync, more perfect for each other. Their relationship was the reason he'd turned his own life around. The reason he'd reformed himself from badass to choirboy. It had taken him a lot of years, but he wanted what they had. He wanted a partner. He wanted someone to come home to every day. He wanted love, too.

The way he saw it, if Dominic and Claire Russo couldn't make it, no one could.

"If I get involved, they will most certainly get divorced," Emma emphasized again. "I have a real knack for finishing off relationships." She gave a bark of laughter, as if she'd made a terrible joke. "My track record for helping couples stay together sucks, to use a vulgar American term."

She'd let her guard down. She certainly wasn't talking like the haughty debutante he'd thought her to be. She looked up at him with hopeless eyes.

He squeezed her arm. "We'll just do the best we can."

"You aren't listening," Emma said desperately.

She straightened then, as if remembering whom she was speaking with—Go Get 'Em Gabriel, as she'd nick-named him at the wedding. "Fine. I'm taking Claire's side," she said tersely. "Why can't she have a baby?"

"I never said she can't . . ." Gabe fumbled. "But it has to be a mutual decision. And Dominic says—"

Emma stood and tried towering over him by putting her hands on her hips. "It's not fair for Dominic to hold his sperm hostage. If Claire wants a baby, she should get to have one. End of story."

Gabe stood, as well, and showed her who towered over whom. "It takes a couple to raise a child, Emma."

"Come into the twenty-first century, Gabriel," she replied. "Fathers are optional."

He got angry, ready to deliver a sermon she wouldn't soon forget. *Fathers optional, indeed.*

She thwarted him, though, by turning on her heel and marching out of his kitchen, leaving him with nothing but his anger and her lukewarm cup of tea.

As Emma stomped down the stairs, she heard Gabriel swearing, his brogue thick and his words harsh. *Good.* She felt bloody proud about putting his big Scottish arse in its place. Of course, unlike her mother, she didn't really believe that fathers were optional. It just felt good to tick him off.

The dull headache at the base of her neck got incrementally worse. The headache had first surfaced when Claire slammed the pot against the wall; Gabriel had made it worse by forcing her into an impossible situation. *Penned in from all sides.*

She made her way back to the restaurant and upstairs to the flat. Claire wasn't there, which was just as well. Emma needed a few moments alone to pull herself together. She paced the floor, going over it in her head. She'd always prided herself on being Claire's yes-friend— loyal, supportive—what every woman needed. Yet something wasn't right.

She went to the desk in the corner and sat down, putting her head in her hands. She looked down. A ledger lay open. She sucked in a breath.

There it was in black-and-white—red, actually Dominic's side of the story. She shouldn't snoop, but she'd been thrown in the middle of it, almost like the pot hitting the wall.

The restaurant stood on shaky ground, the negative numbers stacked up against it. A bad shipment of meat. The last quilting retreat canceled due to bad weather, meaning no tourist pounds. Not enough revenue coming in on a regular basis. Claire and Dominic's livelihood hung in the balance and tipped precariously toward no return.

This definitely isn't the time to have a baby.

Emma's stomach turned on her. Maybe she should've eaten more than a nibble of a scone. Or maybe she should've gotten all the facts first before making any declarations. A short time ago, she'd assured Claire that she was on her side. And now?

And now . . . Emma didn't know.

Gabe hiked to the top of the bluff to blow off steam. Emma and her idiotic idea that fathers were optional. What a crock of shite.

Gabe hated to think where he might've ended up without his own father. His mother had died when he was only a babe. Only recently had he realized what his father had gone through. His da had been *all*—father, breadwinner, spiritual leader for his church. Gabe hadn't missed his mother, never knowing her, but maybe he wouldn't have been such a handful if she'd been around. He felt terrible for what he'd put his da through. Gabe had always believed Da's flock had come first, that he saw Gabe as an inconvenience, but lately he'd gotten a clue. His da had done the best he could—and it had been pretty damn amazing. Look at how when Dominic's ma passed away, Da took Dom in, too. Hell, his da deserved sainthood. Later today, he'd call and tell him so.

Gabe turned the corner and headed toward the cemetery, which overlooked the bay. He pressed on, trying to keep the thought of Emma from wedging itself back into his mind. She was so damned attractive, acting as if she didn't have any idea. With her green eyes, cinnamon hair—*There it is again: cinnamon*—and her rocking-hot body. The damnedest thing was that the society-girl thing she had going on turned him on, too. He rolled his eyes at his own imaginings and pushed her out of his mind again.

With his boots crunching in the snow, he rushed on. It was a little morbid but he liked coming to the cemetery; it gave him perspective. The graves grounded him in the assurance of the past. With the ocean as a backdrop, it made him think of life's endless possibilities, too. *Yeah, I'm turning into a sappy fool.*

As soon as he stepped through the white picket fence, he saw he wasn't alone. Seven-year-old Mattie MacKinnon stood by one of the graves over a mound of sea shells and a tiny snowman.

Gabe approached him slowly and squatted down to

his level. "Afternoon, Mattie. Did you get out of school early?"

Mattie nodded. Gabe didn't expect a verbal answer; Mattie seldom spoke. Ever since witnessing a tragic accident that killed all the men on a fishing boat, he'd been almost entirely mute. And then he had to go and lose his father to leukemia. So young to have suffered so much.

Cait Buchanan, his adoptive mother, was one of the few Gandiegowans who treated Gabe with civility. She had told Gabe that although Mattie was young, he was allowed to come to the cemetery by himself whenever he needed to spend time with his da, who had passed away.

Mattie's grandda . . . well, that was a huge secret that Gabe and all the rest of Gandiegow kept. Mattie's grandda was the famous actor Graham Buchanan and Cait had married him before Gabe had arrived in town. Of course, Gabe had been forced to swear on a stack of Bibles that he wouldn't tell anyone that Graham hid out in Gandiegow. Gabe was happy to oblige; he'd met Graham once and he seemed like a decent, down-to-earth bloke.

Gabe settled in next to Mattie. "Okay if I rest here a moment?"

Mattie glanced over at him and shrugged.

He pointed to the seashells. "May I?"

Mattie nodded.

Gabe picked up a medium-sized white one, turned it over, and examined it. "I like to come up here to think. It's peaceful. A good place to work things out."

Mattie gave him a knowing look. The poor kid probably came here to get a break from Cait's grandma, Deydie, and her gaggle of quilting ladies—Bethia, Rhona, Ailsa, Aileen, Amy, and Moira. It was a constant buzz when it came to the women of Gandiegow. And exhausting.

They also had the biggest hearts Gabe had ever

seen. *Except when it comes to their new doc.* He guessed it wasn't such a bad thing that Mattie spent so much time with the quilters, especially since Cait was such a fine person. She'd definitely been the only one who had tried, sincerely tried, to make Gabe feel welcome. She'd also been instrumental in bringing Dominic and Claire here.

Gabe gently placed the shell back where it had been. "How about I walk you home?"

Mattie tipped his head to his father's gravestone, as if to say, *I'll see ya later, Da,* then walked off with Gabe, kicking the snow with his boots like all boys do.

"I try to get out and walk to the top of the bluff most days. Can I come by and get you if you're not in school?" Graham was out of the country, making a film. Gabe figured the kid could use another male in his life. "I'd like the company."

Mattie nodded again.

They walked along in silence toward Graham's mansion. It sat on the bluff above the town, close to the ruins of Monadail Castle, a good stretch between it and the cemetery. Gabe kept a slow pace because his stride was twice that of the boy's. He glanced down. He was a good kid and seemed relatively happy, considering the crap that had happened to him.

When they got to the back door, Gabe stopped. "Shall I be leavin' ye?"

Mattie nodded, but then the door opened and there stood Deydie, as old as the rocks on the bluff, with a broom in her hand.

"I was wondering when ye'd be back," she said to Mattie. She dipped her head at Gabe in deference but not with any true warmth. "What can I be doing for ye, Doc?"

"Just seeing Mattie to his door, is all." Gabe gave her

an extra-friendly smile. If he could win Deydie over, he was sure the rest of the village would follow.

Deydie frowned at him, as if to work out whether she should ask him in or not.

Gabe made a rash decision. "Can I speak with you a moment, Ms. McCracken?"

"I told ye, me name is Deydie." She waggled her broom as if she might smack him with it. No mistaking it: Deydie, Cait's crotchety gran and Mattie's stand-in great-gran, was a force to be reckoned with. She turned to Mattie. "Go get Dingus and take that dog out." She stepped out on the porch and lifted her eyebrow.

Gabe jumped into the thick of it. "As the town doctor, I was wondering if Mattie has had any therapy to help him overcome his mutism."

Deydie scowled at him like it was none of his damned business, but then finally answered, "Caitie and Graham had him seeing a man, *a therapist*, in Inverness last summer, but they let the lad take a break when school started." She leaned in like she might be confiding in him, but the glower on her face said otherwise. "Ain't nothing wrong with wee Mattie. He's just a mite quiet— that's all."

Mattie opened the door and his sheltie went tearing out into the yard, yapping for all of Gandiegow to hear.

"Thank you for the information," Gabe said. He turned to the boy. "Remember, I'll be by for us to take our walk."

Mattie smiled back and then ran off after the dog.

"Ye're not going to meddle, are you?" Deydie swished her broom.

"No." Gabe took a step back. "I just thought Mattie might be missing his grandda and he might enjoy spending some time together."

"Gandiegow doesn't like meddlers. But ye can come by some and get the boy for a walk. As long as you don't meddle." Deydie nodded and then shut the door in Gabe's face.

He exhaled, not realizing he'd been holding his breath during the exchange. That woman was downright frightening.

Aye, the town had made it perfectly clear, too: Gandiegow did not take well to strangers. He wondered how long before they would embrace him or at least accept him as their physician. *Bluidy hell.* Small towns were not easy, especially when you weren't one of their own.

But he had little control over whether they accepted him or not. This town was only a small part of the growing list that constituted his problems. He didn't know what he was going to do about Dom and Claire, how he was going to solve their issue. Especially if Emma insisted she wasn't going to help.

Another picture of Emma Castle came to mind—of her in her tailored, overcrowded blouse. He exhaled deeply, fantasizing about undoing the buttons and burying his face in her chest. Damn, the image banging around in his head was going to kill him. But the image that affected him more was the lost look he saw on her face as she explained how she'd given up marriage counseling.

God, he needed to get a grip. Neither his mechanic skills nor his medical ones could fix what ailed him—his attraction to her.

Chapter Four

Emma went downstairs and found Claire up to her elbows in soapy water, humming a lilting tune. Emma breathed a sigh of relief; the Russos must have resolved their problems.

Claire twisted around and smiled like she'd discovered the perfect scone recipe. "I've figured it all out."

"What?" Emma looked around, but Dominic was nowhere in sight. "What have you figured out?"

"I don't have anything to worry about," Claire cooed. "I just need to remind Dominic what's important to him."

A sinking feeling came over Emma, like she'd fallen into a pit and dirt was being shoveled on top.

Conniving Claire is back.

The girl who'd gotten them in a heap of trouble at boarding school. The girl who'd convinced Emma to help fill the headmistress' office with wads of paper from the floor to the ceiling. The girl who'd procured pruning shears and shaped the bushes in the quadrangle into phallic statues. And poor Jenny Montague should've thought twice before stabbing Conniving Claire in the back. Claire used a hair dryer to get revenge, blowing a kilo of flour under the crack of Jenny's dorm door. When Jenny returned, all her things were buried in dust.

"Don't you want to know what I've figured out?" Claire said.

No, not really. "If you must."

"I just need to flash Dominic the girls." She laughed. "He won't be able to resist. That man is like dough in my hands whenever I give him a wee bit of flesh to ogle."

Good. Child's play. Maybe Claire wasn't reverting back to her avenging younger days.

The restaurant's front door slammed.

"Is that him?" Claire wiped off her hands.

Emma peeked into the restaurant. Dominic was wheeling in a cart of supplies.

"Yes, but—"

"Good." Claire slipped off her apron and undid the top three buttons of her sweater. "This should do it."

The girls made an appearance, enough cleavage to make a eunuch sweat.

"Claire, we need to talk," Emma tried.

But her friend was too busy hiking her skirt above her knees to listen. She grinned up at Emma. "Dominic does like my goodies. I think I'll go and give him a little taste of what he's going to miss." She pranced from the kitchen like a Scottish doe in heat.

Emma followed her into the dining area, planning on stopping her, but Claire had already leaned her hip up against the counter. Dominic kept his head down while he unloaded a box of sausages from the wagon.

She captured his hand. "Do you need any help with your meat?" she purred.

His head came up. His shocked look turned into a glare. Emma had never seen him like this. No playfulness, just outright anger.

"I'm busy, Claire." He reached past her and grabbed a case cutter to break open the next box. "You're in my way."

Claire's face fell. Her mouth opened, but she shut it without a snipe back as Dominic stomped through the swinging doors to the kitchen.

Emma thought about the negative ledger upstairs and hoped Claire would now be in the right frame of mind to listen to reason. But her hope was short-lived.

Claire huffed, straightening out her ruffled feathers. "I'll just have to *up* my game."

"Your relationship with Dominic is not a game," Emma said.

Claire stared right through Emma. "You and I need to make a trip to Inverness for reinforcements. Aye, new lingerie. That's what this calls for. We'll go shopping in the morning, as soon as the rush is over."

Emma would not conspire with her best friend this time. Some things were too important. It would do no good to call her on the carpet about the state of the restaurant. Claire could, at times, be shortsighted—sometimes unable to see much farther than her own wishes. Dominic, Emma, and everyone who cared for Claire couldn't help but play along because she was so lovable. But there were limits. Emma didn't know what to do. When that girl got something in her brain, there was no dislodging it.

"I need to stretch my legs," Emma said. *And think.*

For a moment, Claire snapped out of it, giving Emma a worried frown. "Are you all right?"

"We need—" Emma tried once again, but Claire cut her off.

"It's your parents, right? We'll get to that. I promise." But in the next second, Claire was back to concentrating on the swinging doors of the kitchen.

So much for my problems. "I'll be back." Emma grabbed her coat, hat, and scarf, and went outside.

The late-November wind had picked up and the

waves were crashing against the containment wall, which served as the support for the boardwalk, as well. She wandered down it with no destination in mind, glancing at the buildings and cottages but mostly staying within her own thoughts.

She felt like an anchor had been dropped on her chest. She was certain Dominic felt the same. She had to convince Claire to give up her irrational notion of having a baby now. But how? If Emma had thought she'd felt stuck in her career in LA—*stuck in a career she didn't believe in*—well, being stuck in Gandiegow was far worse. Especially under such dire circumstances.

Her best friend needed a competent marriage therapist to help her. Some professional who believed in marriage-ever-after. And that wasn't Emma.

If it were anyone else in the world but Claire, Emma would book a flight, make her excuses, and run as fast as she could to Saint Martin or any other tropical location. *Lie on the beach. Watch cabana boys. Sip mai tais. And hide out.*

But no. Claire was her best friend, the sister of her heart. Emma was stuck in Gandiegow until either Claire got her way with Dominic—which would most certainly happen, if the past was any indication of the future—or the Russos destroyed their relationship and let their marriage wash out to sea.

Emma's problems—her disappointed parents and her uncertain future—would have to wait. She wrapped her scarf around her more securely and walked toward the General Store to look for a pair of warm boots. At least she could fix the problem of her frozen feet.

Then an idea hit Emma. It was so small, she couldn't even call it a plan. But if Claire insisted on going to Inverness tomorrow, Emma would tag along. Not for a thong or a bustier; she had no need, since her sex life bordered on celibacy. No, the automobile ride would be the perfect time to confine Claire, make her listen to reason, and maybe Emma wouldn't be caught in the middle anymore. Yes, the drive to Inverness would be the perfect time to knock some sense into Claire's ruddy head.

Emma stopped midway through the boardwalk and leaned over the railing, gazing out at the rough sea. For a moment she was lost in it. The waves were on a mission with their endless pursuit of the shore—just like Claire's relentless pursuit to have a baby, come hell or high water. One wave started way out and didn't break, but waited until it was almost on top of Emma. She should've stepped back from the railing, made a run for it, but she was too mesmerized. The wave crashed over her, soaking her from head to toe. Then her arm was yanked back by a mighty force.

An old woman shook a gnarled finger at her and glared at her with rheumy eyes. "Are you addlebrained?"

Another elderly woman stood there, too. "Lass, you can't lean over the barrier with the sea as it is. You'll get carried away." She smiled kindly at her. "Ye must be Claire's friend. Emily, is it? I'm Bethia."

"Emma," she corrected. "Emma Castle." Even though she was cold, soaked, and embarrassed, Emma's proper English upbringing kicked in. She stuck out her hand. "How do you do?"

The first woman stared, frowning, from Emma's chattering teeth to her frozen, shaky hand. "I'm Deydie Mc Cracken. If we don't get you back to Quilting Central and get ye dried off, ye'll die of a chill. Ye're as skinny as a measuring tape."

Bethia took her hand and shook it. "Welcome to Gandiegow. Come now. Deydie's right. Let's get you inside."

Emma obediently walked behind the women, taking

stock of them. Deydie was barely five feet, if that. Her white hair was done up in a loose bun, and below her long, dark skirt peeked a pair of heavy black boots. Bethia, slighter and taller with her silver hair bobbed short, wore a calico-print dress under her gray peacoat. Not Laurel and Hardy, but almost.

Only a few feet away, the women stopped in front of a storefront with the facade dolled up in painted-lady fashion—pale orange, dusty peach, and sage green.

"Do you know how to quilt?" Bethia asked.

Deydie pushed open the door before Emma could answer and ushered her into the warmth.

The room was gigantic and beautiful, with several long tables bearing sewing machines and brightly printed fabrics. One wall, covered in felt, had quilt blocks stuck to it, which two ladies were rearranging in a pattern. Some women stood in the back, ironing, while others mingled by the coffee machine. More leaned over green mats, cutting fabric with rotary blades. Only one man was there, an elderly gentleman bent over a long monstrous contraption with a huge sewing machine in the middle. The place, though homey, was somehow elegant and inviting. Emma knew how to sew but didn't know the first thing about quilting. Just seeing this place made her want to learn.

Bethia motioned to the far wall. "The necessary is over there."

"Go dry off," Deydie barked. "Then come meet my ladies while you warm up in front of the hearth. We're getting ready to start the Gandiegow Doctor quilt." She rolled her eyes with true disdain. "The new doc isn't one of us though."

An uncomfortable prick ran up Emma's spine. "You mean Gabriel?"

"Aye, the outlander," Deydie hissed.

"But he's from Edinburgh, isn't he?"

Deydie's wrinkled face scrunched up into a scowl. "So far south, he might as well be a Brit. Now get going." She gave Emma a polite shove.

Emma trudged to the loo, feeling uneasy. She was the actual Brit in their midst. Could they not hear her accent and know from where she hailed? What were they saying behind *her* back?

Inside the powder room, she discovered a stack of fluffy violet towels. She wrapped her hair in one and then used another to scrub her face and clothes. She hated to admit it, but quite unbidden, sympathy for Gabriel washed over her. Why she felt anxious for such a scoundrel, she didn't know. Maybe being ostracized was exactly what he deserved for his womanizing past. She deliberately put him out of her mind while she finished wiping the ocean from her person.

When she was done, she pulled the towel from her head and peered in the mirror. Her hair had gone from wavy to the ringlets she detested. "Great." She ran her fingers through her hair.

Preoccupied, she pulled open the door and ran smack-dab into a hard chest.

Tea spilled over the front of that chest. But a droplet sprayed onto her white tailored blouse, too.

She gazed up into a pair of summer blue eyes, getting a little lost. *Perfection.* Until she regained her senses and realized they belonged to the dreaded physician.

Gabriel.

He'd changed into a black shirt and black pants, and wore a satisfied grin. On closer inspection, she realized his eyes weren't on her face, but on her clinging, still-ocean-wet blouse.

The glint in his eyes danced. "Did I miss the announcement?"

She crossed her arms over her chest. "I'll play along. What announcement?"

"The wet-T-shirt contest. Or, in your case, the wet-blouse contest."

She dropped her head to stare at her own chest. Sure enough, her nipples pushed against her damp blouse with so-very-happy-to-see-Gabriel enthusiasm. As she tugged the wet fabric away from her breasts, her cheeks burst into flaming, high-octane embarrassment. All the while, she cursed herself for not wearing a camisole underneath.

"Why are you here?" she growled, despite the fact that a real lady didn't growl.

He steered her in front of the roaring fire. "Ye've got nothing there to be ashamed of." He motioned to her blouse. "Quite the opposite, actually. Besides, I'm a doctor. I've seen plenty of breasts."

"You're a rogue," she muttered.

He gave her a strange look, like maybe she was right, all the smile leaving his eyes. He nodded and gave her what almost could've been a bow. "If you'll forgive me." He motioned to the other man in the room. "I must catch George—George Campbell, the local tinker. His brother, Kenneth, needs him to stop by." Sure enough, the older gentleman was putting his tools away.

"Wait!" she said, then felt instantly mortified. Proper English ladies didn't shout after gentlemen either. *Then again, Gabriel is no gentleman.*

"Yes," Gabriel said.

She took a bite of crow. "I'm sorry about before."

He raised an eyebrow and took a step closer. "For what?"

She shifted from one foot to the other. "I shouldn't have said fathers were optional."

"Glad to hear LA hasn't turned you into an airhead."

Emma decided he deserved a small explanation. "My

mother tried to convince me that fathers weren't necessary. Hence my father's absence during my own childhood. If anyone understands the importance of fathers, it's me." She had an empty hole in the middle of her chest where she knew her father should be.

Pity filled Gabriel's eyes. She hated being pitied more than being called Princess.

"But I've turned out just fine," she said, with added steel in her voice. "Actually, better than fine."

"Aye. You have, Emma." Compassionate Gabriel was patronizing her and unbalancing her all at the same time. Go Get 'Em Gabriel would've been easier to take.

She had to stop him. "You may go now." She dropped her head, effectively making her gesture do double duty—pointing out that George was headed toward the door and dismissing Gabriel with a nod.

It worked. Gabriel's compassion paled, and in its place anger flashed. He nodded again, doing that eighteenth-century-bow thing. He sauntered away, taking his blue eyes with him. She watched as he walked to the door. And jumped when Deydie spoke.

"Making googly eyes at the doc, are ye?" Deydie made a sour face at Gabriel's backside.

Bethia tsked her friend. "Be charitable, Deydie. He's our healer."

Emma couldn't help but glance once more as Gabriel and George walked out of Quilting Central together. Her face felt flushed, hot, and bothered. *Hightailing it to the beach is looking better and better.* "I'm not making googly eyes at anyone," she declared to the old women beside her.

Bethia patted her hand. "It's best not to protest too much, dear."

Deydie, the Scottish warrior, stood directly in front of Emma. "I made myself clear. That lad's an outsider."

Emma hated to tangle with the locals, but they were missing something very important here. "I'm an outsider, too."

Emma always had been and it was okay with her. From family. From school. From work. Actually, she was more comfortable being an outsider than belonging. She had accepted that was her place in life.

"Nay," Bethia corrected. "Ye're family."

"Aye," Deydie concurred. Her voice carried no hint that she had softened in any way, but simply had accepted that things were the way that they were.

Bethia gently took Emma's arm and pulled her closer. "Ye're Claire's oldest friend. That makes you one of us."

Emma became even more unnerved. Normally, people didn't welcome her. They usually stood back and regarded her with skepticism. Starting with her parents.

Something had to be wrong with these two if they wanted to include her.

Deydie took Emma's other arm. "Come and meet the other women." A group waited for her.

All of a sudden, Emma felt swallowed up, claustrophobic. She had to make a run for it before she was asked to do something else that made her uncomfortable. First it was Gabriel insisting she fix Claire and Dominic's marriage. Now it was the women of Gandiegow who wanted her to become one of them.

Emma stepped away. She knew it was rude but she couldn't get out of Quilting Central fast enough. Not even long enough to give Deydie and Bethia a proper goodbye or a nod of thanks for the dry towel and warm fire. She hustled to the door and went back out into the cold. Claire was the only real relationship Emma needed, and she wanted to keep it that way. Any more than that, and she wouldn't be able to handle it.

*   *   *

Claire watched the timer in the flat's kitchen, anticipating her evening. Her marriage might be a little sour right now, but nothing would stop the excitement growing inside of her. As she bent over the oven and pulled out the cranberry scones, Emma appeared, quite wilted. Claire gave her friend her best Scottish smile. "I'm so glad ye're back. Can you adjust that cooling rack so I can set these there?"

Emma shot her a quizzical frown. "Why aren't you helping Dominic with the dinner prep? We always help Dominic. I thought that was one of your golden rules."

"Nay," Claire said, "not tonight. He'll have to go it alone. I made you a sandwich. You'd better eat before we go." She pointed to the refrigerator.

Emma gave her a sidelong glance. "What do you mean, *before we go*? Why are you bailing on Dominic?"

Claire shrugged.

"You two have argued before but you were still able to work together."

It did feel strange not to be downstairs in the thick of the dinner. But Claire had an important date tonight. She felt as giddy as if she'd landed a new prizewinning scone recipe.

Emma motioned to the cooling pan. "And what is all this?"

"Scones."

"I can see that. But what about your other golden rule? Everything fresh-baked in the morning?"

"Oh, these aren't for the restaurant," Claire clarified.

"Then who are they for?"

She smiled. "We're calling on Amy and Coll." And baby William. She couldn't wait to get her hands on that bairn.

"And they are?"

"The MacTavishes. Gandiegow's newest parents," Claire confessed.

"Oh."

"Don't look at me like that, Emma Castle. This is what we do in small towns. We take care of one another." Claire pointed to the table where she had stockpiled canned food, vegetables, and baked goods. Yes, it was enough for twenty people, but Amy and Coll could use the provisions.

That's when Emma's overall appearance registered with Claire. "What happened to you?"

"Tidal wave," Emma said flatly.

"Well, go change. We need to get going." Claire stacked the warm scones into a basket as Emma left the kitchen.

When Emma came back, she looked warmer, dressed in dark corduroys and a green sweater.

"Your hair is still curly," Claire pointed out. "I thought you hated it like that."

"I used the blow-dryer, but I need to wash out the salt water. I figured we didn't have time for that."

"You figured right."

Claire and Emma loaded the groceries into sacks and carried them down the stairs. When they got to the restaurant, Dominic trudged through the kitchen's swinging doors, carrying a knife, cutting board, and prosciutto. Claire stopped breathing. Even after all these years, she still had it bad for her Italian meatball. For a second, their eyes met like they had thousands of times before—a recognition of the souls. But then Dominic masked his emotions and Claire could only see disdain. Or maybe it was disappointment. Either way it felt like he'd carved out a piece of her heart with the knife he held. But she wouldn't let him see; she came from a long line of strong Scottish women, dammit.

One of Emma's bags slipped and instantly Dominic rushed to her rescue, leaving his knife on the chopping block, catching the sack before it hit the floor.

"Thank you, Dominic," Emma said, still the polite lass she always was.

"Not a problem." Dominic opened the door for them. But as Claire walked through, he gave her a pointed look for leaving him in the lurch. "You're not going to reconsider?"

"Are you?" Claire shot back, knowing they spoke of entirely different things.

Emma touched Claire's arm. "Go on without me. I'll stay and help Dominic."

Claire opened her mouth, but Dominic jumped in first.

"No, Emma. I'll be all right. Gabe said he'll be here soon to help."

Why did a pink blush fill Emma's cheeks? Claire would have to remember to ask her about that later.

Dominic went inside, leaving them to get the bags settled into the wagon.

"Claire, this is a lot of food," Emma said. "I'm surprised Dominic didn't complain about you giving away the restaurant's goods."

"You know Dominic. He's passionate about feeding people." In this one area only, Dominic didn't hold the financial reins so tightly. It was important for her husband to feed people, whether they could afford it or not. To him, food equaled love. And no one loved like Dominic Russo.

Claire stared at the restaurant door and longed to run back inside and tell Dominic that she wanted things to go back to the way they were. But in the next second, wanting her own baby outweighed that urge—stronger than ever. She took it as a sign she shouldn't give in. Dominic would have to be the one to cave. He needed to give her a baby. She could feel she was right all the way to her toes. And her toes never lied.

With the wagon filled, she and Emma each grabbed a side of the rope handle and dragged the goods across the village to the one-room cottage of baby William. Coll answered the door and ushered them in. He took care of the groceries while Claire introduced Emma to Amy.

Since she and Dominic had arrived in Gandiegow six weeks ago, Claire had spent a lot of time with Amy in the small cottage. This cottage had no room for a large crib, changing table, or other extras; just a small two-person table, two chairs, and one cradle beside the bed. Propped up on top of the poinsettia quilt was her new friend, Amy, with her cropped dark hair held back with a headband. The wee one was at her breast.

Claire went straight to the baby and ran her fingers lightly over his whisper-soft hair as he nursed. She wondered if their own baby would have dark hair like Dominic's or turn out to be a carrottop like herself.

"Ah, Amy, ye did well," Claire said. "He's so beautiful." She turned to Emma. "Get over here and see the wee lad." Her friend stood over by the door as if worried about the babe's privacy. *Which is ridiculous.*

Amy looked at Emma and smiled. "'Tis okay. He's just having his dinner."

Emma nodded and walked toward them. Claire grabbed her arm and dragged her closer.

"Isn't he something, Emms?" Claire couldn't help but gush. Her praise made Amy beam.

Emma clasped her hands in front of her. "He is beautiful. I've never seen so much hair on a baby before," Emma said.

"He looks like he's wearing a baby wig, doesn't he?" Amy laughed.

"Aye," Claire said. Baby William's eyes were shut as he fed. "It's remarkable, isn't it, that one so young knows how to get his food? He's lovely, Amy."

Claire turned to Coll, who wore a goofy grin. "Och, Coll, with that grand smile on your face, you're acting as if you're the one who invented childbirth yourself."

"He's a strapping lad," Coll said proudly.

All of Claire's emotions burbled out. "We're going to have a baby, too."

"Oh, that's wonderful news," Amy exclaimed. "When arc you duc?"

Claire felt stupid, but she stood her ground. "Well, Dominic will have to deposit some sperm first."

Coll, who'd just brought his mug to his lips, choked on his tea.

Amy laughed. "I'm sure that'll be no problem for Dominic."

Coll came to Amy and kissed her head. "If you're sure it's all right, then?" He looked at the doorway, as if he were being called off to war.

Amy turned to Claire and Emma to explain. "Coll wants to make sure the shipment came in correctly at the pub today." She turned back to her husband. "You go. I'll be fine. Claire and Emma will sit with me until I get tired."

"Aye," Claire said. "We've nowhere to be."

Emma's eyes called her a liar. Okay, maybe they should be helping Dominic with the dinner hour, but visiting the new baby during *his* dinner hour seemed much more important.

With one more glance back, Coll eased through the doorway and left.

A surge of jealousy overcame Claire. It rankled that

Amy got to have a baby in her early twenties. Claire would be thirty-one on her next birthday. It wasn't fair. At this rate, Amy would be a grandmother before Claire's first bairn was born.

The baby let go of the breast and Amy repositioned him on her shoulder.

"Here, let me," Claire said.

"Thanks, if you don't mind. I could use a quick trip to the loo."

"Not at all." She eased the baby from Amy's arms and held him close, swaying, gently patting his back.

Emma looked embarrassed as Amy refastened her nursing bra, but had the sense to help Amy from the bed.

"Thanks," Amy said. "I'm a little sore. And stiff." She hobbled off to the bathroom.

Emma turned on Claire. "I don't like that look in your eye."

"What look?" Claire gazed down at baby William and placed a kiss on his precious forehead. He smelled great. He felt perfect in her arms, too. Amy was a lucky duck. If something happened to Coll, Amy would have a bairn to remember him by. Just like Mama had had her when Papa had died.

Amy returned from the loo and offered to make tea, but Emma insisted on waiting on her instead. Which was good, because Claire had no intention of putting down the sweet babe.

"I hope my auntie can come and see the wee one before the end of the week. Her neighbor said she'd give her a ride from Fairge, but her neighbor has been under the weather."

Emma brought a cup of steaming-hot tea to Amy. "I hope her neighbor doesn't have anything contagious."

"I think we're safe. I believe it's gout," Amy said.

Claire cooed and hummed to baby William as his mama recounted every detail of the labor and delivery for them. Claire only half listened—that Amy MacTavish surely did love to talk.

"So we named him William after my da," Amy finished. "Of course, the Gabriel part is after our doc."

"What was that?" Emma perked up like a dog who'd heard *squirrel*.

"William Gabriel MacTavish," Amy said. "Have you not been listening?" She smiled at Emma good-naturedly.

Claire wondered what was wrong with Emma. She suddenly looked like the walls had closed in. Was Emma holding her breath?

"Are you okay?" Claire asked.

"Yes, well, I'm just surprised," Emma finally said. "About naming the baby after Gabriel."

"Doc MacGregor was incredible. So gentle. So understanding. He was wonderful to me. But more importantly, he kept Coll from passing out." Amy laughed, but then yawned. "We're so lucky to have him here in Gandiegow."

"Claire," Emma prodded, "we should let Amy rest while the baby sleeps."

"But you haven't even held him," Claire argued.

Emma raised an eyebrow at her. "Like there was ever a chance of that?"

"Fine." Reluctantly, Claire handed baby William back to his mother. Amy tucked him into her arms and gazed down at him lovingly.

"He really is beautiful, isn't he?" Amy said.

"Aye," Claire answered, unable to keep the longing from her voice.

Emma grabbed their coats. It took all of Claire's strength to drag herself from the cottage, away from the newborn.

To hell with Dominic's obsession with the restaurant's books. She understood the state of their finances perfectly, but there were more important things in life than turning a profit. Claire would just have to convince him to man up and give her what she wanted. And it wouldn't cost him a cent.

When Emma and Claire got back to the restaurant, all the customers were gone. Dominic was nowhere in sight, but Gabriel was there, clearing tables. He said hello to Claire but didn't make eye contact with Emma. It stung, but she guessed he was still angry from earlier when she'd dismissed him from her presence at Quilting Central. She glanced at him once more, then followed Claire upstairs to the flat.

Once inside, Claire stripped off her coat. "I think I'll go soak in the tub." She hugged Emma. "That was a nice evening. Don't you think?"

Emma thought they should be downstairs, helping with the dinner dishes. "Sure," she finally answered. "Nice."

Claire glided down the hallway and disappeared into the loo.

As Emma settled onto the sofa, the door creaked open to the flat. She turned around to see Dominic in the doorway, looking haggard, which wasn't easy for the big, hearty Italian that he was. She stood.

"Where's Claire?" he asked.

Emma pointed down the hall. "The tub. Are you all right?" She'd been fond of Dominic from the very beginning. He'd always given her a warm bear hug and kind words, treating her like a beloved sister. She took a step toward him now.

"Don't." He put his hand up in roadblock fashion. "I've only come for a few things." He grabbed a pillow, two quilts from the basket near the couch, and a book from the table. "I'll be getting out of your way and back to cleaning up."

He was gone without giving Emma a chance to say another word. She understood; he was too distraught for niceties.

Claire appeared in her bath towel, water dripping all over the hardwood floors. "What was that? Did I hear someone?"

Emma winced, not wanting to say, but finally did. "Yes. Dominic."

"Where is he now?" Hope radiated in her desperate eyes. "Was he looking for me?"

Emma went to stand by her. "He grabbed some things. I think he's taking your words to heart and sleeping downstairs."

Claire burst into tears, her good mood from the evening with the baby ruined.

Emma walked with her down the hall to the Russos' bedroom, grabbing her pajamas off the hook by the door. "Get dressed while I make you some herbal tea. It should help you sleep. We have an early morning."

Claire sniffed and took the pajamas from her. "Early morning. Yes, the baking. But you sleep in. I'll be fine alone."

"I've missed working with you in the kitchen," Emma insisted. "I'll be up with you. Which scones are we making?"

"I'll have to check the schedule." Claire was definitely distracted if she didn't know which scones were on for tomorrow. Scones were Claire's life, always first and foremost in her mind. Claire prided herself that she had a scone recipe for every day of the year and was always on the hunt for something new to try.

Emma had an uncharitable thought toward the precious MacTavish family—Amy, Coll, and baby William. They seemed so nice but they might be to blame for Claire and Dominic's problems. Dangling that beautiful baby in front of Claire in her present state of mind couldn't be healthy. Not for the Russos. Not for the people of Gandiegow, who had to deal with them every day. And definitely not for Emma and Gabriel, who loved Dominic and Claire the most. Baby William might be the sweetest babe in the whole world, but he'd rained down a heap of trouble on all of them.

Dominic spread the blankets over a stack of pallets next to the hundred-pound sack of potatoes. Not the most comfortable bed and not his first choice. But dammit, what could he do? He couldn't trust himself to be near Claire. It didn't make any difference how mad he was—her naked and him horny was a recipe for disaster. A bambino disaster. The storeroom was a good compromise. Here he wouldn't accidentally ravish his wife and get her pregnant. He had only one reason for postponing a child: It came down to economics. Cold, hard cash and the lack thereof. Claire understood how financially strapped they were as well as he did. But for some reason she wasn't in the state of mind to care anymore. Why wouldn't she see they had to wait to have a baby?

He stretched out on the pallets but lost his balance and rolled off. He pounded his fist on the floor. *Why did I ever come to this godforsaken village?*

This town put those blasted baby thoughts into Claire's head. They hadn't been here five minutes before every bastard in Gandiegow had wanted to know when they'd be having their first *bairn*.

First bairn.

He pounded the floor again and yanked the blanket from the pallet. The floor was hard and cold, but it was as good a place as any to spend a sleepless night. Maybe he was punishing himself more than he was punishing Claire. But dammit, he wasn't giving in. Not this time.

Chapter Five

When Gabe woke the next morning, he had a problem. A big one. Actually it was a three-part problem.

Emma Castle.

The hard-on she gave him while he slept.

And when the hell would she get out of town—and out of his life?

His obsession with her was beyond his ken. She wasn't at all what he wanted in a woman. She was too high maintenance. Too prim. Too much.

He rolled out of bed and rushed to get ready. If he hurried, he could get coffee and scones from the restaurant before he saw his patients. *If there are any.* This afternoon, though, he planned to make a house call and see how Amy and Coll's baby was getting along.

Another reason to get to the restaurant was to check on Dom and Claire. Was it too unreasonable to hope Emma had changed her mind and performed a miracle overnight with those two knuckleheads? Or maybe Claire and Dom patched things up for Emma's sake because she'd come to visit. *Yeah, I'm living in a dreamworld.* Both Russos were as stubborn as a resistant strain of strep. A pang of sympathy for Emma overcame him. Here she'd come all the way from LA to see her friend, only to find the Russos in a row. It had to be tough for her.

Gabe shoved his feet into his boots and stepped outside. A sheen of ice coated everything. He reached back inside the doorway and grabbed the trekking pole to help manage the ice. It wouldn't do anyone any good if the town's doctor broke his neck. That is, if they ever bothered to come see him.

It was bitter outside. A Scot himself, he should be able to handle the cold weather, but he was still adjusting to the Highland's brutal winter climate. As he maneuvered down the path from the doctor's quarters to the restaurant, the tantalizing smells of breakfast welcomed him. Claire had a gift when it came to scones. He had wondered on more than one occasion if she hadn't slipped in a narcotic to make them so addicting.

As he opened the door and stepped inside, he let out a *"Brrrr."* Everyone turned to him. Even *her.*

Emma!

He stopped in his boots and gaped. She stood there, staring back at him with a crisp white apron tied around her waist and a notepad in her hand.

Her Majesty, taking the MacDougal brothers' order?

Gabe couldn't wrap his brain around it and what he knew about little Miss Prim and Proper. Wasn't she more likely to be the one giving the orders than taking them? *Huh.* Still holding eye contact with her, he felt a goofy grin spread across his face.

"Claire," Thomas MacDougal hollered, breaking the moment. "Where've ye been hiding this lovely?" He waggled his eyebrows at Emma and gazed at her with a greedy once-over.

A lion roared inside of Gabe's chest. *Ah, hell.* He knew Claire could handle these horny bastard fishermen, but Emma was too refined, too fragile.

Lochie, Thomas's brother, grabbed Emma's hand. "Oh, my *luve* is like a red, red rose, that's newly sprung in June."

Gabe sprang into action, advancing on the MacDougals' table. Emma put her hand up, stopping him.

She unhinged Lochie's hand and hollered to Claire, too. "Bucket of ice water for table one." Sounding just like a seasoned waitress.

The MacDougal brothers laughed and Emma smiled. No harm done. But Gabe chose the far end of the counter to linger close to the MacDougals, in case their ardor got out of control again.

Claire started a new pot of coffee. "Gabriel MacGregor, don't expect Emma or me to serve you. Get your arse over here and take care of yourself."

"What happened to the days when women were at a man's beck and call?" he kidded.

Claire put her hands on her hips. "All those men died off."

"Of starvation," Emma added as she passed by.

"Well, I can't stand for that. I'm wasting away as it is."

As if stealing the opportunity, Emma skimmed down his body with her evergreen eyes, searching for emaciation. She seemed satisfied with what she saw. *As well she should.*

He lumbered behind the counter to fix a cup of coffee and to grab a cherry scone.

Emma strolled into the kitchen with a tray of dirty dishes.

"I'll put your breakfast on your tab, Gabriel." Claire wiped down the counter. "You know, the one where you clean up the kitchen for us girls. We have an errand to run."

Gabe nodded. "Fine. I'll be back in a bit. Office hours, you know." He would wait around at the surgery for a while and then put a sign on the doctor's quarters to let everyone know he was at his second job: scullery maid at the restaurant.

Emma returned. He walked over to her and was as bad as Thomas and Lochie a moment ago. He couldn't help but drink her in. "Damn." This dichotomy she had going on—upper-crust meets French maid—sucked him in and turned him on.

"Keep your opinions to yourself," she hissed.

"You don't know what my opinions are," he countered back.

"I can guess. You think it's funny that I'm waiting tables."

"Oh, right. You've caught me," he laughed. It was a good thing she didn't know where his dirty mind had gone: He'd like to peel that apron off her slowly and get down to her soft middle.

Emma glanced back to where Claire was arranging silverware. "We need to talk," she whispered to Gabe.

"About what?"

"The Russos," she said.

He checked his watch. "I have to run right now. Stop by later."

Emma chewed on her lip. "It'll have to be much later. I'm going with Claire to Inverness. On an errand." She didn't seem happy about it.

"Aye. She told me."

Shock flooded Emma's face. "She told you about the lingerie?"

Gabriel laughed. "No. But you just did."

"Effing A." Emma's hand flew to her mouth and her cheeks turned all shades of red, spreading downward to her neck.

He laughed harder. "Be careful. Or you might get your pretty little mouth washed out." And because he was feeling a little devilish, he added, "You might need a spanking, too."

Emma straightened. "I'd like to see you try."

Aye, I would like to try. It would be entertaining as hell.

He shouldn't be flirting with her. He wondered as she huffed off if maybe he'd pushed her too far. But she'd said she wanted to talk to him later. Maybe there was a cease-fire in their future.

On the way back to the surgery, he saw Mrs. Bruce juggling her youngest baby in her arms while she dropped a letter in the postbox. His own mother popped into his thoughts. Had his mother yearned to have him as badly as Claire wanted her own child? He'd never considered it before. His mother had been years older than Claire when she'd given birth to him.

Gabe would never forget how Amy glowed when she looked upon her babe's face for the first time, then the look she'd given her husband. It was a moment of pure love. It filled the room, more completely than the air that surrounded them. Had his mother looked upon him and his da that way? Coll's exuberance had been priceless, too, as he strutted around the cabin at what he had done, or at least his hand in it—the proud peacock. Gabe witnessed how fatherhood, from the first second even, could change a man. Being a father was one of the most important things in a man's life.

Suddenly, Gabe's feelings shifted. Dom had it all wrong. He was missing out by putting off having a child. Gabe could see Claire was perfectly right. *Now* was the time to have a baby.

Life was short, dammit. Gabe's mother had only had a year with him before she'd died. Claire deserved her baby. Money shouldn't be a factor. Hell, Gabe would pay for his niece or nephew if they'd let him.

A strange kind of peace came over him. He and Emma

were now on the same side and they could work together to make sure Dominic saw the logic of having a child now. A baby would fix everything. The bairn would glue the Russos together forever. Gabe was counting on it.

Emma checked out the last customer and closed the cash register drawer. She was exhausted but not from working all morning. She blamed the ocean for keeping her up half the night with the endless waves crashing against the containment wall. Give her sirens, dump trucks, cars roaring down the street any day—those noises she could deal with. Mother Nature slamming against concrete all night? Not a chance.

As she hung up her apron, Dominic showed up to prep for the lunch crowd, scowling like the prime rib had been left out all night to rot.

Emma nodded to him.

"Mornin'," Dominic groused, glaring at Claire.

"How did you sleep last night?" Claire purred.

"You know damn well how I slept. Terrible." He pointed to the storeroom.

"Stop yere whining." Claire hung her apron on an empty hook. "Ye could've been in your own bed with yere willing wife."

Emma would have to remind Claire she could catch more sperm by being nice than by badgering her husband. The couple faced off, the tension as heavy and thick as the Alfredo sauce on today's menu. Because harsher words were about to fly, Emma stole upstairs.

A few minutes later, Claire joined her. "Get your coat. We're going."

Claire had a superior air about her. She must've won the battle downstairs, or at least had fewer casualties. Dominic was sharp. If he'd had a good night's sleep, he could handle his wife. Emma had seen it before. The two of them were meant for each other. Dominic was a strong man and had a way of taming his somewhat wild wife and making her, *well*, manageable.

Emma did as she was told and grabbed her coat. When they walked back downstairs, Emma saw Claire glancing around for Dominic. His swearwords rang out from the kitchen. Claire stomped out the front door.

Outside, the sky was gray and the air thick with moisture. They picked their way carefully along the boardwalk coated by last night's sleet and snow. White birds circled above and every few minutes they'd swoop, snatch a fish, then take it to the snowy shore to eat. Ah, a lovely mottle of entrails and blood on the beach. *A picturesque Highland scene.*

Emma glanced over at Claire as they trekked along. "How exactly are we getting to Inverness? Did you and Dominic buy a car?"

"No," Claire said, not offering more.

By now they'd reached the parking lot at the edge of town. Claire didn't go to one of the parked vehicles but went to an ancient postbox painted green instead.

"Och, Claire," Emma said in her best snarky Scottish imitation, "are we mailing ourselves, then?"

Her friend smiled sarcastically and opened the small red door on the front of the postbox. "Ye're not as smart as ye think you are, Emma Castle. It's not the post. It's where we store the keys to the community autos."

Sure enough, five sets of keys lay in the innards of the green postbox.

"Who maintains the autos?" Emma asked.

"The village. We pay as we go. There's a sign-out sheet at the grocery."

"Clever."

Claire retrieved a set of keys and plodded off to the blue Subaru. "Come on. We've got a lot to do."

Emma got in the car, rehearsing in her head the speech she was going to deliver to Claire: *patience, compassion, and compromise.* Emma had spent the past three years being in the middle and it was very unpleasant. *Especially when divorce was inevitable.* A sick feeling swept over her—the sticky feeling of a broken marriage and what that ultimately meant.

Dominic and Claire—*together*—had been a constant in Emma's life while she'd been drowning in a sea of breakups. The Russos had given her a small inkling of hope that marriage could survive. Not like her parents' marriage of convenience, but one of love, commitment, and possibly even happily-ever-after. With Dominic and Claire not being *Dominic and Claire*, Emma's world felt precariously off-balanced, tilted. She just might drop off the edge and never find her way back.

Claire reached over and squeezed Emma's hand. "I can feel it. Dominic and I are going to be fine. This little errand is going to remind him just how *fine* we really are." She slid the key into the ignition. "I just need to remind that Italian Stallion what he loves most in life."

"And what's that?" Emma dared to ask.

"My body." Claire revved the engine and they were off.

But it was slow going up the hill because of last night's sleet. "Tonight I'll get Dominic straightened out," Claire said cheerily. "By this time tomorrow, everything will be back to normal. Better than normal," she added emphatically. "Ye'll see."

Emma did not *see.* She opened her mouth to say so, but Claire derailed her.

"How long do you think you can stay in Gandicgow with me? It's been ages, years really, since we've had a proper visit."

"It depends," Emma hedged.

"On what?"

On how stubborn you can be. How long I can stand being in the middle of this mess.

And then there was the other factor Emma didn't even want to examine. *Gabriel.*

The auto made it to the main road and she breathed a sigh of relief.

"I'm waiting," Claire reminded her. "How long can you stay?"

For Emma, it was safer to go back to the rehearsed speech in her head. The problem was, she'd given up marriage counseling and the words she was about to say . . . sounded as if she hadn't.

"Claire," Emma finally tried, "you know you have it all wrong, don't you? Your problems with Dominic have nothing to do with spicing up your sex life. Whether you want to admit it or not, it's more complicated than that."

"Hogwash," Claire said. But in the next second, she chewed her lip, not looking anything like the confident woman Emma knew her to be.

"Here's the thing." Claire sighed heavily. "I need a little sex advice. Or ideas. Something new for Dominic to sink his teeth into."

"Too much sharing," Emma reminded her.

"I know ye're not a prude, so stop acting like one," Claire said. "I need help." She sighed heavily again, motioning to her whole body. "Dominic is the only man I've slept with in more than a decade. Surely there's something new in sex I haven't tried yet."

"Plenty of diseases," Emma offered.

"Ye're not taking this seriously. You've had tons of lovers. You must have something up your sleeve. Some new tricks."

Oh, bollocks. Emma cringed. She didn't even have any old tricks with the minuscule amount of experience she'd had beneath the sheets. The truth was, she was a big fat liar. And for good reason. With Mum the world's leading sexpert, who could blame her for lying about her sexual exploits?

Starting when she was fourteen, it seemed like her mum had hounded her daily about celebrating her womanhood and doing *it*. At fifteen, to get her mother off her back, Emma gathered a bunch of sordid details from an erotic novel and regaled her mother with a make-believe sexual encounter with the captain of the cricket team. Unfortunately, Mum decided to tell the story on the next episode of her talk show to point out the importance of young girls embracing their sexual identities. Thank goodness she'd kept the boy's name out of it.

After that Emma felt she had to keep lying—even to Claire, who seemed to look up to her because of her "maturity." Eventually, Emma had tried to erase the lies by having casual sex, but the experiences had fallen way short of her partners' expectations and her own. If only now she could take back every tall tale.

"Emms, you can't let me down," Claire begged.

Emma shored herself up, thinking about her past clients. "If there's one thing I've learned over the years, it's that sex is not the end-all."

"Bollocks," Claire said. "It's the great communicator. The only way to get and hold a man's attention. It's the one thing men truly care about, too. You're the one who told me that."

More crap Emma had spewed. "I was wrong," she admitted. But she couldn't admit to the rest, not now. She had to keep the focus on Claire. "Men care about a lot of things that we don't give them credit for." She thought for a second. "Like respect."

"I respect Dominic," Claire defended. "He just doesn't respect that I want to have a baby now."

"Backing Dom into a corner when he's clearly against it isn't the way to show him respect." As Emma said this, she felt unnerved. She was no longer a marriage counselor, but she could be a friend. She reached over and touched Claire's arm. "I saw the restaurant's ledgers. You can't afford a baby right now. Can you in good conscience press Dom? You and I both know how finances can stress him out. You told me how upset he got when he sprained his arm and couldn't work for a few weeks. Remember?"

"Things got a little tight, but we were fine," Claire argued.

Emma tried from a different angle. "I think he's under more pressure here. You two have always worked for others. This is your first time as the proprietors. Have you considered what it might do to Dominic, as a man, if the restaurant fails?"

Claire harrumphed and clutched the steering wheel with the force of vise-grips. "You don't understand what I'm going through."

But Emma did. Time was against them. They were both thirty and the clock was ticking. A constant thud that never went away. The good news for Claire: She was married and Dom loved her. Emma, on the other hand, had zilch. No one. No prospects. No leads. No nothing.

Emma's only consolation was her mother's voice ringing in her head: *Children serve no purpose until they are of the age to contribute to society.*

She doubted her mother's "wisdom" on so many levels. But in this one instance, Emma let her words serve to curb her own appetite for wanting a child. She was tired of talking of babies with Claire—a brick wall on the subject—and was happy to sit quietly for the rest of the trip. Especially since her friend was clearly angry with her.

When they got to Inverness and parked, they were

both still in a lousy mood. Emma followed Claire down the sidewalk and watched as her friend's spirits lifted the closer they got to the intimates shop.

Before they opened the door to A Slip of the Tongue, Emma grabbed Claire's arm. "I'll be across the street having coffee." She gave her an imploring gaze.

Claire shook her head determinedly. "Fine. A great friend you are, making me do this alone." She made it sound like Emma was letting her down, when in reality Emma didn't have the stomach to help Claire let Dominic down.

Much later, Claire showed up with three small bags and a satisfied grin. "The deed is done. We need to run to the grocery while we're here. I have a list."

"All right." Emma wasn't sure where the two of them stood.

"Get that look off yere face. We're still friends, Emma," Claire said. "You just need to work at being a better one." She took Emma's arm good-humoredly as they made their way to the car.

"You know good friends try to protect one another from making stupid mistakes," Emma lectured.

But Claire only smiled, unable to hear the truth.

"Fine," Emma said. "It's your marriage. I have no stake in it." But that wasn't necessarily true.

At the market, Claire talked excitedly about her irresistible lingerie and how Dom wouldn't be able to keep his hands off her. "He did say one time, though, that the sexiest outfit I owned was me naked." She went silent after that.

Emma could've pointed out the obvious but it would've only fallen on Claire's stubborn, deaf ears. If Dom refused to sleep in the same bed with her, then the *irresistible* teddies and G-strings would be worthless—money and energy wasted.

By the time they got back to Gandiegow and the restaurant, it was dinnertime and Dominic had a few customers. Emma noticed Gabriel wasn't there to help. She did catch, though, the mischievous glance Claire shot her husband.

"Meet me upstairs later." She gave him a wink. "I've something to show ye."

When she disappeared, Dominic turned to Emma. "What's that all about?"

Emma went to the sink and stuck her hands in the dishwater. "I wash my hands of it." And scrubbed a saucepan. After a bit, she went to the dining area and served the few customers that were left, and then finished the rest of the dishes. She said little more to Dominic, giving him space to concentrate on his business. She feared he had Claire's shenanigans on his mind, though, because the crease between his brows stayed bonded together. Emma focused on giving him her mental and moral support—for whatever that was worth.

When she'd done all she could do at the restaurant, she slipped out the back door, not sure what to do. Now that Claire had her sights set on luring Dominic back into the marriage bed, Gandiegow felt damned uncomfortable. She couldn't be in the next room while Claire and Dominic had wild, crazy sex. Emma felt lost and, yes, alone. *What have I gotten myself into?* She had no home anymore. She'd terminated her lease in Los Angeles with a hefty penalty. Her mother's house in London surely wasn't home; it hadn't been in a long while. Emma belonged nowhere. To no one.

She trudged along the path until she got to the boardwalk. It was after eight and her stomach grumbled. She wished now she'd sneaked in a bite at the restaurant when she'd had a chance. Besides the pub, the only place with the lights still on was Quilting Central. She remembered the kitchen and decided to go there.

Only two steps later and she saw Gabriel come around the corner, carrying his medical bag. Her breathing involuntarily stopped.

"What are you doing out?" His breath was visible in the frigid night air.

She nodded toward Quilting Central. "Looking for food." Her unruly stomach took that moment to grumble—loudly.

He raised a questioning eyebrow. "What about the restaurant?"

"Don't ask," she answered.

"Come back to the doctor's quarters. We'll have a bite to eat; then we can have that talk you wanted to have."

She hesitated. He affected her in ways she didn't want to think about. Maybe being alone with him wasn't wise. Just then her stomach growled again. *Oh, bugger.* "All right."

They walked back to his place side by side.

"So, why are you out and about?" she inquired.

"Checking on Amy and her baby."

Mentally Emma rolled her eyes. *Don't get me started on that baby.*

She slipped and he caught her arm. She spun into him while he pulled her close. For a second her chest rested against his. Time warped into a still-life photo. Two lovers wrapped in each other's arms, staring into each other's eyes. The streetlamp provided the right amount of light in the dark of night—as cozy as being under the covers with a flashlight, but this wasn't some child's play. And then, as if a blowtorch had set her blood on fire, her center melted and pooled in her nether regions. An area she'd completely given up hope on.

She started to reach a hand up to push his hair away from his eyes so she could see him better.

He pulled away, clearing his throat. "Are you okay?"

"Yes," she said stupidly.

She glanced up at him and he stared straight ahead, his expression as stony as the rocks on the bluff above them. Immediately, cold seeped into her body and she felt mortified. She must've imagined the intimacy they'd just shared.

A few seconds later and they were at the doctor's quarters. He held the door open for her, and she wavered. Coming here wasn't a good idea. The air seemed to hum when he was around her and she didn't know how to handle herself.

"In or out, Emma." His deep Scottish baritone gave away nothing of what he was feeling.

Two could play at this game. She put her reserved British emotions back in place and stepped over the threshold. The smell of beef met her nose, and her mouth watered. "It smells delicious."

"Stew," he offered. He sat on the pew at the bottom of the stairs and slipped off his boots.

The unusual seating gave her the perfect opportunity to land on a neutral subject. "What is the story behind the pew? Was it here when you moved in?"

"Nay. I brought it with me. It's from my grandfather's church." He ran his hand over the polished dark wood before reaching down and pulling a pair of sock slippers from a box underneath. "Here. Put these on." He frowned at her snow-covered sneakers. "Boots, Emma. You have to get some boots."

"I promise. Tomorrow." She pointed to the spot next to him. "May I?"

"Aye." He scooted over.

Tentatively, she sat next to him. "So, you come from a

long line of pastors?" She glanced over at him. "Why didn't you go into the family business? I had to."

A wave of anger or pain, she couldn't tell which, swept over Gabriel. If the war raging on his face was any indication, Emma had poked at a sore spot.

Quickly, she laid a hand on his arm to undo what she'd done. "Sorry. I didn't mean to dig."

"It's okay." He shoved his feet into a pair of moccasins.

"Do you want to talk about it?" She flinched. *How very counselor-like of me. Old habits do die hard.*

"Nay." He pointed up the stairs. "Let's get our tea."

She rose. "Yes. Let's."

"You go on up. I'll be just a minute. I have to put this away." He picked up his medical bag and headed toward the surgery.

She walked up the stairs and went into the kitchen. It hit her again, just like before: She loved it. It was the quaintest kitchen she'd ever seen. Yellow-checked curtains over a farmer's sink. A tiny red Formica drop-leaf table with matching red stainless-steel chairs. Open cabinetry with unmatching but charming plates, bowls, and mugs. Had Deydie and the quilting ladies decorated for him? Remembering the old woman's remarks about outlanders and outsiders, Emma decided no.

She went to the stove to check if there was water in the kettle and turned on the burner. Like she owned the place, she lifted the lid on the pot and smelled the beef stew. "Yummy."

Gabriel cleared his throat. "I'm glad I started it earlier."

"Yes, me, too. Thanks for the invite to dinner." Then she noticed what he wore—a Dr. Who T-shirt and jeans. "Your normal doctor attire?"

He looked down at his shirt. "It puts the patients at

ease." He pulled down two teacups and saucers and sat them on the red tabletop. "So, you wanted to talk about the Russos?"

Emma took down a couple of plates. "Are these okay?"

"Fine," he said. "About Claire and Dom—"

She stalled. "Not on an empty stomach." She was so tired of Claire's irrational state of mind and being thrust into the middle. She looked up at Gabriel apologetically and shrugged. "Can't we just have a peaceful dinner? I need a break from them."

"Aye, a break it is." He leaned against the wall.

She kept her head down, fussing with their place settings, making them perfect, knowing he watched her.

The teakettle whistled and he seemed to snap out of it. "Do you mind taking care of that while I take care of the stew?"

"Not at all. Making tea is my specialty." She walked past him and grabbed the kettle while he sidled past her and snatched up the ladle. A perfect dance, as though they'd worked in the kitchen together forever.

When they finally sat down to eat, a sense of contentment overcame her—something she hadn't felt since she'd arrived in Gandiegow. Or in a long time, for that matter.

Gabriel shocked the hell out of her by grabbing her hand and saying a quick grace. When he finished and glanced up, he didn't apologize for not warning her. "Force of habit," he said.

She kept her head down, blowing on her stew, waiting for the blush to leave her cheeks. She liked holding his hand for those brief seconds. And if God were truly watching, He wouldn't appreciate how her body had warmed at Gabriel's touch and how fuzzy her brain had gone while Gabriel said the short prayer.

She peeked up at him. The man was way too good-looking for his own good. He glanced over and caught her staring—again. He didn't chastise her this time, only smiled.

He tore off a piece of bread. "So, what should we discuss during our feast?"

"There's no love lost between you and the quilters of Gandiegow."

He dipped his bread in the stew. "Wow. How does it feel to twist the knife deep in that open wound?"

She smiled and shrugged. She was only speaking the truth.

He didn't seem to hold it against her. "I have no idea what I've done to them, except not be from here. You know that small-town thing where they don't accept outsiders."

She reached out and patted his hand good-naturedly. "It's worse than that, Gabey."

"Oh?" He gave her a little frown. "And don't call me *Gabey*."

"Only if you quit calling me *Princess*."

"Deal. Now, what have I done to make all of Gandiegow treat me like I have the plague?"

She grinned. "They consider you an outlander."

"Are ye sure they didn't say Lowlander? That I am," he said.

"I'm sure. Deydie said it plain and clear."

He gave her a derisive bark. "And what about you, Ms. London England, the true outlander? I'm surprised they haven't strung you up yet."

She buttered her bread with superiority. "I have connections. I have Claire."

"Claire? I've known her forever, too. I'm practically married into the family," he said.

"Ah yes, right. But for some reason they've decided that I'm one of them."

"God's teeth, these people. I just don't understand

them. Dominic isn't faring too well with them, either. Did they say anything about him? He has a stake in this town with the restaurant and all. Do you know where he stands?"

"I don't know." She took a bite of stew and changed the subject, not ready yet to talk about Claire and Dominic. "Do you have big plans for Christmas?"

She thought it was an innocent question, but Gabriel looked even more unhappy about the inquiry than he had talking about the strange ways of the people of Gandiegow.

Gabe sat there a little stunned. What was it with Emma Castle that she could ferret out the two points of contention he had with his father? Not going into the ministry as his father had wanted was one, and Christmas was the other. She certainly had a way of tearing open one's soft underbelly and exposing the deep issues. She was either a gifted therapist or a psychic.

"Are you heading home to Edinburgh to see your father?"

There, she did it again. "Nay." Gabe didn't know what to say, if he should tell her anything.

"Are you all right?" She touched his arm, and it warmed him. "Gabriel, did I say something I shouldn't have?"

He liked the way she said his name and didn't really mind the concern in her eyes. It looked sincere.

"I'll probably be staying here for Christmas. I am, after all, Gandiegow's doctor." But it was more than that.

She took a second to rub his arm soothingly and then took her hand away. The sympathetic smile she gave him said she knew he wasn't telling the complete truth.

He took a sip of tea and then put the cup down. *What the hell?* "My father and I get along fine on most things but are at odds when it comes to Christmas," he finally confessed.

She shook her head. "How can that be? You're both religious, right? He's a pastor, and you say grace." She stared at his hand for a long moment, as if reliving their hands joined in prayer.

"My father observes the old ways. Traditionally in the Church of Scotland, Christmas is celebrated very quietly."

She put her spoon down and leaned closer. "Really?"

"Aye," he said. "My father would argue that nowhere in the Bible is Christmas celebrated or even mentioned, even though the New Testament covers the thirty-three years of Jesus's life and then another thirty or so years after his resurrection."

"Interesting. I've never given any real thought to the holidays from an academic or historical standpoint."

"That's not even to mention how my father abhors the commercialism of Christmas." He took a bite of his stew.

"So, where do you stand?" she asked.

He shrugged. "I want to go all out for Christmas. As a kid I saw others celebrating it in a big way and I wanted that, too. Now I can."

She smiled at him. "Still a kid at heart?"

"Maybe," he said, smiling back. She was easy to talk to when she wasn't taking a bite out of his ass. "How's your food?"

"Delicious. Thank you so much."

They chatted easily for the rest of the meal about their lives, little stories—nothing big and nothing to do with the Russos. If Emma wasn't going to bring up Claire and Dominic, then Gabe decided he wouldn't bring them up again, either. Who was he to muck up their truce and spoil their pleasant evening together?

When they finished, she cleared the table while he filled the sink with water. "I'll just leave these to soak and do them later." He pulled down two wineglasses. "Merlot?"

"Yes, that sounds good."

As he poured the wine, he thought about other evenings spent with other women. Normally, he would've worked out in his head how to take things to the next level. With Emma, he was just enjoying her company. It didn't mean that he didn't think about seducing her every other second; he just wasn't acting on it.

He handed her a glass. "To what should we toast?"

She looked a little sheepish. "A place for me to spend the night?"

Holy shite! He spilled his wine down the front of his shirt.

Chapter Six

Claire lay draped across the bed in her hooker red peekaboo lingerie. A few strings of ribbon covered her crotch and stars barely hid her nipples. Dominic would undoubtedly peel those off with his teeth. She'd blown the budget at A Slip of the Tongue. She shouldn't have, with their finances the way they were, but guilt be damned. This was an investment. *One baby to order.*

She glanced at the clock again. Surely Dominic had wrapped things up downstairs by now. He loved it when she put her slut on. She repositioned her legs, making sure his favorite part was the first thing he saw when he came through the door.

Twenty minutes later, she was done waiting. She grabbed the whip out of the second bag and went in search of her absent husband.

Downstairs, she found him disinfecting the tables and chairs in the grand dining room. He hadn't seen her yet, so she cracked the whip.

He jumped, knocking over a bucket of bleach water. She smiled and waited. She loved it when his eyes came alive for her.

He only glanced in her direction for a moment, as if she was wearing nothing more than a dirty dish towel.

He knelt down and mopped up the spilled water. "Dammit, Claire, you scared the shit out of me. Get some rags and help me clean this mess up."

She flinched but forced herself to recover. Bigger things were at stake here than her pride.

"Dominic," she purred. "You've been naughty." She cracked the whip again. "Come here, sweetheart, so I can make you pay."

He growled at her. "Forget it, Claire." He grabbed an old tablecloth behind the bar and spread it over the mess. "I've work to do."

"Yes, there's work to do," she said, humming with sexuality. "Upstairs between my legs."

"I'm not giving in," he said resolutely to the floor. Finally, though, he turned to her.

Then she saw it—coolness. No, frigid-cold ice. Not a trace of desire in his hard beautiful eyes. Dominic's frown spoke of frustration. And a heaping dollop of stubbornness.

"Go to bed, Claire." He bent over the watery floor.

Her tough-girl act faltered. "But ye'll be up later, right?"

He only scrubbed the floor harder.

She stared at him, bewildered. In times past if she'd so much as grinned at him in that special way, well . . . Dominic would've been finishing up with her by now, bent over the nearest table. She peered down to her near-naked breasts.

"Ye let me down," she muttered to them. "We'll just have to try harder next time—that's all."

Emma grabbed a dish towel and mopped up Gabriel's shirt and chest. His hard chest. She licked her lips. "You'd better get that T-shirt off or Dr. Who will be ruined. Do you have any club soda?"

He pulled his shirt over his head and she almost collapsed into the nearest chair. That hard chest gave way to a six-pack. She remembered the dish towel in her hand and blotted away at his naked chest, pretending not to notice how gorgeous he was. Her cheeks felt as bloody red as the wine.

He stilled her hand, holding it against his chest with her only inches away from him. "I'm good," he said.

"Yes," she had to agree. She looked into his hooded eyes and for a second didn't mind at all that he'd captured her. Then she remembered how easy it was for him. A few come-hither glances, a few charming words, a few smiles, and women fell at his feet. Well, not Egghead Emma. She was much too smart to be lured in. She let go of him and stepped away.

"Right." He backed away, too. "I'll just go find another shirt."

She rummaged through his cabinet for club soda but didn't find any. Next she went to his restroom, looking for shaving cream. She found some and rushed back to his shirt and covered the stain with it.

He came back into the room with a sweater covering his beautiful chest. "What are you doing?"

"Your shirt might be saved. We need to get this in the washer now in hot water."

"Here, in the hallway closet." Sure enough, behind the pocket doors was a stackable. "How do you know how to deal with stains?"

"Well, this princess has played hostess to tons of Mum's parties. Just some tricks of the trade. Plus, Nessa, Claire's mother, made sure I knew the basics." She held herself up straight. "I can take care of myself. I even know how to darn socks."

"Is that so?" He looked intrigued, but then a devilish grin came over his face. "Care to take some work home with you?"

"Not on your life." She dropped the shirt in the washer. He added soap and turned it on.

It was surreal. First the two of them had worked on dinner together and now the laundry. What was next— putting clean sheets on his bed?

She blushed and rushed back to the kitchen.

"About your sleeping arrangements for tonight . . ." he reminded her. "I have a solution."

She bet he did. *A girl gets a little at loose ends on where she's going to sleep, and Gabriel is right there with a solution. His warm body in his big bed.*

She turned away from him and put her hand up. "Forget I ever said anything. I'll figure out something."

Out of her peripheral vision, she saw him reach over and take one of her curls. He pulled it gently, not hurting her, but just enough that she turned toward him.

"I've got a place for you to sleep tonight." He twirled her hair around his finger. "Before you get on your high horse, though, it's not here with me." He dropped her lock of hair. "Come. Let's get your coat."

Outside, the air was calm but so very cold. He'd given her no more clues about where he was taking her. Also, he was acting the true gentleman, which was at complete odds with the Gabriel of the past. But she hadn't changed; she was still Egghead Emma. She couldn't expect him to put the moves on her. Besides . . . she didn't want him to anyway. Not at all.

Gabriel led her to a one-and-a-half-story bungalow with a sign out front that read THISTLE GLEN LODGE. The metal sign was a Nine-Patch quilt block.

"It's one of the quilting dorms," he explained. "Next door is the other one."

That sign read DUNCAN'S DEN and had a Fish and Tackle quilt block in shades of green-and-brown plaid.

"Duncan's Den is a strange name for a quilting dorm, isn't it?" she remarked.

"Nay. Duncan was one of the locals who recently passed away. This was his house. He donated it to the Kilts and Quilts retreat effort."

"Oh," she said, feeling dumb.

"It's okay. You couldn't have known." He opened the door to Thistle Glen Lodge and waited for her to come inside.

She walked in and found the entry decorated in a cheerful yellow-and-blue plaid. The pillows on the window seat were fashioned with a coordinating yellow-and-blue floral print. "Very feminine." She touched the curtains.

"After we get you settled, I'll leave a note at the restaurant for Claire to let her know where you are, in case she wonders."

"She has my mobile number," Emma said.

"I'll do it, anyway."

Gabriel pointed for her to go down the hallway. "You should have everything you need. I know the ladies keep extra toothbrushes and paste in the linen closet."

Emma gave him a questioning look. "And you know how?" Did he crash one of the quilting retreats? *And host another pajama party?*

"I stayed a couple of nights here when I first arrived."

She frowned at him, unable to help the images of naked quilters running their hands over Gabriel's six-pack.

A slight blush colored his cheeks. "I know what yc're thinking, Emma. The floors were being refinished at the doctor's quarters. And, no, there wasn't a retreat going on at the time. Just like there isn't now."

A veil fell over them. They'd been alone together for the whole evening, even shared a couple of intimate moments—if she'd read them correctly. But now the air between them became sexually charged and she was pretty sure she wasn't reading this one incorrectly. He tilted his head a little to one side. She gazed at his lips. Possibility rested there. She worried . . . no, hoped . . . no, bordered on panic that he might kiss her.

She stepped back and bumped into the hall table, and plopped down with her bum resting on the top. "Are you sure it's okay with the ladies that I stay here?" she squeaked.

He took her hand and pulled her back to her feet. "Ye're safe with me."

Which was pretty much saying he wasn't attracted to her, and she was imagining all sorts of scenarios that only existed in her mind. The magic was gone.

"Thanks." She smoothed down her slacks, not meeting his eyes.

"I'll drop by Deydie's, too, to explain what ye're about. Now stop worrying."

"Thanks for thinking of this," Emma said awkwardly, waving a hand vaguely at the dorm, as he walked to the door and left.

God, he'd almost kissed her. Gabe leaned against the front door, wanting to bang his head against it, but that would only summon her back to him. And he'd barely escaped. His evening with Emma had gone from pleasant to as awkward as a first date. She made him feel like a gangly teenager—before he'd learned his way around a woman.

He probably just needed to get laid, plain and simple. But he couldn't without breaking his promise to himself. The next time he took a woman to bed, he would be committed to her and only her. There were no halfways, no gray areas, no rationalizing a little nookie to get him through, and he knew it.

Suddenly the door opened and Emma stood inches from him, his gloves in her hand. She looked shocked. She opened her sweet lips to say something, and that was all the encouragement he needed. He stepped inside and pinned her against the wall and kissed the hell out of her. He even tangled his hand in her hair to keep her where he wanted her. His pent-up frustration fed on her lips. He expected Little Miss Prim and Proper to protest and put up some resistance, but instead she melted into him, letting him do what he wanted, letting herself become part of him.

He shoved himself away from her, breathing hard. "Ah hell, Emma. I'm sorry. I never . . ." He grabbed his gloves from her clutched hand and fled into the night.

What is wrong with me? Emma Castle wasn't even remotely the kind of woman he wanted.

The old Gabe must've resurfaced to grab onto the first piece of ass he saw and liked. He knew the kind of lass he wanted to settle down with: either a girl from the country or one from a small town. One who was sweet, shy, and unsophisticated. Hardworking, strong-loving, without emotional baggage. He knew it was old-fashioned, even archaic, but he wanted to be laird of his own castle, with a woman beside him who understood that he needed to be *the man*. He didn't need a strong woman, like Emma Castle; he planned to be strong enough for the both of them, whomever he ended up with.

He pulled on his gloves and tramped through the village. *Damned old habits.* He'd have to try harder to be a better man.

He rushed to Quilting Central to let them know that he'd put Emma up at the dorm for the night. He'd taken some liberties by stowing her there and he knew it. He just needed to talk to the quilting ladies and square it with them. But when he got to the expansive building on the boardwalk, all the lights were out. In the distance across the cove, he could see Deydie's lights were off, as well. As he walked in that direction, he pulled out his pocket notebook and ripped out a page. He would slip an explanation under Deydie's door so she'd know about Emma when she woke in the morning. It probably wouldn't stop the tongue-lashing he'd get from Deydie, but he hurried to her cottage, anyway.

It was after eleven when he dropped off the note. He quickened his steps to the restaurant, and at least one light, thankfully, was still on. Relief flooded him. He needed someone to talk to about what had happened with Emma. Surely Dom would tell Gabe what he'd already diagnosed about himself: It'd been some time since he'd been with a woman; that was why he'd kissed Emma the way he had. Dom would probably prescribe an adult magazine and time alone to fix the problem.

Gabe quietly let himself into the restaurant but didn't see anyone. Surely Dom wouldn't have left the lights on. Gabe headed toward the storeroom.

Inside he found Dom lying on a pallet of quilts on the floor. He was flipping through a cookbook.

"What in the hell are you doing here?" his foster brother cursed.

"I should ask you the same thing," Gabe said. "You should be upstairs with yere wife."

"Sod off." Dom went back to his book.

Gabe wandered over to a bushel basket of onions and picked one up. "Hiding out here is not helping yere marriage, brother."

"You talking it to death isn't helping it, either." Dom slammed the cookbook shut. "Turn off the lights on your way out." He pulled the North Star quilt over his large frame and closed his eyes.

It looked ridiculous, Dom lying on the floor like some

dog. "Come back to the doctor's quarters with me to-night. You can have the spare bedroom."

Dominic rolled over and cursed. He pulled a potato out from underneath his back and hurled it across the room, nearly hitting Gabe's shoulder.

Gabe took one more crack at reasoning with Dom. "You must be breaking several health codes by pretending to sleep next to the food ye're planning to serve . . ."

That got his attention. Dominic sat up and huffed loudly. "Fine. I'll go back to the damn doctor's quarters with you. But you'd better not keep me up all night with your incessant talking."

The bedroom felt stuffy. Claire threw back the covers and climbed out of her husbandless bed. She opened the window and gazed at the moon. It looked like a big cheese pizza, the yellow hue accentuating the craters, with the cheesy reflection bouncing off the water like a ball.

Earlier she'd slunk off to bed like a whipped pup, her ego taking a beating from Dominic's rejection. She stuck her head out the window now. She'd been charting her cycle since coming back to Gandiegow, and she was ovulating this very minute. Ripe. Ready.

The view out her window spoke to her, giving her hope, rejuvenating her. Tonight anything was possible.

Many times she'd woken Dominic up in their bed the way she had in mind now. If he wouldn't come to her, she'd just go downstairs to him. Then, while he was still half-asleep, she'd guide him back to their bed and have her way with him.

She shut the window. Quietly, she snuck down the stairs, making sure not to make a sound. With all the lights out, she had to be extra careful not to trip and alert her husband of the impending booty call.

At the doorway of the storeroom, she slipped off her cotton nightgown and walked through, naked. With no windows in the room, it was pitch-black. She made her way to where she'd seen the pile of quilts, and reached out to caress Dom's crotch.

It was hard but it wasn't Dominic. "What the . . ." She held on to a large potato. She yanked her hand away. "Damn it."

The storeroom walls closed in on her. Utter loneliness descended into her being. On its heels came fear, which instantly turned into a crushing panic. And with it a memory so strong that she dropped to her knees.

Running into her parents' room, expecting to find her father home from the sea, but the room had been empty. A terrible storm raged outside, so much so, Claire knew not to leave their cottage. She waited for hours for her mother to return. Later, she'd found out why Mama had been called away. She and the others had been told the terrible news—fourteen fishermen had died that night when the Rose *sank. Changing Gandiegow and their lives forever. Her mother had returned, but Claire never saw Papa again.*

A sob slipped from Claire. It felt as gut-wrenching as if it had happened yesterday. With so many families devastated by the accident, the town couldn't help them. Mama had to move them to London for work as Eleanor Hamilton's housekeeper. At eleven, Claire had believed her life was over. But then Emma had been there. They'd become everything to each other. Claire still felt like an outsider in the outlanders' world, but Emma seemed to understand and eased her pain. She owed so much to her friend.

Claire sniffed and wiped away her tears as she stood. Everything would be okay. Emma was here with her now. And Dominic wasn't a fisherman; he hadn't drowned tonight. She willed herself to breathe steadily.

"But where is he?" she said to the potatoes and the empty storeroom.

The answer came to her in a flash and her temper flared. *The pub.*

Anger and jealousy burned behind her eyelids, red and hot.

She stomped out, snatching her nightgown from the floor as she passed. "The women of Gandiegow had better keep their oven mitts off my husband. Dominic belongs to me."

The next morning, Emma roared awake—literally. A Hoover—no, an army of Hoovers—rumbled in the adjacent bedroom and down the narrow hallway. She jumped out of bed and opened the door.

Deydie ran over her foot with the infernal vacuum cleaner. The old woman shut off the machine and looked contrite. "Sorry, lassie. Impromptu quilt retreat. We just got word that Cynthia from Iowa Star Quilts can pop in for a long weekend to teach the Top Method of Foundation Paper Piecing."

"Paper what?"

"Paper piecing. It's a great way to make detailed quilt blocks. Aye, it's a lot of fun." Deydie grabbed Emma's arm. "Run to Claire's now and get us some scones. We've no time to stop for breakfast. My Caitie put a notice on the Internet and thirty women will be coming on the chartered bus from Edinburgh this very evening. It's a lot of stress for me ole bones, but I'm right happy to be doing it. Come now. Hurry." She shoved Emma toward the door.

She only took a moment to slip into her Dolce &

Gabbanas. Whoever said small-town life was quiet and lazy had apparently never stayed in Gandiegow.

Deydie leaned out the door and shouted to her, "And tonight I'll be giving ye your first quilting lesson. I have a plan. Aye, I do." When Emma glanced back, the ancient woman had a secretive smile on her wrinkly old face.

"What plan is that?" Emma hollered back.

The old woman pointed a gnarled finger at her. "Scones. Go on with ye now."

Emma hurried along, first worried about what Deydie might be up to, and then upset she'd left Claire in the lurch by sleeping in. Another of Claire's rules rang in Emma's head: *The scones wait for no one.*

But Emma's main preoccupation and worry this morning was that she could still feel Gabriel on her lips, assaulting her in the most delicious way. She had to admit that from the day she'd met him, she'd wondered what it would feel like to be on the receiving end of one of his kisses. She'd known even back then that his pheromones made her a little dizzy. But she'd imagined his kiss to be engaging and tender; in real life, his kiss had been demanding and consuming, and she'd gone from surprised to on fire in two seconds flat. To have his body crushed up against hers was the most passionate experience she'd ever had. In that moment, she wouldn't have cared if he'd stripped her naked and made love to her against the wall for all of Gandiegow to walk by and see.

Though it was bitter cold this gray morning, she unzipped her jacket to cool off. She had to put the steamy Gabriel MacGregor out of her mind. That kiss had been a fluke. He had even apologized for it, looking so terribly sorry to have kissed Egghead Emma. He must be pretty hard up here in this small town—his options not what he was used to in the big city. She would've felt sorrier for him if she wasn't already sorry for herself; that kiss had been the most exciting thing that had ever happened to her in her whole, unsatisfying life.

At that, she made a deliberate effort to switch off all thoughts of him and put her thoughts on Claire.

Emma wondered if Claire and her lingerie had gotten lucky last night. Of course she had. Claire always got exactly what she wanted. Always.

When Emma arrived at the restaurant, everything looked under control. Another woman was there, helping, taking orders. Claire stood at the cash register, waiting on a couple of fishermen wearing black wellies.

"Sorry I'm late," Emma said, stepping behind the counter.

"Don't fash yourself over it." Claire had dark circles under her eyes, confirmation that the lingerie had worked.

Emma didn't approve of Claire manipulating her husband. But if Dominic and Claire had worked things out and were back together, then bully for them.

The fishermen left, and Claire lit into her. "Why didn't you come back last night? I didn't know where you were until this morning, when I came down to warm the ovens."

"I assumed you were *busy* with Dominic." Emma raised an eyebrow to get her meaning across.

"I wish." Claire grabbed a rag and wiped down the counter, not meeting her eye.

"What do you mean, *I wish*? What happened?"

"You mean what *didn't* happen." She looked up, and this time Emma saw the rawness of rejection in her eyes.

Emma had the childish urge to say *Told you so*. Instead she wrapped an arm around her friend. "Are you all right?"

"What you do think? I miss my husband and I want a baby." Claire crumpled. "And I have no idea where Dominic slept last night. He wasn't here. He could've been in any woman's bed. I checked the pub, hoping he was drinking alone, but he wasn't there."

"Did you see if he went to Gabriel's?" Emma hoped that's where he'd gone.

Claire's face lit up. "Yes. That has to be where he was."

Emma gave her a squeeze. "What can I do to help? I mean with the breakfast crowd." Then, "Oh, damn. Deydie needs me to bring scones over to Thistle Glen Lodge. A retreat is coming this evening."

"So I've heard." Claire grabbed a pastry box and started filling it. "Moira stopped by to tell me. And stayed," she added. She looked up at Emma. "Stop feeling guilty. It was just a wee morning rush."

"I'm a terrible friend," Emma said.

Claire rolled her eyes and filled an insulated carafe with coffee. "Only if you don't help me make Dominic fork over some sperm."

"You know I can't. This is between you and him."

"I know, I know. Don't worry. I've come up with a foolproof plan. Just you wait and see." Claire shoved the box and carafe at her. "Here, get these to Deydie before she takes her broom after you."

Dominic took the money from the last customer and thanked him. The lunch crowd had been a tad larger today. He pulled out the receipts and scanned them.

With the sudden quilt retreat this weekend, the restaurant's fate didn't look nearly as grim as yesterday. Maybe there could be a stay of execution; maybe they wouldn't have to pull up and move back to Glasgow or Edinburgh and work for someone else. "If only the town would support the restaurant more."

If he could hold on to the few regulars he had and grow them little by little, and no more retreats were canceled, Pastas & Pastries might just make it. Maybe in three to five years, if things kept improving, he could give Claire what she wanted.

Claire. God, how would he appease her in the meantime?

The restaurant stood empty, with tables that needed to be cleared. He grabbed a rubber container and bused each one. Using his hip, he pushed open the kitchen doors.

And froze, coming close to dropping all the dishes.

Claire bent over the sink, with her backside to the door, her buck-naked ass facing him. She turned around. From her fiery red hair to her bare feet, the only cloth she wore was an apron. When she shifted, one of her big, luscious breasts fell out.

He set down the dishes and wiped the sweat from his brow. "Oh God."

"No, it's just yere lusty wife. Come over here and give me and the girls a squeeze." She jutted her chest out to emphasize which girls she meant.

He took a step toward her, then another, but when he lifted his foot the third time, he stopped midstride. It took everything in him to utter the next words. "No, Claire. No baby. Not yet." He breathed heavily. "Why can't you understand? We've got no money for a babe."

Claire untied the apron from around her neck and let the front flap fall. She spilled out, and he almost fell to his knees.

"You're too damn beautiful for your own good."

With a sly grin, she reached behind her to undo the tie at her waist. He licked his lips in anticipation. He had to have her. He took another step toward her.

But when he did, he saw the look of triumph cross her face. She had him by the balls and she knew it. Normally, he didn't mind being weak for his wife. But more lay in the balance than making love to her.

"Dammit, Claire, I love you," he yelled. He gestured

to the kitchen. "But this isn't going to happen. The restaurant isn't standing on its own legs. It's still a babe." As he said it, her face fell, and her pain devastated him. Her seductive tricks were much easier to sidestep than her eyes welling with tears.

"Dammit," he muttered, stomping from the room and straight out the front door, not caring about the cold weather outside.

Claire had done it. Made the decision for him. He would stay indefinitely at Gabe's. The farther away he stayed from Claire and her raw emotions, the better.

Claire pulled herself together and tied the front of her apron back up. She wouldn't fall apart. She came from stronger stock than that. The Douglases were a clan of warriors. She held her head high and made her way to the steps heading up to the flat.

She'd just have to pull out the big guns. "I love you, too, you big idiot. I didn't want to have to do this to ye," she said to the walls while ascending the stairs. "Ye'll not like it one bit, either."

It was one thing to be in Glasgow, where she had to take care of herself. But she was home now and Gandiegow had her back. It was time to bring them into the fight.

Chapter Seven

G abe drove the Land Rover over the hill to the old
factory that sat less than a mile out of Gandiegow.
He hadn't gone into the restaurant this morning because
he couldn't face Emma. He'd been a cad last night, kissing her the way he had, and he was a coward this morning. Instead, he'd called Lachlan McDonnell and told
him to expect him after morning office hours at the
newly dubbed North Sea Valve Company.

The McDonnell, as he was known, was a renowned
engineer for these parts, and had decided to give new life
to the sixty-plus-years-empty factory and turn it into a
budding enterprise for the town. It was a tall task, but
Gabe could see the genius of it. The North Sea was right
outside Gandiegow's doorstep, and with the North Sea
oil fields growing like they were, an oil-valve company
close by was perfect. At Gabe's first glimpse of the factory, though, he thought the McDonnell would definitely
have his work cut out for him. The building was ancient,
with missing windows here and there. The roof could use
a few shingles in spots and seemed to slope oddly on one
side. Gabe pulled into the parking lot and retrieved his
toolbox from the back of the Land Rover.

He walked into the factory, confident that working

with his hands was just the thing to keep his mind off how he'd taken advantage of Emma's sweet lips last night. Of course, he'd left a note on the surgery's door, explaining where he was today, along with his mobile number in case he was needed.

The McDonnell met him inside and pounded him on the back. "So good of you to come. I really need the conveyor motor up and running today. Are you up for the task?"

"Aye." Gabe knew nothing about making valves, but he knew a hell of a lot about repairing motors and engines. Working at the factory today was just what the doctor had ordered: an afternoon of being useful.

The McDonnell led him through the double doors to the factory floor. The place was a mess, but it looked grand to a mechanic like him. "Here it is. If you need anything, Ross and Ramsay are just over there." At that the McDonnell left him with the crippled conveyor.

Three hours later, Gabe lay on his back under the motor, sweating. The motor had seized up and he'd done everything in the book to get her back in working order. He grabbed the wrench near his head and ratcheted down a bolt. For the hundredth time, he told himself he wasn't hiding out from Emma. He just needed time to get his head screwed on straight after last night's debacle and before seeing her again.

Gabe's hand slipped and the wrench cracked his knuckles. "Dammit."

"I heard that all the way over here," Ross said. Ross was one of the fishermen, brother to Ramsay, whom Gabe had dehooked the other day. "Did you break anything, Doc?"

"Nay. Just my pride." He put the wrench on the bolt one more time and torqued it. "So, Ross, are you going to give up fishing and work at the factory when she's up and running?"

"Fishing's in my blood. Ramsay might, though, as clumsy as he is."

"Och, brother." Ramsay stood in the middle of the room with a piece of molded sheet metal propped on his shoulder. "We can go outside and settle once and for all who's the clumsier of the two."

Gabe shook his head at these lads, who were always blustering for the position of top Scot, though Ross was older by a year.

The McDonnell came up beside Ramsay. "Back to work, lads. There's too much to do for all this chitchat."

Gabe agreed and grabbed another bolt. He'd had a sleepless night and it was all Emma's fault. He must really be hard up, because he couldn't stop the replay in his mind—pushing her up against the wall, kissing her, possessing her. Why in blazes had he caved and sought out her lips? He was a man with principles now, not some horny wanker.

He put his mind back on his work, grateful he had something to occupy him. This job was doing triple duty. It helped keep his mind off Emma and built up his social capital with the natives, and, hell, he loved working with his hands.

Unfortunately, that thought brought him full circle back to the reason he'd come here today. *Emma*. He shouldn't want to get his hands on Emma Castle. And see what magic he could work there.

"It's four o'clock," the McDonnell said. "Put your tools down. It's time to go home and clean up."

"If it's all the same to you, I'd like to stay and work," Gabe said.

The McDonnell shook his head. "Nay. It's all hands

on deck. The quilters from Edinburgh will be here shortly. They'll need every one of our strong backs to get their things to the quilting dorms."

The quilting dorm. Emma. Gabe wondered if she had anywhere to go tonight. But he had to stay out of it. Emma's sleeping arrangements had nothing to do with him.

Emma sat in Claire's parlor and was in no hurry to get to Quilting Central. When she'd returned with the scones that morning, Deydie had been too busy to talk but promised to get with her later. Emma had a bad feeling about it.

Claire came out of the loo. "Get a move on, lassie." She looked too calm and confident for a woman whose world was crumbling all around her.

"What are you up to?" Emma asked, watching her friend closely.

Claire flipped her hair. "Don't worry yourself."

"What is that supposed to mean?"

"It means I have everything under control."

A shiver, and not a good one, traveled up Emma's spine.

"Come now. The ladies of Gandiegow are expecting us to attend their retreat. I don't want to let them down." Claire handed Emma a box filled with goodies for the quilting ladies.

"Fine." But they would talk about this later.

They arrived at Quilting Central just as the Edinburgh ladies were trooped in, several of the village men hauling luggage behind them.

Emma stepped inside and saw Gabriel lingering on the other side of the room. "What's he doing here?"

Claire gave her a sly grin. "What's that tone I hear? Are you crushing on poor Gabriel?"

"Rubbish. Proper Englishwomen do not crush."

"Are proper English women supposed to blush when they are lying through their teeth?"

Emma turned away from Claire, taking her blazing-hot cheeks with her. "Where do you want this box?"

Claire pointed to the table where the other food had been laid out. "After all the women are gathered, Father Andrew, our Episcopal priest, will kick off the retreat with a prayer. He's over there by the fire. He's new to town, too."

Father Andrew was young, in his late twenties, with sandy blond hair. He was talking with Rhona, Gandiegow's only schoolteacher. Emma wondered how he was faring, being new to town, too.

Deydie waddled over to them and took Emma's arm. "Good. I'm glad ye're here. How are you with straight stitches?"

"Pardon?" Emma asked.

Bethia joined them. "Emma, how are ye adjusting to life in Gandiegow? It's a far cry from London, but we have loads to offer."

Emma opened her mouth to tell her that she was only here for a visit, but Deydie yanked her arm, wanting her attention.

"Yere straight stitching? With a machine?" Deydie pointed to one of the sewing machines on the table.

Bethia cleared her throat.

Emma felt like a doll being tugged back and forth. "My straight stitches are fine, I guess. Claire's mom taught me how to sew." She eyed the old woman cautiously. "Why?"

"Good, good." Deydie broke into a smile, which was almost as frightening as her scowl. A terrible gleam of mischief played in her eyes. She leaned around her to speak to Bethia. "I have an idea."

Emma saw her wink at Bethia before she spoke again.

"We're awfully busy with the retreat," Deydie hedged. "Christmas is coming up faster than a rising tide."

"Nay, Deydie," Bethia warned.

Deydie bobbed her head up and down. "We need you to take care of something for us, Emma."

Bethia shook her head.

Deydie went on. "We're going to put you in charge of the Gandiegow Doctor quilt—the top of it, anyways," she added.

"No." Emma shook her head more emphatically than Bethia. "I don't plan to be here long enough to make a quilt." She looked over at Gabriel and saw he was staring back at her. She turned away, really blushing now.

She couldn't make something for him. Especially a quilt. It was too personal. Too intimate. Nessa used to say, "Quilts are love made tangible." But Emma couldn't wrap her mind around Gabriel wrapping himself in a blanket she had made for him. A comfort to him on cold winter nights. Would he be reminded of her? Would he remember her fondly? Or would he hide the quilt away, not wanting to think about the kiss they'd shared last night, the one he felt he should apologize for. A kiss that caused regret in him instead of a smile. Emma's face heated more. She would most certainly burst into flames if she didn't set the ladies straight right now. About sewing, anyway.

"When I said I know how to sew, I meant little things— darning socks, a throw pillow, a simple blouse." Emma waved a hand toward all the craft and creativity going on. "Not anything like all of this."

Rhona broke away from Father Andrew and joined them. Moira, too, the same woman who had helped Claire with the breakfast this morning.

Moira gazed at her shoes. "We'll help you with the quilt."

The gray-headed Rhona was more direct. "No one in this town gets away with not being connected to Quilting Central in one fashion or another."

Emma peeked over at Gabriel one more time and felt panicked. He might be considered perfection on so many levels. "But if I made the Gandiegow Doctor quilt, it wouldn't be nearly good enough."

Deydie patted her arm a little roughly. "It'll be good enough." Emma waited for her to add *for an outsider*.

But what Deydie said was, "For *him*."

"But—" Emma tried.

"We need ye, lass. Ye and Claire." Deydie grabbed Claire's arm, as well. "Ye see, with this retreat popping up like a winter storm, we'll not have time to finish the quilt for the doc."

"It's a tradition, dear." Apparently, Bethia had bailed on Emma and gotten on board with Deydie. "The first Christmas a doctor is here, he gets the Gandiegow Doctor quilt as a present."

Deydie pulled her closer. "Straight stitches is all ye'll need. Nothing harder than sewing the pieces together. Simple as gooseberry pie."

"I'm not a quilter," Emma argued. "And there's nothing simple about gooseberry pie."

"Ye'll be a quilter by the time we're done with you" Deydie cackled. "Moira will be your teacher."

Moira gave her a sheepish smile. "Aye."

Emma turned to Claire. "You have to help, too. I'm not making it alone."

Claire grinned like the kid who'd gotten out of chores. "Good luck with it. I'll not have time to help ye. I have the scones, the restaurant. But you enjoy yourself." She patted Emma on the back.

"Clairrrre." Whining wasn't becoming of a lady, but Emma did it, anyway.

Deydie harrumphed. "Ye'll not be alone in it, lass." She motioned to the whole room. "You have all of us."

At that, Father Andrew cleared his throat and the room went silent. "Everyone, if we could all bow our heads."

Emma bowed her head. It was a prayer about loving work with loving hands, eloquent and to the point. When he finished and the room resounded with an *Amen*, she looked up and saw Gabriel glance at her.

"Bloody hell," she muttered, turning away.

Claire shook her head. "You can't cuss in the Church of Quilting."

Deydie pulled Emma over to a machine and pushed her into the chair. "I'll get ye started. It's important you make the seams exactly a quarter inch. Ye'll use this special presser foot as yere guide." She gave her a scrap of fabric and showed Emma how to position the foot up against the edge to get the seam the right width.

Emma stared at the pile of blue-and-white-print fabrics cut into pieces beside the machine next to her. She felt overwhelmed and caught in Deydie's web.

"Surely there's someone else," Emma tried one last time.

Deydie smacked her on the back good-naturedly. "Ye'll do just fine, lass."

Emma knew what the old woman was doing, but she didn't know her well enough to make the accusation. *You want this quilt screwed up because you don't like your new doctor.*

"'Tis easy." Deydie took the pieces and arranged them in a block. It was pretty. "Sew these together. Then make another random block." She shook her finger at her. "Don't try to make a pattern with the blue prints. We want this quilt to be scrappy."

Yeah, Emma thought. *A mess. A clear message to their doctor that he doesn't deserve anything better than their scraps.*

Deydie looked up then and hollered, "Not there, Ailsa." She turned back to Emma. "Ye've got everything you need. Moira, watch her." And the old woman rushed off.

Great. Emma stared at the blocks and for a moment thought about leaving. Not just Quilting Central, but Gandiegow altogether. Fast, before the quilting ladies could tackle her. She looked up and found Gabriel gazing at her intently. A warm flush came over her, perhaps a full-on flood. It settled into her unmentionable areas — probably just like it had with all the other women before her who had fallen for his charms. He had the power to melt a woman's underthings right off her. She gave him a weak smile and picked up the first pieces of fabric. If the women of Gandiegow didn't care how this quilt turned out, then Emma wouldn't, either. "Jolly well, then." She started sewing.

Slower than a purposeful turtle, Emma stitched that first seam, keeping the quarter-inch foot squarely on the edge. When she finished, she held up the two pieces, now sewn together, and inspected them. "Not bad for a beginner."

"That's very good." Moira handed her another two blocks. "Later I'll show you how to chain-stitch the blocks so you can make them faster."

"Ye'll have to speed it up," Deydie barked from directly behind her. "We need it done by this Christmas, not by next."

Emma tried to ignore her, making sure her seams were straight, and finally completed the first block — a blue-and-white star with extra points. Moira took it from her to press.

Out of the corner of Emma's eye, she noticed Claire

going from woman to woman, speaking animatedly to the females of Gandiegow. What she said to each one caused initial concern in their eyes; then they would pat Claire's arm and give her a hug.

"What are you up to, Claire?" Emma murmured.

"Excuse me?" Moira lay the pressed block beside her.

"Nothing." Emma positioned the fabric into the next block.

Deydie's hand hit the table, making the fabric jump. "Faster, lassie." She huffed away.

Emma picked up two more pieces and realized her troubles were only adding up—enough troubles to piece into her own mess-of-a-life quilt.

Her dead career, her parents, Claire and Dominic's marriage, whatever Claire was up to right now, the Mac-Tavish baby, Deydie, and the Gandiegow Doctor quilt.

And at the top of her list right now, the doctor himself.

When Emma looked up this time, Gabriel had his back to her while he talked to an older gentleman. Her relief at not being examined by the doctor from across the room was only temporary, though. Her thoughts went back to him pushing her up against the wall and kissing her. Heat filled her face, chest, and other private areas. Yes, the doctor was at the top of her list.

And here was the problem she had with Gabriel: She didn't know if it was just all in her mind. Should she forget that kiss had ever happened? Or should she face the problem head-on and kiss him again—as an experiment—to see if the chemistry between them was real?

Deydie hobbled over to where Gabe stood with the Mc-Donnell. "I need ye to start singing."

"What?" Gabe looked to the McDonnell to see if this was normal behavior for the old woman.

The McDonnell laughed. "Deydie, you can't mean me. Ye know I sing as well as a walrus with a sore throat."

She turned her glower on Gabe. "'Tis time to quit resting on yere laurels and earn yere keep. Sing a carol to keep the out-of-towners busy." She harrumphed. "Ye're not terrible. I've heard ye at church. We've a situation." She pointed to a woman by the fireplace who had a cell phone to her ear. "We just need one song until our master quilter finishes her call."

"What am I supposed to sing?" Gabe asked.

"A Christmas carol," she urged.

"It's a little early, isn't it?"

"Close enough. Now get on with it," she growled.

It wasn't the most pleasant of requests, but . . . he did want the town to be more receptive to him, so he broke into "The Twelve Days of Christmas."

"On the first day of Christmas, my true love gave to me . . ." He looked over, and Emma stared back. He motioned to the packed room as the rest of them turned his way. "Come on, everyone, join in. *A partridge in a pear tree.*" And thank God they did, or else he would've looked ridiculous.

Emma's eyes stayed glued on him, all kinds of emotions playing on her face. Mostly she seemed perplexed. He could've used a big smile from her for encouragement. He only got frowning. Was he off-key and didn't know it?

"On the second day of Christmas . . ."

Also, for the past fifteen minutes, he really had been trying to figure out what Emma Castle was doing behind a sewing machine—*Emma!* Since he'd arrived in Gandiegow, he'd observed the quilters and how much talent, time, and patience it took to stitch a seam, let alone make a whole quilt. It was a real craft. As hard as repairing any engine. He couldn't wrap his mind around Emma sitting behind that machine like she belonged there.

"On the third day of Christmas . . ."

And wouldn't Emma consider sewing beneath her station in life? Miss Designer Suits toiling behind her machine held a certain homespun appeal, and he had to admit that it turned him on to see her across the room, picking out fabrics and piecing them together.

"On the fourth day of Christmas . . ."

The McDonnell pounded him on the back and winked, nodding toward the town's newest quilter. Gabe shot him a couple of daggers. He couldn't stop the song to tell the older man that he didn't feel that way about Emma. Gabe couldn't even call her a friend. An acquaintance of more than a decade, maybe.

"On the fifth day of Christmas . . ."

But something was definitely amiss, because he felt like he'd taken a cricket bat to the chest.

He put Emma out of his mind and continued on with the song by rote. It was then that he noticed the crowd that had gathered around him. The other men of Gandiegow had come to stand next to him, a surprising show of solidarity. The quilting women of the village joined them, too, one by one. It looked as if the town had rehearsed this Norman Rockwell moment and performed it especially for the retreatgoers.

He saw the master quilter put away her phone and enjoy the rest of the song from her place by the hearth. Emma, he noticed, dropped her head down like she'd been caught spying. It was best she was done staring at him; he was done staring at her, too.

When the song ended, he headed straight for the door, not saying a word to anyone. And making sure not to look back to see *her* behind the sewing machine. He needed to talk to Dom. He needed help and he needed it now.

As he walked down the boardwalk, a shout came from the pier.

"Doc, come here and give me a hand." It was Ramsay with a large crate.

Gabe rushed over to the pier and took one end. "What's in here?"

"Fish."

"Isn't it late to be out? And dangerous, too?"

Ramsay smirked at him. "Nah. I'm fine."

"Where are your brothers?"

"John is home with his wife and kid. I don't know where Ross is off to."

"Aye." Gabe adjusted his hands to get a better grip.

"I thought the ladies might enjoy fresh fish for their retreat. If our chef will fix it up for them, of course."

"I'm sure Dom would be happy to oblige. I was just going that way." Gabe groaned.

Ramsay laughed. "Not too heavy, is it?"

"Nay." Gabe forced a weak smile back.

At the restaurant, Ramsay helped unload the fish into the cooler for the next day's fare but then stuck around, not giving Gabe a chance to talk to Dominic alone.

"How about we head over to the pub for a dram?" Ramsay suggested.

"Gabe, you go on without me," Dom said. "I have to get prepared for tomorrow."

"I'll stay and help," Gabe offered.

"No. Showing you what to do will only take longer."

"But—" Gabe tried.

"Go," Dom insisted. "I'm terrible company."

Gabe promised himself that later he'd lecture Dominic and tell him that he wasn't the only person in Scotland with problems. At least Dom's problems could easily be fixed: take his wife to bed and give her a baby.

Gabe's problems, though, lingered at the opposite end of the spectrum. There was a bed he wanted to crawl into, with a certain woman whom he shouldn't want. He needed to find a way to eradicate thoughts of her from his mind.

"Good idea, Ramsay," Gabe acquiesced. "I could use a strong drink."

Chapter Eight

The next morning, Emma cornered Claire in the restaurant. "What was going on between you and the other women last night? What were you saying that had them looking so concerned?"

"There isn't time for talking. The retreatgoers will be starving. Frigid Highland air burns more calories than hours of exercise, ye know."

Emma wasn't buying it. Claire was definitely dodging her questions. But why?

"Go on now," Claire said, shooing her with her hands.

"Just know that this talk isn't over." Emma stowed the huge batch of scones along with fresh fruit in the wagon and hurried to Quilting Central.

A storm was brewing out in the ocean, making her move faster down the boardwalk. When she got to Quilting Central, she hustled the scones inside and set them up on the food table.

Deydie and Bethia roamed over and each took a blueberry scone as the retreatgoers filed in.

"Ye better get back to work on that quilt, lassie," Deydie said. "It ain't going to make itself."

"Ye were planning to stay, weren't you?" Bethia said kindly.

"I guess." Emma thought about how Claire didn't want her around.

Deydie poured her a cup of tea. "Stay hydrated. Quilting is a marathon, not a light jog around the village," she cackled.

From across the room, a woman about Emma's age smiled at her and gave a little wave, but then went to help one of the out-of-town quilters.

"May I ask who that is?" Emma said.

"It's me granddaughter, Caitie Macleod Buchanan." Deydie motioned to the whole room. "All of this was her idea. She's a smart one, my Caitie."

"It's quite an enterprise," Emma agreed.

Deydie grabbed a broom and swept the crumbs by Bethia's feet. "Ye're getting the floor all dirty." She turned on Emma with a glare. "Ye do have to actually use the machine to get the damned doctor's quilt done, ye know." She shoved Emma toward her work area.

Deydie toddled off to the long-arm quilting machine, gathering some of the local women around her. She looked almost like she was directing traffic, giving each woman specific instructions. Dread came over Emma. She had the feeling that Claire's goings-on last night and Deydie's machinations today were connected. Maybe Emma should go back to the restaurant and force Claire to tell her what the town's women were up to.

But as Emma rose, Moira joined her, taking a seat.

"I'm going to teach you how to chain-stitch today," the shy woman said.

"All right." Emma sat back down, knowing she should be grateful for the instruction, but what she really wanted was to get to the bottom of the mystery playing out in front of her.

Moira tapped the fabric. "I usually get several pieces

lined up and ready to sew." Her soft voice brought Emma's attention back to the task at hand.

While the morning workshop began, Moira gave Emma her private lesson. She demonstrated how chain-stitching the quilt pieces—sewing pieces one after another without breaking the thread in between—could be a huge time-saver. Emma mastered the technique quickly, gaining more confidence with every stitch. Her seams were straight and bore the correct quarter-inch width. By late morning, her shoulders were stiff. She stood and stretched, examining the work she'd done on Gabriel's quilt. *No. The Gandiegow Doctor quilt.*

But that's when she noticed something strange happening at the doorway of Quilting Central. The local women were grabbing their coats and filing out one by one.

Dominic had made an early start this morning and had already been to Inverness for the extra supplies needed for the spur-of-the-moment quilt retreat. He'd also been up late planning the catering menu and prepping what he could. But, hell, what else would he have done with those hours? He certainly wasn't spending it with his wife.

When he walked into the restaurant loaded down with sacks, he was surprised Claire wasn't there with the last of her late-morning customers. Either she had stepped into the kitchen for more scones or into the privy for a moment. He greeted customers as he walked through, but stopped at the kitchen doors. What if Claire was up to more tricks? Surely she wouldn't be lying on the prep table, prepped for him. Or, even worse, she could be in one of her foul moods and standing near the recently sharpened knives. He gritted his teeth and pushed through the swinging doors.

She wasn't in there, either. He set down his bags and began unloading and sorting the supplies into three groups—restaurant fare, retreat fare, and crossovers. He stashed the cold items in the cooler, keeping an eye on the dining area, and began fixing the retreat's lunch before starting the restaurant's.

Just as he got into a chopping rhythm with the paring knife, Claire came into the kitchen with a load of dirty dishes. He braced himself. But she only beamed at him. No hostility, no latent sexuality. In the far depths of her eyes, and only for a second, he caught something that made him worry. But she seemed so like her old self and in a good mood that he chose to ignore it. Maybe she'd decided to come to her senses.

"Morning," she said brightly. She leaned over to see what he was doing. "What do ye need help with first—the catering or the lunch prep?"

She dazzled him with nothing more than being herself. He looked down blankly at the knife in his hand and the chopped tomatoes on the cutting board and had to focus—yes, he'd been slicing them for the spring salad.

"I have it," he finally replied, remembering to breathe. God, he'd better get laid soon or he might accidentally cut off an appendage while chopping vegetables. "You still have the breakfast crowd."

"Are ye sure?" She looked the vision of sincerity.

He was glad she was done playing games. Thrilled to have his wife back. He was getting hard. "Yes, I've got it under control," he heard himself saying. "Leave the dishes. I'll take care of them later." Right now he couldn't be near her and get anything done.

Claire nodded and walked out of the kitchen, back to the dining area.

He breathed a sigh of relief. Tonight he would sleep in his own bed. Or, even better, he wouldn't sleep at all.

He stared at the dishes in the oversized sink, then at all the food that needed to be prepared. "Horny bastard," he said to himself.

He lit into the vegetables with a fury and soon had salad for the restaurant and the retreat. Next, he made thirty-five sandwiches, filling a large platter for the quilting women. All the work he had to do couldn't stop the emotions bombarding him. He felt so thankful that this war of wills with Claire was finally over. He'd won.

But had he? She hadn't said everything was back to normal. Fear swept through him.

Had she given up on him? He broke into a cold sweat.

But there was no time to find out. He put on the tortellini soup for the lunch crowd. By eleven thirty, he was ready. Thomas and Lochie stopped by with the cart to pick up the quilting retreat's lunch. Dom made sure the trays were secure and settled, then grabbed his own trays to fill the side counter with today's specials.

When he stepped into the dining area, he almost dropped his armload of food.

A packed house?

Every table filled?

Families. Couples. Every stool along the bar occupied.

Dom had expected there to be about the same number of people as yesterday, maybe fewer because of the extra hands needed at Quilting Central. He looked to Claire, dumbstruck. She didn't look dumbstruck or shocked or confused at the turnabout in business. His wife had a triumphant gaze on her face.

"Claire," Dominic growled. "May I see you in the kitchen?"

"Why, of course." She sauntered past him, swishing her peasant skirt and apron as she passed.

On the other side of the door, where the whole town couldn't hear, he pinned her against the wall with his gaze. His groin, though, wanted to pin her there with his body. "What is going on out there?"

"I don't know what ye're talking about." Beaming with satisfaction, she tilted her head to the side with a grin.

"Why are all those people here?"

She walked over and ran a finger down his chest. "Be a good boy and don't argue about a full house." She walked on and picked up the next tray for the salad bar. "Do you want me to stay and help?" she said sweetly.

He needed space from her more than he needed her help. "No. Go."

"Have it your way," she said. "I'll be upstairs in the shower, if you want me."

Great. Just the image he didn't need haunting him for the rest of the afternoon. He watched only a moment as she headed for the stairs, her hips swaying slightly. He went through the swinging doors to the dining room to deal with the locals.

It didn't take long to figure out how she'd gotten them all there. When Leslie Murray stepped to the cash register, she gave him a sly smile.

"Och, Dominic." She tsked and motioned to the room. "There's no need to worry. You don't have to be frightened of having a wee bairn. We'll all be right here to help ye." Leslie leaned in as if to share a secret. "Don't forget that the *tryin'* for a bairn is the fun part."

Good God. What had Claire told these people?

One by one, the good people of Gandiegow winked at him and cajoled him. "Bairns are a gift from God," one said. "It'd be grand to have a wee babe at the end of summer," said another. By the time the last customer left, he wanted to wring Claire's neck.

He stomped up the stairs, leaving his horny self behind. He marched into the bedroom just as Claire was slipping a dress over her smooth, curvy body—no bra, and only a scrap of hot pink lace for underwear.

His mouth went dry. For a long moment he could only stare, not remembering what it was he wanted to rail on her about.

Rail on her. Yes, that would be good. Lay her on the bed and rail on her. When he took a step toward her, she lifted the hem of her dress.

"Should I take this off?" she purred, sex and phero-mones pouring off her. "Or do you want me to leave it on?"

That stopped him. Oh, she was sure of herself, wasn't she? And after she'd embarrassed him in front of the whole town! Dominic ground out the words like he'd put them in a mortar and taken the pestle to them. "What did you tell them, Claire?"

"Nothing much. That you might be scared of becom-ing a da. It's pretty common. They all understood." She smiled at him prettily.

"It was a dirty trick," he muttered. "Just because you wrangled them into being here today doesn't mean we'll have money in the coffers tomorrow to support a child." He wouldn't admit to her that what she had told the vil-lage rang a little true. He might be scared. And why not? Any sane person *should* be scared of that kind of finan-cial burden. When a child came into the world, a world of responsibility came with it. A child would depend on him to care for it, to provide for it. Forever. But what if some-thing happened to him? To Claire, too? His mother had left him when he needed her most. No home. A confused teen. The MacGregor family had taken him in, God bless them, but it hadn't been the same as having your own madre. He wished he could see her just one more time.

He shook his head vehemently. "You shouldn't have

done it, Claire. You shouldn't have dragged the village into it."

"Ye're right. I shouldn't have had to." She dropped the hem and advanced on him. "Ye're a bonehead, Dominic Russo." She stepped past him and out the door.

Her perfume remained behind.

Throughout the afternoon, Emma noticed Caitie watching her, always with a pleasant smile on her face but too busy with the retreat to break away. At precisely three o'clock, though, she saw the woman make her way purposefully to Emma. She didn't look a thing like her grandmother, Deydie, but she sure had a gleam in her eye that Emma recognized, one that had *favor* written all over it.

She introduced herself as Cait in a Scots-American accent and shook her hand. "I was wondering if I could have a minute of your time."

"Sure." Emma turned off her machine, expecting Cait to take the seat beside her.

But she stayed on her feet. "It's about Mattie. Have you met him, my adopted son?"

"No." Emma rose, but got that creeping feeling she was going to be put in an awkward situation. Surely she wouldn't be asked to babysit.

Cait motioned to the overstuffed sofa. "Let's go sit by the fire and I'll tell you his story." She took her arm and guided her to the hearth.

Emma gazed around at all the Gandiegow quilters, and they all had eyes on her. Of course. What else could she expect from a close-knit community? They must've known about this little ambush beforehand. At least that's what it was feeling like. She had the urge to dig in her heels and put a stop to whatever she was being dragged into. Mattie's story might lead to something worse than babysitting.

As Cait got comfortable, she gave her a wistful smile. "Mattie is a great kid. My husband is Mattie's grandda. He's gone a lot on business."

Emma nodded.

"About two years ago, Mattie witnessed a terrible accident off the rocks just outside the cove. Tragically, all the fishermen on board the vessel drowned. Then his own da died of leukemia."

"How awful. I'm very sorry for your loss."

Cait touched Emma's arm. "Thank you. We're doing better—adjusting, accepting. It's Mattie, though. He's spoken only a few words since the drowning. We had him in therapy during the summer break and it helped. Before my husband left this last time, Mattie even whispered goodbye to him. We were thrilled. He seems to be coping and adapting to life without Duncan—his da."

Yes, Duncan's Den, one of the quilting dorms.

"We want Mattie to continue therapy."

"Therapy can be a comfort." Emma didn't exactly believe it, but thought she should say it, anyway.

"But here's the problem. Mattie's therapist has suspended his practice to finish working on his book."

Uh-oh.

"Which brings me to you. Claire told me ye're a therapist."

No.

"I spoke with my husband on the phone last night and he's as excited as I am that you've come to our little corner of Scotland."

She must've seen the panicked expression on Emma's face, because Cait's words picked up speed. "I know you're on holiday, but we were hoping you would at least meet Mattie. Evaluate him."

Emma clasped her hands in her lap. "I don't know what to say."

Cait stared her down, giving her this knowing look.

Bloody hell. Cait must know. Sure. She would've checked out Emma, her credentials, and her background. That meant that she knew about the series of papers Emma had written early in her graduate studies about children and effective therapeutic techniques.

Right now, Emma worked hard to keep a smile plastered on her face. She'd given up her interest in child psychology when her mother had pooh-poohed it. The expectation was for Emma to be a marriage therapist, end of story. She'd done what her mother expected. And look what it got her.

Cait's eyebrows furrowed. "We wouldn't expect you to do this for free, of course. We would pay you double the normal rate, as you would be doing us a favor."

Emma formed her words carefully. "Did Claire also tell you I'm taking a break from counseling?" *Like, a forever break.* She glanced over at her sewing machine and the partially finished quilt. She'd gained a lot of confidence making blocks, but her confidence as a counselor was shot.

The door flew open, and Moira came in with a kid who had dark red hair.

Cait grinned at him. "Oh, there's Mattie now."

Yeah, like that wasn't planned. She wondered if Gabriel knew about this, too.

Cait grabbed her hand. "Emma, please. I know I've put you on the spot, but just take a minute to meet him. Then give yourself a little time to get to know him. I can't tell you how important it is to the whole town to get Mattie back to where he was—or at least a little closer."

Deydie's voice reverberated in Emma's head. *Ye're one of us.* If Emma really was considered to be part of Gandiegow, then she would have to at least meet the boy.

"All right," she finally said. "But I can't make any promises."

Cait squeezed her hand and stood. "You're a godsend."

As Moira and the child walked over, Emma became more tightly wound. She was afraid she'd be like a spring and pop out of her seat and flee out the door. She wasn't a therapist anymore. Why did these people keep putting her in these uncomfortable situations?

Cait hugged Mattie to her side and spoke to him. "This is Emma Castle."

He nodded, not looking unhappy to meet her. He hesitated for a second, then stepped out of his mother's arms and produced his hand for Emma to shake. Very grown-up for one so young.

"It's nice to meet you, Mattie." What else could she say to the child?

Cait pointed to the kitchen area. "How about you and Emma have a cookie while I get the next workshop going?"

Mattie regarded her closely, and Emma realized she'd have to watch herself with this one. Those big eyes of his caught everything.

"Yes, that would be nice." When Emma rose, Mattie surprised her by putting his hand in hers and leading her away.

Okay, now what was she supposed to do? Research had proven that children were not little adults; children used completely different thought patterns. And what little she knew about trauma-induced mutism she could fit on an index card. They all acted like she had no choice but to step in and fix Mattie. Did his mother not know that Emma could do more harm than good? She would have to get Cait to sign an informed-consent waiver before she did anything.

They grabbed a cookie each and cups of cocoa, then sat at a small round table nearby. She didn't get a chance to say a word to the boy because Deydie rushed over.

"Mattie, run up to the big house and let out that dog. I've been too busy to get back up there."

He glanced at his cup of cocoa.

"Drink up," the old woman said. "But hurry. If that dog poops on your grandda's clean floor, I'll take the broom to him. Now get going."

Relief swept over Emma that she wouldn't have to do this right now. She didn't like being unprepared, let alone being put on the spot. She really needed time to process Cait's request.

Deydie nudged her. "You go with him. I expect you back here later, though. Lots of work to do." She looked none too happy about it. "Nothing wrong with the boy," she muttered to herself.

Mattie looked over the edge of his mug for Emma's reaction as he took a big gulp. She made sure to keep her attitude in check about the expectations being laid upon her. All the Gandiegow quilters were still watching her. The connivers. They wanted her to perform a miracle. And that just gave her one more thing to worry about.

The two of them grabbed their coats and stepped out into the cold. It wasn't quite three thirty, but it was already getting dark. Some early Christmas decorations had been hung up by the businesses on the boardwalk while Emma was sewing up a storm today. The hours behind the sewing machine had kept her brain occupied, but now she couldn't help but wonder what Gabriel had been up to. She hadn't seen him at the restaurant this morning, either.

She gazed down at Mattie, feeling awkward as they ambled along in silence. She wasn't sure what to do. Was it better to remain quiet or to make small talk? She would feel so much better once she had the chance to do a little research on his condition. They walked all the way to the end of town and then Mattie pointed to the path leading up behind the last cottage.

"Do you live up there?" she asked.

He nodded. That was the end of the short conversation. She followed him up the path to an honest-to-goodness mansion, a stone castle, really, which had been built close to some ruins. *What a beautiful setting,* she thought. . . . Until under the outside light of the back door, she saw a familiar man knocking.

Chapter Nine

Gabe knocked on the door and stood back, waiting. This was probably a dumb idea. If Deydie answered the door and gave him another earful, he wasn't sure his residual headache would allow him to be polite. Ramsay had drunk him under the table last night. He knocked again.

He'd promised Mattie he would stop by and get him. He needed to keep that promise. He'd spent all day at the factory again, which hadn't exactly occupied his mind as much as he'd hoped. He was sure that walking with Mattie would be just the thing to clear his head. Besides, he liked the kid.

The snow crunched behind him and he turned around. He couldn't believe he'd made them both materialize.

Emma brushed back her hair and squared her shoulders, but she wasn't fooling him. He clearly saw the relief spreading over her face at the sight of him. His chest expanded—confusing—but he was glad to see her, too. And he shouldn't be.

"Hallo. What are you two up to?" Gabe asked.

Mattie tilted his head up to Emma.

She cleared her throat. "I walked Mattie home."

"I see." He gave her a quizzical look, but she didn't

explain further. By her uncomfortable behavior, she must've been wrangled into evaluating Mattie.

"What are you doing here?" she asked Gabe pointedly.

"Mattie and I have a sort of guy thing we're supposed to do together," he said.

"Well, I'd better leave you to it." She looked ready to sprint down the bluff.

Mattie reached over and snatched her hand, stilling her.

"I don't think ye're allowed to leave," Gabe said, smiling. "What do you say, Mattie—should we take her along?"

Mattie nodded but reached for the door handle. Gabe looked to Emma for an explanation.

"He's supposed to take the dog out." The words barely slipped from her mouth before the sheltie bolted from the house.

Mattie grabbed a leash and ran after him, leaving the door wide-open.

Gabe pulled the door shut. "I guess Dingus is coming with us."

"To where?" she asked, pushing back her hair once again.

For a moment, he was mesmerized by her cinnamon hair glowing under the light above the door. He recovered quickly, though. "We're just going to take a walk along the bluff. Maybe to the cemetery, if Mattie feels like it."

Dingus ran and jumped on the boy, which gave him a chance to get the leash over his head. Mattie turned to them and motioned for them to hurry up.

"Shall we?" Gabe took her elbow and guided her in the right direction. She didn't jerk her arm away, but she did put distance between them.

Emma had always been direct with him, but it looked like she was going to pretend the hell-bent kiss they'd shared had never happened. *Fine by me.*

They caught up with Mattie and walked along the path that led up to the cemetery. Emma seemed to relax incrementally. Gabe did all the work on the conversation, keeping up a one-sided narrative with Mattie about school, the upcoming Christmas pageant, and if he had any homework due tomorrow.

Gabe finished by telling him about his day at the North Sea Valve Company. "Maybe the McDonnell will let your school come to the factory when it's up and running. You'll have to wear a hard hat, though. It's the rules."

Mattie looked back at him and smiled, like wearing a hard hat would be the pinnacle of the field trip.

Gabe glanced over at Emma and mouthed, *Your turn.*

Her shoulders stiffened but she spoke, anyway. "Mattie, did your mum tell you why she wanted us to get acquainted? That she wants me to consider continuing your therapy while I'm here? Which won't be very long at all."

What the hell was that? Gabe frowned at her. Didn't she have any finesse? Kids had to be handled carefully, cajoled. She should've just tried to make a little small talk with him and not be so direct. She was putting Mattie on the spot by asking him such an asinine question. He was just a kid, after all.

She squatted down to his level, keeping eye contact with him, treating him with respect. "You understand what I'm talking about, right?"

Mattie stared at her face for a long moment, searching. When he seemed satisfied with what he saw there, he nodded.

"Good. It's important you know the truth." She reached out and touched his arm. "Here's the deal, Mattie. My specialty has been marriage therapy. I don't have a lot of experience with children."

She may not have experience with children but her instincts were spot-on, if Mattie's reaction to her frank communication was an indicator. Apparently, she did know what she was doing.

"So, here's what's going to happen. I'm going to do a little research first." She brushed the hair back from the kid's eyes. "I know a lot of therapists. And if it's all right with you and your mum, I'd like to speak with the therapist you saw over the summer. Would that be okay?"

He nodded again, but then Dingus pulled on the leash. Mattie was dragged off.

She finished what she was saying, although the boy was out of earshot by now. "But the best we can hope for is for you and me to become friends." She acted as if that would be the only possible outcome.

Gabe reached down and helped her back up. As she rose, she was so close that he breathed her in. Her cinnamon hair smelled like tangerines. Much more intoxicating than the whisky he'd drunk last night with Ramsay. He forced himself not to stare at her lips, which he didn't quite pull off. He couldn't help but want to kiss her again.

She stepped back and looked around to locate Mattie. She seemed satisfied he was out of earshot, and turned back to Gabriel with fire lighting her eyes. She poked him in the chest. "You could've warned me that the town was going to expect me to work with the boy. I thought they actually accepted me, but they were just getting ready to waylay me."

He stepped back, too. "What makes you think I knew anything about this? If you haven't noticed, I'm not anywhere close to being in Gandiegow's inner circle. Or even their outer circle, for that matter."

"You certainly didn't seem surprised to see Mattie and me out on a wintry stroll together."

Up ahead, Mattie steered Dingus into the cemetery.

Gabe shrugged. "I put two and two together. That's all, Emma. If I'd known the town was going to do this to you, I promise I would've said something." Hearing the words come out of his mouth, he was taken off guard. It sounded like he cared about her, wanted to protect her.

A guilty expression crossed her face.

"What?" he asked. "You could do a lot of good for the boy. You have talent. What's wrong?"

"Nothing," she said.

Gabe didn't think it was nothing, but she looked closed on the subject. He watched as Mattie took the dog to his da's grave. He stopped Emma from going farther by touching her arm. "Let's wait here and give him some privacy."

He never should've touched her. The kid was their chaperone but even that couldn't stop the sexually charged air between Gabe and Miss Priss from ratcheting up a notch. He changed his mind—he couldn't pretend the kiss hadn't happened. He had to straighten Emma out and explain how things would have to be between them.

"We need to talk," he said.

Major worry played on her face, furrowing her eyebrows. "Don't say anything that we'll both regret."

"We have to clear the air, Emma, and now is as good a time as any."

Her back stiffened. "Fine. Do your worst."

"I shouldn't have kissed you the other night. I don't know what got into me."

"Desperation?" she offered stiffly.

"I promise it won't happen again."

If he'd thought his declaration would make her happy, he'd been wrong. She glowered at him.

"It was a one-off deal," he added.

Anger radiated from her like sparks off a roaring fire. "Excellent," she muttered in a whisper. It wasn't a whisper between lovers. It sounded like a threat.

Well, good. At least they'd gotten that straightened out. Gabe felt much better that Emma would no longer be a problem for him.

She glared at him one more time, then turned toward the cemetery and hollered. "Mattie, it's time to head back."

Emma stomped off. *A one-off deal, her pedicured foot.*

Gabriel might have regretted their kiss, but he was totally wrong to think it wouldn't happen again. He didn't control her. Emma *would* kiss him again—get *him* all hot and bothered, then douse him with cold water like he'd done to her. That's what the rogue deserved. To hell with being a proper English lady. Men like him explained why good women like her *snapped*. If Mattie hadn't been there, she would have.

Fuming, she kept on walking, wondering if she could get away with murder. Of course, now that her libido had been unleashed and she knew what she'd been missing, she didn't want to go without. So, first she would abuse Gabriel's lips to her heart's content. Then she'd toss the smug bastard to the curb.

Mattie and the doctor caught up with her. As they headed back to the mansion, there was no chatter from Gabriel. She said goodbye to Mattie at the door, but didn't wait around while the boy put the dog in the house. The doctor could see to that. She had to get away from him, stat.

In those few minutes as she walked off the bluff, she formulated different ways to make Gabriel pay. Would she sneak into the doctor's quarters in the middle of the night and kiss him awake? Or would she do what he'd done to her and back him up against a wall and kiss him until he cried uncle?

Or until he cries out my name.

Emma went to the restaurant to get something to eat

before returning to Quilting Central. But when she walked in, the place was packed, every seat taken. How could so many people be here with a retreat going on? She looked around. Where was Claire? With a crowd like this, someone had better be here to help out.

Emma found Dominic in the kitchen, filling eight bowls with pasta.

"What's going on out there?" She pointed to the dining room.

He glanced up. "I don't know. I think the locals are coming in shifts from Quilting Central."

Emma grabbed a tray for the bowls he'd filled. "I'll take these in, but then I'll need to run and tell Deydie I can't work on the quilt for her tonight. I won't be gone but a minute."

He shot her a determined look. "Don't bother. The rush is actually helping to keep my mind off yelling at Claire. You go on. But could you take the cheesecakes to Quilting Central, since you're going?" He motioned to the box on the far counter. "I just pulled them from the cooler."

"Sure. But are you certain you don't want me to stay?"

"I'll be fine. Besides, I expect Gabe to be along anytime now." Dominic took the filled tray from her and headed for the swinging doors.

Emma took the box and left the restaurant, hurrying down the boardwalk. With the snow falling on the village and the recently added strings of garland and multicolored blinking lights, the town was looking more and more like a winter wonderland. When she walked into Quilting Central, Mattie waved to her as she maneuvered her box in the door. She didn't dare wave back, but smiled at him instead. She immediately set out the cheesecake on the food table and grabbed a plate for herself.

When she looked up, Gabriel was watching her from across the room. She turned away. Then she was mad at herself. He didn't have the upper hand with her, and she needed to make sure he understood that. When she glanced back, though, he held a wrench, working on the long-arm quilting machine with George Campbell.

As she finished her dessert, she saw Claire talking to Ailsa and Aileen, Gandiegow's matronly twins. As Emma started toward them, Deydie grabbed her by the arm.

"It's about time you made it back. The Gandiegow Doctor quilt has been waiting on you," the old woman said.

"I need to have a word with Claire first."

"Nay. Claire can wait. I need you to get to work." Deydie tapped the man's watch strapped to her arm. "Time's a-wasting, missy."

"Fine. But tell Claire I need to speak with her right away." Emma went to her machine and started sewing. But a minute later, Cait was at her side with a folder in her hand.

"Well?" she asked.

"Mattie seems like a nice boy," Emma said honestly.

"Then you'll try to help him?"

"I'll need a few things from you first."

Cait handed her the folder. "I've already contacted Mattie's previous therapist and faxed over the paperwork giving you permission to speak with him. He's expecting your call for a time to set up a visit. He's only in Scotland for a few days. Then he's off to Budapest. Also in the folder are the standard consent and release forms to treat a child. Did I miss anything?"

Emma flipped through the pages, a little disgusted with herself for having the backbone of dental floss. "No, it looks like it's all here." There was a business card with the therapist's number on it. "You do realize I may not be of any help to Mattie, don't you?"

"Nay, I don't believe that for a second," Cait said. "Claire says you're a wonderful therapist. Besides," she added cheerily, "Gandiegow is a magical place. The impossible happens here every day. I'm living, breathing proof of that."

Emma worked very hard not to roll her eyes. "We'll see."

Cait patted her on the shoulder. "We're all counting on you." Then she walked away, leaving Emma to mull over that frightening bit of truth.

She got to work, but sewing didn't hold her attention. Claire was up to something again, flitting from one person to the next. But tonight was different from last night. Instead of Claire receiving smiles or hugs, her frowning face had the village quilters frowning back. There were no soft expressions of compassion like last night, only anger and outrage from the women of Gandiegow.

Gabriel's deep baritone came from behind her. "What are you working on?"

She froze. "You wouldn't believe me if I told you." It took a second for her to dispel the illogical thrill he'd stirred inside her with only a few words. She slowly turned to face him.

"You could try me," he offered.

"Top secret Gandiegow business." She nodded toward Deydie. "I don't want to get on her bad side. Have you seen that woman wield her broom?"

He studied her closely. "That frown between yere eyebrows says something else is going on."

She plastered on a smile. "What frown?"

He pulled out a chair and sat beside her. *Oh no.* She felt light and fluttery and feared she might honest-to-God swoon. So much for showing him that he didn't have the upper hand with her.

"I see it, too," he said softly.

She stared into his perfect summer blue eyes. So, he saw the depths of forever, too? Then he nodded toward Claire and the outrage she was causing among the townsfolk.

"Oh yes," she said, feeling like an idiot.

"What do you think is going on?" he asked.

Emma had seen this before. Claire had always had the ability to sway people to her side. "I wish I knew."

"I'm afraid it won't bode well for Dominic," Gabriel said. "I overhead a couple of the villagers plotting."

"About what?"

"I'm not sure. When I heard Dom's name and looked their way, they clammed up."

"Interesting." Emma surveyed Claire, who was now by the espresso machine, her bumble bee–like flutter making emotions fly. "Have you been by to see Dom today?"

"No."

"He's swamped with customers right now. You should go help." *And give me a break from your pheromones.*

"I will. Come with me." He stood and offered her his hand.

She stared at it. Deydie and her demands were one thing, but Gabriel and his big, outstretched callused hand was another. Sure, he might've offered it to her innocently enough, but didn't he know the quandary he'd put her in? The man was hard enough on her body *without* physical touch. But her hand automatically clasped his.

Heat shot through her with a sizzle and a pop. He smiled as he helped her up out of her chair, and she felt like she'd gone on autopilot and would follow him anywhere. At the last second, she grabbed the folder Cait had given her.

He let go of her hand, but her insides still remained as

gooey as the inside of Claire's éclairs. *Proper English ladies do not drool over handsome Scottish rogues.* End of
story. But Gabriel was a doctor now. She'd have to check
her Proper English Ladies' handbook about rogues becoming physicians.

As they walked to the restaurant, her sputtering
thoughts drove her crazy. Was this the moment? Should
she take this opportunity alone with him and just do it —
kiss him? Or maybe find a secluded place to waylay him.
Or should she wait until her attack was completely
planned out first and take him off guard, too? Within
minutes, though, they'd arrived on the restaurant's doorstep and she'd made no definite decision.

She tugged his sleeve. "Wait."

He stopped and gazed down at her as she stepped in
front of him. She'd do it now and get it over with. Yes,
that would work. Better now than later. Unfortunately,
she'd waited too long for that same element of surprise
that he'd pulled on her, because his eyes hooded. And
she feared *he* might kiss *her* before she could kiss *him*.
She had to be the one to do it.

He leaned down, but when he did, the door opened,
smacking them together. His lips hit her ear. Her lips hit
his shoulder.

"Damn it all," he growled.

"Sorry, mate," Ramsay said. "Didn't see you there."
He nodded toward Emma. "You, either." Then he realized what had been going on between them and grinned.
"Carry on." He hopped off the porch and sauntered up
the boardwalk.

What a disaster. She looked down at her feet.

"Still no boots?" Gabe asked, shaking his head in disappointment.

"I'm getting to it," she bit back. "What are you going
to tell Dominic when we get inside?"

"I don't know." He challenged her with his eyes. "What are you doing to help the Russos fix their problem?"

"I told you that I'm neutral. I'm the Switzerland of Gandiegow." But she wasn't neutral, really. She just hadn't told Gabriel that she was on Dominic's side yet.

"Has Claire said anything to you?" he tried.

"I couldn't tell you, even if she had," Emma said. "Confidentiality."

"Careful, Emma. You're sounding like a therapist." He frowned at her, and she didn't like how that made her feel.

"Stop looking at me that way. You know as much as I know," she said.

"And what do you know?" he asked.

She shrugged, thinking about the restaurant's ledger-in-the-red. What right did she have to divulge the Russos' finances to another? *None*. If Dominic wanted Gabriel to know the state of the restaurant, he'd surely tell him. She pushed her hair over her shoulder. "Are you going to open the door or not?"

"Just a minute, Emma." He leaned against the door. If someone else tried to come through, they'd have to move a veritable brick wall. But he didn't look like he wanted to resume the kiss that had started a few moments ago, either. "I need to tell you something. I've had a change of heart since the last time we spoke of them. I think Claire's right. They've been married for ten years and they should start a family. She's not getting any younger."

Emma's own unused eggs shriveled up a tiny bit more with his words. "You make her sound as if she's decrepit," she said. "There's plenty of time." Maybe she was just assuring herself.

Gabriel frowned down on her. "Ye're acting pretty weird about this. I thought you'd be happy that I had switched sides. What is it that you're not telling me?"

She harrumphed. "That we'd better get inside. My feet are freezing. And besides, Dom is expecting your help."

"Fine, but we're not through speaking of this." Gabriel opened the door and let her walk in.

Sure enough, the crowd had not dissipated; in fact, it looked larger. Villagers stood around the cash register like a mob, boxing Dominic in and bending his ear. He had a fierce Italian grimace on his face, as though he were trying to smile through some kind of jaw pain.

"Come on." Gabriel steered Emma by the elbow over to the group.

"It's time to start a family, lad," a tall Scotsman said. "A bairn will help to settle you in. It'll make a man of ye."

Dominic looked like he might take a swing at the guy, but said nothing.

"A wee babe is nothing to fash yereself over. I'm certain he'll grow into a great one such as yereself." A round woman caressed Dominic's biceps.

Dom flinched.

Gabriel put himself between them and his foster brother. "Sorry, but I think it's time to close up now, folks. Dom has to get food ready for the retreat."

Emma saw the outrage on every Gandiegowan's face. *What right did* he *have to tell them what to do? He was an outsider.*

She smiled sweetly at the townsfolk. "Dominic has promised to teach me how to make pasta carbonara." Not looking back, she grabbed Dominic's arm and dragged him through the swinging kitchen doors, leaving Gabriel to herd the others out the front.

Once on the other side, Dominic hung his head.

"Cheer up, old chap." Emma patted him on the back. "You can stand strong against them. It's only a hundred to one." She smiled at him, but he only stared back.

"Correction: a hundred to two." She gave his arm a

reassuring squeeze as Gabriel came through the swinging doors. He looked at her hand on Dominic's arm and a strange look crossed his face.

For a second she thought Gabriel was jealous, but that was laughable. She rolled her eyes at him. "Push up your sleeves and get started on those dishes while I scrape."

Gabriel frowned at her but spoke to Dominic. "Emma and I have it from here. You head back to my place for some peace and quiet." He motioned to the exit.

Dominic nodded and pushed himself away from the prep table and through the swinging doors.

"I'll lock up behind him." Gabriel followed him out.

Emma leaned toward the door so she could hear what Gabriel said to his foster brother.

"God doesn't pile on more than we can carry."

If only that were true. Emma feared Dominic might be crushed under the weight of this load.

Chapter Ten

Gabe paused at the locked door of the restaurant for a long minute, jealousy poking at him like a very large, very painful hypodermic. Emma's hand resting on Dominic's arm almost got *Dom* punched. It didn't matter that she was only consoling him. The lion inside Gabe wanted to pounce. Was he going mental?

All he knew was that he didn't want her touching another man. Gabe wanted her soft touch for himself. Her tender words. Her understanding eyes. Maybe he *was* mental. Emma should put her therapeutic talents to work on *him*. Gabe imagined lying on her office couch. Maybe with her on top. Or with her underneath. It didn't matter.

Dammit. He shouldn't feel this way. He'd settled it earlier with Emma by the cemetery. Their kiss had been a one-off.

But then he'd almost kissed her again.

Gabe was a prick. Dom—his *brother*—needed his help and understanding, not his petty jealousy. Gabe pushed away from the door and walked back into the kitchen. Emma glanced over her shoulder and once again his breath caught. Right then and there he came to a decision. He'd have to take a break from this town. Meet other people. Maybe go to a bar in Inverness. Anything to keep him from ravishing Emma. When was she leaving Scotland, anyway?

She turned back around, her long, luscious hair cascading down her back. As she bent over the sink, unwanted, lustful thoughts slammed into his chest again. If only he could sidle up behind her and nuzzle her neck and do all sorts of wild, unmentionable things to her body.

Instead, he grabbed a towel and picked up a large stockpot to dry. He heard her muttering to herself.

"It's now or never." She wiped her soapy hands on her apron with her eyes fastened to the floor.

"Emma, are you okay?" he asked. "Is something the matter?"

She shook her head, then brought her eyes up to meet his. She looked both frightened and determined. As she took a step toward him, she untied the apron and let it fall to the floor.

He backed up. "What are you doing?"

She came closer. "Don't worry your pretty little head about it."

Surely it wasn't one of her mother's asinine techniques. He took another step back, gripping the large metal pot in front of him. "What about the dishes?"

She only smiled. For the first time, he actually believed the rumors he'd heard about her. Dom had told him that, according to Claire, Emma had been with dozens of men, that she was a master seductress. The gleam in Emma's eyes said she was on a mission and that mission was *him*.

Gabe wasn't the type of man to back away from a woman. Hell, he was the type of man to take charge and have her begging for more. But that look in Emma's eye said he might be the one doing the begging for a change.

And for a second, he wanted to see where this might lead.

But no. He couldn't let this happen.

"Emma, stop," he tried. He bumped into the chopping block.

She took the last step toward him, relieved him of the stockpot, and rested her body between his thighs. God, she was killing him. He couldn't breathe. She sighed as her arms snaked up around his neck. Involuntarily, he bent his head down.

Coll busted through the doors. "Doc MacGregor? Amy needs you."

Emma dropped her arms and stepped away, mortified. Her face felt like she'd singed it on the hot grill. She turned toward the sink.

Gabriel cleared his throat as if getting his bearings also. "Sure, Coll. I'll get my bag and meet you there."

She heard Coll leave.

"Emma?"

"I'll be fine. Just go." She couldn't look over at Gabriel. "I hope everything is all right."

"Aye." He waited a second longer.

She kept staring at the sink and didn't get the courage to turn back around until she heard him leave through the double swinging doors.

She was such an idiot. A failure. Egghead Emma had no skills when it came to seducing a man. Especially a man like Gabriel. Book smarts only got a woman so far. She never should've tried.

"Imbecile." She picked up the apron off the floor and shoved it into the basket with the dirty towels. She would keep her mind on the job at hand.

Wash the dishes.

Wipe the counters.

Get the heck out of Gandiegow as fast as I can.

But it wasn't that easy. She glanced over at Mattie's folder on the stool. It felt like a ball and chain right now. But if she jumped right in—talked to the other therapist, did a little research, met with Mattie a few times—her obligation would be satisfied. Then nothing would be holding her to this town.

Except for Claire.

Bloody hell.

Emma scoured the dishes within an inch of their lives, running the water as hot as she could stand. The only thing she lacked at this moment was a strategy to get her through her stay in Scotland. Tonight, after she finished up at the restaurant, she would figure out a way to make it easy on herself. Something short of taking a cold swim in the ocean every time her thoughts landed on the town's doctor.

She picked up the last dish, the stockpot Gabriel had dried, and held it close.

She wasn't one of Gabriel MacGregor's bubbleheaded groupies, those girls who succumbed to him at a single word uttered in his sexy baritone burr. For one thing, Emma was smart. But how smart had it been to put the moves on Gabriel. *Playing with fire.* It was stupid to tempt her psyche into thinking she could kiss him again and come away unscathed. The one skill she had going for her was self-control. She could choose where she spent her time while she was forced to remain here. She would do what she'd done for the past ten years. Avoid the doctor at all costs.

She hung the stockpot on the rack and trudged up the stairs. Gandiegow was a small town. She wouldn't be able to completely dodge Gabriel, but she could make certain they weren't alone again. Emma let herself into the flat and collapsed on the couch.

Not five minutes later, the apartment door opened and Claire sauntered in. "Hiya."

Emma sat up straight. "Can we talk for a minute? I noticed you with the quilting ladies tonight. What was that all about?"

Claire didn't meet her eyes. "Just a bit of gossip." She produced a yawn. "I'd better get to bed. The scones wait—"

"For no one," Emma finished. "Yes, I know. But what is going on?"

"Don't worry yereself with it. It's only a bit of harmless chitchat."

"Clairrrre," Emma warned.

"Let it go, Emma." She flounced off to the bathroom, closing the door on the subject with a *whoosh*.

That girl is up to something. Emma just didn't know what.

That night, Emma wanted to sleep, but she was so restless. And when she did drift off, it was one crazy dream after another. Flooded kitchens. Her hands bruised from sewing piles of quilt blocks. And the worst were the hooded eyes of a particular Scottish warrior who kissed her until she liquefied into a hot toddy. Then the church bells were ringing.

She turned off the alarm and dragged herself out of bed to help Claire in the kitchen. An hour later, Moira stopped by to pick up breakfast for the retreatgoers, who would be heading home soon. Just as the third batch of scones came out of the oven, the fishermen showed up. Not a few, like on the other day, but droves of them.

"This is strange," Emma remarked. Claire only smiled.

Thirty minutes later, more Gandiegowans descended upon the restaurant.

"Claire, we're here." The woman waved as she came through the doorway. "We stand behind you, lass, in yere hour of need."

*   *   *

Claire dodged Emma's questioning eyes. She didn't need
to explain anything to her. Besides, she wouldn't understand that Dominic needed to be brought down a peg for
not coming back to their bed and giving Claire the baby
she desperately wanted. The sour faces of the Gandiegowans around her guaranteed that her husband would
pay dearly. She feared a lynching might be in the works.

Guilt coated her like the icing on her cinnamon scones.
So she'd fibbed to the villagers. So what? Even if he
hadn't said *A baby will make you fat, turn you into an old
fishwife*—the first thing that had popped into her head—
he was being just as awful to her. She was so angry at her
husband; she just hadn't realized how angry it would
make the women of the town. But it was only a wee
stretch of the truth, wasn't it? She ran a hand over her
stomach. She would get fat after having a baby. Surely
Dominic worried about that, too.

Emma delivered three cups of coffee for the Armstrong brothers—John, Ross, and Ramsay—and then
barreled in Claire's direction.

"Why are all these people here?" Emma whispered.

Claire shrugged. "I told you the Highland air makes
them hungry."

Emma pulled her over to the side, frowning. "You know
what I mean. What did you do?"

"Nothing."

Emma slammed her hands on her hips. "Don't insult
me. I know you better than anyone."

Claire rolled her eyes. "I may have mentioned to
them—" The timer went off in the kitchen. "Gotta run."
She bolted. Emma tried to follow but, thank God, she
was waylaid by Lochie and Thomas. Maybe Lochie would
recite more poetry, and Emma would forget about questioning her further.

Claire carried fresh-out-of-the-oven scones to the dining area and delivered them off the baking sheet to the growing crowd. If this restaurant was back in Glasgow, the Health and Safety Executive would've shut them down for exceeding the legal number of patrons. But this was Gandiegow, her home, her people.

Moira slipped back into the restaurant and grabbed an apron and an order pad.

Claire set the baking sheet on the counter. "Has the bus left with the quilters, then?"

"Aye," Moira said. "I'll be able to work for a bit, but then I'll need to get home to my da. He didn't have a good night."

Claire patted her arm. "We'll be okay if you need to go to him now."

"I'll only stay a while. I would like to drop a scone by to Da before I go to church, though."

"That would be fine, Moira." Claire had always seen herself as long-suffering, growing up without her own da. But she'd had Emma and an easy life compared to the toils of Moira.

Moira's father, Kenneth Campbell, hadn't completely recovered from a fishing accident and lingered painfully between infections. But he was a lesson for all. That man had the most optimistic outlook for one so sick. Claire had seen him smile through the pain, time and again, while she delivered food to them at the cottage.

She should do more for Moira than give her a part-time job and friendship. Maybe she could help her ease out of herself, possibly even help her find a man.

Just then she noticed Emma, eyes narrowed, headed in her direction. Claire didn't wait around for more of her best friend's questions. She hightailed it to the kitchen through the swinging double doors.

And ran smack-dab into Dominic's powerful chest.

Claire looked up into his caramel-colored eyes. He smelled wonderful. But she was angry with him.

He stepped back and frowned. "Are you okay?"

"I'm grand. Thanks for asking." A month ago, he would've jumped at the chance to pull her into his arms for a midmorning kiss. It hurt that he didn't now.

He walked away into the storeroom while she stared after him. *Damn.*

She trudged back into the dining room and spoke to the room. "Time to close up, folks."

Emma sidled up to her and glanced at her watch. "It's early still."

"Not if we're going to make it to church on time."

"I'll just stay here and clean up," Emma said.

Claire touched her arm. "Everyone attends church in Gandiegow. No exceptions."

Emma ran upstairs and put on her best dress. *Everyone attends church. No exceptions.* She took extra time fixing her hair. Not because Gabriel would be there, but because she wasn't sure what the churchgoing etiquette was here in Gandiegow. She'd been to church only a handful of times in her life—Claire's wedding and a couple of funerals. She knew she would feel as out of place as she had in the past. Dressing nicely, looking her best, always helped her cope with the unknown. She wasn't trying to attract anyone.

Claire rushed past the open door of the restroom. "Ye'll have to go without me. I can't find my shoe."

"I'll help you look," Emma offered, anything to delay.

"No, go. It's best if Deydie only takes her broom to me, instead of to the both of us."

"If you're sure."

"Hurry," Claire said.

Emma slipped on her red pumps, pretty sure they

wouldn't be the best thing to wear along the slick board-walk. But she would be careful. She grabbed her red purse and headed out.

The walk was indeed slippery, but she made it to church and inside on time. Bethia greeted her with "How are ye this fine morn?" Then she looked down and frowned at Emma's shoes.

"I know," Emma said, trying to head off the repri-mand.

"*Pretty* can be dangerous here, lass. We have to be practical."

"Bethia, don't waste yere breath." Gabriel's voice pulsed from over Emma's right shoulder. "The lass doesna have a practical bone in her body."

Emma spun around. "Why are you so obsessed with my feet?"

"Apparently, you've never seen frostbitten toes." He raised a superior eyebrow.

Bethia chortled. "Or perhaps he's one of those lads who fancies feet."

Gabriel shook his head. "Just concerned for another human being's welfare is all."

"Well, you can stop being concerned about me. I'm grand." But her insides warmed that Gabriel cared for her. Her face turned as red as the heels she wore and the red clutch purse she held.

"Ye look a bit feverish," Bethia said, amusement play-ing in her eyes. "The doc may need to give you a good going-over."

Emma didn't dare look up to see Gabriel's reaction to Bethia's conniving. Emma was already smoldering—and in church, too. "Shouldn't we find our seats?"

She didn't wait for their answers, but took off for the sanctuary. Self-consciously, she made her way down the aisle and found a pew for her and Claire. Bethia walked past and sat with the other quilting ladies. Emma expected to see Gabriel walk by next, but he didn't. As nonchalantly as she could, she glanced at the pews beside her, then behind. He wasn't seated anywhere.

Organ music began and the churchgoers stood. The choir entered from the narthex and processed down the aisle with Father Andrew leading the pack. The choir marched two by two, and that's when Emma finally saw Gabriel, the caboose of the choir, his baritone voice strong and clear. Emma tried not to meet his eyes as he came near, but she couldn't help it. He had the audacity to nod to her as he passed. Her face heated up again.

But not three steps later, she saw him smile and nod to Mattie, too. Maybe he was just friendly to everyone.

Father Andrew took the pulpit and began the service with a prayer. Emma probably should've bowed her head like the other parishioners, but instead she boldly studied Gabriel. He had his eyes shut, looking sinfully handsome in his choir robe. When the prayer was done, he said, "Amen," with the rest of them.

Emma sat, but Gabriel stood and went to the lectern as Father Andrew took a seat off to the side. Claire slid in beside her.

"I finally found it," she whispered.

Emma nodded toward Gabriel. "What's up?"

"It's the first reading," Claire explained. Deydie turned around and glared them into silence.

Gabriel opened the Bible and read a passage. Emma stared at him in awe. He honest-to-God glowed. She looked around, but no one else seemed shocked at the transformation. He was no longer the rogue of his youth, the man who had slaked his lust at Claire's wedding. He was very much the sincere, mature adult. Was this who Gabriel MacGregor really was?

Seeing him like this did explain a lot. His reticence to

seduce her. His care and compassion for others. His insistence on fixing Claire and Dominic's marriage. Either Gabriel was a changed man or Emma had been wrong—incredibly wrong—all along.

He closed the Bible and strode back toward the choir. Emma forced herself to concentrate as Father Andrew gave a lovely sermon. The ritual of the service was beautiful and fascinating. The combination of the music, the prayers, and the simple but sincere sermon brought a peace over Emma. One she had never experienced before.

When the service was done, Claire excused herself to go speak with Moira. Although church had been surprisingly nice, Emma didn't feel comfortable hanging around afterward. Besides, someone should help Dominic with the lunch crowd. She wrapped her coat tightly around herself and rushed out the door. Three steps later, she slipped, her ankle twisting, and went down, her red heels no match for the icy boardwalk.

"Oh, mother bugger!" she shouted over the waves crashing against the retaining wall. She broke out in a sweat.

"Dammit, Emma." Gabriel squatted down beside her.

"How did you get here so fast?" Her bottom hurt almost as much as her ankle. She must've cracked it against the concrete when she'd fallen.

"I was trying to catch up to you and couldn't get here fast enough to stop it." He slipped off her shoe. With gentle hands he probed her ankle through her tights.

"Ouch." She tried to push her skirt down to cover her thighs.

"Hold still." Instead of examining her further, he scooped her into his arms and stood like she wasn't five foot eight and a healthy weight.

"What are you doing?" She wiggled in his arms, but that only made him hold her tighter. "Put me down."

"Stop thrashing about. You need to be checked."

Her ankle and backside hurt like a son-of-a-wanker . . . but it didn't stop her from instantly noticing how wonderful he smelled. Something woodsy, male, intoxicating. The combination of the real pain she felt mixed with Gabriel's scent was doing strange things to her. But despite everything, she relaxed a little in his arms and breathed him in. Soon enough she'd be out of his arms and at the surgery. She decided to be gutsy and take advantage of being held. She laid her head on his shoulder. "I'm a little dizzy," she said by way of explanation.

"I didn't see you hit your head." He turned to look at her, which put their faces very close together. He seemed to be breathing her in as well. His eyes dilated.

"Well, I didn't hit my head." But being so close to him made her light-headed, something she wouldn't admit.

"I see," he said in a teasing manner.

"I must be dizzy from the pain in my ankle. And my bottom."

"I'll check your *bottom* out later." He had a slight grin on his face. "In private."

"Stop it. We were just in church. You were a saint in there."

Seriousness shrouded his face. "You have a way of leading me astray," he admitted, the teasing gone, the determined Gabriel fully returned. "I'm a God-fearing man, Emma—weak, maybe, but certainly not dead."

Had he just admitted he was weak for her? A little sizzle shot through her. Then he walked right past the path leading to the surgery.

She lifted her head. "Where are you taking me?"

"To Inverness. You need an X-ray," he said.

"I'm fine." But it did feel like her ankle had swelled to the size of a beach ball in a matter of minutes.

He guided her head back to his shoulder. "I'm the doctor. We're going to get it checked out properly."

When they arrived at his Land Rover, he put her down. "Lean against me while I unlock the door."

She did as he said. Instead of letting her hobble into the vehicle herself, he picked her up again and tucked her into the backseat. She reached for the seat belt, but he was already on it and buckled her in.

"I'm not completely helpless."

He shot her a look that said she most certainly was. "Elevate your foot." He shut her door. He came back with an ice pack and handed it to her. "It's for your ankle."

She remembered the makeshift ice pack he'd made by hand for her after their accident. "Since when do you keep ice packs in your vehicle?"

"Since you came to town." Gabriel reached over the seat to readjust the pack over her injury.

Her ankle hurt, but she was definitely distracted. So much for her plan to keep her distance from Dr. Gabriel MacGregor.

Dom left church after Communion, not waiting for the final prayer. God understood chefs. He had to get back to Gabe's and unload his refrigerator.

Dom had stayed up half the night chopping veggies and generally prepping for today's lunch. He wouldn't be caught off guard again. Today he was ready for the appetites of the good people of Gandiegow.

It didn't take long to get everything over to the restaurant, start pots heating on the stove, and get the salads lined up in the cooler. Gabe should be here any minute

to help, as promised. And Claire—*who knows?* He had
no idea if she meant to help him today at the restaurant
or not.

Dom went to stand by the door, ready to open it for
the after-church flood. The Highlanders really knew how
to eat. Through the paned glass he only saw the waves
bobbing the tied-up boats by the dock. He grabbed his
coat, stepped outside, and gazed down the boardwalk.
No one milled about. The final announcements at church
must be running long.

He lumbered back to the kitchen to stir the sauce and
waited. He watched the clock for twenty minutes. As the
seconds passed, a harsh reality set in. He had a pretty
good idea who might've orchestrated this boycott.

Once again he grabbed his coat and headed out into
the cold. He knew of only one place to find his wife.
When he got to the door of Quilting Central, he could
smell the food. It hit him like a punch in the stomach—
the aroma savory, but the betrayal thick.

He opened the door and stepped inside. The whole
town was there. Including his wife. The chatter ceased
and all eyes fell on him. Their frowns, too. Except for the
one person he sought. She gave him a smug *And I
showed you* face.

The punch in the stomach a moment ago felt like
child's play compared to his wife's antipathy toward him
right now. Dominic only stayed a second, just enough
time to feel the gravity of the message being conveyed
by one and all. *The ranks have been closed. You're not
one of us.*

Dom turned and left. He hadn't belonged anywhere
in a long time. Not since he was fifteen. Not since his
madre had died. She'd worked so hard, leaving their village in Italy when he was six for a better life, better op-

portunities. He remembered how proud his mama was to have her own little Italian restaurant in Edinburgh. And then for her to die so suddenly—sixteen years later, Dom still felt the loss. Gabe's dad had tried to make Dom feel at home, welcomed, but the truth was that Dom had felt like an outsider since the day he'd stepped foot in Scotland. He was still the olive-skinned new kid at school. Gabe had been a true friend through the years, of course. And then there was Claire. When he'd met her, everything changed. She made the world feel right again. He was at peace. As though he'd come home at last.

But since coming here to Gandiegow, it had all gone to hell.

He kicked a chunk of ice off the ledge of the boardwalk into the water. Well, Claire had done it now. She'd caused real financial damage to the restaurant. Possibly the final nail in the coffin. But that feeling of desperation was nothing compared to his greater worry. Where was their marriage headed?

For a long time, he stood outside the restaurant, leaning over the railing, watching as the chunk of ice got smaller and pulled farther and farther out to sea.

Gabe glanced over at Emma as she dozed in the front seat beside him. According to the scan, her ankle wasn't broken but badly sprained. The first thing he planned to do once he got to Gandiegow: buy her a pair of boots. And ice grippers. Maybe even bubble wrap to keep her safe.

It was dark by the time the Land Rover descended the hill into Gandiegow. The few Christmas lights really added to the exterior charm of the village. The interior charm still needed work, as far as he was concerned. When he shut off the engine, Emma roused.

"Are we here?"

Damn, she looked beautiful when she woke up. "Aye, we're home."

She scrunched up her face like she took umbrage with the word *home*.

"Come on, sleepyhead. Let's get you settled in for the night." He jumped out and went around to her side of the car. He slid his arms under her legs and lifted her out.

"What are you doing? I have crutches."

"I'm not going to chance it. I can't afford to spend all my time at the hospital in Inverness, getting you back to rights. Now put your arms around my neck."

She frowned at him stubbornly.

"It's easier to carry you that way than throwing you over my shoulder."

"You wouldn't dare."

"Haven't you seen me heft one of Dom's hundred-pound sack of potatoes?" he warned.

She slid her arms around his neck. She didn't put her head on his shoulder like earlier, and he was disappointed.

"How am I supposed to manage the stairs to Claire's flat?" she asked.

"You're not. You're going to have to stay at the quilting dorm."

"Have you cleared it with the ladies?"

No, he hadn't. "It won't be a problem."

"What about my crutches?"

"After I get you settled, I'll come back for them."

As they walked by the restaurant, he noticed the lights were off.

"I wonder what's going on there," she said.

"I'll check into it. But first—"

"You'll get me settled into the quilting dorm. I know." She laid her head down on him then but popped back up. "I'm just resting, so don't get the wrong idea."

He gently laid her head back on his shoulder. "I dinna say a word. Ye've had a tough day." She'd handled the accident and subsequent trip to the hospital well. He admired that about her. She might come off as a princess, but she had the fortitude of a royal trooper.

He got her to Thistle Glen Lodge and hated to put her down, but he did, carefully, on the sofa by the hearth. "What do you need first—a warm fire, food, or drink?"

"Crutches," she said matter-of-factly.

"A drink it is. You have to stay hydrated to keep the swelling down." He walked into the kitchen.

She spoke loud enough for him to hear. "Maybe we should've had your hearing tested while we were at the hospital, Gabriel. I can manage on my own. I've managed for my entire life."

He came back in with her water. "And you've done a fine job of it, too." He gazed down at her wrapped ankle.

"I need the crutches. I need to get to the loo."

He scooped her up again, and she gasped.

"You are not taking me to the restroom."

He lifted an eyebrow at her.

She swatted at him. "Put me down."

"Be calm," he said. "I'll get you there, but I won't stay."

"Some things a lady just has to do for herself," she muttered.

In the restroom, he righted her on one foot, then went for a chair to set in front of her. "Use the chair for balance. Call out when you're done. I'm going to see if the ladies left any food in the refrigerator." He shut the door to give her privacy.

A few minutes later, he heard the sink running and then she hollered, "I'm ready."

He carried her back to the couch.

"What's the verdict on the food?" she asked. "I'm hungry."

"We struck out in the kitchen. They must've cleaned it all out after the retreat. I'll run and get you something." Either at his place or the restaurant. "Let me get the fire going first. I don't want you to catch a chill." He pulled a multicolored Diamond quilt off the chair and laid it over her bare legs, her tights still in his coat pocket from when she took them off at the hospital. He wasn't sure yet if he was giving them back—payment for his services.

In the fireplace, he piled wads of paper, twigs, and finally logs. When he held the struck match to the wood, the fire caught instantly. The bellows had it roaring within minutes. When he stood and turned around, she was smiling at him.

"What?"

"Nothing, really. You're very skilled and useful is all, Dr. MacGregor."

"Aye." What else could he say? He couldn't help but think about the fire he'd like to start between them right now. His lips on hers. Her lying back on the couch. Getting cozy and hot. He stood and backed away from her. "I'll find us some dinner."

She looked surprised. "Us?"

"I have to eat, too, lass. Lugging you around has given me quite an appetite." Grinning, he laid a quilt magazine in her lap, leaving her to chew on that thought.

Before he went to his place or the restaurant, he decided it was best to stop in at Quilting Central to let them know how the patient fared. When he opened the door, he was surprised to see the building was packed with Gandiegowans, two tables set up with food.

Deydie lumbered over to him. "I hear Amy is having

a tough time with the baby. It's the colic, isn't it? Coll had it when he was a wee babe. His mama about went crazy with him screaming like a banshee. I bet that was Amy's baby I heard last night. The poor thing sounded as if he were trapped in the fishing nets."

Amy and Coll did have their hands full with the baby. He was indeed having an early and bad bout with colic.

Deydie slapped Gabe on the back. "Well, Doc, am I right?"

Claire rescued him by running over. "Is Emma back?"

"Aye. What is all this?" He motioned to the crowd. "Is there some town get-together I didn't know about?"

"No." Claire paled.

Deydie took over for her. "Just an impromptu village potluck."

"What about the restaurant?" he said pointedly to Claire. "Why is it closed? And where is Dom?"

"I don't know." She slammed her hands on her hips. "And I don't care."

He leaned close, trying to calm his anger. "Dominic is your husband. You'd better start acting like you care. I'm on your side about this whole baby thing, but I'm warning you: You'd better not screw up the good thing you and Dom have going."

She frowned at him. "Mind yere own business."

"What are ye going to do for baby William?" Deydie asked. "Any doctor worth his salt would know to put a colicky bairn on a boat. The rocking motion soothes the wee one, ye know."

He sighed. "Deydie, no disrespect, but I can't discuss another patient with you. You know that. You wouldn't want me to discuss your ailments with—let's see—Mr. MacPherson?" He pointed to where MacPherson stood by the back wall.

She huffed. "I don't know what ye're talking about. I

don't need a doctor at all. MacPherson's whisky fixes all of *my* ailments." She stomped off.

He turned back to Claire. "Do you think Dom went back to my place?"

"Probably," she said sheepishly.

"I'll go and check on him, after I get some food for Emma and myself. I assume as a working member of this community, I'm entitled to some of this potluck?"

"Aye, there's plenty," she said.

"And just so you know, Emma is staying at Thistle Glen Lodge. You may come by tomorrow and see her." *And not before.*

"Fine. I have to get back to the flat and get to bed, anyway. The scones wait for no one."

He'd heard her say it a hundred times over the years, but she'd never sounded so downcast. "You love each other. Fix things with Dominic." That was the best prescription he could offer her.

He filled two plates and took them back to the quilting dorm. There he found Emma stretched out on the sofa, sifting through the magazine he'd left her. He set their plates on the coffee table and then gently propped a pillow under her foot. "I'll fix you a new ice pack. Then we'll eat."

She reached for her plate and almost fell off the couch. "Whoa."

He steadied her. "I said after I fix the ice pack. Ye're worse than a toddler when it comes to listening." *But, God, she makes me smile.*

He brought back the refilled ice pack and settled her plate in her lap. He stopped her when she reached for her fork. "Not until we give thanks." He took her hand.

"I'm not religious." She looked down at their linked palms.

"It doesna matter. I am." He bowed his head and said a few words.

When he looked up, her head was still bowed. She slowly lifted it and he let go of her hand. For a charged moment they gazed into each other's eyes. He broke away first and grabbed his plate.

They ate in silence with the fire crackling in the background. It sounded almost as if they'd put on mood music. It was nice. Nice to eat with someone instead of sitting alone at the restaurant or alone at his kitchen table.

When she was done, she set her fork on her plate and looked up at him. "You've done a wonderful job of taking care of me today. Thank you, Gabriel."

He took a moment to soak her in and then finally answered, "It's been my pleasure." It had been. But he'd better keep it on a professional level. "How does your ankle feel?"

"Do you want the stoic answer or the honest one?"

"Honest, always." He saw the pinch between her eyebrows and he kicked himself for not watching for it sooner.

She frowned down at her foot. "It hurts a lot and is really starting to throb."

He went to his jacket slung over the chair and pulled out the pain meds. "Here, take one of these."

She swallowed it with a swig of water. "What about my crutches?"

"I'll run back to the Land Rover and get them. I'll also stop by Claire's to get your suitcase." It should be easier to drag down the stairs than it had been lugging it up. "Plus, I need to find Dom." With Emma's injury, Gabe had totally forgotten he was supposed to help with the lunch crowd. He also wanted to know what had happened, why the restaurant was closed. "Will you be okay on your own for a while?"

"The stoic answer—I'll be grand," she said. "The honest answer—don't be long."

He chuckled. "I'll refill your ice pack before I go."

Gabe headed to the Land Rover and retrieved Emma's crutches, along with the red heels she'd had on earlier. He hurried to the flat and luckily caught Claire before she headed off to bed. Together they packed Emma's things in her suitcase. He didn't bother to question her any more about the restaurant. He'd talk to Dom and get to the truth. In a separate bag, he shoved all of Emma's inappropriate shoes.

He rushed to his place to make a quick stop and found Dom in his kitchen, drinking alone.

Gabe laid a hand on his shoulder. "What are you doing here? Why is the restaurant closed?"

"What I'm doing is celebrating my early retirement." Dom downed his drink. "The dream is dead. No more customers means no more restaurant."

"What do you mean, *no more customers*? You were swamped yesterday."

Dom filled his glass and gave a mock toast. "Here today. Gone tomorrow." He knocked it back.

"Go to bed," Gabe said. "We'll figure this out in the morning."

"There's nothing to figure out." Dom stood and drifted from the room.

Gabe ran a hand through his hair, feeling like the problems were piling up. But one issue was settled. Somewhere between the hospital in Inverness and where he stood right now, he'd made up his mind. He couldn't leave Emma alone tonight.

He looked down at the sack he still held in his hand. *Emma's shoes.* This was one problem he could solve right now. He went to his bedroom and stowed her damned shoes in the back of his closet. "She'll have to go through me to get these back."

Chapter Eleven

Emma very much liked the pill that Gabriel had given her. Her ankle didn't hurt anymore and she felt all floaty and freer than ever. She scooted down farther on the couch and rested, enjoying the buzz. The next thing she knew, he had returned and had squatted down next to her, his face close.

"Are you feeling better?" he said in his Mr. Sexy Baritone voice. "Your face is relaxed, which tells me you are."

She reached out and brushed the hair away from his eyes to get a better look. His eyes dilated. She liked the way he looked at her. And she didn't care that he made all women feel like this—special. "I feel great."

She wrapped her arms around his neck and pulled him in for a kiss. Unfortunately, she pulled him off balance, their lips crashing together for only a moment before he toppled over.

"Oops," she giggled. "Did I hurt the doctor?"

He stood and scooped her up. "Off to bed with you."

She laid her hand on his face. He had a five o'clock shadow and it intrigued her how it could feel both soft and prickly at the same time. She remembered her mother describing how pleasant stubble burn could feel on the breasts. Emma started undoing the buttons on her dress to find out.

Gabriel stilled her hands with one of his. "What are you doing?"

She tried out Claire's purr on him. "Getting ready for bed, big guy." Emma got her hands free and snaked them around him again, this time playing with the hair at the back of his neck with one hand and massaging his neck muscles with the other. *Mum was right—sluts do have all the fun.*

"Stop, Emma. You're going to hate yourself in the morning. That is, if you even remember." He walked her into one of the bedrooms and deposited her on the double bed.

But before he could get away, she pulled him in for another kiss, murmuring into his mouth, "I need my big Scottish warrior." Then she stopped talking and kissed the hell out of him. Oh, Lordy, how he reciprocated. She loved every second of their dreamy kiss and could feel down in her bones that he did, too. She wondered if this was real or not. Or was she just having another steamy dream about the doctor?

Gabriel pulled away, panting. "God, Emma."

She fell back on the bed, satisfied that she'd gotten to him. "Go ahead and regret that kiss. I dare you." She felt like she could say anything right now. "Join me. I'll scooch over for you."

He ran a hand through his hair.

"You're gorgeous," she said.

"You're not so bad yourself." He took another step back. "I'll get the ice pack and put your crutches beside you."

She laughed as he practically ran from the room. Maybe she could snag him again when he returned.

*   *   *

Gabe stood outside the bedroom, trying to regain his composure. "Dammit." He couldn't deny that he was fully hard. He could deal with prim, proper, and uptight Emma, but he couldn't deal with her being the tempting seductress. She was acting like it was all a game. But he was done playing the field. And he would not fool around with Emma Castle. He just wouldn't. He was done with flings, going through the women on his Rolodex like it was a roulette wheel. He finally understood that sex, love, and intimacy were all connected and it did matter.

He retrieved her ice pack and crutches and snuck back into the bedroom. But he needn't have worried; she was passed out. He leaned the crutches beside the bed and stood over her. "What am I going to do with you?"

She sighed in her sleep.

If only she'd get called away tomorrow, go back to where she came from, and take her tempting body with her.

He lay on the dorm's sofa, staring up at the dark ceiling. He couldn't blame the sofa for his insomnia. He blamed Emma and his sex-deprived pecker. Claire could share a major portion of the blame, too. She's the one who'd invited Emma to come to Gandiegow to "regroup" in the first place. What the hell had she been thinking?

He decided that tomorrow after office hours he would go to Inverness for a change of scenery, talk to other people—just get away from Emma for a while. He had to regain his focus.

He tossed and turned on the dorm's sofa all night. It was hard, literally, with Emma down the hall. He rose early and met Dougal, their postie, opening up the General Store. Dougal had stepped in for Amy until she came back to run things. Which reminded Gabe, he needed to stop by and see how the MacTavish family was doing before he headed out of town for his diversion.

"I'm here to buy boots," Gabe announced.

Dougal glanced down at Gabe's feet. "Those not working for you?"

"Nay." Gabe went to the end of the aisle to look for himself.

The postman followed him. "What size do you wear?"

"They aren't for me." Gabe pulled Emma's red shoe from his pocket. "Do you know what size would fit these?"

Dougal eyed him suspiciously like the shoe belonged to him.

"Red's not my color," Gabe deadpanned.

Dougal took the shoe and examined it. "Here, the size is on the inside."

"Fine. Let's get a women's boot in that and some extra-heavy socks." God, that woman frustrated him. It was so important to take care of one's feet. He'd give her the boots and be done with it.

Dougal pulled out a pair of boots and laid four pairs of socks on the counter. "Is that all?"

"I jolly well hope so." Then Gabe thought about the hydrocodone hangover that Emma was likely to have. "I need chocolate, too." Guessing it might help.

Dougal gave him a questioning look.

"Just ring it up."

"Oh, Doc, I almost forgot." Dougal dug in his postal bag. "A letter came for you." He pulled it out and handed it over.

Gabe saw his father's perfect handwriting on the envelope. He shoved it in his pocket for later. In private. "What do I owe you?"

Dougal gave him the total and loaded the sack with the boots, socks, and chocolate. Gabe paid and got the hell out of there. But before he left, he caught the strange look on Dougal's face. *Oh, the things I do for Emma. Watching out for her is turning out to be a full-time job.*

At the doctor's quarters he grabbed eggs and butter from his refrigerator and a loaf of bread from the bread box. He only gave a cursory thought to Dom, wondering if he was up yet or not.

Next, he rushed over to Thistle Glen Lodge to leave Emma's boots there before she got up. He found her leaning over the counter, stirring sugar in her tea.

Nice ass, he noticed. God, did he always have to be such a pig? He plunked the sack on the table. "For you."

She looked over her shoulder at him. "And that is?"

"Your prescription. I filled it for you." He set the groceries on the counter.

"What prescription?"

He didn't answer but took her in from head to toe. "You look great."

She barked a laugh of derision. "I feel like bloody hell."

He pulled down a bowl and cracked the eggs into it. "For once you're not all polished and buttoned-up like a college professor." She was different from every other woman he'd ever dated. And vastly different from the ideal lass he had in mind for his own happily-ever-after.

"What do you mean *all buttoned-up*?"

"I'm just saying that the rumpled look suits you." His brain latched onto what it would feel like to rumple her himself by sharing a few days alone with her in his bed.

"Thanks for calling me rumpled. Your professional opinion means the world to me, makes me feel so much better."

"Go sit down." He popped bread into the toaster. "Do you want me to carry you to your chair?"

She sighed, exasperated. "I'm managing quite nicely—

thank you." But she winced as she used her crutches to maneuver herself into a kitchen chair. "What kind of painkiller did you give me?"

"Yeah, you probably should think twice before taking hydrocodone again. You had a . . . strong reaction."

As she stared at the tabletop, her cheeks tinged. "I don't remember a thing."

"Sure you don't."

"I have no idea what you're referring to." Her eyes were on her lap, where she adjusted her dress.

"Fine." He would ignore what had happened, too. "After we eat, I have office hours." He moved the sack closer to her. "Come on. Check out your new medical equipment."

As she took a drink of tea, she eyed the bag suspiciously. "It's too small for new crutches."

"Just look inside." He poured the eggs in the pan.

She opened the bag and pulled out the candy. "Chocolate? If this is some holistic medicine you're practicing, I approve." She ripped open the wrapper and took a bite.

"You'll ruin your breakfast," he said in vain as she nibbled some more. "Keep digging in that sack."

She reached in and pulled out the shoe box. It slipped from her hand and spilled out on the floor. "Oh, these are sexy." She held up one black boot, frowning at it. "*If you're a polar bear.*"

"Try it on your good foot. New socks are in the bottom, as well."

She pulled out one pair of thick socks. "Seriously, Gabe, I appreciate the sentiment and all, but what kind of lady wears these?"

"A smart Highland lass, that's who." The kind of lass he wanted. A woman with common sense. A girl who could be practical. He shot her a firm reprimanding glare, driving home the point.

"You mean the kind of woman who doesn't have an ounce of self-respect and doesn't care a whit how she looks." She harrumphed, sounding very unladylike to him.

He softened up a bit. "Come on. Let's see if the boot fits."

She pulled on one sock and one boot. "Well, it's warm. I'll give you that."

He took the toast and slathered on butter. "Do you need a topper on your tea?"

"Yes, thank you."

He poured more hot tea in her cup and set their plates on the table. When he sat down, she put her hand out to him. He stared at it for a long moment, confused.

"You always say grace, don't you?" she said matter-of-factly.

Stunned, he took her hand and said the prayer, and they dug in, sharing their meal, this one as companionable as the others.

Afterward, he cleaned their dishes, knowing she watched him. He spoke over his shoulder. "During my office hours, I'll ask the ladies to check in on you. You need to ice that ankle for ten minutes every hour. Tomorrow, we might start applying heat. We'll have to see."

She got up on her crutches and hobbled into the living room. "Can you hand me my purse?"

"Sure." He slipped on his coat, retrieved her purse, and gave it to her. "Can I get you anything else before I go?" He wouldn't see her again until tomorrow, and it bothered him to leave her like this. But she would be in good hands, and he had to get some distance from her. That kiss last night still hovered dangerously in the air, and he was afraid if he didn't get out of town, he would want to do it again. And again. Yes, hanging out at a pub in Inverness, maybe talking with some other women at the bar, or even catching a movie, would help to clear his lust for Emma Castle from his mind. He had to screw his head on straight at all costs.

She pulled him back to reality.

"No, I'm fine. Thank you." She had said it like she really meant it. "I don't need anything else." She grabbed her phone and started checking her messages.

As Gabriel went out the front door, Emma read the message from Mattie's former therapist. "Well, I guess that settles that." She texted back a note, slipped her phone in her pocket, and reached for her crutches. Today was her only chance to meet the therapist in person—five p.m. at the Bar None, a pub in Inverness. She rose clumsily on the crutches. She'd need every second between now and then to get ready and make it there, even though it was only nine in the morning.

She made it into the loo okay but almost toppled over, trying to take off her knickers. "Bugger that." She had to be careful. She turned on the tap for the shower. What would Gabriel think if he had to come to her rescue again? But this time she'd be naked as the day she was born. She'd die of embarrassment—not only because he'd see her without a stitch on, but he'd probably carry her through the village that way and not give a care that her bare bum was on display for the townsfolk to see.

She wasn't brave like the slutty deb who'd taken advantage of Gabriel's lips last night. No. Egghead Emma was back, shy and awkward as ever.

But she had done it. She'd kissed him and it had been as hot and sexy as the first time. Even more so. He'd turned to putty in her hands, and she loved that feeling of controlling a man—not just any man, but Gabriel—taking him to the edge. And with that, her feeling of power turned on her and she went all squidgy on the inside, her middle melting into caramel.

She put her head under the water and tried to rinse away the lust. That man did things to her that Emma had assumed were impossible. And she'd sure shown him that kissing each other wasn't just setting off a few fire-crackers; it was more like Buckingham Palace's fireworks on New Year's Eve. She'd proved her point. Now what?

The truth hit her. Kissing him was like stepping into sunshine in the dead of winter, and she didn't want to stop. Ever. But Emma couldn't let herself be just another in the long line of women who had succumbed to Gabriel MacGregor's charms.

No. She was made of stronger stuff than that. She would slake her lust, but it wouldn't be with him. Maybe she could find a man in a nearby town—maybe in Inverness while she was there.

With her mind set, she finished her shower safely and dressed in a gray suit and black tights. While she blow-dried her hair, she wondered what had happened to her tights from yesterday. She'd probably lost them at the hospital.

After she rewrapped her ankle, she went ahead and put on the thick wool socks, though her sense of style begged her not to. But he was right: The weather was harsh this far north. With one boot on, she carefully left and closed the quilting dorm door behind her. As cautious as a princess on glass crutches, Emma slowly made her way to Quilting Central. By the time she got there, her arms were screaming from carrying her own weight.

Deydie met her at the door. "Have you eaten yet, lass?"

"Yes." Emma was ready to cast the evil crutches into the fireplace.

"I hope ye're here to work on the doctor's quilt." Deydie glanced over at Emma's neglected place at the sewing table.

"Sorry. I can't. I'm off to Inverness."

Deydie frowned at her and opened her mouth as if to argue.

"For your granddaughter and for Mattie," Emma added.

Deydie bobbed her head in understanding. "Aye. Right."

"How do I get permission to borrow one of the cars?"

"At the store. Just put yourself on the sign-out list." Deydie eyed her carefully. "What did the doc say? Did he give you permission to go to Inverness by yereself?"

"I'm fine."

"Ye didn't answer the question." Deydie frowned. "I could get one of the lads to drive you."

"No. I'll do this on my own."

Deydie glanced at her bad ankle. "Ye better be careful, then, and not wreck one of the cars with yere lame foot." The old woman huffed off.

Emma called after her. "I promise to work on the Gandiegow Doctor quilt tomorrow."

She hoofed it carefully to the store and signed out a car. Dougal offered to get someone to drive her, as well. It was only her ankle that was sprained, but he acted as if she'd gone feebleminded for heading into Inverness alone. Didn't they know that she'd managed on her own her whole life? And in London, too?

She handled the drive just fine and found the pub on the first try. She was glad she'd given herself extra time. Sitting at one of the tables, she spent the next hour using her phone to continue her research on Mattie's condition. In a back issue of *Current Psychology* there was an article on how to heal the effects of trauma. She took notes and vowed to contact one of her former professors and two colleagues who had experience with selective mutism. She was feeling more confident about meeting with Mattie's therapist, looking forward to the challenge of working on such an interesting case.

She looked up as a man sauntered over to her table. She was about to tell him she wasn't interested in whatever he wanted when he spoke.

"Emma Castle? I'm Geoffrey Peterson, Mattie MacKinnon's therapist. Well, former, anyway."

He was tall and very good-looking. He was dressed in a cashmere sweater and chinos, and over his shoulder he carried an expensive-looking messenger bag. He was like a movie version of a mental-health professional.

"I hope you didn't have any trouble finding the pub," he said. "And I hope I didn't inconvenience you by forcing you to come today." He glanced over at her crutches leaning against the wall. "Yours?"

"Yes. Misunderstanding between me and a piece of ice."

He took the seat across from her and shot her a dazzling smile. "Shall we order first? They have excellent food here."

"Nothing for me. I'm not really hungry." She should've been attracted to such a striking man, but she wasn't even remotely interested in anything beyond what he had to tell her about Mattie. So much for her resolution to slake her lust on someone other than Gabriel. For some bizarre reason, it looked like no one else would do.

Chapter Twelve

Gabe was glad to finally be in his Land Rover and on the road, putting Gandiegow in his rearview mirror. He'd spent the day in his office—not seeing patients, but reorganizing the surgery. Again. The only people who stopped by were Ailsa and Aileen, the spinster twins—their words, not his. The ladies wanted him to repair their eyeglasses. *Their eyeglasses!* Of course he did what he could for them, a temporary fix, and promised to pick up new screws in Inverness.

Neither the organizing nor the twins could keep his mind off Emma and her kissing the hell out of him last night. But his plans for this evening should take care of his obsession with Ms. Crutches. He didn't know what he saw in her. Yes, she was beautiful. But there were plenty of bonny lasses to choose from, if not in Gandiegow, then here in the Highlands. Maybe it was Emma's sharp mind. It couldn't be her smart mouth and biting wit. He didn't even want to contemplate how she could bring him to his knees with just the touch of her lips.

He stepped on the accelerator, anxious for his evening in Inverness. But as the miles wore on, his grand plan to forget Emma by chatting up a few women over drinks seemed less grand and more implausible. He didn't have the patience for the type of birds he'd occupied himself with in the past. He would just have to wait for Emma to leave Scotland. It would be much easier to purge the thought of her when she wasn't in such close proximity.

He started to turn the car around and head back to Gandiegow when he remembered his promise to Ailsa and Aileen. He headed on to Inverness. When he got there, he stopped in the first shop he saw. It didn't take long to buy the screws for their glasses. As he was walking back to the Land Rover, he saw a familiar Audi 4x4 parked in front of the pub. The same Audi Q3 whose air filter he'd changed last week.

"I wonder who's here from Gandiegow." He crossed the street to find out.

Inside the pub, he looked around at the crowd milling about and didn't see anyone familiar. When he turned around, though, he bumped into a man who was holding a woman's hand across the table.

"Excuse me." Gabe leaned over to give the tall man room. When he did, he saw whose hand the man was holding—and the smile on her face.

"It was lovely to meet you. Don't hesitate to call anytime." The man let go of her.

Gabe couldn't unclench his fist, but at least he didn't bring it up and connect it with the bloke's face. The guy walked out, and Gabe took the seat across from her.

"Close your mouth, Emma."

"What—what are you doing here? Did you follow me?"

"Happenstance." Gabe pulled the menu from between the condiments. "What's good here?" He gazed at the menu but didn't see a damn thing. He was trying to still his beating heart. *Breathe in and out and she won't notice.*

She pulled down the menu, effectively making him meet her eyes. "I don't believe you."

"Fine. I followed you here to see who your lover is. Believe me now?"

She snorted. "Like Egghead Emma could ever land a guy like that." She grabbed the menu from him and fanned herself. "Did you notice he looks exactly like Hugh Jackman?"

Gabe took back the menu and buried his face in it. "Aye, a wolverine in sheep's clothing." How could she not know that she could get that bozo, or any man in this room, with a flick of her long cinnamon-colored hair and a come-hither glance from her evergreen eyes.

She pulled down the menu again. "Do they have fish and chips?"

He pulled up the menu and asked nonchalantly, "Who was that, anyway?"

She smiled at Gabe mischievously. "Wouldn't you like to know?"

He was done messing around. He reached over and snatched her crutches from behind her. "Spill the beans, lassie, or you'll have a tough time making it back to the Audi."

"Fine," she huffed. "That was Mattie's therapist from last summer. Cait wanted us to meet."

"To what end? A *setup?*"

Emma shook her head, clearly exasperated. "You're being ridiculous, Gabriel. We were discussing Mattie. I don't know what it is to you whom I meet with. Now give back my crutches." She thrust out her hand.

Satisfied, Gabriel handed them over and then waved to the nearby waitress. "Two fish and chips and two Cokes." He placed his elbows on the table and leaned in. "How's the ankle? I'm not happy you ventured out today. You should be at the dorm, resting."

"It's fine." But the crease between her eyebrows said otherwise. *Either that or the crease speaks to how she feels about me.*

"When was the last time you iced your ankle?"

"I said I'm fine."

"You're so stubborn." He stood and left Emma with her mouth hanging open again. He went to the bar and spoke to the attendant. "Can I get some ice in a plastic bag?" He pointed to where Emma sat. "I'm a doctor and she needs ice on her ankle before she can drive home."

The attendant made up a bag and gave it to him. Gabe went to the table and squatted down beside Emma.

She tried to scoot away, but he caught her thigh.

"Hold still." He carefully slipped the ice bag in between her Ace bandage and the thick socks he'd given her. He looked at his watch. "We'll take that out in ten."

She crossed her arms over her chest. "You are such a bully."

"No, just a damn good doctor. I plan for you to be dancing by Hogmanay, our New Year's Eve."

She shook her head. "I know what Hogmanay is. I'm sure I'll be gone by then."

"It looks to me like you're just settling in." He pointed to the folder sitting beside her on the table.

She snatched it up and put it in her bag. "Can we talk about something else?"

"Sure. What do you want for Christmas?" he asked, throwing her off guard.

"Three French hens," she said mulishly.

"You seem more like the *five golden rings* type."

"Is that still how you see me?" She sat back and frowned. "Do you have a partridge in a pear tree lodged in that thick brain of yours?"

He thought about it for a second. She was much more down-to-earth than he'd ever imagined. "No. I was wrong."

That earned him a look of surprise.

He couldn't help adding, "I believe ten lords a-leaping are more your style."

She didn't get a chance to react, as the waitress arrived with their food.

"Well, I've been wrong about you, too." She glanced down at her ankle. "You're not the wastrel I thought you were, either."

"Careful, Emma. My thick brain might get the wrong idea and think you're hitting on me."

"Not in a million years," she said confidently.

Oh, he so wanted to bring up last night and remind her who had hit on whom. But that would be a Pandora's box better left alone. So many questions surrounded Emma Castle. Not the least of which was why her kiss could get him harder faster than any other female he'd ever laid lips on. He couldn't ponder it, because in the end, it didn't matter that she affected him. Emma wasn't for him.

"Eat up," he finally said, and dug into his meal.

Claire paced. Emma had gone to Inverness and wouldn't be back until *who knew when*. Hanging out at Quilting Central held no real appeal; she never should've thrown her husband into the Cuisinart for the villagers to puree. And she definitely had to steer clear of Dominic now—surely he'd heard the lie she'd told about him. There was nothing quite so daunting as a pissed-off Italian. Except maybe an irate Scot. Perfect rivals and perfect lovers. One of the reasons the two of them had such heated arguments. And then great makeup sex afterward.

A brilliant idea hit Claire. She'd go see Amy and her baby. She wouldn't go empty-handed, either. From the walk-in cooler, Claire gathered plenty of Dominic's delicious food and fixed a hefty box for the MacTavishes. She put on her coat, loaded the wagon, and set off. About halfway through town, she heard the squall of a babe above the crashing waves.

She gave a mental shrug. No big deal. Babies cry. It was all part of raising a wee one. Claire pushed on, but the closer she got to Amy's, the louder the baby's wail became, and the more apprehensive she felt. She was beginning to see why the neighbors had started to complain that baby William had gone from being ever so lovely to a right-loud little banshee.

When she reached Amy's doorstep, William was screaming bluidy murder. Claire hesitated. She could still turn back and no one would know any different. But she wasn't a coward. She could handle it. She was a tough Scottish woman. Resolved, Claire knocked on the door. The baby screamed on. The winter wind whipped around her. She knocked again. The baby screamed some more. Finally, a ragged Amy answered the door.

The afterglow of giving birth was gone, replaced by zombielike circles under her eyes and an I-don't-give-a-shit demeanor on her sleep-deprived face. She wore blue sweatpants and a Just Kill Me Now sweatshirt splotched with spit-up spots down the front.

"Come in. Don't look at the place." Amy shuffled back in the room. "Coll had to rush off to Glasgow to see his uncle in the hospital." She went to the cradle, picked up the little terror, and thrust him at Claire. "Can you hold him for a bit? I have to get a shower." The word *shower* sounded like her last lifeline to sanity.

"Sure." Claire reached for him. Baby William pulled his legs up toward his tummy and screeched again—so loudly that Claire thought her eardrums would burst.

Without a backward glance, Amy trudged off to the loo.

Claire tried cuddling with William, but he was having none of it. Then she tried singing her own mama's precious lullaby, which only made him scream louder. The one thing that seemed to appease the little guy, but only a very little, was swinging him from side to side, while she hummed. It was the longest—and loudest—thirty minutes of Claire's life.

Amy finally reappeared from the bathroom with dripping hair but wearing clean clothes. She still looked haggard and utterly exhausted. "Here, I'll take him."

William cried on but seemed to calm a little in his mother's arms.

It was only then that Claire got a real look at the cabin's disarray—dirty dishes, baby clutter everywhere, and diapers soaking in a pail outside the restroom door.

"It's a mess. I know." Amy laid William down on the bed and changed his nappy. Afterward, she washed her hands and arranged pillows on the bed. "I'll try to nurse him. Maybe that'll help."

She propped herself up and pulled him into her arms. Between screams, he rooted around at her breast. He finally found what he wanted and got a few moments of comfort between half sobs.

"I'll take care of the dishes," Claire offered, "and whatever else needs to be done." But in truth, she wanted nothing more than to run from the cabin.

"That would be grand," Amy said. "But I could really use a cup of herbal tea first. Do you mind?"

"No problem." Claire made the tea and spent the next fifty minutes trying to bring Amy's previously cozy little cottage back into some semblance of order. But it wasn't long before the baby was wailing again. His mother's ever-patient care just couldn't stop his colic.

Claire's nerves were near shot when Moira arrived. Claire had never been so happy to see another person in her whole life.

Moira looked to Claire, then to Amy, and frowned.

She spoke quietly to her friend. "I thought you would call. I waited. I would've come sooner, but I assumed you were sleeping."

Amy laid the now-sleeping babe beside her. "I knew you had your hands full with your da. I'm managing."

Moira touched Amy's shoulder. "The circles under your eyes say otherwise."

"We've been grand. Claire came and took care of us."

"'Twas nothing," Claire said. "I only did a few things."

Moira grabbed an apron off the chair. "If it's fine with you, I'll take over now."

Her words were music to Claire's poor abused ears.

"I'm grateful you stopped by," Amy said. Claire could read the truth of it in her eyes.

She took her opportunity and got out, not needing to be told twice. Nobody could've made a quicker exit. Her parka wasn't even zipped for the first fifty feet from their doorstop. Then the baby started crying again.

Claire didn't know how Amy dealt with it. That poor girl needed round-the-clock help, not just a few friends dropping by here and there. Especially with Coll gone. Claire would organize it all and make it happen; Amy would get the help she needed.

Visiting Amy today had been a real wake-up call for Claire, too. Perhaps there were some things that she was unprepared for. She tilted her head to heaven and said a little prayer. "I think I still want a baby, God. But if it's not too much trouble, could you make it a nice, quiet one? Please?"

Of course, she knew all along that babies were a lot of work, even the quiet ones. How was she to deal with a wee bairn? A quiet baby still nursed in the night. A quiet baby still needed twenty-four-hour care. How could she be up all night and still get up to make the scones?

Everyone knows that the scones wait for no one.

*   *   *

While Dom packed food from the restaurant's kitchen into individual containers, he wondered where Claire was. No matter what he did, he couldn't get her off his mind. She'd ruined their only chance at having a restaurant. No one had shown up for lunch or dinner again today.

But he wouldn't let the food go to waste. He'd been in Gandiegow long enough to know who needed the food and who didn't. Even though the restaurant was gasping its last breath, he loved feeding people. It had always given him a rush.

He retrieved one of the wagons, loaded it up, and headed off to Mrs. Hume's house first. When he arrived, her brood of children squealed and cheerily unloaded the wagon as if the items were the hottest toys of the season. Next he stopped by Mr. Menzies'. It took a while to convince the old man that it wasn't charity, that if he didn't take it, the food would go to waste. It was the perfect thing to say to a frugal Scot. He used the same reasoning with Kenneth Campbell. Dom went to a few other cottages before making his last stop at Amy and Coll's one-room cottage near the edge of town. He'd heard Coll wasn't back from Glasgow yet.

Outside he could tell there were problems within. The bambino had a set of lungs on him, wailing like a siren. When Dom knocked, Moira opened the door.

"I've brought food," he said above the child's cries.

"But Claire has already brought us some," Amy said. The poor thing. She looked wiped out.

"I'll put it in the freezer, then." Moira took the box.

Dom slipped off his coat and ambled over to where Amy held the boy. "Here, give him to me. You look like you could use a break." He didn't know anything about babies, but at least he could hold him for a while.

"Are you sure?" Amy said.

"Yes."

"You'll have to support his head like this." Amy demonstrated how to cup his head to keep it from lolling.

Dom carefully took the child into his arms and held him close, looking down upon the wailing face. "You're not such a tough guy."

The baby stopped crying instantly and stared up at Dom like he was trying to bring him into focus.

"You need to learn that tough guys have respect for their madres. You love your mamma, don't you, little guy?"

The baby just stared at him.

"I thought so."

"That's amazing," Amy said breathlessly, in case her words might break the spell and make the babe scream again.

"Ye've got a gift, Dominic Russo," Moira said.

He didn't know what all the fuss was about. This baby stuff didn't seem too hard. He just had to show him who was in charge. "Amy, I've got him if you want to get out for a while." Dom took the child over to the rocking chair. "I think the two of us have come to an understanding."

"I would like to go to the store and see how Dougal is doing. Maybe pick up the receipts so I can work on the books?" Amy looked questioningly at Moira.

"I'll stay, too, in case his nappy needs changing."

"Are you sure?" Amy said again.

"Go on now."

"I'll take my mobile. Do you promise, Moira, to call if he needs me?" Amy said.

"Bundle up," Moira said firmly. "We don't want you to catch a chill."

"I won't be gone long. I promise." Amy grabbed her

coat, kissed the baby's head, and looked worried as hell, but finally went out the door.

"Tea?" Moira asked.

"We're good." He looked down at baby William, who had drifted off to sleep.

Moira busied herself around the cabin. She stripped the bed and started the sheets in the washer under the counter. She worked quietly and efficiently, just like she did for them at the restaurant. What a nice, helpful woman. He wondered why she wasn't married yet. It probably had to do with her shyness.

Amy returned in short order, with color restored to her cheeks. The walk to and from the store had done her good. "Is he asleep?" she asked.

Moira finished with the bed, pulling the comforter over a clean pair of sheets. "Yes." She turned to Dom. "Can you try to put the babe in the cradle without waking him?"

"No problem." He rose steadily and confidently laid the little one down. William didn't rouse.

Moira picked up her parka and handed Dominic his coat.

"Promise to call if you need anything," Moira said.

"Sure." Amy smiled that bright smile she'd had when Dom had first met her. "But, Dom, I'm putting you on speed dial."

"He's a fine boy," Dom said, not knowing what else to say as he and Moira left. They walked back through town, Dom pulling the rope handle of the wagon behind him.

Suddenly Mrs. Bruce hailed him. "Oh, Dominic? Can you come in for a moment? I need help with my boy, too."

"What the . . ." Dom said.

"Amy told me what you did for her screaming bairn.

Guthrie's colicky, too, though not as bad as the MacTav-ish baby."

"How did—"

"News travels fast in Gandiegow," Moira said quietly. She touched his arm. "I think you should help. Ye've got a gift."

"So you say."

"Will you?" Mrs. Bruce held the door wider, and the baby's cries made Dom's ears ring. "I'm about to lose my mind."

"Sure." *What the hell?* And he laughed. With the restaurant in the shitter, he was due for a career change, anyway.

From Italian chef to baby whisperer.

Chapter Thirteen

Emma didn't understand why Gabriel insisted he follow her home from Inverness to Gandiegow. She'd finished dinner with an espresso, after all, and was perfectly fine to drive. She'd only yawned a few times during their meal. She gazed in the rearview mirror for the hundredth time in the past hour, and there he was—her guardian angel, Gabriel. Even though it irritated her, she had to admit it was comforting to know he was there, in case her car slid off the slippery roads.

Her thoughts drifted to the cabin they'd shared on her first night in Scotland. Oh, how things would go differently between them now. Now that she knew he was a bloody good kisser. For a moment, she allowed her fantasies free rein, but then stopped herself. Yes, they had chemistry between them. But she was a civilized woman and didn't have to act on her baser desires. She forced him from her mind. Or at least she tried.

But for the rest of the trip back, she couldn't help but replay the comfortable dinner they'd shared tonight. They seemed to always call a truce when sitting across the table from each other. There had to be a psychological reason why food brought them together. Was it because of their two best friends and the food that Dominic and

Claire had fed them over the years? It was something to consider. She'd love to discuss it with someone—someone like Gabriel.

When they finally made it back to the village, it was late. Gabriel hopped out of his auto and was at her car door before she had time to grab her crutches from the passenger's seat.

"Do you want me to carry you to the quilting dorm?" he asked.

"Of course not." But her underarms ached and it wouldn't have been awful to be in his strong arms again. "A woman has her pride, you know."

"Sure. But my father would say, pride cometh before a fall."

"Too late." She lifted her bad ankle. "Already did that."

"Aye." He kept a slow pace beside her as she hobbled along on her crutches. "I'm just glad we're finally on the same page, the same side now."

"What?"

"You know, the Russos. That we're both rooting for Claire to get herself a baby."

Emma thought about Gabriel putting himself between Dominic and the townsfolk, protecting his foster brother. Since Gabriel had Dominic's back, surely it wouldn't hurt for him to know about the ledgers. "About that." She hesitated.

He stopped. "What?"

She came to a stop, too, leaning on her crutches. "The restaurant is in serious trouble, Gabriel. I saw the books. I'm no longer on Claire's side. She has it all wrong. They can't bring a baby into the world when their finances are so precarious."

His eyes turned dark under the streetlamp. "Money be damned—they need this baby. A baby will glue those two together. Forever."

She shivered. "Having a baby is no way to fix a marriage." It was stupid to think it could.

"A baby is a blessing, and part of its job is to keep people together. The cold weather has clearly addled your brain. Let's get you to the quilting dorm." He started walking.

She caught up to him, maybe wielding her crutches a little too quickly on the snow and ice. He turned and reached out and steadied her from slipping again. But she wouldn't thank him.

"Have you seen the latest divorce rates? Through the roof." Her pitch sounded shrill to her ears, but she didn't care. "Your logic is flawed. Bringing a child into a broken marriage isn't good for anyone."

He glared at her. "Dominic and Claire's marriage is not broken." Pain crossed Gabriel's face like he had a stake in the Russos' happiness. "Married couples have disagreements. They *will* work this out."

They were outside the quilting dorm by now. "I think you're wrong. Claire is being selfish, and Dominic is being sensible."

"No, ye're wrong. Ye know nothing about it." His brogue seemed to have thickened. He looked like he wanted to shake her. Or maybe kiss her. Or maybe both. He opened the door for her instead. "Good night."

"You're being unreasonable." She maneuvered herself inside. "Just like Claire."

"And you wouldn't know true love if it smacked you in the face." With that he closed the door and wouldn't let her get in the last word.

"Like you would," she said to the empty entryway. "Jackass."

She huffed off to get ready for bed. Their nice evening had been flushed down the toilet along with the little truce they'd had over their meal. So much for good food and good company.

She didn't sleep well at all; she blamed the espresso. The next morning, she headed off to see Claire at the restaurant. She couldn't help out with customers, but she could be there for moral support. She felt a little guilty for saying out loud that Claire was selfish, but she had no other explanation for why her best friend couldn't see the cold, hard truth.

The breakfast crowd was thick and buzzing. Claire didn't seem to be enjoying the extra sales of her scones or the nice things that the customers were saying.

"Are you okay?" Emma asked as Claire filled her coffee.

"I'm tired. Tired of everything."

"Can we spend some time together today?" Emma asked. "I've missed you."

"I promised to help out at Quilting Central. What about you?"

"Yes, I have the Gandiegow Doctor quilt to do." Emma's heart wasn't in it. She wondered if she'd see Gabriel today, too. And if they would argue again. "I'm also going to try to meet with Mattie."

"You're seeing patients in Gandiegow now?" Claire asked.

"It's a favor. Just an evaluation." Which wasn't exactly true. Between talking with Mattie's old therapist and the research she'd done, she had a pretty good idea which direction to go with the boy.

But the meeting didn't happen. Mattie had caught a cold, and Cait declared him housebound until he was better.

Instead of seeing Mattie, Emma sat behind her sewing machine all afternoon, wondering if Gabriel was ignoring her. Shouldn't he check up on her injured ankle? But what she really hated was that she missed him. And that working on his damned quilt was making her a better and better quilter—that really annoyed her, too. Her skill was showing now in every stitch. And for what? A pigheaded doctor who didn't care one fig about her. Pride wouldn't let her screw up his quilt, though he didn't deserve her effort. Even Deydie was impressed with her quality of work.

After she finished for the day at Quilting Central, she holed up at the dorm, working out a treatment plan for Mattie, preparing for when they did have their sessions together.

One day turned into two. In the morning she sat at the restaurant with Claire during the breakfast rush. Then in the afternoon she worked on the quilt. Then two days turned into three. Every evening, Emma and Claire dined at a different house by invitation, staying away from Dominic and the restaurant. Emma was getting more and more worried. Claire didn't want to talk about it, and Emma could only watch as her best friend's spirits sank.

Maybe Gabriel had it right. Maybe true love had to be saved at all costs. In her whole life, Emma had met only one couple she could say had the telltale marks of true love—and that was Claire and Dominic.

For the first time in her life, an empty place resided inside of her. Not the loneliness of her childhood growing up without loving, attentive parents. She'd come to terms with that long ago. This was new, different. It felt more like a hole had been chiseled in her chest, more specifically, right in the middle of her heart.

She sighed. For just this one moment, she would admit the truth. She wanted true love, too.

*   *   *

At the restaurant, Gabe unloaded the box onto the counter.

"What's all that?" Dominic asked, coming from the kitchen into the dining area. He carried a tray with a stack of clean napkins and silverware to roll.

"Christmas decorations." Gabe had found the box in the attic. Doc Fleming had left him a plethora of holiday decorations. "I thought we could spruce up the restaurant. Maybe that will bring in the business."

Dominic picked up a stack of receipts. "Breakfast is going well." His sarcasm was as thick as cranberry sauce.

"We just have to get back the lunch and dinner regulars."

"Yeah, like that's going to happen." Dom sat at the counter and prepared the silverware.

In the center of each table Gabe set a miniature wreath, and in the center of the wreath he set a votive. At a smirk from Dom, he said, "You know how much I like the holidays."

"Martha Stewart."

"Grinch," Gabe countered back. Unconsciously he glanced around, looking for Emma on her crutches. Crap, he'd done it again. Even though he'd managed to stay away from Emma for the past few days, she was always on his mind. It wasn't easy avoiding her in such a small town. Lucky for him, he had the restaurant to hide out in, at least during lunch and dinner. The rest of the time, Gabe spent on the Armstrong brothers' boat, helping repair their engine. Oh, and of course, he'd stayed busy at the office. *Not*.

A twinge of guilt hit him. He should have been checking Emma's ankle. But being near her drove him nuts. Still, he had a responsibility.

Dom ambled off into the kitchen and came back a

while later with a large sack that he dropped next to Gabe. "You might as well deliver these to the fishermen at the dock while you're there. No sense in food going to waste."

Gabe finished decorating the last table, put on his coat, and grabbed the sack of sandwiches. "I'll see you back here for dinner."

"Sure," Dom said. "It'll be just you and me again."

Gabe would see about that. When he got to the dock, he stopped by every tied-up vessel and handed out food. "Compliments of Dominic Russo." None of them turned down the sandwiches, which Gabe thought was encouraging.

When he climbed aboard the Armstrongs' boat, he found only Ramsay there. "Where are the other two?" Gabe asked.

"John slipped home to *see* his wife, Maggie." Ramsay waggled his eyebrows. "Ross ran up to the North Sea Valve Company to help the McDonnell. Ye're stuck with me."

"Here." Gabe tossed him a sandwich. "Last one. Now hand me that wrench and we'll see if we can't get this engine running."

Ramsay handed him the tool before tearing open the paper to get to the food. He took a bite. "Aw, hell, this is good."

"Enjoy it now. The restaurant won't be here long." Gabe undid one of the bolts and then the next.

"What do you mean?" Ramsay said around another bite.

"I mean Dominic will have to shut down, since he doesn't have enough customers." Gabe looked up at him pointedly. "Lunch and dinner pay the bills."

Ramsay put his hands up. "Don't blame me. My sister-in-law said she'd skin us alive if we went in there for anything other than breakfast."

"What did Dominic ever do to all of you?" Gabe knew what he himself had done to them—he'd had the audacity to take their beloved doc's place. But Dominic? He'd done nothing more than feed them well.

"Maggie said that Olive said that Rosemary told her that Dominic had disrespected the women of Gandiegow."

"Horseshit," Gabe said. "That can't be true."

"Try telling that to Maggie."

Gabe frowned. "Oh, I see how it is here in Gandiegow. The women tell the men what to do?"

"Nay." Ramsay's face turned red.

Gabe went on. "I can see why John might want to do as his wife bids, because he shares a warm bed with Maggie, but I'm not sure why you and Ross would follow her orders." Gabe paused for effect. "I know for a fact that in the rest of Scotland, single men do as they damn well please." He knew he wasn't playing fair, but hell, the women of Gandiegow hadn't played fair with Dominic, either.

Gabe shrugged and went back to the engine, but caught the expression on Ramsay's face as he angrily tore off another bite of sandwich.

Good. Maybe the restaurant wasn't sunk after all.

The next day, just as Emma got settled behind her sewing machine with her crutches balanced against the chair next to hers, Gabriel sauntered in like the king of Quilting Central. He didn't look right or left but came directly to her and moved her crutches, taking the seat beside her. Without saying a word, he turned her chair to face him and carefully lifted her leg, resting it on his thigh. If she so much as shifted her bad foot, she could've caressed his crotch with the wiggle of her toes.

She brought her eyes up to meet him. "What are you

doing, Gabriel?" Her voice sounded frantic to her ears, though she tried to keep herself together. Hard to do when Dr. Handsome was fondling her leg.

He slipped off her thick wool sock. "Doing my job. Checking up on my patient."

She mustered up some sarcasm. "The saintly country doctor, eh?" He undid the clasps of the Ace bandage and began unwrapping. She tried to look indifferent, but there was just something titillating about having her foot in his lap.

"Have you been applying heat?" His burr felt as warm as her thick wool sock.

"No." But she sure felt bloody hot all over right now. He'd be blind not to see her fiery blush.

"You should."

She felt lightheaded. "I should what?"

"Apply heat. Three times a day." He ran his hand gently across her ankle, then farther up, his hands doing a slow rub on her calf.

She couldn't help herself; she closed her eyes and sighed. "You're good at this." It didn't matter that his hands had practiced this particular skill on hundreds of women, maybe thousands. He'd perfected the hell out of it.

"I'm just trying to increase the circulation in your foot to speed up the recovery."

"Don't stop." It felt like he was seducing her, and it was working.

There was a loud harrumph over Emma's left shoulder.

"Stop playing handsies with her foot," Deydie commanded.

Gabriel's fingers halted. "I'm not playing *handsies*. I'm examining Emma's ankle. She should've come by the surgery already."

"It looks fine to me," Deydie said, though the ankle was clearly black-and-blue.

Gabriel reached for the bandage and rewrapped Emma's foot. "I'll bring by some Epsom salts for your soak."

"Ye most certainly will not." Deydie put her hands on her wide hips. "It's not proper for you to be at the dorm."

"You forget you put me there when I first arrived. Besides, Emma is a grown woman," Gabriel argued.

"And I'm right here," Emma interjected. She turned on Deydie. "I appreciate your concern, but I'll be fine."

Deydie jabbed a finger at him. "He has more than doctoring on his mind."

"I promise I can handle it." Emma turned on Gabriel, and she, too, saw his sly grin. "And you, Dr. MacGregor. I'll get my own Epsom salts, thank you very much."

He didn't look deterred. She'd have to try another tactic. The massage was nice, but it was time to put him in his place. "You may go."

Yes, her upper-crust dismissal did exactly what she'd intended it to do: ticked him off royally. His anger gave her something else to focus on besides how good his hands had felt on her leg. She could grow attached to a man with hands like that.

"I have things to do," he said stiffly, like leaving was his idea and not hers.

"Yes, I'm sure." She turned back to her machine and picked up two pieces of blue batik fabric. It took every scrap of her energy to not watch him as he stomped to the door. *Or limp after him to apologize.*

Claire broke away from Ailsa and Aileen and hurried over to her. "What was that all about?"

Deydie and her salty tongue beat Emma to it. "The doc was taking liberties."

Claire burst into laughter. "Gabriel has been known to do that a time or two. But never with Emma."

It stung. But it was true.

Deydie chewed on her lip. "Well, maybe me old eyes saw it all wrong."

Now Emma wanted to correct them both. In fact, she wanted to shout it to the whole blooming room: Egghead Emma and the gorgeous doctor had shared two earth-shattering kisses.

But who was she kidding? They wouldn't believe her.

"Back off, please. I need some space," Emma said. "I'm trying to make a quilt here."

She put the presser foot down and started sewing, ignoring them. What did they know, anyway?

She worked for the next several hours, keeping her hands busy with Gabriel's quilt and forcing her thoughts to Mattie's first session.

At 3:10 p.m., Cait brought Mattie to her.

"Hi, Mattie." Emma shut off her machine. "Are you feeling better?"

He nodded. While she stacked up the blocks, he threw away the pile of extra threads she'd accumulated throughout the day. In a perfect world, she would've chosen his house on the bluff for their therapy sessions, because he would've been most relaxed there. But her dependency on the crutches wouldn't allow it.

"Are you ready to head to the dorm?" Earlier, everything had been organized. Claire had set out a tray with snacks and Emma had laid out drawing materials—pencils, markers, finger paints, and paper.

As they made their way down the boardwalk, Mattie kept glancing over at her with a pinch between his eyebrows.

She stopped and gave him her full attention. "Are you worried about me falling again?"

He nodded.

"I promise I won't." She smoothed back his hair. "I'm pretty good on the crutches now." Emma made a mental note to have Cait meet her at the dorm in the future — for Mattie's sake.

At the quilting dorm, he held open the door for her and seemed relieved when she finally settled herself at the table.

"Grab a snack and get comfortable." She poured them both a glass of milk. He fixed them each a plate with two cookies.

She plugged her smartphone into the speakers and started the classical music. His face scrunched up.

"Not your cup of tea?" she asked.

He shrugged.

"Eat up." She found a pop station, and he looked happier. *So far, so good.* When they finished with their snacks, Emma got down to business.

"I know you've done a lot of play therapy with Dr. Geoffrey. I've got a new game. What do you think about making ourselves into superheroes?" She gave him a sheet of paper. "We have plenty of stuff to draw and paint with. Remember, with your superpowers, you can achieve anything. So in your drawing, Super Emma wants to see what you want to get out of therapy. I'll do the same. When we're finished, we can compare."

Mattie pulled the paper in front of himself. Determinedly, he drew three smiling people: a man, a woman, and a child who wore a cape. The child had his mouth open as if he were speaking. The family stood at the edge of the ocean, a boat off in the distance.

Emma drew a stick figure of herself holding a boy's hand. The boy had a smile on his face. In the background, she drew a lot of stick figures to represent all of Gandiegow around them, supporting them.

"Are you ready to trade?"

He gave her his picture, and she pushed her page toward him.

"Oh, Mattie, this is so good." She was impressed how he was able to articulate through his drawing what he wanted. He wanted to be able to speak. "Take a look at mine, and then we're going to make up stories about our superheroes on the page."

He leaned over and examined her drawing.

"I've never been a good artist. But can you see that Super Emma only wants her patient to be a happy camper?"

He nodded.

She tapped his drawing. "Well, Super Mattie has already accomplished some great things with his powers. He already has a happy family. I've seen how your mum looks at you—as if you invented sunshine."

He smiled at her like he knew exactly what she was talking about.

"Right." It was too early to ask him about the boat in his drawing. But in future sessions they would come back to his picture to dig deeper and also use the drawing to gauge their progress.

"Are you ready to make up a story and have our superheroes solve all kinds of problems?"

His eyes twinkled.

"In a small town, not so very far away, there was a—"

The front door opened.

"Emma, are you here?" Gabriel hollered.

"We're in the dining room." She would've liked to have headed him off at the pass, but she didn't even get her crutches in hand before he sauntered into the room.

"Don't get up," he said. "I brought your Epsom salts." He looked about. "Hey, Mattie." His expression changed as he took in the scene. "I didn't mean to interrupt."

The boy jumped up and pulled him over to the table, shoving a clean sheet of paper in front of him.

"Oh no," Gabriel said. "I'm here on doctoring business." He held up the salts.

Mattie opened his mouth and a very soft and very breathy sound came out. "Stay."

Emma was stunned, but she had to hand it to Gabriel—he didn't make a fuss. He acted like it was the most normal thing in the world.

Gabriel smiled at Mattie. "Emma would have to say it's okay." They both turned to her.

"First of all, we're being superheroes, so it's *Super Emma*. And I guess it would be all right." Gabriel did, after all, have professional training. What else could she say? They'd ganged up on her, too.

Gabriel ruffled the boy's hair. "Let me get Emma's ankle soaking in some water. Then I'll put you both to shame. I'm the world's best finger painter." He left the room.

"I bet he's fibbing," Emma said.

Mattie grinned and set up a spot for Gabriel. It gave her a moment to wonder what it was about Gabriel that put Mattie at ease, comfortable enough to speak. Was it because he reminded him of his father, who had passed away? Or perhaps his grandfather?

The doctor returned with a pan of water and set it at her feet. He squatted down and undressed her ankle, as gently as if she were a hummingbird. He placed her foot into the warm bath salts.

"There." He sat beside Mattie, directly across from her. "Now what should I draw?"

"You have to show us what superpower you'd have."

"Ah, that's easy. Prepare yourself to be amazed."

He poured the three primary colors onto the page

and swirled them around with his fingers until he had a brown mess. "Ta-da. What'd I tell you? My superpower is that I'm an amazing artist!" He grinned at her, then at Mattie, waiting for his reaction.

Mattie's shoulders shook with silent giggles. It was so infectious that Emma giggled, too.

Gabriel held the page up, the paint running down it. "I tell you, it's good enough to hang in a museum."

Mattie shoved his new completed picture in front of Gabriel. It was a decent enough interpretation of the house next door. He'd spelled out DUNCAN'S DEN on the bottom. Mattie's old house.

That sobered things up.

Gabriel looked from the picture to the boy. "That's really good, Mattie. You did a fine job."

The boy beamed.

Emma wiped her hands and looked at her phone for the time. She'd told Cait they'd be done at four. "We should clean up."

Gabriel took her hand. "You're soaking. Mattie and I have this." He dropped it but his painted handprint, *his mark*, remained behind on her.

She gazed down at her hand, a little mesmerized, but snapped out of it quickly enough.

"All right. But you two had better do a good job. I don't want Deydie to yell at me if you don't."

Mattie nodded with understanding.

Just as the boys finished tidying up, Cait arrived with Dingus on a leash. The dog immediately jumped up on Mattie.

"Can you take him outside?" she said to the boy.

Mattie wiggled into his coat and grabbed the leash from her.

"Thanks, kiddo," she said, as the dog ran out the door, pulling Mattie. "How did it go?"

Emma sat back in her chair. "He said the word *stay*."

Cait smiled at her warmly. "I knew you'd be good for him."

"Gabriel was the one who got him to talk. Mattie said the word to him."

"It was a team effort," Gabriel corrected.

"Well, I'm thrilled. Graham—his grandda—will be, too." Cait pulled them both into a hug, Emma sitting in her chair, Gabriel hovering above her. "Monday after school, then?"

"Yes," Emma said. "Monday."

"I'd better go see where those two ran off to." Cait pulled her gloves back on and walked down the hallway, leaving Emma and Gabriel alone.

Dominic sat at the small desk and entered the last several days of receipts—all of them from Claire's shift, of course, none from his own. He had made his way up to the flat as soon as he saw Claire go into Quilting Central. He needed time with the restaurant's books—alone— and had waited until the coast was clear.

When he was done, he turned to stare out at the sea through the frosted window. Despite the treatment he'd received from the townsfolk, there were so many advantages to living in Gandiegow. For one, he liked living close to the ocean—the vastness and continuity of it calmed him. It was proof, right outside his door, that God existed. Secondly, Gandiegow's smallness gave him the chance to really get to know his customers. And he loved living where people understood and appreciated being close to the source of their food. Buying fresh fish from the fishermen's boats had only been a pipe dream when he worked in the big city. But here the fishermen would sometimes even bring in their catch for Dom to cook and serve up right away for them and their families.

At least when he'd had customers.

With a sigh Dom checked their balance one more time. He had just enough to pay the farmer for the special order he'd committed to weeks ago, something he had hoped would kick off the first in a long line of self-sustaining ventures for the restaurant. He should really cancel the order, but the local farmers were struggling, and Dom understood firsthand what one canceled order could mean: life or death to a small business.

So, it was time to pick up the weaned piglet that awaited him. Dom planned to use kitchen scraps from the restaurant to feed him, and outside the restaurant he'd readied a lean-to near the dryer vent, which would keep the little porker warm. He had imagined taking the pig to the school as a way to teach children about animal husbandry, and then, when the time came, he would serve fresh pork to his customers.

Claire crossed his mind for the hundredth time that day. He'd wanted to surprise her with his latest idea, but that was before everything went to crap between them. In times past, she'd always understood his passion about food; shoot, she'd shared that passion. Her support always meant so much to him. But this was something he'd have to do alone.

He checked his watch. Time to go. He grabbed the checkbook and his coat. He would be back in no time at all. With his pig.

Emma took her foot out of the pan and watched as Gabriel opened his mouth. She put up her hand. "Not a word, Dr. MacGregor. The water is cooling off."

She wanted to quiz him on where he'd been the past few days and ask him if he'd ditched her on purpose. But she couldn't; he'd think she'd missed him. Missed his face. His smile. And how comfortable he made her feel.

Gabriel grabbed a towel and wrapped her foot in it gently. "I'll dump this out. Let's soak it again in another hour."

"You said three times a day," she complained.

"We're making up for lost time." He gave her a comical frown. "Castle, you make a horrible patient."

"I do not." But he was halfway out of the room with the pan of water by then.

She rearranged the art supplies, keeping herself busy, trying not to wonder what would happen next. Would Gabriel stay or would he go?

He came back in. "Well?"

"Well." What could she say? *Please don't leave. Keep me company.*

He sat down at the table across from her and appeared ready to speak. But in that moment, the front door to the dorm opened. He jumped to his feet, as if they had been caught in the act, and went to stand in the doorway to the kitchen.

"Miz Castle, are you here?"

"In the dining room," Emma called out loud enough for the woman to hear down the hall.

Two women came in, one twenty, the other in her forties. They looked so much alike that they had to be related.

"Miz Castle, I'm Annie and this is my daughter, Sophie." Annie had worry lines between her eyebrows, while Sophie's face was a mixture of listlessness and discomfort. "I've come to see what you can do for Sophie."

Gabriel looked from one woman to the other, frowning. Emma understood. Shouldn't the doctor be the first person to turn to for help?

Annie was no dummy and nodded toward Gabriel. "No disrespect to the doc. It's not a body problem, ye see. Sophie just isn't herself."

The young woman looked even more uncomfortable but didn't object.

"Sophie," Emma said, "may I ask what's bothering you?"

Sophie shrugged and turned away.

"Maybe I should leave," Gabriel said.

"No, stay," Emma said. "We may need your expertise, as well." *There. That should appease him and help establish his bona fides.*

"Aye," said Annie. "We need all the help we can get. Me and her father don't know what to do. Sophie is usually so cheerful. But then when the days get short . . ." She put her arm around her daughter's shoulders. "I don't know what it is. But like clockwork, it seems, when the cold and snow hit, she gets the terrible blues. She's got no energy and all she wants to do is sleep."

Pretty cut-and-dried; Emma saw Gabriel's comprehension, as well, but he nodded as if to defer to her. *The expert.*

"I believe it's SAD," Emma said.

Annie frowned at her like she was a little off her rocker. "Aye, 'tis sad."

"Sorry. I meant *seasonal affective disorder*."

"I don't understand."

Emma explained. "It's a type of depression that occurs at the same time every year, most frequently the winter, probably due to a lack of sunlight. We can help her with bright-light therapy." She looked up at Gabriel.

"I can order a lamp for her. She might also benefit from a course of melatonin, but I'd have to evaluate her first."

"Thank you, Dr. MacGregor," Emma said, setting the precedent.

"Aye, thank you, Doc." Annie made a kind of curtsy to Gabriel, but then took Emma's hand and shook it. "Thank you, too, Miz Castle."

"Please call me Emma."

They talked for a few minutes, setting a time for Sophie to meet with her.

At last the woman said goodbye and took her daughter's arm, heading them down the hallway. After the front door shut, quiet ensued for a long moment.

Gabriel leaned against the doorframe. "I think maybe I should make an appointment with you, too."

"What are you talking about? She was just looking for a little advice."

He pushed himself away from the frame and walked toward her.

Unwittingly, she held her breath.

"It's like this." He squatted down by her foot again. "I've been here more than three months and have done everything I can to ingratiate myself with these people." He picked up her leg and massaged her calf once again, making it hard for her to concentrate.

She closed her eyes. "Your hands have definitely ingratiated themselves with me."

He continued on. "What magic do you hold, Emma Castle, that everyone here loves you instantly?"

Everyone? She shook her head, opening her eyes, and found he was gazing into hers. It was too much, so she closed them again, getting lost in the magic of his caress.

"Share your secret with me," he went on in his deep burr.

She sighed. "I guess I'm just in the right place at the right time. Unlike the past three years." Then she thought out loud. "I never should've been a marriage counselor. I don't even believe in the institution."

He stopped massaging.

She opened her eyes again. "Keep going. You're working out all the soreness."

He frowned at her with a disappointed expression and stood, towering over her. "Ye're wrong about marriage, Emma. It's the foundation of a fulfilling life. Everything builds upon it."

She scoffed.

He pulled a chair so close to hers that when he sat, she could smell his woodsy aftershave. "Marriage is a public declaration that you love each other." He stared deep into her eyes, searching hers, almost as if he were using his powers to sway her into seeing it his way. "Weddings bring the community into the relationship. Everyone at the wedding has a responsibility to help the couple stay together. Like you and I do with Dom and Claire." He nodded as if that fact couldn't be argued. "Marriage is about bringing people together so they won't have to go it alone. Life is hard. It's nice to know someone is there by yere side, sharing the load." He leaned in, his face the picture of earnestness. "Don't you want someone to grow old with? That one person who will love you forever?" He looked like he wanted it more than anything else in the world.

"Gabriel," she said, "what you're asking me to believe in doesn't really exist." But as soon as she said it, she began to doubt herself.

He reached out, captured her hand, and held it tight. "Marriage is the best place to raise children—where parents can model love and commitment. And, in turn, their love and commitment reassure their children that they are safe and will be protected from the outside world. I know there are a lot of divorces out there. But real love does exist. I've seen it. At my father's church, there are couples who've been married forever; they got it right. And up until now, Dominic and Claire had it right, too. I'm sure all couples go through a rocky patch. This is theirs. I think you and I have a responsibility to lift them up and carry them over their rough spot. Don't you?"

She stared down at Gabriel's hand linked to hers. "I

used to think Claire and Dom were the exception. . . .
But with them falling apart, now I don't know if such a
thing is possible for anyone. I *am* sure that bringing a
baby into poverty is wrong. It just won't work."

He stood up. "Money isn't everything." He turned and
walked away. "I'm going to get us some dinner."

He got away too fast; otherwise she would've tripped
him with her crutches for good measure. "You haven't
convinced me of anything," she hollered, as he went
down the hall. But he did have her thinking. Maybe even
softening in her convictions. It was almost as if his views
on marriage were either starting to rub off on her, or
strong enough for the both of them to believe in.

Chapter Fourteen

There had been talk of it all over town. Claire absent-mindedly rearranged her scone recipes on the table at Quilting Central, thinking about what the other ladies had said. She just didn't believe it. *Dominic quieted colicky William?* How could that be?

Dominic had never been particularly interested in small children. Actually, more standoffish on the occasions when they'd been around a toddler or two. Where had he acquired this skill?

Bethia touched her arm. "It'll be all right, Claire. We'll get Dominic straightened out."

"Damned right we will." Deydie swept the clipped threads into a pile on the floor. "Ye're as skinny as a needle. Ye *need* meat on your bones. Don't know what yere husband was thinking."

Claire felt her cheeks flush. She opened her mouth to come clean about the lie, but the door to Quilting Central blew open.

Mrs. Lister stood there, holding a screaming baby in one arm with a four-year-old hanging on to the other. "Bethia, can I leave Agnes here with you? Stephen is at it again. I'm going to run him over to the restaurant and have Dominic get him to sleep. With Big Stephen out on the boat, I'm not sure what I'm going to do if I don't get some sleep."

Bethia pushed herself up from the table and spoke above the wailing baby. "We'll have a grand time." She took the little girl's hand and led her to the tray of sandwiches. "When Dominic gets the babe down, you nap, too. I'll drop her home later." Mrs. Lister nodded and hustled out with Stephen screaming.

Deydie whacked Claire's backside with the broom. "Close yere mouth. Ye look like a gaping fish."

"But—"

"Go see for yereself if ye don't believe it." Deydie swept on.

Claire sat there for a minute longer and then dumped her recipes back into her bag. "I guess I'd better. Seeing is believing."

Gabe stepped outside, filling his lungs with cold air. He certainly never worried about being bored around Emma. *First, she acts like the most amazing woman I've ever met, and in the next second she says something stupid like she doesn't believe in marriage.* What was he supposed to do with that? And why did he feel the need to convince her, anyway? He headed toward the restaurant at a brisk pace, confused as ever.

Just as he reached the door, Claire came up behind him.

"Are you here to get dinner, too?" he asked.

"Nay. I've come to seek the truth." She walked in ahead of him.

Although all the lights were on, Dominic wasn't in the dining room. Gabriel and Claire walked toward the kitchen. He held the swinging doors open for her, but she stopped midstride at the threshold. Gabriel couldn't believe his eyes, either. Dominic had a baby asleep on his shoulder while with his free hand he stirred the simmering sauce on the stove. He glanced over at Gabe, not acknowledging Claire.

"Don't ask. Even though there'll be no customers again tonight, it's just hard to break old habits. Like cooking dinner." He didn't say anything about the babe as he shifted the spoon to the rest, then pinched several spices and sprinkled them in the sauce.

Gabe stepped around Claire, who was standing as still as a pillar of salt. "Well, you'll have two orders at least. Mine and Emma's."

Dominic returned to stirring. "Fill a pot with water, will you?"

"Sure." Gabe went to the sink and washed his hands.

Claire took another step into the kitchen. "How? When?" she sputtered. "Why?"

"Not so loud, Claire," Dominic chided. "The baby's sleeping."

"But . . ." she tried. "Only a little bit ago that baby was screaming like there'd be no Christmas. How did you do it? How did you calm him?"

He shrugged, the baby remaining as relaxed as a bobber on the water. "Babies can smell fear, I guess."

"But . . ." Claire's eyes were misting up.

"I'm not afraid of a few tears," he said pointedly. He wasn't speaking only of babies.

Gabe saw anger flash in Claire's eyes as he carried the full pot of water to the stove.

"I'm not crying," she insisted.

Dominic nodded toward the child. "And this doesn't change anything."

The bell over the front entry rang. Then a voice hollered out, "Dominic, are you here? We're hungry."

Dominic looked at Gabe quizzically. Without asking

permission, he transferred the babe to Gabe's shoulder and went to the dining room. Gabe and Claire followed.

Five fishermen stood there—Ramsay and Ross Armstrong, Thomas and Lochie, and Abraham Clacher, an old bachelor fisherman, who was holding a gutted fish in his hand.

Deydie appeared at their side and pushed her way forward. "What are ye all doing here?"

Abraham ignored her and heaved the fish at Dom. "Make sure to put extra butter on it when you throw it on the grill."

Gabe knew that Dom would've normally told the old man where he could shove his cooking instructions—*he was the chef*—but he looked too stunned to do more than to take the fish.

"I'll have whatever Italian dish ye're cooking up in there," Ross said, glancing over at Deydie nervously. "Smells good."

Ramsay nodded. "Aye. The same for me."

Claire seemed at odds with herself, a myriad of emotions playing on her face as she looked from Dom's relieved expression to the cocky grins on the fishermen's satisfied faces.

Deydie had no such dilemma. She thrust her hands on her hips. "I saw ye all coming this direction. Ramsay Armstrong, does Maggie know ye're here?"

"I'm a grown man. My sister-in-law doesn't own me. I eat where I please." He cut a glance at Gabe.

Deydie turned her glare on Gabe. "Ye've had a hand in this, haven't ye?"

Gabe didn't admit to anything, only readjusted the lad on his shoulder. If Deydie hadn't been glaring at him so, he might've been able to relish the feel of a sleeping babe in his arms.

Claire slunk out the front door, glancing at Dom long-ingly. Dominic took the fishermen's orders with pleasure shining on his face.

"We'll just see about this," Deydie huffed. Then she stomped toward the door, too.

Gabe went into the kitchen with Dominic right behind him.

He pounded Gabe on the back. "Looks like I owe you, brother." He laid the fish on the counter. "And if Deydie's glare was any indication, whatever you did to get them here was at great peril, too."

"What do we do about the baby?" Gabe asked. "I have to get food back to Emma."

Dominic narrowed his gaze at Gabe for a long moment, but then said nothing. Finally, he pointed to a pallet in the corner. "Lay him over there. His mamma will be by to get him later."

There was a squeal in the opposite corner. For a moment, Gabe wondered if there was a second baby under Dom's care. But it didn't exactly sound like a bairn. "What's that?"

Dominic looked up and smiled. "That's Porco, the pig."

Gabe laid the child down and then went to the opposite corner of the kitchen to the cardboard box. Sure enough, a pink piglet was stretched out on a blanket. "What are you going to do with it?"

"Pork cutlets." But an unsure frown crossed Dom's face.

"I doubt it." Gabe remembered what had happened when Dom had tried to raise a chicken, a turkey, and a duck. None of the poultry made it to the table, either, but a local petting zoo in Glasgow had been thrilled.

"It's an economical solution," Dom said. "Raise fresh food, serve it to the customers."

"The water's boiling." Gabe went to the cooler and pulled out the leftover lasagna and the roasted vegetables. After he sacked everything, he turned to Dom. "Write this up for me, will you? I'll be by tomorrow to pay."

Dom waved him off. "It's on the house."

"No, it isn't." Gabe headed out of the kitchen. He waved to the fishermen as he hurried out the door.

But out front, he didn't head down the boardwalk. Impulsively, he took the path behind the restaurant.

He would make an overnight bag for himself. He would stay at the dorm with Emma again. He felt like a prat for leaving her to her own devices for the past three days with her foot sore and swollen. It would only be for a couple of days, until she could put a little weight on it again. Or until she was well enough to go back to Claire's. To devil with how Deydie felt about it, too. Gabe was Emma's doctor, and she needed him.

It didn't take long to gather his shaving cream, toothbrush, and clothes. As an afterthought, he picked out his favorite CDs to play during dinner, and grabbed a bottle of wine for them to share.

When he got back to the dorm, Emma was stretched out on the couch, her cell phone to her ear, and a cup of tea on the side table. "I have to go, Mum. The food is here. Yes, I'll let you know. Bye." She glanced at the load in his arms. "What's all that?"

"Dinner," he answered.

"In a duffel bag?"

He dropped the bag. "I'm going to stay here for a couple of days to watch over you."

"Gabe, you're off your trolley." She held up her teacup. "I can manage fine on my own. I've been alone for the past three days and I'm getting along famously."

"Your foot should be better by now. I want to keep an

eye on you. We might need another X-ray of that ankle," he said.

"Then I'll ask Claire to come stay with me."

"Do you really want to bother Claire in the middle of the night if you need something? With her getting up so early?" Gabe walked past her. "I'll warm up the lasagna and bring your plate to you. We can eat in front of the fire tonight. But first, music."

He went to the stereo, ignoring her muttered protests about not being *in the mood*, and inserted the CDs. It didn't take long for him to fix their food and get a picnic set up for them in front of the hearth. He sat next to her and stretched out his hand.

As if it were second nature now, she automatically took his in hers. He bowed his head and said grace. Afterward, he poured them each a glass of wine and handed one to her.

"What should we toast to?" he asked.

She frowned at him. "For the warden to go home and leave the prisoner to her own devices."

Her hair had fallen in front of her face and he pushed it back over her shoulder. "The warden shouldn't have left the prisoner alone in the first place."

She gave him a sheepish look.

He clinked her glass. "To good company, it is."

"You're an exasperating man."

"And you're a delight. Now dig in."

As they ate, they both praised Dom's excellent pasta, and, once again, shared a pleasant meal. Gabe mused that eating was perhaps the best thing that they did together. *Except maybe kissing.* He put her lips out of his mind and told her about the pig at the restaurant. He explained his sunny forecast for the pig's future and long life. Emma's laugh was infectious. Once again he wished for a woman in his life to share all his meals with. A nice Scottish girl, with a big appetite, who knew how to laugh.

In the loo, Emma rested on the side of the tub, stalling. She should've been readying herself for bed, but her nerves were trying to get the best of her. She hollered through the door, "It's ridiculous for you to stay here with me."

He laughed. "Ye're repeating yourself, lass. Time to come up with some new material."

The last time he'd spent the night with her, she'd accosted him. And at the cabin in the woods, that hadn't been tiddlywinks she'd been holding in her hand when she woke up in the morning. God only knew what she would do to him this night.

"Please, Gabriel," she tried, checking her fingernails.

"Begging doesn't become ye. At the count of three, I'm coming in to brush my teeth. One . . ."

"Go away." She hopped to her good foot and grabbed the red plaid nightshirt from the towel rack. She stripped off her sweater and bra as fast as she could.

"Two."

"Give me a minute." She pulled the nightshirt over her head. It wasn't hers—she'd found it lying on top of her things—but she wasn't going to say no to it. It was definitely warmer than any of her silk pajamas. She'd have to pay Gabriel back for the nightshirt and the boots and the socks—all the things he'd bought for her. She splashed water on her face and reached out for the hand towel.

"Three." The door opened, and she got a handful of Scot. "Whoa."

She jerked her hand away. "Dammit, Gabriel."

"I counted slowly." He handed her the towel.

"Have you never heard of privacy?" She scrubbed her face, too embarrassed to look up at him just yet. When she did, she stopped in midscrub. She gaped at his pants. The exact match to her nightshirt.

"I . . . you . . ." she sputtered.

"Ye look nice, Emma." He wore a black T-shirt, too, but she couldn't stop staring at his pajama bottoms.

She held the nightshirt fabric away from her body. "This is yours?" It was too intimate.

He laid a hand on her shoulder. "I worry you're not warm enough at night. I thought I would share."

Not warm enough? She was sizzling on the inside at his words and caressed on the outside everywhere his shirt touched her skin. "But—"

He stepped around her and grabbed her toothpaste. "I have to get up early. Ramsay wants me at their boat before they take off. In case they have any problems with the engine."

She leaned against the wall. "You don't mind that they are taking advantage of you? That you're their mechanic?"

"Hell, Emma, if it weren't for the extra little jobs about town, I'd go nuts for lack of anything to do."

Well, that explained why he was giving her ankle extra attention—he was bored. The thought helped to settle her nerves and, at the same time, oddly angered her. She grabbed her crutches and stumbled from the restroom.

Instantly he was there, steadying her. How many times had he done that for her since she'd come to Scotland? She was used to being on her own, independent, doing things for herself. His support felt both weird and comforting. Maybe she shouldn't have had that second glass of wine with dinner. She stared down at her feet.

"You're tired," he said.

"Yes." That's what it was.

"I'll help you into bed," he said.

She looked up at him then. "Where will you sleep? Where did you sleep the other night?" *The night I kissed you senseless.*

"The sofa."

"The love seat? No, Gabriel." She frowned at him. "There are plenty of beds, upstairs and down."

"All right." He followed her into her room and helped her settle into the double bed, pulling the covers over her.

"Good night," she said as he stood by the light switch.

He turned it off and she heard him go back in the bathroom. A few minutes later, she heard him come back in her room and climb into the bed directly across from hers.

"I meant there are plenty of beds in the other bed-rooms."

"I don't like to sleep alone?" he offered.

"So I've heard," she said, wrapping the covers more tightly around herself.

How in bloody hell am I supposed to get any sleep tonight with the sexiest man in Scotland not six feet away? All toasty in his bed . . . in matching pajama bottoms. Oh, gads!

She almost wished she was the type of woman who would have the nerve to crawl into his bed with him and take a trip around the world for the heck of it. But she wasn't. Egghead Emma was much too smart to do something as stupid as that.

Gabriel came so close to turning her own words back on her. She had more of a reputation than he did when it came to *not sleeping alone.* At least he had to have some sort of connection with the women he'd slept with. Dominic made it sound like Emma was just out to do as many men as possible. Gabe still had a hard time believing it, especially after getting to know her better since she'd arrived here in Gandiegow.

He rolled onto his side, watching her from across the room, using the moonlight to make out her features. He'd done so well avoiding her the past several days. Yet here he was, only a couple of feet away from her now.

"You know," he said, thinking to tease her, "maybe we should switch. This bed is too small for me."

"Not on your life," she said.

"Then what about making room for me over there?" He shouldn't have said it, but he couldn't help himself.

"Sorry. I have restless legs syndrome," she quipped. "I'd keep you awake all night long,"

He groaned. *Oh, God.* He imagined all sorts of ways in which she'd keep him awake all night and RLS wasn't one of them. Maybe her legs wrapped around him? *Oh no.* He grabbed his blanket and got out of bed.

"Where are you going?" she asked.

"I can't take the heat, so I'm getting out of the kitchen," he muttered.

"Huh?"

"I'm going to another bedroom to sleep." He only made it a few steps.

"Don't go," she whispered. "I don't like sleeping alone, either."

Oh, hell. "Okay. I'll stay for a while." He sat at the bottom of her bed and pulled the cover from the lower part of her bad leg.

"What are you doing?"

"Shhh." He carefully located her calf and began massaging it.

"You know," she said softly, "you could always become a masseur if this doctoring thing doesn't work out."

He chuckled. "Thanks."

For a moment, he allowed himself the fantasy of letting his hands roam higher. Maybe even crawling in beside her, kissing her, loving her until dawn. He'd have to be careful not to hurt her ankle. He'd be tender. Attentive. Anything to hear her moaning with satisfaction.

No.

He shook his head. He wouldn't take advantage of her. He'd already done too much conniving. He'd insinuated himself into her bedroom. He was even rubbing her calf with not so honorable intentions.

He pulled the cover back over her foot.

"Don't quit," she pleaded.

"We both need our sleep." Not that he'd be getting any with this hard-on. "Good night, Emma." He picked up his quilt and went to the bedroom next door, leaving the doors open between them.

After he crawled in bed, he laid his hand on the wall, the wall they shared. "Call out if you need me."

"I'll be fine," she answered back.

Gabe closed his eyes, but it didn't do any good. He still saw her. Once again, he wondered: When would Emma be leaving his corner of Scotland?

He must've drifted off somewhere amid his thoughts, because he came awake with a start at the sound of a cry. He jumped out of bed, got tangled in the bedcovers, and stumbled. He ran into her room.

"Help!" she cried, thrashing about. "I'm drowning."

He leaned over and shook her shoulders. "Emma, wake up."

"Stop! Help!" she gasped.

He gathered her into his arms. "Wake up, luv. 'Tis only a dream."

She came awake, her eyes wide in the moonlight. He stroked her hair down the length of her back, and she relaxed into him.

He kissed her temple and held her close. "What was that all about?" he whispered.

"Bad dream. My parents were in a speedboat," she said breathlessly. "It was so real. I was tied to the boat like a skier, except I had no skis."

"Oh, Emma," he said.

"They drove the boat too fast and I couldn't keep my head above the water. I couldn't breathe and I couldn't get them to stop." A sob slipped out and she tried to stifle it.

"Shhh. It's okay now. No boat. No water. It's just you and me. Now scooch over." He slid into the bed and pulled them under the covers until they were lying down. He tucked her in the crook of his arm with her head lying on his shoulder. "The bad dream is over. I'm here now."

"It was so real. They weren't paying any attention to me, even though they were the ones who'd tied me there. It didn't make any sense."

"I know, luv." He caressed her arm. "Nightmares seldom do."

She cuddled closer. "I know dreams can be the subconscious' way of working out our problems."

Is that why I keep dreaming of you in my arms, night after night?

"Do you think it was the phone call from earlier?" he offered.

"Probably."

He rubbed circles onto her arm now. "Do you want to talk about it?"

"No. Yes." She paused for a second. "I don't know."

"What did they say? In the phone call, I mean."

"They want me to fly to New York tomorrow for a TV appearance." She sounded as meek as a mouse, which wasn't like her. "They want me to apologize on camera for what I did."

"No!" Gabe saw red. *How dare they?* He kissed the hair on her head fiercely. "I hope you told them where they could put that idea."

"They're my parents," she said. "I've never told them no."

He turned his head so he could see her better. "It's just, ye're a grown woman with a life of your own."

"But they have a point. I hurt their *brand*. I owe it to them to fix things."

"What do you want to do?" he asked.

"I'm still figuring that out." She was quiet for a long moment.

"May I give you my opinion?"

She gave a small laugh. "It's not like you to ask my permission."

"I think you're a talented therapist, Emma." Pride swelled within him. "I've seen how you've handled Mattie and Sophie. You have the potential to help a great many people. The problem is that you've hidden your talents away. For some dumb reason, you think your parents are more important than you are. They aren't. Just because they make the most noise and shine their light so annoyingly bright doesn't mean that what you have to give the world is any less important. In my opinion, ye're worth a million Eleanor Hamiltons and Dean Castles." He brushed her hair back from her face. "Yere parents shouldn't be asking ye to serve their needs. No longer, is what I say. They can take care of themselves."

She patted his chest. "You're a good man, Gabriel."

Her hand stilled. It was as though they simultaneously realized they were snuggled together like two turtle-doves. The air became electrically charged everywhere their skin touched. She turned toward him, sliding her hand up to his face, shifting her body, coming closer to his mouth. "Thank you," she murmured. Then she kissed him.

The kiss wasn't the inferno of perfect chemistry as before; it was so much more. Tender, sweet. Utterly consuming. It captivated him—hell, *she* captivated him like no other. He held back and let her lead; it wouldn't be honorable if he seduced her after her bad dream. But that was exactly what she was doing to him.

She deepened the kiss, slipping her tongue into his mouth, and shifted until she was on top of him—careful of her ankle, he noticed. She fit him absolutely perfectly in every way. His body molded to hers; her body molded to his. He thought he would die from restraint. He wanted nothing more than to roll her over and make love to her.

Just this once, he could let go and forget his convictions. Tomorrow he could go back to being a better man . . .

"No, Emma." He pulled away, gasping for air. "We should stop."

She laid her forehead on his, her breathing shallow, too, as if they'd both climbed a Highland mountain. "I know." She rolled away from him.

Instantly he felt cold, but it was good. It cleared his head. If he'd let things continue down the path they'd been going, he would've been taking advantage of her and he would've let himself down in the process. He wanted to make love to her—but not at the risk of everything he'd worked so hard to achieve. His new life, his newfound principles. He swung his legs over the side of the bed and sat up.

She touched his arm. "Gabriel?"

He twisted toward her, expecting her to thank him again. "Yes?"

"I'm leaving tomorrow."

For the hundredth time, Claire glanced at Emma's note lying on the cash register. It might as well have been a neon sign pointing to the neglect of her best friend.

Gone to New York to see my parents.

The note made Claire's stomach ache—more guilt piled on the massive heap she'd already accumulated. The only reason Emma had come to Gandiegow in the first place was to get comfort from her best friend. Poor Emma. Claire had done nothing but dump her own problems on top of Emma's mess of a life. Claire had let her down, plain and simple. She should be with her when she saw her parents, support her. But that was impossible. Even if she had the money for airfare, Emma wasn't answering her phone or replying to her texts. Claire had no idea where she was in New York, how long she was going to be there, and if she was ever coming back to Gandiegow. What was Claire going to do?

Loneliness enveloped her. Which was crazy, since most of Gandiegow had paraded in and out of the restaurant all morning. The last of the customers were still sitting at the counter. Claire couldn't wait to close up. But what would she do then? Hanging out at Quilting Central had become unbearable since she'd told the lie about Dominic. She certainly couldn't stay here—Dominic would come in soon for the lunch shift. She missed him. But she couldn't bear it if another one of the village mothers brought her child here for her husband to calm. She was still reeling from seeing him yesterday evening with a bairn tucked into his shoulder like it belonged there.

Her heart ached for him, for their life, and for their love. It had all come so easily up until now.

Finally the McDonnell and Mr. Sinclair paid for their coffee and scones and left, leaving Claire all alone. She went into the kitchen and ran the water in the sink. From behind her, she heard the swinging doors to the kitchen swoosh open. She turned around and Dominic was standing there with his damned piglet in his arms. Jealousy overtook her. And for a piglet, no less!

Dominic nodded toward her without anger, without yearning, like they were two acquaintances. She wondered at what point she'd lost the ability to make her husband ache for her. He tucked the pig into the box in the corner. *Yet another baby he's put to sleep.*

"I thought you were going to keep the pig in the lean-to out back," she said.

Dominic shook his head. "I saw the weather forecast. Porco stayed with me at Gabe's last night."

"What does Gabriel think of the pig staying above the surgery?" It was better to speak of the pig than to pine over how ruggedly handsome her husband looked this morning as he donned his crisp white apron. Or to think about how he should've been home last night in bed, beside her.

Dominic turned to her, looking determined. "Claire, I have something to say."

Her heart leapt. He was finally going to end this feud between them.

"It's about Gabriel and Emma."

Her hopes plummeted and her gaze dropped to the floor, lest he see her hurt. She screwed a frown on her face and lifted her head. "What about them?" She sounded bitter, but there was nothing she could do about it.

"I think Gabe is getting attached to Emma."

"What? No. Ye're crazy. Gabe has never liked Emma. Think back to all the times he wouldn't come over if he knew she was to be there."

"Something is happening between them. And I don't want *you* to do anything that's going to ruin it for him."

She felt like he'd taken the paring knife to her heart. Did he think so little of her? "Why would I do anything to ruin it?"

Dominic leaned against the cutting counter, looking gorgeous but serious. "I know how fond you are of Gabe. But I'm worried about you exacting revenge on him because he convinced some of the fishermen to return to the restaurant for lunch and dinner."

"I would never exact revenge on Gabriel." She was glad the fishermen were eating Dominic's food, but she couldn't bring herself to say it.

Her husband, though, gave her a hard stare, as if he didn't believe it.

Claire huffed. "Well, I know for a fact that Emma thinks more of the mud on the bottom of her shoes than she does of Gabriel."

"I believe you have it wrong. Have you not seen what passes between them? I'm just asking you to stay out of it, is all. Let nature take its course. Gabe deserves to be happy." He stared at her for a long moment.

"Go ahead and say it, Dominic. At least one of ye men deserves to be." She grabbed her coat off the hook, trying not to cry in front of him, and practically ran from the building.

At one time and not so long ago, she and Dominic had been the perfect couple—always in sync, always in tune with each other, always passionately in love. Their relationship now felt like a war zone. How had it come to this? She knew their finances were crap, but it didn't take much to live here in Gandiegow and raise a babe.

The tears ran down her face and she tried to wipe them away before anyone passing saw her misery. What if she never got Dominic back? What if she'd ruined it?

In another minute Claire found herself in front of the kirk. She stepped inside, intending to light a candle for their relationship, but Father Andrew was there, winding garland around the candles.

"How are ye today?" Father Andrew asked.

"Fine," Claire answered automatically. "Do you need a hand?"

"Aye. I didn't know this was a two-person project until I started."

She grabbed the other end of the garland and wound it through the candles on her end while he did the same from his side. The church was quiet, solemn, perfect for Claire to reflect on her sins. She had the sudden urge to confess everything, especially throwing Dominic under the proverbial bus for the villagers to run over. She opened her mouth to say something when the door rushed open. Moira dusted the snow off her jacket and stomped her feet.

Father Andrew smiled. "I'm glad you could make it. Are the rest coming?"

Moira nodded just as the door opened again. Deydie, Bethia, Rhona, Claire's second cousin Freda, and what felt like the whole damned town flooded in. Why were they here? *This isn't Sunday.*

The women took off their coats, and Deydie took charge. "Okay, ladies, let's get to polishing those pews. Ailsa and Aileen, I want you to work on the floors. Make them sparkle, dammit."

Father Andrew shook his head. But everyone accepted that Deydie would always be Deydie. Not even God would take on the task of changing her.

Father Andrew turned back to Claire and explained.

"The town cleans God's house once a month." He beamed at all of them.

Bethia nodded to Claire. "Many hands make light work."

Claire finished with the garland. She had every intention of sneaking out the front until Deydie snatched her arm and shoved a dust rag in her hand.

"Ye get to work on the altar. Make it shine, lass."

Claire took the rag and went down the aisle, her sins feeling larger and heavier than ever.

Emma woke up in her hotel in New York and struggled into the outfit her mother wanted her to wear. As soon as she was dressed, she and her crutches were whisked away in a limo to the television studio. In her hand she held the itinerary her parents had sent her, the script she was to memorize, and answers to the most likely questions. At the studio, hairdressers, makeup artists, and producers awaited to ready her for her appearance. She was so jet-lagged she couldn't see straight. When she was introduced to come onstage, there sat her father, looking perfectly Hollywood, his black hair with just enough silver in it to show he could be trusted by one and all. Emma knew differently. He shot her a look that said she'd better not screw this up with Dr. Hill, the famous television psychologist.

Dean Castle spoke first about how *children can lose their way* and how *children often feel the need to rebel against their parents*. He spoke about how he and Eleanor, Emma's mother, planned to help Emma through *her current lapse in judgment*. They were going to *spearhead her therapy* and *get her on the right track so she could help couples in no time, contributing once again to the psychological community*.

Emma wanted to vomit. Thank God they went to

commercial break, or she might have spewed on her father's polished Italian loafers. Without the cameras rolling, her father's veneer of parental love fell away. He gave her a disappointed frown, then spoke to the producer, not looking back in his daughter's direction again.

An assistant straightened Emma's jacket. "You'll speak next."

The show went back on the air. Dr. Hill turned to Emma, tucking her long, pencil-skirted legs under her chair. "How do you feel about your poor advice being caught on tape and going viral? Do you feel remorse for what you said to the couple you were *supposed* to be helping?"

Emma saw Robert Frost's two roads in front of her. She was too tired, too disheartened to go down the path less traveled. It didn't help that her father kept shooting daggers at her every time he knew the camera wasn't on him.

Emma caved. Like always.

She recited the mea culpa her parents had written for her. Her father seemed satisfied, but she didn't get a chance to speak with him afterward as she was whisked off to the next appearance with her mother across town at *Mom Talk*.

After that she had an hour at the hotel before a late lunch with her parents and their publicist. If only this nightmare-of-a-day would be over. Then three more days of morning shows, talk radio, and late-night appearances with her parents.

Emma lay on the bed and cried. Irrationally, she wished Gabriel were here to take her into his arms, tell her it would all be okay, and kiss her until none of this mattered. Until he had blotted out the mess she'd made of her life.

But that wasn't how things worked. She was alone in

this world. She straightened her shoulders. She'd gotten herself into this, and she would get out of it by doing exactly what her parents wanted her to do. She rolled out of bed and prepared for her next ordeal.

Just as she was finishing with her makeup, the phone rang. She picked it up. Her mother didn't say hello or ask how she was doing.

"A car is waiting out front to take us to the restaurant." Her mother hung up.

It sounded more like a ransom call from a kidnapper than a parent who cared about her daughter. Emma slipped on her coat and grabbed her purse, taking a second to glance down at her sleek black dress and trendy black pump on one foot and black stocking over her Ace bandage on the other. Gabriel would have a fit about her wearing a pump with her crutches. But what was Emma to do? Her mother needed her to dress appropriately.

On the way to the restaurant, everyone was silent. But her mother's tight mouth and her father's squint gave them away. They were still furious with her. Acid churned in Emma's stomach and she was certain she wouldn't be able to eat a thing. She wished she were back in Gandiegow, sitting in Gabriel's kitchen, having a relaxed dinner.

At the restaurant, the limo driver helped her out of the car and to the doorway, but then she was on her own. The maître d' showed them to the table where the publicist sat, looking bored.

Emma went to prop her crutches against the chair next to her, but a server ushered them away. Her hopes sank. A quick retreat would now be impossible.

Another server came to take their drink orders. Emma felt like she could use a whisky, but resisted. She needed her wits about her when dealing with her parents.

As soon as the server left, her mother pulled out a contract and thrust it at her. "We need your signature on this."

"What is it?" Emma picked up the papers, examining them. "Is this a contract for another book?" She still owed them chapters on their current work in progress.

"Yes." Her mother took a sip of chardonnay. "Your father and I are trying to put a positive spin on this disaster of yours."

Her father drummed the table with his fingers. "The book is about you, Emma. As we discussed on air today, your mother and I will help you get back on track, and this book will tell our story."

Holy crap . . . This was too much. Gandiegow's brand of in-your-business insanity was looking better and better against these *business arrangements* her parents had to offer!

Emma stood. "I have to go to the loo." It was the most assertive she'd been in the past twenty-four hours. She motioned to the server who'd taken her crutches. It wasn't a pretty exit, but she finally succeeded in trudging off to the bathroom for solitude.

When she got there, she collapsed into one of the boxy black chairs and put her head in her hands. She wouldn't whine about having a crappy childhood; she knew she'd grown up in great privilege. But couldn't they act like they cared for her just a little? Deydie and Bethia came to mind. Those two women reminded Emma of Claire's mother, Nessa. Deydie and Bethia didn't hesitate to treat Emma like family. The whole town of Gandiegow had, in fact. Even the doctor.

Her phone rang. She looked at the number and didn't recognize it. Normally she would have let it go to voice mail, but she was happy to do anything to stall, anything to keep from going back to the cold, impersonal table with her parents.

"Yes," she said.

"We need you." Gabriel's baritone brogue warmed her, even though he sounded upset.

"Why? What's going on?"

"Claire is missing," he said. "I don't know where she is."

"I'm on my way." Emma hung up. Her heart raced.

She hobbled back to the table as quickly as she could but didn't sit down. "I have to go."

Her parents both blinked up at her, annoyed.

Her mother spoke first. "Sit down. I ordered you the lamb."

Emma hated lamb. "It's an emergency."

Eleanor scoffed. "Seriously, Emma, what kind of *emergency* could you have?"

"It's Claire."

For a moment, her mother looked confused, then realization dawned. "Oh, that little Scottish girl."

Oh, good grief. She wanted to yell at her mother that Claire had lived in their house *for seven years.* That Claire's mother, Nessa, had been their housekeeper, working her fingers to the bone for Eleanor until she passed away.

"Yes," Emma finally said, not trusting herself to say more.

Her father pushed the contract toward her. "You haven't signed this yet. We have more appearances here in New York for you to do, too."

"You'll have to do them without me." Emma snatched up the contract and shoved it in her purse. "I'll take it with me and read it on the plane."

"Where are you going, Emma?" Dean said, perturbed.

"I'm going home to Gandiegow." Emma turned and left, not giving her parents a backward glance.

Chapter Fifteen

Gabe hung up and leaned back on the sofa by the fire in Quilting Central, satisfied with a good day's work. Claire came out of the women's restroom, and he waved to her. "Oh, there you are. I was wondering where you'd gone to."

Claire came over but didn't sit, studying him closely. "I've known you a long time; you're up to something. Spill it. What's going on?"

How much should he tell her? Should he boot up his laptop and show her Emma's television appearances? How her best friend had denied her feelings and lost her dignity for her parents' sake? It hadn't been hard to find out where Emma was and what she was doing. All he had to do was Google her parents and discover what devilment they were up to.

"Come sit for a minute," he said.

Claire plopped down beside him. "What gives?"

"Emma dug herself into a hole and I threw her a lifeline, is all. I need you to play along when she gets back." He explained what he'd seen and what he wanted her to say when Emma came home. "Can you do it?"

"Sure." She sat back and scrutinized him. "Why are you doing something nice for Emma? You don't like her."

"If you saw a dog run over by a car, wouldn't you stop and help it? Even if it was an annoying, yipping dog?" He felt proud of his analogy, though he knew it wasn't exactly true. He didn't think Emma was nearly as annoying as she'd been in the past. Or maybe she'd never been annoying at all. Maybe it had been him and his skewed perception of her. He didn't know anymore.

Claire looked conflicted. "I'll be here for Emma when she gets back, but we need to talk."

He frowned, the one to be circumspect now. "About what?"

"I need to warn you about her."

"She's yere best friend," he growled, knowing where she was headed. "Don't say anything ye'll regret."

Claire stood and backed away from him. He'd never really lost his temper with her or even in front of her, but he was close to doing it now.

She got a determined look on her face and plowed ahead. "Ye're family to me, just like Emma is. You need to be aware that Emma has a past."

"We all do, Claire," he bit off.

"Don't misunderstand. Emma's a wonderful person, but she's had more men in her bed than I have scone recipes."

"Stop," Gabe warned. "Don't go any farther."

She reached out and gripped his arm as if he meant to bolt. "Dominic said you have feelings for her." She frowned at him, perplexed. "I didn't see it before, but I'm sure seeing it now."

"Bullshit. At least not in the way you think," he denied.

"I'm telling you, Emma doesn't do relationships. I know ye're looking for one. She doesn't believe in marriage, either. Which *you* do. She isn't the right one for you."

He jerked his arm away. "Who said anything about the right one? I told you I don't care for her in that way. And you, her closest friend, should be ashamed for . . ." Gabe had been blocking Emma's escapades from his mind, but now he felt . . . hurt? Jealous?

"I love her, but I love you, too. You're like the brother I never had." She crossed her arms over her chest and plastered a stern expression on her face. "You had to be warned."

"Dammit, Claire." He rose. "Maybe you should get your own house in order. Quit worrying about me, and make things right with your husband. What did you do to make the town's women turn against him?"

She paled but recovered quickly. "I didn't do anything."

"Ye're lying, Claire. Your right eye always twitches when you're shoveling out the bullshit."

She rubbed the offending eye. "I have to go."

Gabriel watched as she marched off, and knew he'd have to work harder to get the Russos back together. Claire sure as hell wasn't making it easy on him. When Emma returned, he'd have to force her to help more. Then a terrible thought hit him: What if Claire ratted him out to Emma about how he'd lied to get her home? *Screw it.* He'd done it for her own good.

He opened his phone and texted Emma. Send me your itinerary. I'll pick you up from the airport.

She sent back one letter: K

He wouldn't leave Emma hanging. The second he knew she'd made it through airport security or boarded—as soon as she couldn't turn back—then he would tell her that Claire had been found safe and unharmed. He hated that she was worrying, but he had to get Emma out of harm's way, away from her self-centered parents.

*   *   *

Emma fretted all the way to the airport, worried about Claire. Had she gone for a drive and gotten lost in a snowstorm? Had she slipped and fallen off the board-walk into the sea? *Oh, God, please let her be okay.*

Luck was with Emma. She was able to exchange her ticket and get through security in time to board the next flight. She didn't bother buying a magazine, as she had the contract to focus on during the trip. That was, if she could quit worrying over Claire long enough to read it. She texted Gabriel her itinerary.

Gabriel texted back: Let me know when you've boarded.

Strange. After she settled into her seat, she sent him a quick text to let him know she was on her way. She was about to turn off her phone when she received another text from him.

Claire has been found safe and sound. She's at home in bed.

"What?" Emma said out loud. She texted Gabriel back. Where was she?

She'll tell you when you get home.

Emma stared a long time at the word *home*. It was odd, but she did feel like she was headed home. She let the feeling settle over her as more passengers boarded.

Gabriel texted one more time. Are you okay?

She smiled at her phone. Yes.

I'll see you when you get here. I'll be waiting.

His reply made her smile even more. It almost sounded like he'd missed her, too.

She laid her head back and shut her eyes, feeling more relaxed than she had in a long time. She thought about the peace she'd felt in church last week and hated that she'd missed a Gandiegow service for this dreadful trip.

She was starting to get a clue how screwed up she really was. She'd willingly come all this way to humiliate herself for her parents. But she'd always done what was expected, wanting to please them, hoping if she did what they wanted they'd have a normal family—with parents who cared for each other and cared for her. Emma pushed it out of her mind. She'd think about it another day. Right now she was going home to Gandiegow. To Gabriel.

She fell asleep and didn't wake up until the plane landed in London. On her connecting flight to Inverness, butterflies began to multiply in her stomach. *He'll be waiting.* She had to pull herself together. If not mentally, then physically. With compact in hand, she fixed her face, making herself presentable for the doctor.

As Emma made it through the gate with her Aircast and crutches, she saw Gabriel. His face lit up. Then she noticed he was holding one boot in his hand. It wasn't black, like the last pair he'd bought her, but a shiny red plaid boot. He was wearing a Santa cap and grinning like seeing her was the best present ever.

She pointed to his plaid treasure. "What's this all about?"

"An early Christmas present. I figured you wanted to feel more feminine."

She gazed up at him. "What I'm going to feel is more Scottish. Are you trying to turn me into a Highland lassie?" She smiled and reached for the boot. But he didn't immediately let go, giving her a funny look instead.

"What's wrong?" she asked.

He shook his head. "Nothing. We'd better get going."

She leaned on her crutches and took his arm. "Claire? Is she all right?"

He squeezed her arm back. "Sorry. False alarm. She's fine. I feel terrible about making you come home early."

"You don't look sorry." She gazed into his eyes.

He didn't resemble the person she'd held in her mind for so many years. He was an amazing man. He had a way of soothing her—and driving her crazy—like no other. While she was in New York, she'd missed him, truly missed him. All the anticipation at seeing him again coalesced into one definitive point. They were here together now, and that was all that mattered. She did a most uncharacteristic thing: She went up on tippy toe and kissed his cheek.

He blushed. "What was that for?"

"It's the Christmas season. A time for giving, right?"

A flash of mischief crossed his face. "Well, in that case . . ." He took her into his arms and spoke right before his lips touched hers. "Welcome home." Then he kissed her passionately but, oh, so tenderly.

She should've swatted him away, but she plastered herself up against him in front of the whole airport terminal and kissed him back fervently. She gave herself over to the kiss and floated away with it—thrilled, relaxed, safe, secure, complete. It felt too wonderful to care about anything except for him and what he was doing to her beating heart.

"*Get a room*," some joker said as he passed by.

The statement stopped her midkiss. She pulled away, thinking this would be the perfect time and place, away from the good but nosy people of Gandiegow. She chewed her lower lip and brought her gaze up to meet his, making him read her mind with her pleading eyes.

He stared at her for a long moment, a tortured expression on his face. "Nay, I can't." The way he shook his head almost imperceptibly made her think he was trying to convince himself.

"But . . ." She stopped, the truth hitting her in the chest. *He's gone to bed with half the women in the UK. What's wrong that he won't sleep with me?* She shut her mouth and straightened her shoulders. She was sick to death of being humiliated. She'd had enough of it in the past day to last her a lifetime.

"Never mind." She walked away as fast as she could manage on crutches, completely mortified. Her eyes stung, feeling like they would give way to tears at any moment.

"Wait, Emma." He came up beside her.

She put up her hand but didn't dare look over at him.

"It's not you—it's me," he tried.

"That's original." She kept her gaze straight ahead. "You don't owe me an explanation. I get it. I'm not your type. But, then, what the hell was that kiss all about?"

He grabbed her arm and spun her around yet steadying her at the same time. "No, you *don't* get it." He dragged her over to the side, out of the way of the other passengers and their roller bags.

"It *is* me, Emma, not you. Ye're great." He ran a hand through his hair. "I promised myself that I wouldn't take another woman to bed unless she's . . ." The rest of the sentence seemed to have gotten caught in his mouth. "I have to be in a committed relationship now for me to . . ."

Pain contorted his face, and she wanted to console him. Which was in complete contradiction to the pain *he was causing her*.

He continued. "I've made a vow to change, don't ye see? For me now, sex and commitment have to go hand in hand."

Was that supposed to make her feel better, saying he wasn't interested in a committed relationship with her?

Not to mention that she wanted to have a right good romp in the sack just when the rogue had decided to become a choirboy. *Literally.*

"I'm sorry, Emma."

"Please. Life is full of little disappointments."

He gently pushed her shoulder back against the wall, trapping her there. He bent his tall stature to her level, making eye contact, searching her face. "But if there were any other way . . ."

She stepped out from his large hands. "You can't do that, Gabriel. You can't just seduce me with your eyes and not expect me to want you back."

Anger crossed his face. "I could say the same of you, lass."

"Maybe you should've sent someone else to pick me up from the airport."

"Maybe." He slung her bag over his other shoulder. "But you're stuck with me. Get over it."

Everything had gotten turned upside down. Moments ago, she'd been happy to be back in Scotland. Thrilled to see him. But in a matter of minutes, she wished she were anywhere but here.

They walked to the Land Rover in an uncomfortable silence. It didn't get better once they were in the vehicle. He looked like he couldn't be rid of her fast enough. Deposit her at the quilting dorm. Steer clear of her at all costs. Now and forever. Amen.

She didn't know why it hurt so much. Egghead Emma should've known better than to open up and let him in. She'd given him a wide berth for the past ten years. What was another decade without him?

Just thinking about Gabriel's easy smile not being in her life made her physically ill.

"Pull over," she said.

He did, bringing the auto to a stop. She stumbled out, leaned against the car, and sucked in the cold Highland air.

He came up beside her and laid a hand on her back. "What can I do to help?"

She shook her head, afraid to say anything lest a sob escape from her soul. After a long minute she spoke. "I'm okay." *I'm not.* "Let's get to Gandiegow."

Back in the car, he wouldn't leave her alone. "Is it your stomach? Your head?"

"It's probably jet lag."

"Tell me where it hurts," he insisted. "How am I supposed to diagnose you if you won't talk to me?"

"I don't want to be diagnosed. Just drive." She was afraid of what it really was and refused to name it. She didn't believe in love—at least not in the way that others blindly accepted its existence. Emma believed in cold, hard facts. And the fact was that Claire and Dominic had the only healthy relationship she'd ever seen.

"Ha," she said bitterly. Look at the Russos now.

"What?" Gabriel said.

"Leave me be." She closed her eyes and laid her head against the window. A tear slipped out. She quickly brushed it away before it went down her cheek.

"Ah, bluidy hell," he muttered. "I made you cry."

Like a flash, her emotions shifted from hurt to *I'm going to strangle him if he utters another word.* "You've gone batty. Maybe your guilty conscious is making you see things."

"What do I have to be guilty of? Having principles?"

"No, for leading me on." For kissing her like he wanted her. For making her fall for him and his bloody charms. *Wanker.* Then she got madder. "Are you trying to imply that I don't have principles?"

He raised a knowing eyebrow.

"Hell and damnation," she muttered. *Claire must've told Dominic, and Dominic must've told Gabriel about the made-up trysts.* Her embarrassment knew no bounds. He wouldn't believe her denials, so she decided to use those stories for their intended purpose—as her shield. "You're so right," she said. "Best not to get mixed up with me, big boy. I've had a lot of men to compare you to. You might not measure up."

Oh, my mother would be so proud of me right now, Emma thought. She hated herself for playing this part, for humiliating herself—once again. But her days of being honest with Gabriel were over.

Gabe gripped the steering wheel so hard, it was a wonder it didn't crumble. He glared at the road in front of him. Now he was the one to feel ill. He'd always thought Claire's stories about Emma were totally exaggerated. For the first time, he could see that Emma Castle was indeed her mother's daughter. He had to believe it now— Emma always told him the truth, no matter what. He had to accept that she honestly didn't believe in love. She was only interested in sex for sex's sake.

He finally had to face his own truth, and it had been coming for some time now. He'd been trying to turn sophisticated, worldly Emma Castle into a sweet Scottish lass. It wouldn't work. Now he had to stop trying. He wished Emma well, but he had to let her go.

But how could he do that? He'd grown attached to her, and life without her would be like losing his leg. *Or my heart.*

Well, as long as Emma was in Gandiegow, he would just have to stay busy helping others, more than ever before. He'd be so booked that he wouldn't have time to notice her, to see how beautiful she looked, or worry about what she was doing. He wouldn't have time to miss her at all. Emma would be just another one of the quilting ladies, as far as he was concerned.

Satisfied, he turned on the radio and sang along. When they arrived in Gandiegow, he took Emma's things to the quilting dorm but remained aloof, thinking about all the things he could do with his time now that he wouldn't be spending it with her.

Ross and Ramsay would help him scrounge up more work on the boats. Then there was always the factory. Surely the McDonnell could give him more to do.

Staying busy would be just the thing to get Gabe's priorities back in line and help him to forget about his damnable crush on Emma Castle.

Chapter Sixteen

Claire sighed resignedly, resting her head in her hands and watching Emma at the next table over. For the past two days, Emma had sat there like some lovesick seal whose mate had swum off without her. She kept staring at the door to Quilting Central, even though Gabriel had left some twenty minutes ago.

And it irked, really irked her that Dominic had been right about Emma having a thing for Gabriel. Claire thought she'd never see the day when Emma Castle would be cowed by love. If it wasn't love, it sure was one helluva crush. Emma had been moping around ever since returning from New York. So much so, in fact, that she'd barely questioned Claire about her supposed disappearance.

Claire had been wrong about Gabriel, too. He seemed to be in just as much a state over Emma, although he hid it well by keeping his distance from all of them.

How had Dominic seen it before her? Had Dominic always been this astute when it came to matters of the heart? She'd certainly never given him credit in the emotional department. Maybe she was the bonehead and not him.

Moira slipped in beside her. "Hey, Claire."

Claire frowned at Emma a second longer, then gave Moira her complete attention. "What's up?"

"I wanted to say something about Dominic." Moira spoke so quietly that Claire wasn't sure she'd heard right.

"What about him?" She couldn't share one of his secret recipes; he'd chop her in two. She also didn't feel like talking about her husband, as chagrined as she felt now.

"I know folks were upset about what he said to ye. But in good conscience I have to say I think he's a remarkable man. I'm ever so grateful for all he's done for us. I thought you should know."

"What do you mean *all he's done*?"

"The way he's been feeding the village." Moira kept her eyes glued to the lint on her jeans. "He's helped so many of us that I'm sure we'll have a better Christmas because of him."

Claire felt like a heel. Yes, she was the bonehead. Why had she tried to punish him?

"Ye're a lucky woman, Claire Douglas Russo. It's more than me that's sayin' it." Moira stood up. "I'd better go. My da is expecting me."

Claire gaped at her. Moira was quiet, but she sure had a way of getting her point across. Claire realized that even if she couldn't save her marriage, she had to fix things between the village and Dominic. She didn't know how to go about it without being skewered by the villagers, but she would have to come up with a plan. Claire grabbed her coat and headed back to the restaurant.

She found Dominic in the storeroom, taking inventory on a yellow pad. She wasn't surprised to see him; his pig was sleeping in his box in the back corner of the kitchen. She grabbed her white pad and began making a list of the things she needed for her scones, keeping one eye on Dom.

He glanced over at her. "Have you given any thought to what I said about Gabe and Emma?"

"Aye." Why did he only want to talk of them?

"Gabe has turned as pleasant as a riled polar bear this past week. Do you know what's going on?" He gave her a pointed look like she had been the one to upturn the sugar canister.

She waved him off. "I didn't do anything. Emma's not saying much, either. She's been too busy moping. She said something about being on opposite sides but wouldn't elaborate."

Dom put down his pad and fully turned to her. "Maybe it's time you and I stepped in. If we can get them to work together, then maybe they can work out their differences and Gabe will be tolerable again."

"What do you have in mind?"

"Let me call Amy first. To see if she'll help. She owes me. Then we'll work out the details."

Claire smiled. It was the first time in a while that she'd seen the old gleam in her husband's eyes. Not for her, mind you, and it hurt that she wasn't the one who'd put it there. But the truth was that she wanted Dominic to be happy—whether she made him that way or not.

Emma sat across from Mattie at the dining room table in the quilting dorm. He put his hand in the fabric bag again and drew out another old-fashioned key.

"Is it the key to one of your happy words?" She was thrilled to have come up with this game, because Mattie seemed to have taken to it. There was no pressure; he could decide whether to speak or not.

He smiled at her, holding the key in the air. "Grandda," he said quietly.

"Is the magic-key game your favorite?"

He nodded. He'd said seven words this session, using all the keys. Next time they met, she'd tell him the magic keys were so magical that they could be used over and over again in the same session.

Cait helloed from the door and came into the dining room with Dingus pulling on the leash. "Are you ready to go, little monkey?"

Mattie threw himself at her while Dingus jumped up on him. "Mama," he said.

Cait gasped and hugged him back, then looked over at Emma, mouthing *Thank you.* "Get your coat," she said to Mattie. "Can you let Dingus run a little outside while I talk to Miss Emma?"

Mattie smiled up at her, but before he grabbed his coat, he threw himself at Emma, too. She caught him in a hug. This boy was the one bright spot in her life. Her mother had been wrong about children; they were a blessing, not a hindrance. A minute later, Mattie was out of her arms and out the door.

Cait took Mattie's chair. "I don't know what to say. I knew you'd help him, but I never imagined he could make this much progress so quickly."

Emma beamed at her. "I know. It's remarkable. He said seven words today. Including *grandda.* Will his grandfather make it home for Christmas?"

Cait took Emma's hand and squeezed it. "I've got to tell you something about his grandfather."

God, Emma hoped it wasn't bad news. Mattie had had enough sorrow in his life.

Cait smiled at her. "Don't worry. It's just a secret, one that few people know."

"Okay."

"Mattie's grandda is Graham Buchanan."

Emma tried to process her words. Surely she'd heard wrong. *Graham Buchanan?* "As in the movie star? No."

"Aye. He's working on a film in New Zealand and will be home in a week."

"No," Emma said again. "Here in Gandiegow?"

"Yes."

"But no one's said a word. Not Claire. Not Dominic." *Not Gabriel.* "No one."

"Because we all protect him." Cait laughed as if that statement was an inside joke. "But the news is coming out. I wrote Graham's biography and the book will be out next year. And to keep the disruption to a minimum for Gandiegow, when the book is released, Mattie and I will join Graham in New Zealand while the clamor dies down." She gave Emma's hand another squeeze. "Can I count on you to keep our secret, too?"

"Heavens, yes. Gladly." Emma understood what it was like to live in a famous family, and she wouldn't wish it on anyone. "But if it's been kept a secret for so long, why let it out of the bag?"

"Graham made that decision for a lot a reasons. I agree with him that it's best to do it this way, where we can control when and how it happens. And prepare for it. I knew you'd understand." She gave her hand one more squeeze and then stood. "I'd best go find out what those two ragamuffins are up to."

"Cait?" Emma said. "I think that boy of yours is special."

"I know." Cait shot her one more smile and then left.

Emma barely got a contented sigh in when her phone beeped. *So much for basking in the moment.* She checked the text. *Amy.*

I really need help. I'm struggling with depression. Come in when you get here.

Postpartum depression could take down the best of them. Emma rose and limped across the room to get her coat.

Within minutes, she was out the door, hurrying down

the boardwalk as fast as she could. Since returning from New York, she'd hobbled to the restaurant in the morning for her tea and scones; then she would rush off to Quilting Central to work on the Gandiegow Doctor quilt. Not that she particularly wanted that task, but she had agreed to do it. She might be a liar, but she wasn't a shirker. Unfortunately, as soon as she would get her sewing machine turned on and her pieces lined up, one of the villagers would invariably come over, sit down, and bend her ear. She'd counseled Mrs. Bruce about dealing with one of her strong-willed children. She'd spoken with Freda confidentially about how to love another when that love wasn't returned. She'd encouraged Maxie to talk to her husband about their bedroom problems instead of sweeping them under the rug. Emma knew Quilting Central wasn't the best place to practice psychology. She'd joked to herself that if the villagers didn't quit soon, she'd have to find a spare building and set up proper office hours instead.

The trek to Amy's gave her too much time to think. Emma had only gotten a few glimpses of Gabriel—at a distance as he went into the doctor's surgery, or those rare times when he came into Quilting Central either to work on the long-arm quilting machine or to find one of the villagers. It was always painful to see him. But it hurt even more that he was avoiding her, never meeting her eyes, and certainly offering no words to her, kind or otherwise.

She arrived. Emma knocked on Amy's door and went in as instructed. She looked around. The baby was asleep in his cradle beside the bed. Emma saw Amy slide a magazine under the covers and don an unhappy, faraway expression. Her first impression? That Amy had not only misdiagnosed herself, but that there was mischief afoot. She walked over to the bed and sat down beside her.

"What's going on?" Emma said. "How are you feeling?"

"I'm just so depressed." The cheerful Amy was a terrible actor. "You know, with Coll being gone and all."

Emma knew Claire had arranged around-the-clock help for Amy and that things had been going well. Amy had even ventured out several times to the store by herself and to Quilting Central. She wasn't depressed—she was up to something. Emma could feel it in her bones.

There was a knock at the door, and Gabriel came in. He looked just as surprised to see Emma as she was to see him.

Amy popped up out of bed. "Bathroom break." She hustled off to the loo.

Emma felt all jittery, like she was about to jump out of her skin.

Gabriel stood at the door, frowning. "I was told there was an emergency here."

She flipped her hair over her shoulder. "I fear it's nothing more than a little conniving by the natives."

"I see." He seemed to be soaking her in, but then his expression turned to stone. "I'll be going, then." He reached for the door handle but stopped. "Remind Amy about what happened when the boy cried wolf."

Emma opened her mouth to say that she would, but Gabriel was already gone.

Amy came out of the bathroom sheepishly. "I'm feeling better. I think I'll lie down while the babe is asleep."

Emma grabbed her coat and nodded, too afraid of what she might say. But once she was outside, she wondered who else might have been in on the plan to throw her and Gabriel together.

The next day, she went to Quilting Central earlier than usual, hoping to get more work done on the Gandiegow Doctor quilt. But instead of sewing, she had two separate hour-long conversations with Gandiegowans about their troubles. As she turned on her sewing machine, she received a text from the McDonnell.

Can you stop by the factory for a wee chat?

Emma was immediately suspicious, as she'd never had more than a *hallo* or a *goodbye* from the larger-than-life Scot. Especially after yesterday's debacle at Amy's. But she couldn't refuse him if he did indeed need her, could she?

When? she texted back.

The McDonnell wrote: Be here at two sharp, my afternoon break.

She checked her watch, then grabbed her coat.

"Where are you off to, missy?" Deydie stood over her with her hands on her hips.

Emma shut off her machine and rose. "I have an appointment at the North Sea Valve Company." She'd have to hurry if she was going to check out a car from the store and make it to the factory on time.

"I'll go with ye. I need to speak with Freda. She seems to be spending all her time there these days." Deydie waddled off after her coat.

Emma no longer needed her crutches, but she still wasn't completely back to normal. She and Deydie hurried to the store as fast as they could manage and got the Audi that Emma had taken to Inverness. Unfortunately, images of Gabriel sauntered through her mind—how safe she'd felt with him in his Land Rover behind her.

Good thing Deydie was there. She kept up a constant lecture. "If ye don't work harder on the doctor's quilt, we'll just have to bundle up the pieces of fabric for the doc on Christmas day, and a two-hundred-year tradition will be broken."

"I would be happy to work on it"—*that's a stretch*— "if you could run interference with your buddies. Have you not noticed? Everyone keeps distracting me from working on the quilt."

Deydie put her hand up like she didn't want to hear it. "Stop yere whining. We all have to multitask."

Emma started to tell her that she couldn't both sew and make eye contact with her patients.

She stopped cold. *Her patients.* She'd only been kidding before when she'd thought about setting up office hours. But something shifted. She really was providing a service for these people, helping them, but with that thought, panic settled in. Followed by terror.

No.

Her new career path could not include the title of *therapist*.

She'd sworn off therapy forever. If she did remain a therapist, then she would have to admit that she was her parents' daughter. *Bloody no.*

Deydie frowned at her. "What's wrong with you? Ye're as white as the backing on Bethia's Garden quilt. Didn't you eat?"

Emma bit her bottom lip. "I'm fine." She had to get the hell out of this town. They had her all topsy-turvy. Yes, that was what it was. It was all Gandiegow's fault.

At the factory, Ross met them at the door, looking a little shocked. "Well, this is a treat, Deydie. What can we do for you?"

"Out of my way, Ross. I'm here to speak to Freda." Deydie pushed past him and went through the big double doors.

"What a sweet temperament that ole woman has, eh?" Ross grinned and pointed to the doors. "The McDonnell is waiting for you in his office. I'll take you back."

Emma was led into the belly of the beast. The factory floor was littered with equipment, parts, and packaging, but Ross assured her that by spring the factory would be up and running.

"Ah, here it is." He opened the door for her and stood back. As soon as she crossed over the threshold, the door shut.

She turned around to see what was going on and from the other side of the door came a scraping sound, like a large metal cabinet being dragged in front of the door, blocking it. "What in bloody hell . . ."

"Ah, shit," a familiar baritone burr said from within the office.

She spun around and dropped her purse as Gabriel's head peeked out from under the desk.

"What are you doing here?" She bent down to pick up her personal items scattered on the floor between them.

He reached for her wallet at the same time she did, and they almost conked heads.

"I'm here because the McDonnell asked me to check the cables under his desk." Gabriel picked up a couple of her pens and a pad of paper from the floor. "I believe someone is trying to bring us together, Emma. First Amy and now the McDonnell. The SOB."

"How are we going to convince them that their efforts are in vain? Whoever they may be?" She snatched a tampon from under the desk before Gabriel got to it and shoved it back in her purse.

"I don't know." He picked up her hairbrush and dropped it in with the other contents.

They both stood. But when he handed over the last item—her lip gloss—their fingers accidentally brushed together. His eyes met hers, and in that moment, she knew their hiatus from each other was over. Like the fibers of twisted yarn, their fingers intertwined while they gazed at each other. Something ignited then. They became like a lit match to dry tinder.

He pulled her into his arms as she dropped her purse to the desk. She fisted his sweater in her hands and pulled him down to her lips for a long, overdue, smoldering kiss.

She thought she'd died and gone to heaven. Even heard the choir singing.

But it wasn't a choir. *Those are voices yelling.*

She heard the metal cabinet scraping away from the door. She did push away from him then as the door swung open.

"Doc!" yelled Ross. "It's Ramsay. His arm! He's bleeding everywhere."

Instantly Gabriel reached in his pocket and pulled out his keys. He thrust them in Emma's hand and said, "Get my medical bag out of the Land Rover." He rushed off, following Ross.

Emma ran from the office as best she could in her Aircast. When she came back with the doctor's bag, she found a group huddled around Ramsay, who was leaning over a long conveyor in the center of the factory floor.

"Emma, set the bag beside me."

Gabriel seemed in control and in command.

"Can you hand me items as I need them?" He didn't wait for her answer as he pulled out rubber gloves and shoved his hands in them. He examined Ramsay's arm. "Saline solution first."

Emma handed it to him and he poured it into the wound.

"Oh, mother ducker, that's cold," Ramsay said, gritting his teeth.

The McDonnell brought him a chair. "Sit. You look a little pale." He placed a box under Ramsay's arm to catch the blood and brought another chair. "For you, Doc."

"Is he going to be all right?" Ross asked.

Ramsay looked up at his brother and gave him a weak smile. "Stop yere fashing like an old hag. I'll be fine. It's just a wee cut."

To Emma, it didn't look *wee* at all. The gash was long and deep, ugly, angry tissue bulged out as Gabriel continued to flush the wound with solution.

"Ye're the clumsiest oaf I've ever seen," Ross said, clearly worried for his brother.

"Shut yere trap," Ramsay said, grinning over his shoulder.

Without looking up, Gabriel asked, "How did it happen?"

"I dropped my wrench and put my arm through the conveyor trying to catch it. Unfortunately, while it was running."

"Gauze, Emma," Gabriel said.

She handed it to him and he patted the area dry.

"My suture kit is in the inside pocket."

Ross paced back and forth. "Och, most fishermen get tangled up in the nets, but not my brother. He's bested by a conveyor."

She located the kit and noticed the McDonnell, Deydie, and Freda wiping blood from the equipment.

Gabriel reached in the bag and pulled out two vials and a syringe. "Lidocaine and something to keep it from burning." He turned away from Ramsay as he partially filled the syringes, as if his full-grown patient couldn't handle the sight of a needle. Then Gabriel injected both along the edge of the laceration. He discarded his rubber gloves, put on new ones, then organized his equipment.

"Will it leave a scar?" Ramsay asked. "Scars are pure gold with the women."

Ross swatted him hard on the back. "Ye'll never change, will ye?"

"Yes, you'll have a scar. Now hold still." Gabriel went to work, sewing up Ramsay's arm with stitches held together with little knots.

Deydie hovered, watching avidly. Gabriel had to ask her repeatedly to step out of his light.

"Those are some nice stitches there." Admiration resounded through Deydie's scraggly voice. "Stitches as even as any quilter's."

Gabriel spoke to the McDonnell. "Can you get Ramsay some water? He'll need it to take an antibiotic now."

"I'll not need it, Doc," Ramsay said. "I'm tougher than nails."

"Ye're a sissy," Ross scoffed.

"Ramsay, you'll do as you're told. Keep those sutures dry. And stay off the boat." Gabriel made it sound as if there'd be an ass kicking if he didn't follow his orders to the letter.

"Aye," Ramsay acquiesced.

"I'll make sure of it," Ross concurred.

"Good." He turned toward Emma and pointed to a box in the bag. "Can you get the bandages for me?"

She nodded. She'd never thought of being a nurse before, but she liked being his. She found the small box of sterile dressing and handed it over. Within a few minutes, Gabriel was done. He wrote down directions on how to care for the wound and made Ramsay promise to call tonight if there were any problems.

"Ross, drive him home," Gabriel finished.

"I think we've had enough excitement for one day." The McDonnell shoved the last of the bloody paper towels into a garbage bag. "Let's see if the pub will open early for us."

"Good idea," Ramsay said, grinning despite the blood staining the front of his shirt and pants.

"Not you." Gabriel glared at Ross. "Make him rest. I mean it. Tie him down, if need be."

Ross shook Gabriel's hand. "Ye're my kind of doctor."

Deydie was all beams for the doc, as well. "The first round's on me."

The Gandiegowans' mouths opened in shocked amazement.

The McDonnell found his voice first. "In all the years I've known ye, ye've never offered to buy a round of drinks."

She frowned at each one of them. "I'm only paying for the four of ye, not the whole village." She patted her pocket. "Quilting has been damned good to me this year. And I think we could all use a dram."

"Sure," Gabriel said, smiling back at them.

Emma had the distinct feeling things were going to get better now for Gabriel. Who would've guessed that to be accepted as the town's doctor, all you had to do was know how to wield a needle—and get the nod from the head quilter.

Gabe left the factory, driving the short distance back to Gandiegow alone in the old Land Rover. He felt conflicted, elated, and confused. It felt so good and so right to hold Emma in his arms and to finally kiss her again. But was that only because he'd made her the forbidden fruit?

He wanted a woman who was easy to be around, with no baggage to overcome. A sweet, small-town Scottish lass, not a Brit who had a condo in Los Angeles. Emma didn't fit the bill. She was London—pedicures and the shopping scene. He was dirt under the nails and a whisky by the fire. They belonged to two different worlds. *But that London girl sure knows how to kiss.*

He pulled into the parking lot with the others. Deydie and Emma got out of the Audi. Ross helped his brother from their car. The McDonnell and Freda ambled over to Gabe.

"Doc?" Ramsay waved with his good arm. "Are ye sure I can't have just one drink?"

"Go home, Ramsay," Gabe said, joining the group.

Ramsay's color looked better, but it would still be a rough night for him.

The McDonnell pointed to the pub. "Ready to down a few?"

Gabe wondered if he should check in on Dom first. But when they walked into the pub, his foster brother was already at the bar.

Gabe joined him. "It's a little early for you to be here, isn't it?"

Emma and Deydie sidled up to Dominic, as well.

Dominic raised his glass to Gabe. "It's a good hiding place from the mammas. A guy needs a break now and then from babysitting."

"Aye. But what about the restaurant?" Gabe asked.

"I'll head back in a little bit," Dom said. "But you and I both know it's a lost cause. A few fishermen aren't going to turn the place around. If only Claire had been patient. If she hadn't told those lies, we might've been able to think of having a baby in a year or two. Now I don't see it happening." Dom shrugged, defeated.

Deydie grabbed Dom's arm and spun him to face her, scowling. "What lies?"

Gabe and Dom had finally found out from Ramsay what Claire had said to the quilters.

Dom frowned at Deydie. "It doesn't matter."

Deydie glared at him. "Matters to me. Are ye saying that ye're *not* worried about yere wife getting fat and becoming one of us old fishwives?" Her voice rumbled throughout the pub as the McDonnell and Freda joined them.

Dominic shook his head. "That's the farthest thing from my mind. Claire could weigh four hundred pounds for all I care. I wouldn't love her less."

Deydie prodded him more. "So, the reason you won't let Claire have a bairn has to do with money?"

"Yes. Can't raise a family without it." Dominic frowned, pausing a second. "And, to be truthful, I was worried I wouldn't be good with little ones. But the women, they say I have a gift."

Deydie's face was redder than Gabe's Santa cap. "I'm going to take my broom to that lass's backside, I am. Lyin' to us the way she did." Deydie dug in her pocket, pulled out pound notes, and slammed them on the bar. "Get some drinks. I have a debt to repay."

Claire hurried to Quilting Central on a mission. Emma and Gabriel should be well on their way to being back together by now, even though Claire hadn't heard a word from the McDonnell. Maybe Emma and Gabriel hadn't come up for air since being locked in his office. Now it was high time for Claire to quit thinking about them and straighten out her own mess. She had to come clean with the quilters of Gandiegow.

But when she walked in to Quilting Central, she felt something was wrong. Everyone looked up like normal, but instead of being happy to see her, they frowned. Some even glowered.

Deydie lumbered over to her, Bethia hot on her tail. "So have you come to tell us more of your stories?"

Claire had been ready to confess, but it was entirely another thing to have Deydie glaring at her with her mind already made up.

"I—I . . . " Claire tried.

"I—I, nothing," Deydie barked.

Bethia laid a hand on Deydie's arm. "That's enough. Give her a moment to collect her thoughts."

"Time to make up more lies, I'll wager," Deydie argued.

"I'm sorry," Claire managed. "I was coming here to tell you all the truth. I never meant to hurt anyone's feelings."

The others had ventured over. Rhona spoke up. "But is that how you feel about us fishwives?" The crowd leaned in for the answer. "Dowdy? Fat?"

Claire wanted to crawl under the nearest sewing table. She laid her hand on her stomach. "I'm worried, is all. Baking and tasting the scones every day are taking their toll. I'm afraid if I get pregnant, well, that I won't be able to lose the baby weight."

One or two nodded in understanding, but the majority of them shook their heads like they didn't believe her.

"I've been a dimwitted prat," she said. "I've not been a good wife to Dominic, and I've been a terrible friend to you." She gestured to the group. "I hope you'll forgive me."

"There will be consequences," Deydie said. "Consequences."

Deydie went to the hook by the door and grabbed her coat. All the other women followed, each one filing out of Quilting Central. Claire was left alone in the building, her tears sliding down her face. "I know there are consequences." Because she'd become the loneliest lass in the whole of Scotland.

She grabbed her coat and trudged off with no destination in mind. Once again she found herself outside of the church. She went straight to the sanctuary and sat in the front pew. For a long time she stared at the Advent candles, understanding their purpose to mark the coming of Christmas. This year, though, felt less like a celebration and more like a disaster.

"Need company?" Father Andrew asked.

She hadn't heard him approach. "Yes."

He sat in the pew beside her. "Do you want to talk or would you rather sit here quietly?"

"I could use a sounding board, if that's okay."

"Go on." He was a kind man.

"I don't know what to do," Claire said. "When we moved here, I was certain *now* was the time to have a baby. It's been more than a certainty; it's more like an obsession. I'm afraid if it doesn't happen soon, I'll never have Dominic's baby. But I just have to." It might've been the stillness of the church, but for the first time, Claire realized how frantic she sounded.

Father Andrew gave her an understanding look. "Sometimes what we want isn't exactly what we need."

She frowned. "I know. It's crazy. But I have such a foreboding that if I don't get pregnant, something terrible is going to happen."

"Oh?" Father Andrew said in invitation.

"It sounds completely irrational now that I've said it out loud. But I can't make the panic go away." But talking about it helped her get a grip on her feelings, more than she'd had since moving home. "No one should bring a baby into the world because of anxiety. How do I make it stop?"

Father Andrew gazed up at the cross hanging over the altar as if the answer lay there. Finally, he spoke. "We all get anxious but we don't always recognize the real reasons. Sometimes we have to dig deep to find the truth."

"But what do I do in the meantime while I'm figuring it out?" She was afraid she'd always feel like this, that the unsettling ache would never go away.

"Step into the light, Claire. Have you ever heard that

old saying '*Fear is a darkroom where negatives are developed*'? Have faith everything will turn out okay."

"Words are easy, Father. But living it is a whole other matter."

Father Andrew smiled. "Very true. But just give it a try. Send fear on a holiday. And while it's gone, clean house. Maybe when fear gets back, there won't be room for it in your life anymore. Maybe you'll have replaced it with other things."

"Like love?" She nodded toward him. "Thanks, Father."

As Gabe waited at the bar for his drink, he was more than a little conflicted. Kissing Emma in the McDonnell's office had been the most natural thing in the world. He couldn't have stopped himself, even if he'd wanted to. It scared the shit out of him that he had no control over himself where she was concerned. Maybe he would have to face the truth. His resolve meant nothing when it came to her. He could believe himself a big, strapping Scot all he wanted, but the truth was, whenever she was near, he was a pussy-whipped laddie. And she didn't even know how she affected him.

He stayed at the bar even after his drink was set before him. He knocked it back and ordered another. He glanced over at the table where the McDonnell was telling a raucous story to Freda, Dom, and Emma. Emma was laughing so hard that she was holding her stomach while her eyes filled with mirthful tears.

But he couldn't sit over here by himself forever. When his drink came, he stood to join the others like a man. A proud Scot.

The door to the pub flew open and Thomas burst in.

"Dominic," he said, "you're needed at the restaurant."

Dom jumped to his feet. "Is there a problem?"

"I'll say," Thomas said. "You have a crowd. Hungry quilters aren't the most patient and reasonable of people."

"What?" Dom said, rooted to the spot.

Thomas motioned for him to come. "If you know what's good for you, you'll get your arse over there. And you'd better bring help."

Gabe downed his drink and set his glass on the bar, feeling a sense of relief. Today wasn't the day to let his principles fly to the wind after all. He felt good as he went to the door but caught something disturbing out of the corner of his eye—Emma was following Dom, too. Gabe should've expected it. Little Miss Priss would push up her sleeves and get messy—chopping vegetables, waiting tables, and anything else a good Scottish lass with a limp would do. *Dammit.*

At the restaurant, though, Emma's sprained ankle sequestered her to a stool in the kitchen with a knife and a pile of garlic and onions. Dominic put Gabe to work right next to her, chopping tomatoes for the next batch of homemade sauce. Even though it was painful to be so close to Emma and not touch her, it was worth the large smile on Dominic's face. To be making food for the whole village again made his brother happy. And Gabe, too. But . . . he could smell the peach scent of her shampoo from where he stood. *For the luvagod, how many different, good-smelling shampoos does she own?*

"What's wrong?" Emma said. "Why are you frowning?"

He wouldn't look over; he was the moth to a flame when it came to her. He kept his head down and sliced. "Nothing. I'm just concentrating." Only a few hours ago—before Ramsay's accident—Gabe had held her in his arms and kissed her, *really kissed.* But he still had no answers. He moved farther down the counter, away from her. After a few moments, even that was too close. He took off his apron and threw it on the counter.

"I'm going to go check on Ramsay." He practically sprinted to the door.

Dom watched Gabe leave the kitchen, worried about him. Emma looked like she might cry, and Dom was sure it had nothing to do with the onions.

At that moment, Claire slunk in and took up her old spot in his kitchen as the sous chef. He didn't comment on it, but he hadn't gotten over what she'd done to him and the restaurant. When Emma hobbled off to the storeroom, Dom cornered his wife.

"Those two are still miserable," Dom said. Claire looked miserable, too, but he did his best to ignore it. "I have a new plan."

"Sure. Why not?" Claire said tonelessly.

"These are drastic times." Dominic laid fresh basil on the chopping block. "You and I should help alleviate the stress between them."

"How's that?" She passed him the olive oil.

"Because we've been at odds, they've had to take sides. We don't have any choice left. We'll have to pretend we're back together for their sake. Act like we've patched things up. It's the only way to get those two back on the same page."

She lit up. "Does that mean ye're moving back to the flat?"

"Yes, but it doesn't mean I'm giving in, Claire."

Her face fell. "Okay. So, what do you get out of this?"

"I want Gabe to be happy. Those two belong together. He loves her."

"Well, Emma definitely has feelings for him." Claire chewed on her lip. "Though she's too afraid of love to admit it."

"Then you'll help me with this?"

"Aye."

"Good. We'll break it to them tonight after we close. We'll have to *act* like we're back together. Can you do that?"

"Fine." Claire shoved the garlic bread in the oven.

"Thanks," he said.

"Yeah, I'm a real peach."

Chapter Seventeen

Gabe stared at the text message from Dom.

Come to the restaurant. I need help.

Gabe felt a little guilty. He hadn't come back for the dinner rush. He'd had an excuse—checking Ramsay's injury. But then he'd stayed for dinner at the Armstrongs', at the insistence of the brothers three. But staying away had served Gabe's purposes more than his patient's— Ramsay was doing fine. Gabe, on the other hand, wasn't. Every time he had to be near Emma and couldn't touch her, it felt like he was taking a scalpel to the chest.

He grabbed his coat and left to see what Dom needed, hoping to God Emma was gone for the evening.

When Gabe rounded the corner of the building, though, he spotted her arriving at the restaurant's door, too. Her beautiful green eyes turned suspicious as he got closer.

He reached for the knob. "What are you doing out and about?"

"I've been summoned." She held up her phone.

"Me, too."

He gazed at her plaid-booted feet. "I see you're out of your Aircast and keeping warm."

"You didn't add *and being sensible*." She said the last mimicking his deep voice. She tilted her head to the side and smiled. One gloved hand touched his arm and she spoke quietly. "I have to admit that the doctor was right. Here in Gandiegow, sturdy boots are much safer than heels. No matter how stylish those heels are. Thank you for my new boots. I'm very fond of them." She clunked the heels together like they were Dorothy's ruby slippers.

His heart gave a little jolt. It wasn't the first heart palpitation he'd had around her, either. In fact, it had become quite the habit. He didn't need an EKG, but he needed something. "Don't mention it." He sucked in a deep breath, getting his bearings, and opened the door. "Shall we?"

She passed through. But when they stepped into the empty dining area, Dom wasn't there.

"Kitchen?" Emma asked.

"Let's go see."

Halfway across the room, Gabe saw Claire's head appear through the crack of the swinging double doors, then vanish. There were whispering voices, then shuffling.

"What in the name of Prince Albert . . ." Emma had the same quizzical look on her face that he imagined was on his.

They advanced across the dining area. Gabe held open the swinging doors, but she stopped so suddenly, he ran into her. He peeked over and saw—Claire and Dominic were in a clinch, kissing.

Grinning, Gabe turned to Emma to see if she was as elated as he. Surprisingly, she was frowning.

"Why can't you be happy for them?" he whispered as he stepped around her and went farther into the room.

"Well, it's about damn time," Gabe said.

The Russos broke apart.

"So you two are back together, huh?" Emma's voice held sarcasm and misgiving. Gabe didn't understand why she didn't believe it.

"Aye." Claire wiped her swollen red lips.

"I have to check the sauce." Dom looked uncomfortable, not meeting any of their eyes.

Hell, Gabe understood. *What man likes being caught in the act? Even tough guys get embarrassed.*

"So, how did this happen?" For the tone Emma gave them, she might as well have been wearing a white wig and holding a gavel in her hand. "Worked out all your problems?"

Gabe wanted to shake Emma; she was seriously starting to ruin his good mood. He spoke to her firmly. "I think that's obvious, *luv*. These two have decided to bury the hatchet."

"Aye," Claire agreed.

"The hatchet," Emma murmured. The expression on her face said she saw a handle sticking out of someone's back. "And you, Dominic?" She pinned him with her accusing tone. "You've decided it's time to have a baby, then?"

Dom glanced up at his name but quickly went back to the sauce.

Ah, hell. Gabe was starting to get a clue, too, but he wasn't giving up hope just yet.

"We're still working through the issues. But we're getting there." Claire sounded a little unsure of herself, but she'd jumped in and defended her husband, which was a good sign.

"You're moving back home, Dom?" Gabe said.

Claire looked desperate, and Dominic shifted uneasily. He glanced over at his wife, not smiling. "Yes, Gabe. You'll have the doctor's quarters all to yourself again."

Emma grabbed Gabe's arm and dragged him into the dining area.

"Why, Emma?" he said, once they were alone. "Why aren't you happy for them?"

"If they're telling the truth about being back together, then I'm the Queen of England."

Gabe leaned against the counter. "Listen, Your Royal Highness, it's a start. You know as well as I do that changing one's behavior can change one's thought patterns. Sometimes pretending you like someone can turn into the truth."

She frowned at him but wouldn't give him an inch.

"With my da being a pastor, I grew up under the scrutiny of a lot of people. Most of them were friendly, but some were downright busybodies. Da knew the parishioners were driving me crazy. One day he sat me down and gave me this spot-on advice: 'Just pretend. Treat each one like you care for them. Like they're a close friend. One day, you'll wake up and find that you're no longer pretending.'"

She sat on one of the barstools and swiveled away from him. Gabe swiveled her back.

He squatted down to her eye level. "I don't care if Dominic and Claire's problems are ironed out or not. I only care that they are at least trying. Dom moving back to the flat is a good start."

"It's a lie, though."

"I feel the same way you do about lying." He brushed back the hair from her face. "At least you and I are always square with each other. No lies here." He motioned to the space between them.

A funny look crossed her face, but he chose to ignore it. He felt too happy about the Russos' progress. He wouldn't let her suspicion ruin it.

"And what about the strange 'setups' over the last few

days, pushing us together? I'm sure those two have been behind it. It's ridiculous, isn't it?"

"I don't know. But let's go back to my place, pop open a bottle of champagne, and discuss it there," he suggested. "I want to take a look at your ankle, anyway." And because he wasn't a saint, but a mere mortal man, he thought of other parts of her body he'd like to examine, too.

He didn't give her a choice about coming with him. He took her hand and helped her to her feet. At that moment, something changed. It was as if a spotlight had landed on Emma or as if for the first time he saw the truth.

I don't want a Scottish lass.
I want this English filly.

He wanted a relationship with Emma Castle—prim-and-proper Emma. He'd avoided his feelings for her long enough. Ten years too long. He wanted to dive in and see where the two of them would end up. He cared about Emma and planned to show her just how much. To hell with her cynicism about love. To hell with how many men she'd had in her bed. It didn't matter one whit. What mattered was their future together.

He didn't let go of her hand but stood gazing into her eyes. He wouldn't tell her right here and now how he felt, but he knew it flowed from him, because she stared back at him in wonder. For a long moment they stood like that. But they must've inched closer together, because he was leaning down to kiss her, to really kiss her—with everything he felt, playing no games, with no hesitation—when the front door to the restaurant burst open.

"Just the man I was looking for."

Gabe turned and found Father Andrew grinning at him. Gabe pulled away from Emma but held on to her elbow, not letting her get away.

"We're going caroling and we need our favorite baritone." Father Andrew held the door wide for the group of Gandiegowans who filed in behind the Episcopal priest.

"It's a beautiful night," Ailsa said.

"A beautiful night," Aileen echoed.

Gabe looked down at Emma. "What do you say?"

"Do you have any songbooks?"

Ailsa skipped over to Emma, producing a small booklet from her pocket. "I have one right here."

Emma thanked her and took it.

"Hold on to my arm for support," Gabe advised. "I still want you to keep as much weight off that ankle as possible." He leaned down and kissed the top of her head. He just couldn't help himself.

They bundled up, and Dom and Claire waved to them as they set off. Gabe couldn't have been happier; he'd never felt more blessed in his whole life. He'd finally found that special woman he'd been hoping for. Funny that it'd been Emma all along.

They walked through town, stopping at each house. They were greeted warmly, sometimes with a Christmas cookie or a hot cocoa. More often than not, one or all of the inhabitants of the house would grab their coats and join them. They were quite a crowd by the time they were finishing up. With Emma walking and singing beside him, he felt completely content with the world.

Finally, they ended up at the pub, cold but happy. At the bar, the bartender filled shot glasses with Glenfiddich. Gabe was in high spirits. He couldn't wait to take Emma back to his place and tell her how he felt, and then kiss her until she had the exact same feelings for him.

As Father Andrew raised his glass in a toast, two bundled-up strangers stepped into the pub. At the same moment, Emma paled to the color of frost. Gabe grabbed her arm, afraid she might wilt further.

"What's wrong, lass?" he said, pulling her in to his side.

She nodded in the newcomers' direction. "My parents."

He looked again and, sure enough, he recognized Eleanor Hamilton and Dean Castle. They were older than they appeared on television—probably because there were no makeup artists nearby. Also, it was hard work traveling to the northeast coast of Scotland in the dead of winter.

"What are they doing here?" Emma mumbled. She left his side and wove her way toward them.

He went after her. He'd saved her once before from them and he intended to do it again.

There were no hugs and no pleasant expressions of love from the parents to the daughter. Gabe noticed Emma had plastered a fake smile on her face for them. He came up beside her and rested his hand on her back for support.

Eleanor held out a stack of papers. "We brought another copy of the contract. We needed to make sure it reached you safely."

Eleanor said it as though Scotland was a jungle inhabited by savages. Maybe she was right, considering how protective he felt for Emma right now. She seemed to be shrinking before his eyes.

He stepped in front of her and held out his hand to Dean. "Dr. Gabriel MacGregor. Special friend to your daughter."

Emma had enough gumption left to kick him discreetly in the calf.

Dean eyed him closely. "I see." But he finally took Gabe's hand and shook it.

Gabe turned to Eleanor and made sure his brogue was thick as haggis for her benefit. "I've seen ye're show." If she thought he was going to follow that up with a compliment she was mistaken. He put out his hand to her to see if she would take it. "Nice to meet ye."

Eleanor eventually offered her fingertips for him to shake.

"Shall we go someplace quiet?" Gabe gestured toward the door.

"That won't be necessary." Eleanor stepped around Gabe, thrusting the papers out again. "We just need you to sign this, Emma."

"Mum, I've been too busy to go over it." Emma looked worn-out and her emotions were ragged.

"I assure you that everything is in order," her mother insisted.

"Here. Let me hold those." Gabe relieved the papers from Eleanor's grasp. "Since you don't want to talk, we'll be on our way. I need to examine Emma's ankle at my office."

Stiffly, Eleanor adjusted the fingers of her gloves in an effort to remove them.

"Will you stay the night?" Emma asked meekly. "I'm at the quilting dorm. There's plenty of room." She sounded like a hopeful child.

"Absolutely not." Eleanor sniffed. "We're needed back in London. The cabbie is waiting in the parking lot."

"About those papers," Dean said.

"Don't worry yereself," Gabe interjected. "I'll make sure she takes care of them."

Emma shot Gabe a disapproving look, for she must've figured out how he wanted her to take care of them—in the hearth with a blazing fire.

"There's a fax machine at Quilting Central," Emma offered weakly. "I promise to be in touch."

Gabe was proud of her that she didn't commit to signing them.

Eleanor drew back on her gloves. "This is important, Emma. You owe us." Without another word, she turned on her heels and walked out, with Dean close behind.

Gabe rolled the papers and shoved them in his coat pocket before slipping his arm around Emma's waist. He found her trembling. He leaned down and whispered into her ear, "Let's go back to my place."

She nodded, and he guided her to the door. Once outside, she looked up the walk that led to the parking lot. Her parents had already rounded the corner and were gone. Gabe squeezed Emma to him, trying to transfer his strength to her.

At the doctor's quarters, he let her in and followed her up the stairs. Now he would have the chance to tell her how he felt. And how he wanted to be closer to her. He waited until they were in the parlor, standing in front of the Christmas tree, directly under the mistletoe. As he opened his mouth to confess all, Emma threw herself into his arms, nearly tackling him, and kissed the holy holly out of him.

Chapter Eighteen

Emma kissed him with every ounce of her being and with everything she had. Kissed him to forget her miserable parents. Kissed him to forget the troubles between Claire and Dominic. Kissed him because it felt so incredibly good. She didn't care that he believed kissing her went against his principles. *To hell with his bloody principles.* She needed this. She needed him. She tugged at his flannel shirt and pulled it free.

As she undid the buttons, she kissed his chest and burned for access to all of him. She pushed his coat from his arms and let it fall to the floor.

In the back of her mind, she knew he could pull away at any moment, but he didn't. He kissed her back, slipping off her coat, as well, and cupping her breast. His lips went to her neck, feasting on her, so much so that he had her moaning.

"Take me to bed, Gabriel," she whispered breathlessly.

He didn't hesitate, but scooped her into his arms, kissing her passionately as he carried her to his room. He flipped on the light switch with his elbow and laid her on the bed. The room was sparse, the only real decoration the hunter green, brown, and red quilt she lay on. Deydie had pointed out this pattern to Emma—the Bear Claw. It was very masculine and suited Gabriel to a T.

He gazed down on her with more than lust in his eyes. He looked ready to pour his heart out to her, but she stopped him by reaching up and pulling him down for another kiss.

In the past, sex had been disappointing. Terrible, in fact. This time, she was determined it would be different. Every sex manual she'd ever read came to mind—the correct way to stimulate your partner and the best way to achieve the ultimate orgasm. But she didn't want to analyze every placement of her hands. Every thrust of her hips. She just wanted to feel. She pushed the sex manuals from her mind. All she would think about was having Gabriel inside of her, a part of her, if only for a short time.

But what if I screw it up?

The thought did her in. She pulled away and lay back on the bed, feeling stupid, awkward, and shy.

"Are you all right, lass?" He kissed her chin and stroked her cheek. "Did something happen? Ye don't seem as eager as a few minutes ago."

She couldn't tell him that she sucked at the whole bedroom scene. She wouldn't admit that the few times she'd gone to bed with men had been disastrous. She shook her head instead. "Just kiss me, Gabriel."

He did, slowly and thoroughly. Every caress of his tongue felt like a brand, as if he were marking her as his own. Once again she lost herself in him, in them. The rest of the world slipped away and felt inconsequential.

Never breaking the kiss, he ran his hand down her side, pulling her hips closer to him. He kissed her as he touched her through her sweater. He kissed her while the sweater came off. He kissed her as all their clothes fell away and they were naked. Somehow the magic he wove kept her from being embarrassed. She was only cognizant of how he was making her *feel*. Warm and safe, and at the same time burning up like a roaring fire. His hands loving her. His mouth tasting her. His arms holding her. She felt swirled up in him. She was no longer Egghead Emma and awkward in bed; she was pure emotion. Completely right with the world. *Wonderful*. Touching, feeling, and being with him were as important as the air she breathed.

She was dimly aware when Gabriel slipped on a condom; then he was poised above her, looking deep into her eyes. His gaze spoke of deep affection, a future together, and— *Oh, my God*— love. Emma had the urge to bolt, but he was pinning her down. Not against her will and not with his body. He held her there with the strength of who he was, his character. He wasn't scared, and his confidence bolstered her. She had to see this through, had to know how they would be together.

When he opened his mouth to speak, she was pretty certain he was going to say something she wasn't ready to hear. She wrapped her arms around his neck, closed her eyes, and kissed him into silence, urging him back to the business at hand.

Gabriel complied in the most delicious way. He entered her, and she almost died from the sheer bliss of it, the answer to her need almost too wonderful to endure. When she moved, fireworks lit up behind her eyes. She moved again and dared to look up at him. He gazed back at her in wonder and joined her in a slow rhythm, their bodies one, moving together.

He brought her to the edge, backed off, and brought her to the edge again. Every time she moaned, it looked like it would be his undoing. Every time she squeezed the sinewy muscles of his arms, she thought it would be her undoing. The joy and tension grew inside of her and she didn't recognize this woman who was giving everything to the man above her.

She heard herself murmuring his name over and over. He answered her pleas in a mixture of Gaelic and love words, so primal she understood perfectly what he said. Without warning, they came apart in each other's arms, the most exquisite experience of her life. She pulsed and hummed in places she never knew possible. She wanted to shout to the world what had just happened—she'd finally done it. Egghead Emma had had an orgasm! Gabriel's lovemaking had transformed her into a sensual creature. *Oh, sex is more than an act.* She finally understood all the hype. She gazed upon his beautiful face, the two of them suspended in time where no one else could reach them.

He rolled off her, pulled her close, and looked into her eyes. "I love you, Emma."

She froze. *Why the hell did he say that?* She scooted away from him, sitting up, feeling vulnerable and exposed.

"What are you doing?" He reached for her hand. "Lie back down."

She jerked away from him. "I'm looking for my clothes." She reached over the side of the bed and found her underwear.

"What's wrong with you?" he said.

She stopped and shook her head. "What's wrong with me? What's wrong with you?" Her pitch had risen and she sounded oddly like her mother in one of her rants. "You had to go and ruin it."

He sat up now, too. "What are you talking about?"

"What you said." She couldn't repeat it, not for all the crown jewels. "Everything was going along just fine and then—and then . . ." She couldn't finish.

"Then I told you *I love you*." He moved closer to her

and tried to pull her into his arms, even succeeded for a second. "I do love you, lass." He brushed back her hair. "Whether you want to hear it or not, it's the truth."

She wanted to put her hands over her ears and block it out. She couldn't believe it. She didn't dare fall for it. She didn't want to end up like one of her disenchanted couples—brokenhearted, arguing over who should've taken out the trash, exposing all their intimate details and problems to a stranger, with no hope of ever getting back that initial illusion of love. Look what had happened to Claire and Dominic, the happiest couple in the world.

"I don't believe you," Emma said.

He stiffened like she'd disputed his very being. "Oh, you'd better believe it." But there was more to his voice than anger. He seemed to have taken her statement as a challenge, the throwing down of the gauntlet, because he rose from the bed.

She grabbed the rest of her clothes and backed away from him. "I mean it, Gabriel. I can't do this. Sex is one thing. But love . . ." Her words trailed off.

He was stalking toward her. His nakedness only made him look more the warrior. She clutched her clothes to her chest and kept backing away until she butted up against the door. She could've made a run for it, but she was the rabbit who'd frozen in the wolf's sights. He stopped directly in front of her. He didn't lay a hand on her, but she felt firmly held in place just the same.

With hooded eyes, he gazed at her for a long moment. "I'm not discouraged, Emma. Ye're a smart woman. Ye'll come round to my way of thinking." The power, the certainty, the determination he emitted was intoxicating.

She shivered as if he'd caressed her. The clothes she held in her arms tumbled to the floor.

God help her, nothing could stop what she did next.

She wrapped her arms and legs around him, kissing him as she climbed onto his erection, joining them as if it was meant to be.

"Aye," he growled, with her bum firmly in his hands as he made love to her, using the door as leverage.

Afterward, he carried her to his bed and they made love again. Finally, he fell asleep. As he dozed, she lay in his arms, and every worry she'd ever had crowded in, making the king-sized bed feel too small.

It was one thing to have misgivings about love and commitment. That was enough to have her running from Scotland as fast as she could. It was a whole other matter to be an all-out liar. She'd had plenty of opportunity to set Gabriel straight about her sex life. But she'd been too weak to speak up and tell the truth. Now it was too late. She couldn't turn back the clock—admit all—or take back what they'd shared. Her only choice was to move forward.

Isn't that why I came to Gandiegow in the first place—to figure out what came next? To get unstuck? To move forward?

She hadn't come here to fall for the town's doc. Or to get her heart broken.

She'd come full circle, back to the original problem she'd encountered the moment she'd stepped foot in this town. The only way for her to leave and get on with her life was to do the one thing she swore she'd never do again: *marriage counseling.* If only she could bring Claire and Dominic back together, Emma would be free to go.

She slipped out of bed and left. It was three a.m. She knew where to find Claire: at the restaurant, baking scones. Emma stopped at the quilting dorm for a shower first. She pulled on a black turtleneck to cover the evidence of their lovemaking—the stubble burn to her neck and chest. She could do nothing about how she still tingled, how she could still feel Gabriel between her legs, making love so intensely that nothing else mattered. Emma only hoped that Claire was too busy baking to notice the glow on her face of being thoroughly loved.

On the way to the restaurant, Emma reviewed in her mind every technique she'd ever learned about marriage counseling. First she'd work with Claire alone, then with Dominic by himself. After that, she'd meet with the two together. Emma should get something resolved between them by Christmas—one way or the other. She looked up and found she was outside the church, the tall white steeple rising to the sky, the one she'd thought was a ship's mast on her first day here. Because she had nothing left to lose, she tried out a prayer on God, asking for wisdom while dealing with the Russos. "If that isn't what you have in mind," Emma said out loud, "then divine intervention would be grand." She trudged on.

Inside the restaurant, she found Claire in the kitchen, sifting the flour for the scones.

"Good morning," Emma said.

Claire jumped. "Holy shit, Emma, you scared me." She smiled at her then. "I'm glad ye're here. Wash your hands, then grab the butter from the cooler, will you?"

Emma pulled a clean apron from the hook before getting the cold butter to cut into the scones. As she went back in the kitchen, she got an idea of how to proceed.

"Claire, I've been thinking about your mother lately."

"Really?"

"I think it's being here in Gandiegow that's brought her to mind." It was the truth, but what Emma was really doing was pushing Claire a little, trying to get her on the path of self-examination and help her to figure out what was going on. Emma continued, "Your mum would've loved Quilting Central." She had been so like the other quilting ladies—open, loving, and meddlesome. Emma peeked to see if Claire had any kind of emotional reaction.

Claire stopped the sifting and looked up with a sweet smile on her face. "Yes, Mama would've been quite happy to be living here now. She loved to quilt."

"So, is it just me that's been thinking about her, or have you been, too?" Emma tried. Surely all of Claire's upheaval had to do with the loss of her mother and being back in Gandiegow.

"Yes and no. The one who's really been on my mind is my da."

"Really?" Emma said.

"It's the fishermen, ye see. They remind me so much of him. The way they talk. The way they saunter in here, all full of themselves. My da was just like them. And, oh, how Mama loved him."

"I remember her speaking of him. She clearly loved him very much."

"Aye." Claire rubbed her eyes with her sleeve and then grabbed the butter.

"What was he like?" Emma prodded gently.

Claire took a knife and sliced the butter into chunks above the sifted dry ingredients. "What I remember most is that he made my mama laugh. She always had a smile on her face back then."

Emma remembered Nessa later in life as calm and content, but not as a jovial sort of person, not with a constant smile on her face, like Claire. Or at least Claire before she came to Gandiegow.

Claire finished with the knife. "I never thought about it before, but I guess Mama really didn't smile and laugh as much after my da died." She frowned as she took the pastry cutter to the mixture.

Emma remembered what both Claire and Nessa had been like when they first came to live in the Hamilton household—grieving. Those were sad days. But Nessa seemed to put on a brave face and, after a while, she didn't seem as sad anymore.

Emma hated to do it, but she had to dig a little deeper, open the wound as it were, to get to the root of the problem. "Do you think that's why she never married again? Because she loved your father so much?"

Claire looked up with a thoughtful expression. "I think they were soul mates. I think she knew it wouldn't do any good to even look for another man. My da was her everything." She went back to her work and said the next sentence almost to herself. "Like Dominic is to me."

Emma put her arm around Claire and gave her a squeeze.

"I'm okay," Claire said, straightening. "I've spoilt things between Dominic and myself. I have to live with that."

Emma stepped away, giving Claire a few moments to process. She pulled the napkins from the dryer and began folding them.

Claire poured cream into the bowl and began stirring. "You know, Dominic reminds me of my da in some ways. He makes me laugh, just like my da did for my mother. Da was so vibrant and alive. I just couldn't believe it when they said he was gone." She turned toward Emma. "Did you know that he was only thirty-one when he died?" She shook her head. "Thirty-one."

Electricity shot through Emma, enough so that she froze while folding the napkins. She thought about her prayer in front of the church. Clearly, divine intervention was real. "What did you say?"

Claire frowned at her. "I said Da was only thirty-one when he died."

Emma took a deep breath. She'd been such an idiot. Why hadn't she seen it sooner? This was almost textbook. "Claire, how old is Dominic?"

Her friend's frown deepened. "Thirty-one."

Emma put the basket of napkins aside and pulled Claire to sit on a stool. "Do you think that's why you're so frantic about having a baby?"

Claire's eyebrows pinched together for a long moment. She reached up with a trembling hand and moved the hair out of her face. "Is that why I've been feeling this way, because I've been worried about losing Dominic?"

"I think only you can answer that." Emma believed there might even be more below the surface. Maybe Claire was playing out her mother's life by losing her husband in a whole other way. But Emma wouldn't say that. This was Claire's discovery and she had to find her own way through it. Good therapists were only guides, not the ones running the show.

Tears started running down Claire's face. "Emms, I think I wanted a baby so badly because I need a piece of Dominic in case the worst happens."

"So, you remember what Nessa used to say?" Emma asked gently. Claire had to be the one to say it.

"'*At least yere da will always be with me because I have you.*'" Claire said the words as if she were Nessa herself. She turned to Emma. "I forgot she used to say that. I forgot she used to say I was her greatest blessing. Do you remember?"

"Yes, I remember. Your mother was a good woman." Emma put her arm around Claire. "Just like her daughter." The two friends hugged for a long time, both of them grieving for Nessa all over again and hopefully healing some of the pain from the past.

After a while, Claire pulled away. "I've done enough blubbering. The scones aren't going to bake themselves."

"You go up and wash your face," Emma said. "I'll get these in the oven."

Gabe woke and realized Emma wasn't there. He stretched and climbed out of bed, not worried. For the first time since she'd come to Gandiegow, the lion in his chest felt tamed. Contented. It was all settled between them, no matter her skittishness or the fact that she'd slipped out of his bed. She'd be back. He meant to make it permanent.

He took a quick shower, dressed, and reached for his phone to text Dom his plans:

Off to Edinburgh to see Da for a few days. An early Christmas visit. Pass along the news of my whereabouts to the town.

He sent Emma a text message, too, not wanting to wake her, knowing she must be sleeping after the night they'd shared. He smiled at her shoes in the back of his closet as he pulled out his suitcase. *Already partially moved in.* She just didn't know it yet.

Aye, Gabe needed to spend time with his da, and at the same time, he almost couldn't bear to leave Emma here in Gandiegow. Especially now that they'd come to an understanding. But this couldn't be put off. He had to have a man-to-man talk with Casper MacGregor about Emma . . . and a certain opal ring.

Over the years, Da had tried to give him his mother's engagement ring, in the hopes Gabe would finally settle down and take a wife. Da had liked Emma when they met at Dom and Claire's wedding. Gabe was certain he'd approve.

In the depths of his heart, Gabe knew that Emma was the one. He'd meant what he said to her: He had no worries—he knew she'd come round.

They were perfect together. Now he only had to convince her to be his wife.

Chapter Nineteen

Emma sat behind the sewing machine at Quilting Central and picked up the final row of the Gandie-gow Doctor quilt, feeling great satisfaction that her part would soon be done. Then Deydie would finally get off her back. Bethia assured Emma the doctor's quilt would only need a day or so on the long-arm quilting machine. There was still plenty of time to get it finished for Christmas.

But this accomplishment didn't exactly alleviate the anxiety she felt—Gabriel had been away for almost a fortnight, and she missed him—even though she didn't want to. He'd gone to see his father, saying it was something he couldn't put off, and then he'd had to extend his stay to rebuild the engine on his dad's automobile—unplanned but necessary, he'd said in his voice mail. Day after day, he called or texted or sent word in some other fashion. Flowers, which had to have cost a fortune to deliver all the way out here. Some handwritten notes that he missed her. The most unexpected of all: a six-pack of specialty shampoos, each one with a different scent. Any other woman in the world would've been thrilled with his attention. But her emotions were a jumbled mess. She was confused. Scared.

At the same time, she had to admit she loved talking to him about all the little goings-on in Gandiegow, like the uproar over Father Andrew moving the date of the Christmas pageant—a cardinal sin, apparently. It had gone off without a hitch, but at Quilting Central they were still muttering about the nerve of the young priest in meddling with tradition. Emma was starting to appreciate the villagers' devotion to tradition. She looked down at the tradition she was working on, the Gandiegow Doctor quilt.

But tradition wasn't helping her make any decisions yet about her future. All she knew was that she wasn't moving back to Los Angeles. Maybe she'd find a flat in London and give herself some time to think alone. *Alone* was not an easy commodity to come by here in Gandiegow.

Emma stitched the last seam, turned off the sewing machine, and handed off the quilt top to Deydie, who hovered nearby.

"It's about damn time. I don't think you could've gone any slower," the old woman said with a toothy grin. She held it up. "I think ye're going to be a hell of a quilter one day. Yere corners are damn near perfect."

"Thank you." Emma stood and stretched.

"Now get yere skinny arse over to the long-arm quilting machine and get it finished." Deydie handed her back the quilt top and motioned to one of the massive eighteen-foot machines in the corner.

Emma shook her head. "I don't know how to run one of those."

Bethia put her arm around Emma's shoulders. "It's time you learned." She guided her over to the machine, where Moira waited.

A simple lap-sized practice quilt was set up on the machine. Moira showed Emma how to hold and move the handlebars to achieve the proper stitching.

"The stitch regulator should keep the stitches nice and even," Moira explained. "However, it's important to be consistent with your motions. Let's start with anchoring the quilt by stitching in the ditch—sewing directly in the seams. Then I'll show you how to do a meandering stitch. Later we can work on more advanced techniques."

"But what if I bungle it?" Emma chewed the inside of her cheek.

"This is only practice."

At first Emma felt timid about managing the large machine, but it didn't take long until she fell in love with it. The actual quilting of the three pieces—the quilt top, the batting, and the back—gave the final product another dimension, another layer, transforming it into art. Before she knew it, Moira was taking off the practice quilt and showing her how to load the three layers of the Gandiegow Doctor quilt onto the frame.

"What I like to do," Moira instructed, after the quilt was in place, "is to think about the recipient of the quilt while I work on it. My mama taught me that when I was a wee lass. She said it was the perfect way to put extra love into whatever project we worked on."

Talk about the wrong thing to say. Emma had always believed love was out of her grasp. She could recognize it—like in the case of Claire and Dominic—but she couldn't fathom having it for herself. Even though Gabriel had said the *L* word to her, she didn't dare think of him in that way. It was too far-fetched. Now Moira wanted her to do just that. Thinking about Gabriel only made Emma more nervous. It was bad enough worrying about screwing up his quilt, but now her hands shook as she pondered his smile, her stomach squeezing deliciously in on itself. Suddenly, she was reliving their lovemaking. The excitement. The thrill. It had been . . . perfect. He'd made her feel such joy, such safety. Such . . . what? *Love?* Could it be? Her knees trembled.

"I have to take a break." She rushed off to the loo to pull herself together.

She collapsed into the overstuffed chair on the other side of the door and came to a major decision. Yes, she would get the quilt done. Because she'd promised. She had kept all of her promises since she'd come here, and then some. She'd helped Mattie and Sophie and Claire. Emma would finish up this quilt today, no matter what, and leave in the morning, before Gabriel returned. She'd go to London, check into a hotel, and spend Christmas quietly. By herself.

She trudged out of the restroom and back to the long-arm quilting machine, getting down to work. With Moira's guidance, the quilting was indeed done by the end of the day. Moira had her cut a strip of fabric for the binding, showing her how to stitch it in place. The quilt was finished. All the ladies clapped and took a hundred pictures of Emma with the Gandiegow Doctor quilt. It brought tears to her eyes to think she would have to leave this place, but in her mind, she had no choice. She had to reclaim her life.

She hugged everyone because she knew this was goodbye. Sure, she'd come back to Gandiegow to visit Claire in the future, but this was the last time Emma would be a part of the community. She gave them one more wave and then went back to the quilting dorm to settle in to a quiet evening alone. She didn't have the nerve to tell Claire tonight, but would tell her on her way out in the morning. Emma had to get back to reality and face the future. Gandiegow had been a respite from her life. Now it was time to move on.

But Emma felt terrible for her friend. Since Dom had been vindicated, the town had shunned Claire and her scones. But every day, almost on autopilot, Claire went to the kitchen and baked, anyway.

At the dorm, Emma pulled leftover tortellini from the fridge and heated it. Just like all the other nights since Gabriel had left, when she sat at the dining room table, she folded her hands together and said a prayer. She fumbled over the words, but she managed to give thanks for the food.

As she was about to take her first bite, though, the front door opened and Claire came down the hall. "Emma, are you here?"

"In the kitchen." She shoveled in a bite and jumped up, thinking to grab a plate so Claire could join her.

But when her friend appeared, she had a suitcase in her hand.

Emma frowned at the large brown bag. "What are you doing?"

Claire dropped the suitcase on its side and crumpled into a chair. "I'm moving in with you."

Dom didn't understand it. He and Claire had lived in the same flat for the past two weeks but she hadn't spoken a word to him. She didn't seem angry, only subdued. No fire, no energy. This was not his Claire. They worked in the same kitchen, but she wasn't really there. He'd never seen her like this. He had the urge to wrap his arms around her and tell her to come back to him, but she seemed to be slipping farther and farther away. She didn't even comment when he brought Porco upstairs to sleep in the guest room with him.

Has she given up on me? On us?

He needed to talk to Gabe, but he wasn't back yet. Maybe Ramsay would want to get a drink in the meantime. Dom hung up his apron, went into the dining room, and asked.

"Sure, mate," Ramsay said. "I'm happy to throw back a few with you."

"How's the arm healing?" Dom asked.

He held it up. "Itches to high heaven."

The two of them plodded off to the pub. Dom felt comfortable with Ramsay. Not only had he turned out to be a good chap for supporting him at the restaurant, but they'd had some good conversation, too. Dom told him his worries about Claire.

Ramsay was quiet for a long moment. "I remember Claire as a girl. She's always been a hotheaded lass—no offense."

"None taken. I know my wife."

"Let's face it." Ramsay grinned. "Most of us Scots aren't exactly reserved."

"Tell me about it."

"I remember Maggie, John's wife, going through something similar. She got all quiet after her grandmother died. That was the woman who'd raised her. She just needed some time to work through her feelings, I think."

Was it that simple? Was the move back to Gandiegow making Claire miss her mother? Dom didn't want to say it out loud, but was afraid it was something else. What if Claire was working up the nerve to sever their relationship for good? What if she wanted a divorce?

Ramsay clapped him on the back. "Ye've nothing to worry about. Claire loves you. I'm sure of it. Come, now. Your drink is on me."

Over a dram, they talked of fishing and the weather, and then Ramsay had to call it a night, as he had an early date with the nets in the morn. Dom left, too, not in the mood for the crowd that was ramping up.

When he got back to the flat, he started to go peek in

at Claire while she slept, but a slip of paper on the writing desk caught his eye. Dread came over him, but he walked over and read the words, anyway.

I need some time. I've moved in with Emma.

*   *   *

"What?" Emma couldn't believe it. "This doesn't make any sense. You know why you've been feeling frantic. So why aren't you at home trying to fix things with Dominic?"

Claire pushed her hair out of her face. "Because I have to fix me first. Dominic deserves a wife who isn't mental."

Emma pulled a face. "You're not mental. Did you at least talk to him and let him know why things happened the way they did?"

"No. I couldn't. I can barely even think of it yet. I miss my parents so."

"Ah, sweeting." Emma went to her and put her arm around her shoulder. "I'll make you a cup of tea and then we'll talk. All right?"

But before Claire could answer, another visitor arrived. He didn't call out, but she heard the heavy footsteps as they made their way down the hallway. Emma's first thought was that it was Dominic come to retrieve his wife. But Gabriel appeared.

Her breath got trapped in her lungs and her heart broke out into a glorious chorus. She turned all tapioca pudding on the inside and gave him a weak smile.

"Hallo, Emma." His burr was like a soothing bath, washing over her. "I just arrived home and hoped we could have a nightcap together."

"Uhhh," she managed, not exactly the articulate lady she liked to think she was.

He glanced around, realizing they weren't alone. "Hey, Claire." He nodded to her.

Claire looked from one to the other. "Let's not do tea, Emma. I'm not in the mood to talk, anyway. I'll just go to bed."

Emma turned to Gabriel. "Claire just got here." She nodded in the direction of her suitcase.

Claire shook her head and stood. "You go on. I'm tired. You and I, we'll chat tomorrow."

"Are you sure?" Emma asked, searching Claire's face.

Claire hugged her tight. "Have fun," she whispered into her ear.

Emma watched as Claire grabbed the suitcase and disappeared down the hallway to the bedrooms. Anxiety for Claire should've outweighed her excitement at seeing Gabriel, but her insides were doing a dance.

"Come back to the doctor's quarters with me."

She stared at her own clasped hands. She had to tell him she was leaving Gandiegow in the morning. It would be safer to do it here.

She looked up to find him gazing back. "Bloody hell." *Who am I kidding?* She wanted him, wanted to go to bed with him one last time before she left. It would make a nice Christmas present for herself, a memory to pull out on the lonely nights ahead.

"Yes, I'll go with you. For a drink," she made sure to add.

"Get your coat."

Outside, the village paths were empty except for the two of them. Twinkling Christmas lights bounced off the water and lit their way. It was both enchanting and magical. She repeated to herself over and over that it was only sex they were headed for. Great sex . . . but still just a romp in the bedroom all the same.

He held open the door to the doctor's quarters and

she went up the stairs. She made no pretense but headed straight to his room, a woman on a mission.

"What about that drink?"

"Forget the drink." She concentrated on undoing the buttons of her blouse.

He stood there in disbelief as her clothes hit the floor. She glanced over at him. "Either close your mouth, Gabriel, or get over here and put it to good use."

"You don't have to tell me twice," he growled. He crossed the room in two steps and took her into his arms, kissing her. She tugged at his clothes.

"What about foreplay?" he asked, as his lips traveled to her neck.

"Overrated." She pushed his pants to the floor; he stepped out of them.

She backed away and lay on the bed, needing their bodies connected as much as she needed to breathe.

Naked himself, he stood over her and gazed down. "Ye're so beautiful, lass."

She just wanted to feel, not think. "Less talk, Doctor, and more action."

He grabbed a condom, put it on, and came to her. Like a good Scottish warrior, he plundered her, making her gasp with joy—they were finally back together. All the days they'd been apart fell away. All her misgivings disappeared. In this moment, she didn't feel confused or scared. She just *was*.

He murmured Gaelic to her, kissing and touching every part of her body, but it was as if he'd gotten it backward. He didn't need to woo her with his ancient words and loving hands. She was already his.

"*Tha gaol agam ort*," he said tenderly.

She understood him perfectly; he'd told her he loved her again. But Emma, she couldn't put two words together to save her naked British hide. She was close to the edge—and then suddenly went over the top.

"That's right, my luv," he said, caressing her face.

He hadn't come with her, she noticed as her spasms subsided and he began nibbling on her ear. He started a new rhythm between them, slow and languorous.

"I've missed you," he said.

"Shhh." She'd missed him, too.

But she wanted to concentrate on what he was doing to her; it felt nice. She loved how he made love to her.

Nice became heated. Heated turned into all-out need. His breathing became ragged and his composure slipped away. This time he got caught up in his own game and he wouldn't be denied. As she rocked with him, she saw the pain of pleasure on his face. She loved to see him lose control, his hips frantic to meet hers. She opened wider to him, wrapped her legs around his waist, and pulled him deeper inside. It turned her on like nothing else to feel his strength, to know she was the one to bring him to completion.

"Emma," he groaned. "Oh, God, Emma." It sounded like a fervent prayer. He hovered above her and she hugged herself to him, not ever wanting to let go.

From nowhere, a sob slipped out and then another. She couldn't stop herself and she couldn't explain to him what she felt. What they shared was beyond anything she ever could've imagined. The pure joy of feeling complete, knowing it was the two of them together that created something so beautiful and wonderful.

He looked down at her with concern and rolled to his side, pulling her to him. "Don't cry, luv. Please don't cry."

"I'm all right." *I'm not.* The tears wouldn't stop. She'd gone to bed with him hoping for a physical connection. He'd given her so much more. He'd touched her in a much deeper way than the physical. It would take her some time to recover from it, if ever.

He held her close and murmured more Gaelic to her. Eventually, she relaxed and became drowsy.

"Sleep, my luv," he said.

And she did.

Chapter Twenty

Once again in the wee hours of the morning, Emma snuck out of Gabriel's bed. She felt a mixture of elation and embarrassment at what had transpired between them last night. *I cried!* She still couldn't believe it. Then she'd slept like a satisfied baby. She had to speak with Claire. That was the only way Emma was going to figure out what was going on between her and Gabriel.

Emma dressed quietly and stole out of the doctor's quarters. She found Claire in the restaurant kitchen, as expected, but she wasn't making scones.

"What gives?" Emma asked. "Why aren't you up to your elbows in flour by now?"

"I've come to my senses. We have plenty of scones in the freezer to heat. That is, if anyone cares to show up." Claire plastered on a brave smile. "How did you and Gabriel get on last night?" She put her hand up. "Before I hear any details, I need to warn you: You'd better not break his heart. You may be my best friend, but the world needs more men like him. He's a decent guy."

"I know." Emma burst into tears all over again. Claire ran to her and wrapped her arm around her shoulders and helped her to a stool.

"What's wrong?" Claire cooed soothingly. "I wasn't trying to upset you."

Emma gasped for air between each sob. "I don't know what's wrong. That's why I needed to talk to you."

"If Gabriel did anything to hurt you, I'll take the cast-iron skillet to his thick head," Claire said emphatically.

Emma gave her a weak smile. "You just said he's a decent guy."

"He is. But he's still a guy."

Emma shook her head. "Gabriel didn't do anything to hurt me. He did nothing but be wonderful."

Claire gave her a sly look. "Then I take it it went well in the bedroom?"

Emma took Claire's hands but couldn't face her, speaking to the mixer instead. "With him, it was the first time . . . I mean . . . I never felt . . ."

"You two had a wonderful time in the sack. Good for you. So, he was better than some of the other men you've shagged."

In that moment, Emma knew she couldn't go on lying, not for one second longer. "Claire, can we sit at a table? We need to talk."

"Sure." She grabbed her coffee mug and pulled out a chair.

Emma sat across from her. "I haven't exactly been truthful with you." She twisted the edge of the tablecloth in her hands.

"What are you talking about?" Claire reached out and stilled her hands. "You're the most truthful person I know."

Emma pulled away. "I've lied. To you. To my mother. To everyone." She stood and stared at the door.

"Sit back down. Ye're talking crazy."

Emma leaned on her chair back, looking into her friend's eyes. "Gabriel was my first."

"First what? First man that you've loved? That's not news to me." Claire smiled.

"No, he was my first . . ." How was Emma going to say this? "You know. In the bedroom . . ."

"Good grief, Emma. Gabriel is not the first man you've slept with. The whole world knows that."

Emma mumbled bitterly, "Yes, Mum loves to share." She took a deep breath. "I haven't slept with tons of men like I've said. I've slept with exactly three before Gabriel." *Not the triple digits I've claimed.* "But with Gabriel . . . it was different. He was my . . . my first . . . orgasm."

It was hard to get the word out, but once she did, her insides flip-flopped deliciously. She finally understood what all the hubbub was over sex. She never should've undersold the importance of a good roll in the hay to lift one's spirits. Maybe she should've listened more closely to her couples in their therapy sessions when they said their sex lives had been *off*. Hers felt absolutely on, and there was no better drug in the universe than complete satisfaction.

Emma was so caught up in her own thoughts and the details of her new and wondrous sex life, she didn't immediately register the shocked look on Claire's face.

"Three?" Claire's volume was considerably higher. "What the hell, Emma? All those years, I thought something was wrong with me that I wasn't having wild sex."

"I never meant . . ." Emma looked down at her hands, with no real words to defend herself.

But Claire had more to say. "So, the whole spread-eagle thing on top of the grand piano was made up?"

Emma nodded.

"And you never came three times in one night with three *different* men."

Emma shook her head, ashamed of that one. But her

mother had called her a prude in front of Claire, and only because Emma dressed more conservatively than Claire when they went out. Emma never realized that while she was protecting herself from her mother, she had inadvertently been hurting her best friend.

"So, all these years when I've worried I wasn't normal, because I'm satisfied sleeping with the same man for the past decade . . ." Claire's voice trailed off.

Emma reached out to touch her, but Claire backed away, her shoulders stiff.

"I don't need this right now. Between what's been going on with me and Dominic and all the grief I'm reliving over losing my da. And Mama." She spun on Emma, more distraught than she'd ever seen her. "How could you have lied to me over the years? I'm your best friend. Has that been a lie, too?"

"No," Emma said, "I'm a terrible person is all. I never should've—"

The swinging doors to the kitchen flew open and there stood Gabriel, smiling. One after another, emotions slammed into Emma's gut.

First, he made her weak in the knees. Second, it was such a relief to see him; he could save her from Claire's tirade. But then it occurred to her that he had poor timing. He wouldn't save her from Claire—he'd probably join in the crucifixion.

He walked toward her. "There you are."

"Hold on." Claire stepped in his path, stopping him from reaching her. "Did you know about this?"

"Claire, don't." Emma grabbed her arm.

But Claire shook her off with a crazy look in her eye. Emma knew that look. Her Scottish ire had the best of her, her hotheaded temper set to boil. "Did you know Emma was a big, fat liar before ye screwed her? She hasn't slept with hundreds of men like she's claimed. She's been feeding me lies since we were teenagers. Haven't you, Emma?"

Gabriel's eyebrows pinched together. "What are ye talking about?"

Claire put her hands on her hips, but there were tears in her eyes. "She's been playing us for the fool. Tell him, Emma. Tell him that he's the first Big O that you've ever had!"

Gabriel cocked his head to the side as if he hadn't heard correctly. He turned to Emma, searching her face.

Emma couldn't stand to see him judging her. But she was the liar here.

"That's enough, Claire," Dominic growled, standing in the doorway. "This is between the two of them. You have nothing to do with it."

"Oh, really?" Claire yelled. "I think I have a perfect right. They haven't been too shy with their opinions of *our* marriage." She swung around to Emma. "How does it feel to have another person get in the middle of your relationship?" Then Claire turned back to Dominic. "Have ye not gotten an earful from these two?"

"Not really." Dominic shot Gabriel a puzzled expression. "What is it you have to say, Gabe?"

After a moment, the doctor shrugged. "I'm on Claire's side. You know I'll help out financially. She should have a baby. She's not getting any younger."

Claire's intake of breath could've been heard all the way to London.

Gabriel shifted uncomfortably. "That didn't come out right. I mean from a medical standpoint. If Claire is going to get pregnant, she should do it before thirty-five. The problems and complications start to rise exponentially from there." He took a step toward Dominic. "I'll always have your back — you know that. But if ye insist on waiting to have a baby until you have all the money you want, then you're wrong. Some things are more important—like family. You, of all people, should know that."

Dominic looked like he wanted to punch Gabriel.

"But what about lying?" Good ole Claire had brought the focus right back to Emma.

When Gabriel turned toward Emma with that questioning look again, she wanted to crawl under the table. When she didn't speak up for herself, she saw the last remnants of his good opinion of her drop out of sight. Just like she'd strapped cement blocks to it and slung it in the ocean.

What was she supposed to say to him? That Egghead Emma hadn't been able to figure out how to land a real relationship or an orgasm until now? That is, if she and Gabriel were in a real relationship. She was such a loser. And a liar.

But she wasn't the only one who'd lied.

Emma whipped around to Claire. "What about all the lies you told everyone in Gandiegow about Dominic?" Immediately, she felt lower than the lowliest of rats. "I'm sorry, Cla—" Emma tried.

"Don't fash yereself," Claire said coolly. "Now that I know ye, I wouldn't expect anything less."

Emma burst into tears. *Again.* She'd done enough damage for one day. She grabbed her coat and rushed out of the restaurant into the cold morning air.

"What the fuck, Claire?" Gabe muttered, looking at the door Emma had just gone through.

"Don't talk to my wife that way," Dominic warned. He swung on Claire. "Don't think I approve of what you did to Emma, either. It was badly done."

"Gabriel needed to know that she lied about it all, every last sexual conquest," Claire muttered.

Gabe was still in shock. Emma hadn't slept with every Tom, George, and Harry? He'd been her first orgasm?

Unless of course, Emma had lied about climaxing with him, too. She'd have to be one hell of an actor, but still. What other secrets might Emma have been hiding from him? He thought they'd always been honest with each other.

In a funny way, he'd thought he and Emma were both the same, walking the same path, trying to put their pasts behind them, looking for a more meaningful relationship.

With that, the truth hit him head-on, knocking the air from him. From day one, Emma had insisted she didn't believe in lasting relationships. She'd held firm to that belief, never wavering. *Ah, hell!* He'd been kidding himself to think otherwise. Hoping against all odds. The lion in his chest roared, and the small ring box in his jacket pocket felt out of place. He'd been too hasty. He never should've gone to Edinburgh to get it. Christ, he never should've gushed to his da that he'd found his *one true love*. "Lies," he muttered. Lies were tearing them all apart.

"Gabe? Are you or aren't you?" Dom said impatiently.

Gabe frowned. "What?"

"Are you going to stay and help with the lunch crowd?"

"No." Gabe needed space. From Emma and her lies. From the Russos and their stunts. From everything. Dominic and Claire were on their own. Gabe had finally learned his lesson: Don't mess around in other peoples' relationships. Especially if he didn't have a clue what the hell he was doing with his own.

He didn't say goodbye, but before the kitchen doors closed, he heard Dominic speak to Claire.

"You're not going anywhere. Whether you want to or not, you're stuck here with me. The tomatoes are in the cooler."

Emma made it back to the quilting dorm and into the bathroom just in time to throw up. She'd been emotional and queasy since she'd woke up. Vomiting seemed perfectly normal, like the icing on the cake to her horrendous morning from hell. She would get out of town today, Christmas Eve or not. She probably wouldn't get a flight out until tomorrow, but sleeping in the terminal was preferable to staying one more night in this town, with all the residents' stupid heartwarming, gut-wrenching, ripping-the-truth-out-of-her ways.

She shuffled into the bedroom and fell on her double bed. She felt awful—both physically and mentally. She and Claire had had minor arguments over the years, but this breach of Claire's trust would not be easily mended. It might take a long time, if ever. Tears blurred Emma's vision. Claire was the only person in the world who had always been there for Emma. She rolled on her side and held her stomach. She felt like she might throw up again.

She closed her eyes and tried to come up with a way out of this mess. She loved Claire and Dominic. She loved Gabriel. She wanted to make it right with all of them.

Her eyes flew open.

I love Gabriel?

She gasped. *Oh, God, where did that come from? Can it be true? And if it is, when did it happen?*

She jumped out of bed. She had to talk to Claire about it. But then it all hit her again. Claire didn't want to be friends with a big, fat liar. What was Emma going to do?

There was a holler from the front door. "Girl, are you here?" It was Deydie.

"Back in the bedroom." Emma tried to straighten herself up, but she knew she must look a fright.

Deydie waddled into the bedroom while Emma pretended to fuss over the bed, as if making it. As if she'd slept in it last night. *Still the liar.*

"Ye're needed at Quilting Central. Moira embroidered the tag for the Gandiegow Doctor quilt and I need ye to sew it on."

Emma turned to face her, not in the mood to be pushed around yet knowing she risked life and limb by facing off with Deydie. She pressed on, anyway. "Isn't there someone else to do it?"

Deydie glowered at her. "They're busy."

Emma heard the underlying text loud and clear: *You have no obligations, no family like the others.* Now she didn't even have Claire to call her own.

Deydie's frown deepened. "Ye started that project and now ye'll see it through to the end. The quilting ain't over until the fat lady says so, and I say that quilt ain't done yet."

"Fine." What a grand day Emma was having. "Just give me a minute. I need to . . . I need to . . ."

Deydie eyed her closely, scanning her clothes. She opened her mouth to say something, then slammed it shut, her lips forming a needle-straight line. Emma cringed. Deydie had figured it out—*the lass stayed out all night* was written all over her face. Same clothes as yesterday might've worked if Emma were a pauper, but didn't sit well on a girl from London who owned a massive wardrobe and had brought quite a selection with her.

Deydie harrumphed. "Well, I hope at least ye and the doctor had the good sense to do something to keep ye from gettin' in the family way." She frowned at her. "Don't look at me like that. I've got eyes."

A terrible dread came over Emma as she remembered the second time they'd made love, backed up against the door. When she hadn't cared if he used a condom or not. She'd wanted what she wanted, and he'd given it to her.

She turned to Deydie, feeling the blood drain from her face. She worried she might throw up again. She started to warn Deydie to step out of the way, knowing there wasn't time to make it to the bathroom again. But instead, a great freight train roared through Emma's head and the light around Deydie seemed to squeeze in. Then the old woman seemed so very far away.

Emma's last thought was to wonder why everything had gone black.

Chapter Twenty-one

"There, there. That's a lass," Deydie said.

Emma came to, lying flat on the double bed, with the old woman patting her hand. "What happened?"

"You keeled over." Deydie had a worried frown on her face. "I'm going to get the doc."

Emma grabbed her arm. "No!" She composed herself, then schooled her voice. "Please, don't. I'm fine, really. I just need some tea. I might have a touch of the flu." *Still lying*. She needed to get to Inverness and buy a pregnancy test. No way would she buy one here at the store—before she'd have time to pee on the stick, the news would get to Gabriel and have him knocking down her door, demanding answers. Something she couldn't handle right now. "No," Emma said one more time, imploring Deydie with her eyes.

"Verra well, then." Deydie helped her into a sitting position. "I'll make yere tea." As she waddled out of the bedroom, she grumbled, "Never imagined I'd have to stock the dorm with smelling salts. Better pick some up at the store."

Emma was in shock—emotionally and possibly physically, too. She pulled the vintage Sampler quilt with the calming colors from the bed and wrapped it around her, mentally counting the days since her last period. She was due for it today. Or was it yesterday. *Bloody hell.* Could it really be true? She held her wrist to her forehead. Maybe she really did have the flu. Was it safe for her to drive to Inverness? What if she passed out again?

Emma wandered into the living room and sat on the sofa, dragging the quilt with her. The same questions swirled again and again in her mind until Deydie brought in a tray.

"I'll be back in a bit to check on you," Deydie said. "Don't go anywhere."

Emma sipped her tea and ate the biscuits on the tray. Maybe her blood sugar had dropped. That had to be it.

Ten minutes later, Deydie was back. She dropped a sack in Emma's lap. "Git off to the loo with that."

Deydie didn't stop to explain, only hurried off to the kitchen, giving Emma some privacy. She pulled open the bag, peeked inside, and pulled out the box.

KNOW NOW PREGNANCY TEST—EARLY DETECTION. A yellow smiley face was plastered next to the logo.

Emma stared at the box for a long moment.

Deydie hollered from the kitchen. "There's no time like the present, lass."

Emma pushed herself up and trudged off to the bathroom. If she thought Deydie would leave her alone for two seconds, she was wrong.

"Well?" the old woman said outside the door. "Are ye or aren't ye?"

"I can't go if you're talking. Please go away." Emma tried to imagine that she was alone, but it was hard to do with Deydie still issuing orders.

"Run the water," Deydie said. "That should get things flowing."

Emma closed her eyes and it finally worked. While

she waited for the results, she splashed water on her face, trying to calm down.

Deydie banged on the door. "Have ye gone yet?"

Emma looked at the stick; a plus sign had appeared and stared back at her with stark finality. "Oh, God." She collapsed on the toilet seat.

Deydie tapped lightly on the door. "Let me in, lass."

Emma reached over and turned the knob. Deydie bustled in and came to her side.

"Come on. It's going to be all right. We're all here to help ye." Her old voice was kind and reassuring. "We're going to Quilting Central. Ye're going to work on the Gandiegow Doctor quilt and put that tag on. That'll take yere mind off it. For now." She took Emma's elbow and helped her to stand, as if she were the geriatric in need of assistance.

"I think I'll just lie down." *Forever.*

"No," Deydie said. "Ye need to be with people."

Panic hit Emma. "You can't tell anyone!"

"Don't ye worry." Deydie grabbed Emma's coat and held it out for her.

"You have to promise. Not a soul. Do you hear?"

Deydie fixed her collar for her. "Don't worry, lass. Not a word. Now, come. We'll get you squared away."

Claire carefully sliced the tomatoes, knowing all the fire had burned out of her. She should be spitting mad at Emma right now, but she only felt confused. A terrible realization hit her like a rogue wave: She wasn't even close to being as tough as she thought she was. All these years, it was Emma and their friendship that had empowered Claire to be strong, gave her the courage to go out and conquer the world. Emma, who had picked her up as a wee, sad girl and been there for her after her da had died. Emma, the straight arrow. Emma, the one constant in her life.

Claire blinked back tears.

"Are you all right?" Dominic stood farther down the counter, cutting onions. The irony wasn't lost on her.

She couldn't answer him and not blubber, so she nodded instead. What could she tell him, anyway? That she'd lost everything. First him and now Emma.

Dominic wiped his hands on his apron and came to stand beside her. He took a washed green pepper and began coring it. "Are you as mad at them for meddling in our marriage as I am?"

Where did that come from? "I don't know. I guess. It would've been nice, though, if Emma had stood behind me and taken my side."

"Tell me about it," Dom laughed derisively. "Gabe is the one who always says that men have to stick together. Instead, I feel like he took my best butcher knife and stabbed me in the back."

"By taking my side of things?" Claire stated matter-of-factly, with no accusation.

"You know what I mean."

"Aye." She smiled at the tomatoes. "*Bros before hoes.*"

"Clairrrre," he chided.

She looked up at him, and their eyes locked. Claire's heart jolted. It was as if they were seeing each other for the first time. But more powerful, because it felt like old times, too—working side by side in the kitchen, with comfortable conversation between them.

Dominic gave her a long, easy smile, and she knew without a doubt he felt it, too. *Their connection.* Happiness sizzled through Claire. It had always been like this with him. Dominic was the yeast in her dough. The clotted cream on her scones. The absolute love of her life. For the first time in a long time, she felt like they were working from the same recipe in the same cookbook.

Dominic finished with the green peppers and scooped up the onions, tossing them in the sauté pan. He spoke above the sizzle and pop of the vegetables. "How are those tomatoes? I was a little worried they weren't ripe enough."

She cut off a chunk and walked over to him. "Open." He had his hands busy with the sauce.

He did as he was told and she fed him the piece of the tomato, a well-rehearsed dance that had played out a thousand times between them in the kitchen. And like before all the trouble between them, his eyes dilated, then hooded. Her Italian Stallion was back and had sex on his mind. She was thrilled to see he still cared for her, but she couldn't just gloss over what she'd done to him. She squeezed his arm and stepped away with a we-need-to-talk-first smile.

"Ah, Claire . . ."

She held up her hands. "Dominic, I've been a rotten person."

He put down the spatula and turned off the stove, giving her his full attention. "Go on."

She'd hoped he would've denied it, but they both knew it was true. "I've put you through the grater over wanting a baby."

She grabbed the next tomato and began slicing; it was easier to talk if her hands were busy. "I know ye're angry that Emma and Gabe got involved in our marriage. I am, too, but I'm also grateful. It was Emma who helped me to see what was really going on."

"And that is?"

"Ye're going to think this is a wee bit crazy."

"I'm listening." He waited patiently for her to continue.

"Dominic, ye're the same age as my father when he died."

"What?"

"I told you it was crazy."

"I'm fine, Claire. Healthy as a horse." He stepped back with his arms out as proof. "God willing, nothing will happen to me for a long, long time."

"I know." She shrugged. "It must've been coming home to Gandiegow that stirred up the old feelings. Mama used to say how lucky she was to have me to remember my da by. Don't you see? I don't have anything to remember you by if something should happen, except maybe your recipes and kitchen knives." She glanced over at the knives, and shame filled her. She'd thrown pots at her husband's head and crotch and had even waved a knife around like a lunatic.

"Yeah," he said, frowning. He must've been remembering, too.

"I'm so sorry. You did nothing to deserve it. I promise to work at keeping my fear at bay about losing you. I don't want to live without you, like my mother had to live without the love of her life." She looked up at him, desperately wanting him to forgive her.

"Claire." Dominic came to her and wrapped her in his arms. "This has been my fault, too. It wasn't just the money, you know. Even though our finances have been bad enough to scare my sperm." He laughed into her hair at his own joke. "I've had my own fears haunting me. I grew up without a father. What do I know about being a papa?"

She pulled away from him. "But ye're amazing with kids. I've seen you. The whole town thinks ye're a miracle worker."

He laid her head back on his shoulder. "I'm feeling more confident now."

"You know, Father Andrew told me to trust that everything will work out." Being in her husband's arms was a good start, the rightest thing in the whole world.

"Something else," Dom said, kissing her temple. "About the finances . . . I've figured out a few things, too."

"How to get more customers?"

Porco took that moment to make an irreverent snort from the corner.

Claire leaned back and looked into Dominic's eyes. "Ye're not fooling anyone when it comes to that pig. We all know his only job is to be our garbage disposal."

"Yeah, I'm pretty attached to him. Maybe he can be used as a stud at the farm where I got him," Dominic offered.

"We'll see. First, tell me what you figured out about the finances. You know I understand as well as you do about how tight things are."

"I know my wife has good business sense."

"I've just been an emotional mess."

"We'll work together to help you through this. It has to be hard. I still miss my madre just like you miss your father. But, Claire, what I'm finally starting to understand is that we're not in Edinburgh or Glasgow."

She squeezed him. "Duh."

He tweaked her nose affectionately. "We're in Gandiegow. Look around at the people here. They have children and don't have tons of money."

Claire thought of Amy and Coll's little one-room cabin. "Ayc. Everyone makes do."

Dom continued on. "The cost of living is incredibly low here. I think we could do it. I think we could have a bambino and make it work. Right now."

"Maybe," she hedged. "I'm not sure I'm ready. Amy's

little hellion has shown me I have a lot to learn about bairns before we go down that path."

Dominic looked at her earnestly. "I don't want to wait too long. I love you, Claire. I can just imagine my baby in you."

"And my breasts getting as big as watermelons?"

He peeked down at her cleavage. "That, too." He turned serious. "How about in a year? Do you think that would give you enough time? I don't want to wait any longer than that."

"Maybe two. I can train Moira and have her get up early with the scones. You and I both know—"

"The scones wait for no one," they both said together.

Dominic smiled at her tenderly. "I love you, Claire."

"I love you, too, Dominic."

Then their lips met, and Claire's world tilted back into place. She was finally home.

Just as she was being swept up in the magic that was *them*, a worry pulled her away.

"What, my *dolce*?" Dominic caressed her back. "What's wrong?"

She laid a hand on his chest and looked him in the eyes. "What are we going to do about Emma and Gabriel?"

For Christmas Eve, Quilting Central was surprisingly packed. Emma had assumed that everyone would be home with their families, but women filled almost every work space, furiously putting together last-minute projects or wrapping presents. Deydie brought over the Gandiegow Doctor quilt and the embroidered tag, laying them next to Emma on the overstuffed sofa in front of the hearth.

"Just turn under the edges on the tag and hand-stitch it in place," the old woman said.

Emma flipped it over and read:

To Gandiegow's Doctor
Gabriel MacGregor
Pieced & quilted by Emma Castle

Stunned, she looked up at Deydie. "My name is on his quilt?"

"Ye're the one who did all the work. Now get to stitching."

While Emma sewed, she kept her eye on the door, but neither Claire, Dominic, or Gabriel appeared. When Emma was done with the tag, Deydie shoved a box and some Christmas paper onto her lap and made her wrap the package, as well.

Never more than a few feet away, Deydie stood near Emma all day, shoving crackers and tea at her, making sure she was comfortable and cared for. Throughout the day, she kept an endless stream of tasks in front of her, too. When she wasn't fussing over her and working her half to death, Deydie was using her rotary blade to cut out fabric. If anyone stopped by for *a chat* with Emma, Deydie shooed them off.

"Emma's not working today," Deydie said to them. "It's Christmas Eve. Yere problems will have to wait until after Hogmanay. She's taking some time off for the holidays."

Deydie the receptionist. "Not working?" Emma gestured to the projects laid before her. A stash of fat quarters to sort, a box filled with patterns to organize, and thread to arrange by style and color. *Not working, indeed.*

And why would Deydie assume Emma would be in Gandiegow after the New Year?

After the building cleared out and the quilters went home to their families, Deydie plopped a quilting magazine and a shoe box in front of Emma. A big red bow had been taped to the top.

"What's this?" Emma asked.

"A Christmas present from me," Deydie said.

Emma stared at her, dumbfounded.

"Come on, lass, we're going to miss church if you don't get on with it." Deydie took the lid off the box for her. Inside were pieces of pastel cotton fabric—blue, green, pink, yellow, and white—cut into perfect squares and triangles.

Deydie flipped open the magazine to a page marked with a Post-it note. "I thought you could make this for yere next project."

It was a baby quilt made of stars, triangles, and squares. But in the center, there was a quarter-moon with its own special star.

Deydie tapped the middle of the quilt picture. "I'll show ye how to applique that part."

Emma burst into tears.

Deydie sat next to her and took her hand. "Now, now, don't be sad. Working on a quilt will help you accept the miracle ye've been given. It's what I did when I found out I was to have Nora. It's what we all do here in Gandiegow. It'll all work out for you. I promise. My Nora was my greatest blessing. She could be a handful, but she was my shining star." Deydie seemed far away for a second, but she snapped back quickly to the here and now.

"I'm not sad," Emma said. And she wasn't. "I'm just grateful. Thank you for being so kind to me."

"'Tis nothing," Deydie gruffed. "Come on, now. Get back to the dorm and get ready for church. Put on your best dress. Ye'll sit with me and my ladies."

Emma wiped her tears and stood, feeling stronger. "I'll be there."

Deydie shoved a sandwich at her before she left. "Make sure you eat this right away. We don't want a repeat of earlier and have you swooning in front of the whole congregation. Now, do we?"

"Good point." Emma took a bite and headed to the dorm. Even though she was worried about what she was going to tell Gabriel, her bigger worry was Claire.

Poor Claire. Emma being pregnant would be the biggest betrayal of all.

Chapter Twenty-two

At the quilting dorm, Emma sighed heavily as she pulled on her jumper dress, the color of evergreens, the one that matched her eyes. She wondered what color eyes the baby would have.

The baby.

A baby was the only thing that Claire had wanted. And Emma was the one who was going to get one. She didn't know how her friend would bear it. This might be the final blow that would end their friendship. Emma sighed again.

But her insides glowed. *I'm pregnant.* Even though everything had gone wrong with Gabriel, she found herself overjoyed. She would have this baby. That was the only thing in the world she knew for sure. Except that she was going to church right now. What she did tomorrow would be anyone's guess.

When she arrived at the white-steepled building, she hurried inside, keeping her head down. She couldn't face Gabriel right now, or Claire, for that matter. Not yet. She zipped through the narthex and went into the nave, searching for Deydie's pew with the quilting ladies. Bethia was already seated, and Emma joined her.

"Are you feeling all right, lassie?" Bethia's old eyes looked concerned.

"Yes." What could Emma say? Gabriel had impregnated her and Claire would never speak to her again?

While the organist played quiet Christmas tunes, more people filed in. Mattie came down the aisle, followed by Cait and her famous husband, Graham Buchanan. Mattie and Cait waved to her and it eased Emma's anxiety a little. Only a very little. She waved back, then closed her eyes, willing the music to relax her.

Deydie squeezed in beside Emma, leaning over to whisper, "Keep the faith. Ye're doing fine."

Suddenly the music shifted to "O Come, All Ye Faithful" and the congregation stood. It took everything in Emma not to turn around and watch as Gabriel processed in with the choir. Instead, she stuck her nose in the hymnal and sang along, doing well for the first verse. But as he passed by their pew, her head came up automatically. Unlike before, he didn't search her out and nod. He seemed to have locked his head in the straight-ahead position. Whatever she'd been hoping for from him wasn't going to happen, and her stomach dropped. Even more upsetting, now that she'd seen him, she couldn't look away.

Deydie tapped a gnarled finger on Emma's hymnal to draw her attention back to where it should be. Emma tuned into the service as best as she could, and was surprised when it calmed her. Father Andrew spoke about how the baby Jesus had been a blessing to the world and observed that all children were a blessing and the best hope for the future. Emma put a hand on her stomach, warmed by his words, as if they had been delivered just for her.

She turned around and saw Claire sitting three rows

back with Dominic beside her. Why were they keeping
up the ruse that they were back together?

Out of the blue, a clear-cut decision came to Emma.
Right after church, no matter what, she would seek out
Claire and tell her about the baby. No more secrets, no
more lies. She'd be honest with Claire, put it all out there. If
their long-standing friendship was over, at least Emma
would have been honest with her in the end. *And Gabriel?*
He needed to know, too. Maybe she'd write him a note and
slip it under his door. If she told him in person, he'd probably propose on the spot; that Scottish warrior was such a
gentleman. But a child was a poor excuse to be together.
She couldn't bear for him to be with her out of obligation.

At that moment, Father Andrew motioned to the table off to the side. "We have a special treat this evening.
The choir has decided to surprise us with 'The Holly and
the Ivy' on the bells."

Gabriel stood and his eyes fell on Emma. He looked
so vulnerable that she wanted to go to him. However,
before she could blink, a dark mask fell over his face and
only disappointment remained.

Tears sprang to Emma's eyes and fell down her cheeks.
Deydie dug around in her pocket and pulled out a clean
hankie, shoving it in Emma's hand.

On the other side of her, Bethia patted her arm.
Alarm rang throughout Emma—Deydie hadn't kept her
mouth shut.

But then Bethia leaned over and whispered, "The bells
always make me cry, too. They remind me of my daughter,
Ciara."

The music was beautiful. Emma didn't punish herself
further by watching Gabriel, but kept her eyes in her lap.
She loved him, and it hurt so much. They'd probably
never be together because of her lies. At least she'd have
his baby to remember him by. Just like Claire's mother.

But she couldn't stay in Gandiegow another day knowing Gabriel couldn't stand the sight of her. It was more than she could handle. As soon as she got back to the dorm, she'd call a taxi and head to London. For good.

The song ended, and Emma could finally breathe. Father Andrew announced the closing hymn, and the congregation rose and sang. When the service was over, Emma had every intention of sprinting for the door. She did fine hurrying up the aisle, but just as she made it to the narthex, her arm was snagged and she was pulled to a stop.

It was Claire.

"Not so fast, my friend." Surprisingly, she had a pleasant smile on her face. And she'd called her *friend*.

"Claire, I—" Emma started.

Claire pulled her into a fierce hug. "I love you. I'll never let you out of my life. Never."

Tears welled up in Emma again. *Seriously, how many times can a person cry in one day?* She pulled Claire to the side to let others pass by. "I need to explain. It's a long story. It's about my mother." Emma told her everything. "I never meant for it to go on forever. I'm so terribly, terribly sorry."

Claire hugged her again. "No worries. It's all washed out to sea. We need not speak of it again."

Emma loved Claire so much and was so lucky to have her. But she would have to test their friendship further. Now was better than later. "There's one more thing you need to know."

Chapter Twenty-three

Dominic joined them, practically pushing Gabriel on Emma. "I got him, Claire, before he slipped away."

Gabriel had on his choir robe and a grim expression. He looked heavenly to Emma, though, making her heart pound. At the same time, she was sad she'd made a mess of things with him.

Dominic pointed at her. "I like to think that you're the less pigheaded of the two of you. I need you to work things out with him. He's miserable without you. Which makes *me* miserable."

Claire nudged Emma closer to Gabriel, too. "Fix it now. If you don't talk, we'll be forced to lock you in a broom closet next."

"So, it *was* you two." Gabriel gave them a disapproving look.

"Aye." Claire went to stand by Dominic, intertwining her hand with his. The Russos beamed at each other.

"Oh, Claire." Emma was the one to hug her friend fiercely this time. "I'm so happy for you."

"Happy for what?" Gabriel asked.

"They're back together," Emma said.

Gabriel turned to Dominic. "For real?"

Dominic nodded. "For real. Now you two talk. Claire and I need to speak with Father Andrew, but we'll be watching you."

Claire smiled and flipped her hair. "We're going to set a date to renew our vows." She elbowed Emma teasingly. "Maybe make it a double ceremony with you two?"

Emma rolled her eyes as the Russos walked away, leaving her alone with Gabriel. She turned to him. "What should we talk about?" She wasn't ready to tell him about the pregnancy here in front of God and everyone. Claire had to find out first. Besides, Emma was still getting used to the idea herself. A nice text message to Gabriel after she got back to London might be the ticket.

Gabriel looked at her sideways. "Are you feeling well?"

She deflected. "The service was lovely."

"Aye, religion is always a safe subject. We'll talk about politics next."

"I mean, it was pretty. The religious rituals are nice. I think everyone enjoyed them."

His expression softened infinitesimally. "There's more to church than just enjoying the service. Do you really want to know my thoughts?"

"Yes." She really did.

"I think church and the lessons we learn here are the best tools we can have in our toolbox. When life gets tough, we can pull out what we need to get us through our troubles." He paused for a second, as if to reflect on his past and present problems. "But here's the deal about church, Emma."

"Yes?" she encouraged.

He leaned in. "You come from a world where anyone in your social circle can get therapy. Am I right?"

She shrugged. "Sure. All of my parents' friends are either in therapy or used to be."

"A lot of regular, everyday people don't have access to counseling, like the kind of help that you give people." He said the last as if he was proud of her. "Most people only have the support of church and its community."

"Oh." She'd never thought about the accessibility of therapy before. No wonder her table at Quilting Central had been graced with so many Gandiegowans wanting to talk about their problems. Speaking with them had truly been Emma's honor. Although she might have helped them, it had also had been a blessing to her. It was rather nice to feel useful.

She gazed down at the floor and confessed, "I know what you mean. Since I've been here, church has been a real comfort for me." She looked up at him. "It centers and calms me like nothing I've ever experienced."

"Finally, *therapy for the therapist*." He smiled. His warm eyes made her heart pirouette.

She still hadn't been completely honest with him. "Can we go sit? I need to talk to you." She pointed to the empty church.

Gabriel nodded and followed her. Dominic and Claire did indeed keep an eye on them as they entered the sanctuary.

After she settled into a pew, she began, "I want to clear the air between us. I know I lied to you—"

He took her hand. "Nay."

For a moment she stared down at their linked hands—such a simple act made her so happy. She pushed on with what had to be said. "I didn't lie directly, but I let you believe something that wasn't true; that's the same thing as lying, in my book. I have to tell you the truth now, though." She told him about her mother and her desperation to keep her at bay, all the same things she'd finally confessed to Claire.

Gabriel squeezed her hand. "I understand, lass. I've seen yere mother on TV. I'm sure you had no choice."

"But there's more," she said. "I want you to know it all. I've never had a real relationship." *Egghead Emma stepped out from the shadows and came into the light.* Emma could finally accept her true self. "The few times I had sex were with acquaintances. I didn't care about them—I just needed to find out what the fuss was all about. But it did nothing for me. After that, I gave up on sex completely. I decided it wasn't important."

"And now?" he said.

"It is."

"What changed your mind?" He gazed at her expectantly, like he hoped he knew the answer.

She got brave and squeezed his hand back. "You did." She paused for a moment. "I finally figured out that the only sex worth having is with someone you really care about."

"That's exactly what I came to realize, as well. I gave up on meaningless sex because it was just that—meaningless."

She'd come this far and she decided to go the whole way. Spit it out. Put all her cards on the table. "I know now I never would've made love to you unless I truly, well, did love you."

"Ah, lass." He kissed her captured hands.

"Can you forgive me for being closed off, naive, and a liar?"

"Only if you can forgive me for not recognizing sooner how we were made for each other. I avoided you for years because you got to me like no other. *My Emma* never minced words." He leaned over and kissed her tenderly.

His Emma. She bunched his choir robe in her hands and held on tight. She never wanted to let him go.

He pulled away. "Don't cry, my luv."

She swiped at her tears, smiling through them. "I'm not crying. I'm just leaking love."

She took a deep breath. It was no good waiting to tell him about the baby. "Gabriel, I—"

Chapter Twenty-four

Emma stopped abruptly as Dominic cracked open the door and stuck his head into the sanctuary. "It's about time you two figured things out. Father Andrew wants to turn off the lights and get over to Moira and Kenneth's for dinner."

Gabriel pulled Emma to her feet and tucked her into his side.

Dominic held the door open for them. "Claire and I know you want to be alone, but we've planned a special family dinner for the four of us at the restaurant."

Emma looked up at Gabriel. She needed to tell him about the baby. And Claire, too, for that matter. She glanced at the cross hanging over the altar. *Why is God keeping me from telling them this gigantic piece of truth that will affect all of our lives?*

Dominic shot his brother a knowing glance. "Claire won't take no for an answer. Whatever you two have in mind can wait until later, is what she says."

Emma murmured, "That's not what the pot usually says to the kettle." Her stomach took that moment to growl. "All right, then. Let's go eat."

After Gabriel hung his robe and retrieved his coat, the two couples walked back to the restaurant. As they opened the door, the smell of garlic and yummy food hit Emma's nose and made her mouth water. One table had been dressed in a gold tablecloth, garland strung down the center, and candles interspersed in the greenery. Claire lit the candles while Dominic brought in their traditional Italian Christmas feast—Italian wedding soup, lasagna, veal parmesan, tomatoes and basil, orange salad, garlic mushrooms and broccoli, fresh bread, panettone, and struffoli. Gabriel poured the wine while Emma hung their coats on the rack by the door.

Before they all sat down, Gabriel reached for Emma's hand. "Let's say grace." As the four friends made a circle around the table, Emma thought she would burst with the love she felt for them. They bowed their heads, and Gabriel prayed from his heart—grateful for the many gifts they'd received, especially the gift of one another.

"Amen."

When they sat, Gabriel raised his glass. "The first toast goes to the chefs. To Dominic and Claire. For the finest fare and the best friendship."

They all clinked, but Emma managed to set her glass down without a sip. They dug in, and the food was perfection. As Emma reached for a second helping, the door was flung open.

Deydie stood there with two packages in her hand.

Emma stood up first. "Do you want to join us?"

Gabriel looked like she'd asked Genghis Khan to dine with them. He recovered quickly and stood, too. "We have plenty."

Dominic was already pulling a chair over to the table, and Claire was clearing a spot for an extra plate.

"Nay, I have to get back to Graham and Caitie's. I just wanted to bring these." She set the bigger box on Emma's chair but took the smaller one over to Dominic. "Open it."

Dominic stared down at the present, puzzled. "For me?"

"Aye, for you. Now hurry it up. They'll eat all the Christmas pudding without me," Deydie said.

Dominic pried the lid off the box and pulled out the present—a kilt made in the Douglas plaid, Claire's family tartan. He turned to Deydie with a confused look on his face.

"Ye're a fine cook, Dominic. The town got together and decided to make you an honorary Scot. Go put it on. I want to see you in it before I leave."

Claire put her arm around Deydie as he left with his kilt slung over his arm. "You're not the tough ole bird you want us to believe, are ye?"

Deydie cackled. "If it 'tweren't Christmas, I'd take a broom to yere backside for that cheek."

Gabriel came to stand next to Emma, as if he couldn't stand to be away from her. She turned her face up to smile at him, and he put an arm around her waist.

Deydie winked at her. "What'd I tell ye, lass? Everything's going to be okay."

Emma gave her a weak smile. She might have told Gabriel that she loved him, but she hadn't dropped the other shoe yet. *The baby shoe.*

"Deydie, where's *my* kilt?" Gabriel challenged.

The old woman shook her head. "Ye're already a Scot. And any doc that can make stitches as good as ye has a place in my town. Anytime you want to learn how to quilt, I'd be right proud to be yere teacher."

Gabriel gave her a genuine smile. "That means a lot coming from you."

Dominic came out and proudly modeled his new look.

Claire whistled. "You were born to wear a kilt. Spin around so I can get a good look at you."

"The Douglas tartan fits ye well," Deydie said. Then she turned and pointed to the other box. "Emma, that's for you to give the doc. Now I need to get going."

"Wait." Claire grabbed the bread basket and dumped its contents into a napkin, tying the ends. Dominic nabbed a bottle of wine from the rack. They both got to Deydie before she lumbered out the door.

"For ye and yours," Claire said.

"Happy Christmas." Dominic kissed her cheek. "Thank you for the kilt."

" 'Twasn't me, I told ye. It was the town."

"I know," Dominic said, smiling.

Deydie gathered the items into her arms, gave Emma a bolstering nod, and waved to them all at the door with the wine bottle in her hand. "Good night to ye," she said, and was gone.

As soon as the door shut behind her, Claire turned to Emma. "Help me get the dishes cleared. I need to get my man upstairs and de-kilt him."

"What about my present?" Gabriel asked.

"You and Emma can open it back at your place or the dorm," Claire said. "I'm a wee bit impatient to get my husband alone." She gave Dominic a smoldering look as she grabbed the empty bread basket.

"What happened to *it can wait until later*?" Emma asked.

Claire winked at her. "It's later, don't you think?"

Emma picked up the lasagna dish, hoping this was the right time to come clean with her friend.

When the two of them were behind the kitchen doors, Emma grabbed her arm. "There's still something you need to know."

"What, Emms? Is everything okay? You and Gabriel seem happy."

Emma chewed her lip. "I have news and I'm worried how you're going to take it."

"Nothing could spoil this perfect Christmas," Claire assured her.

Emma took her hand. "First, I want you to know that I'd never do anything on purpose to hurt you. You are the sister of my heart."

"I know." Claire looked back at her lovingly.

"But accidents happen."

Claire looked worried, but put on a brave face. "It'll be fine, whatever it is."

Emma took a deep breath. "Claire, I'm pregnant. I just found out."

Claire stood, spellbound. "You're pregnant?" she whispered.

Emma nodded and waited, not able to breathe until Claire said something more.

"Oh, Emma." Claire pulled her into her arms and hugged the stuffing out of her. "I couldn't be happier. Really!"

"So you're not upset with me?" Emma said tentatively.

"Nay. Dominic and I talked. We're going to wait to have a bairn. I'm not ready yet. Amy's baby showed me a thing or two about what it takes to have a babe." Claire squealed. "But I'll love being an auntie and practicing my baby skills on yere wee one." She stopped for a moment. "Does Gabriel know?"

"Not yet."

"Well, you'd better get to it before I blab the news to Dominic and the whole damn town knows." Claire pushed Emma toward the double swinging doors. "Dom and I'll clean up this mess. You go talk to your man."

When Emma marched into the dining room, the men

looked up. "I've been banned from the kitchen." She pulled their winter jackets from their hooks and turned to Gabriel. "Are you ready to go?"

He raised one eyebrow at her. "What do you think?"

"I think it's a yes."

"A resounding *yes.*" He helped her into her coat.

Emma turned to Dominic. "Thanks for everything."

Dominic nodded, but his thoughts seemed to be elsewhere. Perhaps on the feisty Scottish woman washing dishes in the kitchen.

When they got outside, Emma looked up at Gabriel. "Your place or mine?"

"Mine." He took the box from her. "Here, hold my arm. It's getting a little slippery."

She grabbed hold of him and let his strength guide her over the path that led to the doctor's quarters. At his place, they went upstairs into the living room. Gabriel set the box on the sofa and pulled Emma into his arms for a long, tender kiss. He seemed in no hurry, letting the kiss speak for him of love and steadfastness, forever and commitment. When he ended the kiss, he pulled her to the sofa, next to the Christmas present she'd wrapped.

"What's in it?" He beamed at her and she got a glimpse of the boy he once was.

He untied the bow and pulled out the beautiful quilt, unfolding it. He flipped it around, looking as if he were taking it all in.

She smiled, happy with how it had turned out. At a distance, the scrappy blues had come together with a four-sided motif in the center with Log Cabin blocks accentuating its presence. The rest of the quilt had blue stars that Emma thought were stunning. She wanted to take back her less than kind thoughts toward the village quilters. They hadn't wanted Gabriel to have a scrappy mess of a quilt; they'd wanted him to have something unique and special.

Emma loved Gabriel's thrilled expression, too. She stood, taking the other end and holding it up. "It's called the Gandiegow Doctor quilt. It's an old Gandiegowan tradition. Whenever a new doctor comes into the village, they give him a quilt his first Christmas here." She turned the quilt so he could see. "It has baby William's name and birthdate right there. Whenever a new baby is born, a patch will be sewn on with the babe's name." She thought of her own babe growing inside her—*Gabriel's baby*—and her cheeks flushed. *Our baby's name will be on this quilt, too.*

"What's this?" He had found the tag. "You made this quilt, Emma?" He stared at her in wonder.

"Yes." She gave him a sheepish smile.

"This quilt means even more, knowing that you were the one to make it." He pulled her down to his level and kissed her again.

She cut it short, though. She still had to tell him about the baby, before things got too out of hand. Her mouth went suddenly dry. "I'm thirsty. Do you mind fixing me a glass of water?"

"Anything for you, luv." He kissed her hand, laid the quilt aside, and left for the kitchen.

As she slipped off her coat, her phone rang. It was Mum.

"Happy Christmas," Emma answered.

"Yes, I hope it will be. Hold on, I'll put you on speaker."

"I'm here, too," her father said.

Her mother got right to the point. "Have you signed those papers yet? Your father and I have been waiting."

Emma shook her head and smiled at her phone, forgiving them. *They will never change.* That was okay; she would love them, anyway. In that instant Emma forgave herself, too.

For the first time ever, she would speak to her parents honestly about who she really was. "I've haven't been true to myself, Mum and Dad. I've spent my whole life trying to please you." Emma had believed if she did everything that they wanted her to, somehow the family she'd always fantasized about would miraculously appear. She wanted parents who loved each other like Emma knew in her heart lovers were supposed to. Like Claire and Dominic. Like she and Gabriel loved each other. The hard truth was, her parents would never have a happily-ever-after because they weren't wired that way. And that was okay. For them, but not for Emma.

"I can't tell you how grateful I am to both of you for guiding me toward psychology. For the first time, I see I can really make a difference, that I can really help others."

"Emma?" her mother said in her firmest tone. "What are you trying to say?"

"Mum and Dad, I love you. But I won't be working with you in the future. You're on your own."

"What?" her parents said together.

"And there's something more. I have a Christmas present for you, actually. You're going to be grandparents."

Gabe stopped in the doorway, water sloshing over the top of Emma's glass. *Emma is pregnant?* He stared at her, not believing what he'd just heard. Quietly he backed away from the threshold, then dashed to his bedroom and retrieved the small box with his mother's ring in it.

When he got back to the living room, Emma was just signing off with her folks.

"I'll call you after the New Year. Bye."

She turned around and stilled when she saw him. "How long have you been there?"

"Long enough." He walked toward her and then dropped to one knee.

Emma gasped. "What are you doing?"

"What I've wanted to do since I got back from Edinburgh." He took her hand in his and kissed it. "Emma, will ye marry me?" His emotions felt as thick as his brogue. "I've waited so long for the right lass to come along. You can't deny me. You just can't." He was begging, but he didn't care.

She looked worried, and he knew why.

He opened the box and produced his mother's opal. "I'm not asking you to marry me because of the bairn. But God, I'm so happy, I could shout it to the world." He gently put the ring on her finger. "I went to Edinburgh to get this. *For you*. I also wanted to talk to my da about love and marriage." He gave her a sideways grin. "Casper MacGregor is a wise man. He said I could do none better than you. He remembers the long talk that you two had after Claire and Dominic's wedding. He told me all about it. He thinks a lot of you, Emma."

She gazed down at the ring. "Yes, we talked about relationships. He spoke of your mother."

"I know." Gabe looked into Emma's eyes. "But you, my luv, you haven't answered my question. Will you marry me?"

She pushed back the hair from his eyes. "Of course I'll marry you, Gabriel MacGregor. You're the only man for me." Her laughed sounded like it floated on angels' wings. "I never imagined my knight in shining armor would turn out to be a Scottish warrior."

"Aye." He gathered her to him and kissed her. Then it wasn't enough. He leaned down and scooped her into his arms. Never breaking the heated kiss, he carried her into his bedroom.

He'd wanted to celebrate Christmas in a big way, but

never imagined it could be like this. He'd learned Christmas gifts don't always come with ribbons and wrappings: Sometimes the best gifts come by way of love. With Emma in his arms, he'd found the only Christmas gift he really needed.

"I love you, Emma," he said. "Always and forever."

"I love you, too, Gabriel." She wrapped her arms around him and whispered exactly what he wanted to hear. "Always and forever."

Epilogue

Emma put her hand to her back as she took a seat on the sofa, smiling at the now-empty hearth. A fire had been set this morning, but by late afternoon, they'd let it die out; the May sun streaming through the windows had been enough to warm the interior of Quilting Central.

The door opened, and her breath caught. It always did when her husband appeared. She smiled over at him, wondering if he would always have this effect on her.

Gabriel glanced around the room. "Is everyone gone, then?"

"Yes, I'm here all alone."

The baby took that moment to kick. How she loved that feeling, knowing life grew inside of her.

He ambled toward her with that look in his eye, the one that had gotten her into her current state of chubbiness. She looked down fondly at her expanding waistline. Only three and a half more months until they met their son or daughter.

He took her hand and helped her to her feet. "So, was it a success? Your first marriage-enrichment retreat?"

He already knew the answer. The past two nights, she'd talked his ear off about it. The responsiveness of the couples she'd coached. How it was so much better to be on the positive side of marriage. Although she did have to do the occasional couples counseling for her fellow Gandiegowans.

He snaked an arm around her shoulders. "So, my idea was a good one? You do remember that it was my idea, don't you, to have a marriage retreat?"

"How could I forget?" She stretched up on tiptoes and pecked his chin. "Thank you for being my personal brain trust."

"Among other things." He dipped his head down for a lingering kiss and rested a hand on her belly, something he did often these days, always maintaining a connection with both her and their child. "But you've spearheaded all your other ventures."

Yes, she'd held many SAD-awareness seminars in the winter months. Of course, she still worked with Mattie and the quilters who stopped by her sewing machine to talk. Deydie had placed an appointment book beside Emma to remind them all to see her during office hours. For now, she'd set up shop in the formal dining room at the restaurant three afternoons a week. But she was most excited about these marriage retreats. She'd scheduled another one for June.

"Did Claire stop by?" Gabriel said nonchalantly.

The men of this town were worse gossips than the women. "Yes. She came to pick up the platters we used for lunch."

He scooted behind her and massaged her shoulders. "Did she have any news? Anything going on with the Russos?"

She was going to make him suffer a bit. "No, nothing special." Emma paused. "Oh, wait a minute. Yes, there was news. Porco has learned how to shake hands. Claire said Dominic is a very proud papa."

"Oh." Poor Gabriel sounded so downcast. "Are you sure there was nothing else?"

"No. Not unless you're wondering if she told me that they're pregnant."

He spun her around. "You minx. You knew all along."

"Of course Claire told me. We share everything." Emma laughed. "She's the sister of my heart. You know that." She shrugged. "Even though they were going to wait a year or two to have a baby, I guess the universe had other plans."

"It often does." Gabriel beamed down at her, perhaps thinking how the universe had intervened to bring them together. "Are ye ready to go home, Mrs. MacGregor?" His brogue was thick with emotion.

The baby kicked his resting hand and his gaze dropped to her tummy. "You've made me the happiest man in the world. You know that, don't you?"

"If I say yes, do I get a foot rub tonight?" She wrapped her arms around his waist.

He squeezed her affectionately. "Among other things."

"I like how you think, Dr. MacGregor. And, Gabriel?" She leaned back and gazed up into his eyes. "Thank you for loving me."

"It's my pleasure, Mrs. MacGregor. My pleasure." He patted her on the bum. "Now home with ye."

As they walked out of Quilting Central, hand in hand, Emma turned her face toward the shining sun, whispering what was in her heart. "Thanks."

Gabriel squeezed her hand. "Amen."

"Amen," Emma said. Life was good.

Continue reading for a preview of the next book
in Patience Griffin's Kilts and Quilts series,

Some Like It Scottish

Coming from Signet Eclipse in July 2015.

Twenty-six-year-old Ramsay Armstrong pulled the
fishing boat alongside the dock and hollered to his
oldest brother, John. "What's so important that you've
called me back? I haven't pulled the north nets yet." He
threw the rope to his brother.

"I'll take care of the damned nets." John tied off the
boat. "I have a job for you, and it can't wait."

"Do it yereself!" More often than not, Ramsay got
stuck with the crap jobs in the family.

"I had planned to." John ducked his head and, stepping aboard, muttered, "Maggie won't let me."

Ramsay grinned. "Yere wife telling you what you can
and can't do." He pounded John on the back. "There's a
reason I'm still single, brother."

"Nay." John shook his head. "Ye're an arse, Ramsay.
That's why ye're still single. No woman would have ye."

"So what's this job you need?"

John didn't meet his eye. "It has to do with the boat
maintenance."

"I thought we set enough money aside for it."

"I thought so, too, but a revised quote came in. The
price has gone up. Way up."

"By how much?"

John shook his head.

Ramsay frowned. John never shared the actual numbers with him, always keeping him in the dark, always treating him like the babe in the family. "So what's this have to do with the favor you need done?"

"Ross and I'll take care of the boat while ye're doing it," John hedged.

"Spit it out, man." Ramsay was about to knock his brother into the drink. "What do you need?"

John pulled a sheet of paper from his pocket and thrust it at his brother. "It's all there. Her itinerary."

Ramsay took it and opened the crumpled paper. The letterhead read:

Kit Woodhouse Matchmaking, Inc.

Kit Woodhouse, CEO

Real Men of Alaska   *Real Men of Scotland*

Ramsay snapped his head up and glared at his brother. "What the crank is this? Matchmaker? From the U.S.?"

"Read on." John busied himself with two empty buckets, but really he was avoiding Ramsay's glare. He should be chagrined.

It was indeed a detailed itinerary—beginning with when this woman would land and the schedule for each day.

"For the next three cranking months?" Ramsay yelled. "Surely, you don't expect me to play nursemaid *for three months* to some sappy matchmaker!" The word made him feel like he could breathe fire.

John hung his head. "I saw her ad for a driver on the Internet. We need the money. I thought you and Ross could run the boat for the summer and I'd put up with driving Ms. Woodhouse around. But when Maggie found out, she nearly chopped off my balls."

"It would serve you right." Ramsay ran his eyes down the length of the paper. "Did you never think to consult Ross and me in your scheme?"

"I'm the oldest; I make the decisions." John acted like he had decades on him, but he was only thirty-five, nine years older than Ramsay.

Ramsay huffed. "Well, ye've screwed up this time. You'd better call it off and tell this woman we can't do it."

"But I signed a contract." John's brow furrowed as he ran a hand through his hair. "Ms. Woodhouse doesn't care who lives up to the contract, as long as somebody does."

Ramsay wadded the paper into a fist. "So you volunteered me."

"Ye better get back to the house and clean up." John started the motor. "You'll have just enough time to get a shower, *and shave*, before you have to rush off to the airport."

Ramsay considered cramming the itinerary down his brother's throat. He stepped off the boat instead, too angry to speak. On autopilot, he loosened the line and pushed the boat away with his foot.

John shouted above the motor. "Be on your best behavior and don't screw this up. We need the money."

Ramsay flipped him off, and then trudged off the dock, shaking his head.

He sure as hell wasn't going to let John's asinine matchmaker interfere with his own plans. In one month Ramsay intended to have enough money to buy ole man Martin's boat. Between the odd jobs at the North Sea Valve Company and helping the surrounding farmers after he was done fishing for the day, he would have enough. *One month.* And dammit, if he didn't get the old codger the money by then, the boat would be put up for auction and go for twice what Martin had agreed to.

Well, Ramsay had no intention of losing his chance to get out from under his brothers' thumbs. He wasn't born the youngest for nothing. He'd learned early on there's more than one way to wiggle out of a chore. He would make short work of the matchmaker, he decided. Three days with him and the interfering ole biddy would be paying him to go back to her nice cushy life in the States, where she belonged.

Kit's plane landed late—way late. Of course she didn't control the weather, but all the same she hated being late. She'd learned a thing or two about how to come into a remote area and set up shop. First and foremost, she had to gain the locals' trust. Getting off on the wrong foot wouldn't do.

After Kit deplaned and made it to the other side of the gate, there was no one there holding a sign with her name on it, no one to pick her up. She waited around a few minutes, in case whoever it was had run to the bathroom. But no one came.

"Dammit." She marched off to baggage claim to get her luggage. After filling up a trolley, she checked one more time at the gate—no one. She pulled out her folder and found the phone number for John Armstrong. When he answered, the background noise of an engine was loud and obnoxious.

"Mr. Armstrong, I thought someone was picking me up."

"Och, I sent my brother Ramsay to fetch you. Is he not there waiting?"

Kit looked around in vain, trying to keep her cool. "No." She started walking, heading for the parking lot. "Do you think he might be waiting outside?"

"Hold on, lassie. I'll give him a call." John seemed to be struggling with something on his end, wherever he was.

Kit stopped and snatched a pen from her pocket. "Why don't you give me his number and I'll call him?"

"Sure." John rambled it off. "I'm sorry about this, Ms. Woodhouse. It's a hell of a way to start out in Scotland."

Tell me about it. "It's okay."

They said goodbye and hung up.

Kit pulled her trolley outside to see if the brother waited at the curb. There wasn't anyone. She dialed the number. As it rang, a phone in the parking lot played the song "Kryptonite." She hung up and dialed again— "Kryptonite" played once more. Exasperated, she dragged the trolley out into the lot to hunt for the owner of the phone.

She dialed once more and followed the song to a muddy Mitsubishi Outlander SUV where the door was open and a sleeping man sat inside. He had earplugs in, an iPod on his knee, and the cell blasting "Kryptonite" beside him. She hung up and stared at him for a long minute.

He was the same type of man she'd fixed up with her shy East Coast socialite clients through her Alaskan operation. *A real man.* He wore a red plaid shirt, jeans, and black wellies. The boots were awful and she couldn't imagine anyone wearing them anywhere beyond a fishing boat. His dark hair was long and wavy and it framed a handsome rugged face that also sported a day-old beard. Very attractive.

But definitely not her type.

She dialed again, but this time as the phone rang, she nudged him. "You've got a call."

He came awake on a slow inhalation and focused a heavenly groggy smile on her. "What?"

She pointed to the seat. "Your phone is ringing. It might be important."

"Oh." He picked it up. "Hallo."

She put her phone to her ear, frowning, while keeping

eye contact with him. "I've arrived in Inverness. I'd like to go to Gandiegow now."

The place between his eyebrows cinched together. "Fine," he said into the phone, a quick flush of pink on his neck. He hung up.

She gave him a curt nod, pleased she'd embarrassed him.

He frowned at her. "They said your flight wouldn't be in until eight p.m. I came out here to rest my eyes."

"It's 8:15."

He glanced at his phone and his brows knit together again. He unfolded his tall frame from the SUV. Scrutinizing her, he leaned against the side and crossed his arms over his massive chest. The puppy-dog sweetness was gone now, replaced by a mutt who didn't like the smell of what was dropped in his bowl. "So you're the matchmaker."

She slapped a smile on her face and stuck out her hand, determined not to let this skeptic get to her. After all, he was obviously not one of the wealthy Scottish bachelors she needed to win over. "Kit Woodhouse at your service."

He considered her hand, and for a moment, she wondered if he might not take it. Just as she was about to abandon her effort at being civil, his hand enveloped hers. It was callused and firm. Normally, she had a good read on a person in the first five seconds, male or female. But she wasn't clear on this guy. He was gorgeous, if you liked rough-hewn and unpolished, which she didn't, but that gleam in his eye hinted at more.

He maintained eye contact with her and held on. "Ramsay Armstrong. Unfortunate brother to John Armstrong, who contracted services with you."

She dropped his hand and shifted her eyes away from

his gray ones. "Why are you the *unfortunate brother*?" She glanced up at his face again. "Or maybe I don't want to know."

He shrugged. "I'm a sea lover, not a land dweller. I understand that I'm to take ye all over the Highlands by auto. *To do yere job.*" He was indeed unhappy with her.

"Yes, I need to fill my stables."

"Yere what? Is it man or beast ye're after?"

"*Stables.* It's an expression. I'm after men." *Great!* That hadn't come out right. Her delayed flight had her rattled. "I need to find eligible bachelors to fill my database."

"Ye know, don't ye, that what you want to do won't work here?" He lifted one of his smug eyebrows.

"What?" She couldn't believe her ears; he'd given voice to her biggest worry. Her father used to say *never let them see you sweat.* But right now, Kit could use more Arrid Extra Dry. She went on the defensive. "You don't even know what I do."

"I have a pretty clear idea."

The man standing in front of her might have a lot going on in the looks department, but he had a lot to learn about Kit and her tenacity. "I'm very good at what I do." She had a high marriage rate to prove it.

"Why are you even here?" he questioned. "If you wanted to fill yere *stables*, as you say, you could've done that with yere computer from the States."

She straightened her shoulders and stood as tall as her five-foot-two frame would allow. She'd endured some stubborn men in her time and now it looked like she would have her hands full with this one. She stood her ground with the Scotsman. "For your information, Mr. Armstrong, I do things the old-fashioned way. I interview my clients and their perspective dates in person." It was the best way to get an accurate assessment of them. "Skype or FaceTime might be considered the face-to-face of the twenty-first century, but I believe in the personal touch."

He raised his eyebrows as if a crude comment was forthcoming.

She put her hand up to stop him. "Computers are for storing databases, not for getting to know one another." It was bugging her that she still hadn't pinned down this Ramsay Armstrong. She decided it must be because he was all brawn and no brains.

He had been leaning nonchalantly against the vehicle but pushed away from it, standing to his full height. He skimmed his eyes over her, from her summer sweater, to her designer jeans, right down to her new Doc Martens.

She wasn't intimidated. She'd learned from her Alaskan adventure to dress properly. For the weather and the culture. *And the natives*. It was best to try to fit in, but not to try too hard.

When he was done with his perusal, he gestured at her like she was nothing more than a mannequin. "You don't look like an old-fashioned kind of lass. You look to me like you saw this outfit in an outdoor magazine and ordered it online."

"Are you trying to provoke me, Mr. Armstrong?"

He shrugged. "I think what you want to do here is a crock of . . ." He stopped himself as if he'd thought better of it and stepped forward. "I don't believe in matchmakers. Haven't ye ever heard *three's a crowd*?"

"All brawn, no brains," she murmured. She wished she was taller, but her feminine stature was no match for him. He had to be six-two at least. She made sure her attitude made up the difference. "You're arguing against history. Matchmaking has been around since the beginning of time. Look it up."

"If ye're so good at this, then how would you match me?" he challenged.

She maintained eye contact. She was going to enjoy putting this arrogant troglodyte in his place.

"First, we'd have to discuss your assets. Do you own a manor house or an estate?"

"Not exactly."

"What do you mean *not exactly*?" It felt good to wipe that smirk off his face.

"I live in a cottage."

She raised her eyebrows. "Is it at least a nice-sized cottage?"

"It's the house I grew up in."

"You still live with your parents?" He didn't look like he'd *failed to launch*.

"I live with my brother, Ross. And of course John, and his wife, Maggie, and their boy, Dand."

Good grief. "That's quite a crew." She bet they were stepping all over each other. But back to the business at hand. She tilted her head back, trying to stare him down. "What about other property? A ranch? Any sheep? Cattle?"

He looked riled, his neck and chest creeping with red. "My brothers and I own a fishing boat."

She shook her head. "Maybe if you owned *a fleet of boats*. Sorry, Mr. Armstrong, I won't find you a bride."

His eyes narrowed. The great hulk of a Scotsman before her stood rod-straight, a warrior ready to make a scene here in the parking lot.

He could bluster all he wanted. Tough guys like him needed to be brought down a notch. Especially if they were attacking how she made her living.

She'd gone on the offensive; now, it was time to help the poor lout out. "I have a list of *Marriageable Attributes*. You should check out my website." She reached in her bag, pulled out a business card, and slid it into the front pocket of his flannel shirt, patting it. She couldn't help but notice he was rock solid, all muscle under her hand. She had the urge to pat a little longer. "Maybe after you review the list on my site, you can work at being a better catch."

He caught her hand before she'd fully withdrawn it, turning the tables on her. He oozed with latent sexuality. "I do fine all on my own. I don't need help to find a mate," he drawled.

The word *mate* hung in the air. He let go of her hand.

Gads. Her imagination raced into overdrive. She was either extremely jet-lagged or she needed a date herself. She hadn't been out in ages, too busy bringing other couples together. From the beginning, she'd drawn a clear line. She chose rugged men for her clients and picked Wall Street suits for herself. That way she was never tempted to mix business with pleasure. She hadn't found a man with the qualities she wanted, but one day she would. As it turned out, her greatest gift—reading people—was also her biggest impediment to finding someone for herself. The stockbrokers and bankers she'd dated so far had only had money and sex on their minds, and little else.

Ramsay grabbed her bags. "Let's get going."

She glanced up and saw his muscles ripple under his shirt. Her breath caught. *Yeah, I need a date.*

He opened the back and threw in her luggage with brute force. She started to protest, but inhaled deeply instead. It would be best to choose her battles with this man. Otherwise, it would be a long, long summer.

She slid into the passenger seat and chewed her lower lip. There was a subject she had to broach with him and he wouldn't like it. But it was important. She turned toward him in the seat.

"Mr. Armstrong—"

"Ramsay," he corrected.

"Ramsay, then." She paused. "We need to talk about my expectations." She scanned his person one more time, really hating those black wellies of his. She steeled herself for what had to be said. "The bachelors I've selected to interview are men of substance."

Almost imperceptibly, he shook his head as if he was barely tolerating her. "Don't confuse substance with worldly goods; they're two different things, lassie. Ye mean men of wealth, power, and standing."

It wouldn't do any good to try to convince him that she knew the difference. Hell, she'd put it in her business plan. "Yes, I'm speaking of wealth, power, and standing, as you put it."

"Then what's the rub?" he asked.

"I was wondering if you might reconsider your attire. Wear something a bit more upscale."

He glanced at her with raised eyebrows. "Ye have a problem with me being a fisherman?"

"No, of course not. It's an honorable profession." She meant it but hurried on. "There's nothing wrong with being casual and comfortable." She gestured toward her own clothing. "But when I interview these men, I'll be dressed professionally."

"I see. And since I'll be with ye, ye'll be wanting me to convey the right image as well." He put his eyes back on the road and jammed the gearshift into drive. "Don't worry, lassie. I'll be dressed for the part."

"Thank you, Ramsay. I appreciate your cooperation." She didn't tell him that everything was riding on this trip. Every dime she'd made and saved. Her sister Harper's fall tuition for graduate school. The cost of community college for her younger sister, Bridget. Kit would have to help her mother with her living expenses now that Bridget had graduated high school and her Social

Security survivor benefits from Daddy had run out. Even Kit's self-worth and ego were on the line. *Everything.* She had to make a go of it in Scotland or lose it all. Her family was counting on her.

As silence filled the car, Kit gazed out the window. It was after nine p.m. and the sun still hung in the sky. The summer days were long in the north of Scotland, with the view desolate and beautiful. The mountainous hills rose out of the earth like giants. There were few trees and she couldn't help but compare it to the Alaskan bush with vast forests of green. The stark landscape around her had a soothing quality, but Kit couldn't tamp down the fear rising within her. Fear of the future and the unknown. In the past, she never let the fear overtake her. She'd always made it through the tough times and she would again this time, too, wouldn't she?

She must've dozed off because she came awake abruptly as Ramsay brought the vehicle to a stop.

"Are we here?" She looked out and saw the roadblock in front of them.

"Nay. But we'll be there shortly." He shifted into four-wheel drive and drove the car down an embankment.

Warning bells should've gone off, but the man in the seat next to her must've instilled a walloping dollop of trust. Or she was too exhausted to be concerned at his sudden foray into off-road four-wheeling. "So do you want to share with me what's going on here?"

"The road into Gandiegow is being repaved. We'll have to go in by boat."

Dread swamped Kit and she twisted her hands in her lap. She hadn't been on a boat since her father died. "Is there another way?" She hated how weak her voice sounded.

He glanced over at her. "Ye have my word that ye'll be safe."

She nodded. He couldn't know what this did to her.

As they rose over the last dune, the water appeared. *Her father's grave.*

Ramsay pulled the SUV to the edge. "There it is."

A wooden dinghy was tied to a post with a long rope, which drooped in the mud. "Low tide, I presume?" She looked down at her new Doc Martens, not happy to have to break them in this way. But more importantly, did Ramsay have a life vest?

Her father used to call her *trout* because she was a born swimmer. But that was before.

Ramsay turned off the auto and shoved the keys in the glove box. He jumped out and retrieved her bags.

They walked through the grass to the edge of the mud. There Kit hesitated.

Ramsay shook his head and muttered, "New shoes." He dropped her bags, scooped her up, and began trudging toward the boat like she was nothing more than a piece of luggage.

She gasped. "What are you doing?" She clung to him for dear life as he walked her toward the water. "Stop."

"Ye're lucky I don't sling you over my shoulder." His wellies hit the water and he held her higher, making sure she didn't get wet.

She could only stare into his determined face, forcing herself to calm down, focusing on his chiseled features, weathered from the sun and wind. His solid arms and shoulders made her feel safe, reassured he wouldn't drop her.

She relaxed just enough to get why he wore the wellies.

Whatever lingering thought she'd had that he'd behaved gallantly slipped away as he none too gently deposited her in the boat. She had to grab the gunwale to keep from falling on her butt.

As he waded back to shore for her bags, she scrambled for the life jacket stored under her seat and quickly secured it around her, buckling it into place. She ignored that it was wet.

He frowned at her in the life vest for a long second before putting her bags in the boat. She didn't care if he thought she was a chicken or not.

He untied the rope from the post and looped it to the front of the dinghy before climbing in next to the motor. "You'd better hold on." He pulled the ripcord and they were off.

Thank God the ocean was calm tonight or else she might've flung herself at him for a stronghold as they bounced through the water. She'd never been afraid of the ocean as a little girl on her father's yacht. How times had changed. How she'd changed. Just another example of what she'd been reduced to.

As the boat zipped through the water, spray shot up, lightly misting her face. She turned back to look at the Scot.

He was the picture of serenity, his face gazing toward the setting sun. He looked like he owned the ocean around him, perhaps a relative of Horatio Hornblower or the nephew of Poseidon. He did look like a Greek god—well, a Scottish god.

Even though it was ten at night, the orange sky filled the expanse. A fishing boat was anchored just to the right of the white sun, which rested on the edge of the earth. Everything shimmered with color. As they rounded the corner, she caught her first sight of the village. For a second, she forgot how unforgiving the sea could be as the scene before her stole her breath away. Arcing around the cove, idyllic cottages painted blue, red, and white nestled like a row of children's blocks. The town glowed from the setting sun, making Gandiegow look alive, a beautiful sleeping beast, nestled under the ancient bluffs.

Ramsay steered toward the dock, dropping the motor

into idle. "Are you ready for Gandiegow?" He cut the power and he tied them off.

She stood and climbed out on her own, proving she didn't need or want his help this time.

He grabbed the suitcases but stopped. "Oh, ye won't be staying at the Thistle Glen Lodge, the quilting dormitory." He looked as if he was baiting her. "Your arrangements have changed. Ye're now at the Fisherman."

"What?"

He had a gleam in his eye.

She didn't know what he was up to, if anything. But she could give as good as she got. She turned the tables on him. "But I thought I was staying at your place. That's what your brother John told me."

And as expected, Ramsay's eyes bugged, looking horrified to have her shacked up with him and his family.

She smiled at him sweetly. "You do have room for me at your *cottage*, don't you?"

"I—I . . ." The poor guy's mouth opened and shut like that of a fish out of water.

She had mercy on him. "Breathe, Ramsay. The Fisherman will be fine. I'm up for anything." She'd even slept a few nights in a tent in Alaska.

"Aye. Right." Relief spread across his face. He stopped in front of a two-story stone building reverberating with noise and turned to her, that glint in his eyes restored. "You do know, don't ye, that the Fisherman is a pub?"

"Sure." She hadn't known until that moment, but she certainly wasn't going to let on now. She walked ahead of him, worrying if she'd get any sleep with it being so loud. The Alaskan bush had been quiet, and once she'd gotten over the worry of being mauled by a bear, she'd slept like a baby.

Before going in, she glanced up at the building one more time. Hopefully, there was a separate bedroom upstairs and she wouldn't be relegated to sleeping behind the bar. She opened the door to the establishment and went inside.

The place was packed with wall-to-wall Scots, mostly men. There were all different sizes of them, from the tall lean types, to the boxy weightlifters, to a few beer guts. But every one of them was as rugged as the bluffs that hung over the town.

Ramsay put his hand on her shoulder and shouted to her. "The steps leading upstairs are over there behind the bar." He pointed to where a very buxom blond woman was pouring shots. "That's Bonnie."

Bonnie had a lot going for her—a tight T-shirt stretched over double-Ds, red gloss on full lips, and men gathered around her like flies to bait.

"I'll introduce you," he said.

But when they stood before Bonnie, Kit could see the other woman's hackles go up and her talons come out. She sneered while Ramsay made the introductions; the man didn't have a clue. Ramsay stood so close to Kit that she could feel the heat coming off of him. And whenever anyone tried to squeeze by, he bumped into her back. None of which Bonnie missed. She looked ready to start a cat fight, but this kitten wasn't interested in making trouble.

"It's nice to meet you." Kit presented her hand.

"I don't think so." Bonnie grabbed a bottle, poured a dram, and shoved it toward Ramsay, all the while keeping her eyes on Kit. "I hear from Maggie that ye've come to steal away all of our men."

Hell. Kit had hoped to head off some of this posturing. She was going to offer her services pro bono to a few local women, to build up goodwill in the community. *Too late now.* Even the sweet-faced young woman nursing a Coke at the end of the bar was giving her the evil eye.

Kit got it. Gandiegow wasn't going to turn out to be smooth sailing. "I'm ready to go to bed," she said to Ramsay, raising her voice over the noise.

There was a sudden hush, her declaration hanging in the air. Bonnie set the bottle down so hard on the bar that the drinks in front of the two customers in either direction shook.

With her face hot, Kit stammered, "I mean, I'm tired. I want to get settled in."

Ramsay, unfortunately, rested his hand on the small of her back and guided her. Was he crazy? Bonnie looked ready to dive over the bar after her.

As they made their way to the narrow steps leading up, Kit wondered if it was too late to call John and get the other brother to drive Kit around Scotland. Ramsay was clueless. And his warm hand on her back wasn't helping her cause.

Bonnie's eyes followed them and her scowl deepened. "Watch yereself, Ramsay," she said.

But Kit was pretty sure it was directed as much at her as it was at him. She felt certain it had only been her first glimpse of the summer to come. Gandiegow might look beautiful from the sea, but she was going to be a bitch to deal with.

ALSO AVAILABLE FROM

PATIENCE GRIFFIN

TO SCOTLAND WITH LOVE

A Kilts and Quilts Novel

Caitriona Macleod reluctantly gave up her career as an investigative reporter for the role of perfect wife. But after her cheating husband passes away, a devastated Cait leaves Chicago for the birthplace she hasn't seen since she was a child...

Quilting with her gran and the other women of the village brings Cait a peace she hasn't known in years. But if she turns in a story about Graham Buchanan—a handsome movie star who stays in his hometown between films—Gandiegow will never forgive her for betraying one of its own. Should she suffer the consequences to resurrect her career? Or listen to her battered and bruised heart and give love another chance?

"[A] lyrical and moving debut."
—*Publishers Weekly* (Starred Review)

Available wherever books are sold or at
penguin.com

S0562